Praise for Lorraine Brown

'Fresh, charming and wonderfully escapist'
BETH O'LEARY

'Utterly charming'
PRIMA

'A magical modern love story'
HELLY ACTON

'A wonderfully engaging tale of love and self-discovery'
MIKE GAYLE

'A charming, romantic read'
SOPHIE COUSENS

'The lovely descriptions made me want to take the first
post-lockdown Eurostar to Paris!'
KATE EBERLEN

'A gorgeous, romantic book packed full of joy'
LAURA PEARSON

'Fresh, funny and just the tonic for dark winter nights'
ZOË FOLBIGG

'It's the ultimate feel-good read'
HOLLY MILLER

'A gorgeous, slow burning love story which had me tearing
up at the end!'
OLIVIA BEIRNE

'A sweet, romantic story, full of heart'
CAROLINE KHOURY

Lorraine Brown previously trained as an actress and has a postgraduate diploma in psychodynamic counselling. She lives in London with her partner and their son. *Couples Retreat* is her fourth novel.

Also by Lorraine Brown

Sorry I Missed You
The Paris Connection
Five Days in Florence

Couples Retreat

LORRAINE BROWN

ORION

First published in Great Britain in 2024 by Orion Books,
an imprint of The Orion Publishing Group Ltd
Carmelite House, 50 Victoria Embankment
London EC4Y 0DZ

An Hachette UK Company

1 3 5 7 9 10 8 6 4 2

A CIP catalogue record for this book
is available from the British Library.

ISBN (Mass Market Paperback) 978 1 3987 1111 2
ISBN (eBook) 978 1 3987 1112 9

Typeset by Deltatype Ltd, Birkenhead, Merseyside

Printed in Great Britain by Clays Ltd, Elcograf S.p.A.

MIX
Paper | Supporting
responsible forestry
FSC® C104740

www.orionbooks.co.uk

For Gabes, the sweetest of travel companions.

Chapter One

Carla Hardwicke Literary Management was situated on the top floor of the sort of Georgian townhouse I sometimes imagined I might live in one day, if by some miracle I sold about a million more copies of my books. One could dream, right?

Arriving in reception massively out of breath after navigating four flights of extremely narrow stairs, I greeted Carla's assistant, Lily, who always wore short, flippy skirts and cute, gigantic black-framed glasses that pretty much covered her entire face.

'Morning,' I managed, recognising that I clearly needed to do something to improve my cardio fitness.

'Oh, hello, Scarlett! Take a seat and I'll grab Carla for you,' said Lily chirpily, zipping out from behind her desk and disappearing into the agency's inner sanctum.

I dutifully made my way over to the slouchy sofas and the coffee table strategically housing my three books, which Lily had no doubt laid out especially for my visit – it was sweet that they'd thought me worthy of such a display, even if it was only for the hour or so I was likely to be in the office. I picked up the shiny, paperback copy of my debut, *Little Boy Lost*, running my thumb over the embossed title, and our names: Scarlett Green and Theo Winters. It still felt strange to see us linked together like that. My other two books had only my name branded across the front of them because Theo and I … well, we'd only written the one book together. Much to Carla's annoyance, I might add. I didn't know what Theo had told her, but I'd kept it very vague, had said something about our working relationship irreconcilably breaking down, so much so that we couldn't possibly write a follow-up together, not then, not ever. She'd been gutted, and I didn't blame her, because our debut novel had sold *way* more than my other two put together. It was a shame on all counts, but then that was what happened when you didn't keep your emotions fully in check.

As I waited to be summoned into Carla's office, I couldn't help but notice a disturbing new office feature: our author headshots mounted on the wall above the reception desk, with each of Carla's achingly photogenic clients arranged in alphabetical order in symmetrical rows of five. I looked a bit 'rabbit in the headlights' in mine. Hardly surprising, I supposed, because it had been taken when all of this first kicked off and the book world had felt like a bit of a headfuck. Not that it didn't now, mind you. Although surely I could knock something more sophisticated and enigmatic than that out of the park at this point? Perhaps I'd get some new shots done and I'd wear a black turtleneck, like Sally Rooney, because then the industry might take me seriously, too. I could even throw on a sassy Hermès scarf, not that I owned one. And I'd definitely get one of those bouncy blow dries, because lifeless mid-brown hair styled in a too-long bob didn't exactly make for a knockout headshot, it transpired, although my green eyes – the one facial feature I had that was in any way interesting, in my opinion – were my saving grace.

As I looked from one headshot to the other, feeling worse and worse about my lacklustre image, I willed myself to avoid the right-hand corner, where the authors with surnames beginning with 'W' were loitering. But generally, if something looked like it might be bad for me, I tended to wade right on in there and do it anyway. So yeah, there he was: Theo Winters. Sparkling away like an A-list film star. Seriously, if there was going to be a movie made about a male thriller writer in his thirties, this would be how he would be described on the casting call sheet: glossy chestnut brown hair with just the right amount of volume at the front; a brooding half-smile, a neatly trimmed beard. A sort of: *Look how casual I am!* meets *Could I BE any more perfect?*

Thankfully Carla snapped me out of my melancholy by appearing in the doorway wearing one of her trademark trouser suits paired with her (also trademark) short, slicked-back, blonde hair. I reckoned her wardrobe probably consisted of rows and rows of the same thing, which I had to admit would make it much easier to get dressed in the morning. Less thinking about the mood and more deciding whether to wear a plain white shirt or a plain white shirt with a grey stripe through it. By the time I was fifty, which was what I guessed Carla was, although of course she would never say, this was the organised manner in which I would like to be conducting my life.

'Scarlett!' said Carla in her well-spoken drawl.

I flew out of my seat. 'Good to see you!'

I loved Carla, but was also sort of terrified of her. She was everything I wished I could be, in work and in life. For example, Carla was ballsy and had zero qualms about telling people exactly what she wanted. I, on the other hand, had this strange desire to make everyone like me by giving them the thing *they* wanted, even if it wasn't remotely the thing *I* wanted.

I stood up, brushed non-existent creases out of my brown corduroy pinafore dress, and walked over to join Carla, glad

I'd gone for my heeled ankle boots over the flats. Somehow the clip-clopping sound I made as I clattered across Carla's expensive-looking wooden floor gave me a boost of confidence – I was a powerful, successful author. I was going to have a productive conversation with my kick-ass agent about how to elevate my career to the next level. A place in the Richard and Judy Book Club would be mine again, and it would be even sweeter than the first time round because I would have written the book all by myself and not with the writing partner from hell.

Giving Carla the obligatory kiss on each cheek – because that's what people in publishing did, I had that down now – I followed her into her huge office, which had funky Perspex furniture, floor-to-ceiling windows and panoramic views of the River Thames in all its glory. Carla flung herself into her Eames chair, swivelling round to face me like a warrior about to go into battle. If this was my office and I had this iconic scene to look at on a daily basis, I would probably feel as though I'd made it, too.

'I wanted to get you in to talk about early sales figures for *The Mother-in-Law*,' announced Carla unpromisingly.

My latest psychological thriller was tipped to do very well, and I'd already mapped out how I'd spend the money I'd not yet earned in royalties. If my publisher's predictions came true, I was going to get beautiful bespoke bookshelves so big they'd cover one whole wall of my two-bed flat in Ealing. And I'd buy one of those huge, squishy corner sofas I'd coveted for at least a decade, which naturally would be covered in smooth teal velvet, as per my favourite Instagram shots of rich people's designer living rooms. I basically wanted the kind of Zoom background that screamed: *I am an intelligent, successful, well-read author!* instead of my current offering, which was more: *Look at the half-decent place I live in that*

I've tried to big up for this shot.

I took a seat, any confidence I'd rocked up with slowly draining out of me. Fuck. In hindsight, if it was good news, she'd have called me, wouldn't she? She would have been yelling down the phone, announcing that I'd exceeded my publisher's expectations, which was no easy feat, since nobody ever told you exactly what these mysterious expectations actually were.

'Sure. What's happening?' I asked, steeling myself internally. How bad could it be? It was a good book, I was certain it was, and what's more, my entire publishing team had told me they thought so, too.

Carla grimaced.

Christ. This was not looking good, not in the slightest.

'I'm sorry to be the bearer of bad news, Scarlett, but it's sold nowhere near as well as we'd hoped,' said Carla in a semi-sympathetic voice.

The book had only been on sale a week and I'd religiously avoided stalking my Amazon rankings or sidling into bookshops to see how many copies were left on the shelves. But now I felt blindsided because I'd naively thought Carla had called me in to brainstorm my next book and my career in general. And OK, part of me hoped she was going to tell me I had a US deal – *The Mother-in-Law* was on submission out there and Carla had seemed positive, although to be fair she'd gone very quiet on that lately, too.

'Do we know why?' I asked, clearing my throat, trying not to sound completely devastated that my beloved book was clearly about to sink without a trace.

Carla exhaled loudly. 'It's a combination of things, I think. The domestic thriller market is a tough one to break at the moment.'

Shit. Really?

5

'Since when?' I asked, daring to query Carla's sweeping statement about the genre I happened to write in, because if what she was saying was true, why had nobody told me before? Why had they let me spend hundreds of hours writing a thing that they didn't even know if they wanted? 'Because apparently last year you only had to write a thriller with the word "woman" in the title and it would fly off the shelves,' I added, determined to get some answers here.

'Well, the industry is constantly changing as you know,' said Carla, not deterred by the fact that I felt like a flower wilting in the heat and probably looked like one, too. 'Uplit is the big thing this year. Readers want hopeful, optimistic, life-affirming stories, apparently.'

'Uplit?!' I said incredulously.

When I'd handed in the first draft of my first solo novel – i.e. the first one I'd written without Theo Winters breathing down my neck – I was told it was too uplit, and that uplit didn't sell. Now look! Also, why did I have to go and imagine Theo Winters being close enough to breathe down my neck? Now I couldn't get the image out of my head. I could almost hear him talking softly into my ear, his voice little more than a whisper, his lips brushing against my temple. Shaking my head and attempting to pull myself together, I poured myself a glass of water from the jug on Carla's desk and drank it thirstily.

'And I'm sorry to impart yet more bad news . . .' said Carla.

Fucking hell. What else could there be?

'Go on . . .'

'I know you've started work on your next book and you told me it feels like it's going well, but you're out of contract and – I don't know, Scarlett. The way things are going, I think it's unlikely they're going to offer you another deal. And I thought I'd say this now because I don't want you to spend the next six months slaving away on a book that simply isn't going to get picked up.'

I bit my lip. This was worse than I'd feared. It was bad enough when a book you'd put your heart and soul into didn't sell, but at least there was still the promise of another newer, shinier one being published in its wake. And maybe that could be THE ONE, and that's what you held on to when you got your royalty statement and you'd not even made a dent in your advance. But this? This not renewing of contracts? This level of rejection was all new to me. And of course I'd seen it happen to author friends, and I'd felt truly terrible for them, but honestly? I'd never thought it was going to happen to me. Because my editor, Sophie, was lovely and in my head we were friends and I'd been under the misguided delusion that she loved me as much as I loved her and that she'd stick by me even if a book didn't sell quite as well as we'd all hoped. Had I been wrong about her all along?

'But they loved *The Mother-in-Law* when I first handed it in. I hardly had any notes!' I protested. 'They said it was ten times more high-concept than *The Babysitter* and that they were really excited about it.'

Carla didn't flinch. 'It's about the sales, Scarlett. You mustn't take it personally. We can't control how well a book does once it's out there, it's down to a whole host of factors and a bit of luck. Don't beat yourself up about it,' she said annoyingly casually.

My phone buzzed in my bag, a timely reminder of exactly why I could not lose my deal. It would be my dad. Perhaps he'd sent me a picture of another piece of medical equipment he wanted me to buy for his house. There was always something, and to stop myself feeling guilty about not living with him anymore, I always bought it for him. But what if I couldn't?

7

'Look,' said Carla. 'I'm not saying this is the end of your writing career, Scarlett, far from it. Let's not run ahead of ourselves. Saturn House is one publisher in a sea of publishers.'

'Hardly a sea.'

I swallowed hard, hoping my default mechanism would kick in and I'd be able to remain calm and unfazed in the face of crappy news. But it felt harder than usual to act like everything was fine when it wasn't.

'And there's nothing we can do?' I challenged.

I was loath to admit it, but for once I needed someone to help me fix this, even if I did pride myself on not needing help from anyone, ever.

'Look, Carla, I can't afford to stop publishing books, so if you want me to switch to uplit, I'll do it. Give me a premise you think editors would get excited about and I'll write it. Anything. I mean it.'

I was aware I sounded desperate, but I wanted Carla to know how important this was to me and that I wasn't going to allow myself to be brushed off. I was a good writer, I knew I was, and there would be another publisher, another book, I was sure of it. All I needed was some guidance from Carla about how to get there, and fast.

Carla sat back in her chair, twiddling her thumbs like a pantomime villain.

'I do have one idea ...' she said. 'Which was why I asked you to come in. But I warn you, you're not going to like it.'

She took a hardcover book out of her top drawer and slid it across the table to me. I turned it over so that I could see the front and immediately dropped it again, as if it had singed my fingers. It was *The Killing Party*, the latest Theo Winters novel.

'Is there a reason you've pushed this testosterone-fuelled

thriller in my direction?' I asked, trying to sound jokey but not even remotely pulling it off.

'I don't want to go into details,' she said, 'but let's just say that Theo is also in need of a career boost. And, like you, he has reasons for wanting more financial security.'

This was interesting. I knew he hadn't hit any bestseller lists since *Little Boy Lost* because obviously I'd checked, but there was always buzz around his new releases, and his press reviews were annoyingly glowing. Could it be there was trouble in paradise?

'How is any of this going to help *me*, though?' I asked, wanting to get back to the rather pressing matter at hand.

Carla placed her hands in the prayer position and looked me directly in the eye.

'I think the two of you should write another book together,' she said.

It took a second or two for this to sink in. My stomach dropped, my mouth went dry. She could not be serious?

'Me and Theo?' I asked, suddenly finding it impossible to do anything as simple as swallow.

'Yes,' confirmed Carla.

'Absolutely not.'

'Hear me out,' she said.

'No. No way.'

Carla raised her eyebrows. 'What happened to "Tell me what to do to save my career and I'll do it, Carla? Anything. I mean it"?'

I flinched. 'And I will do anything. Anything but this.'

'Scarlett. Listen. You wanted my best advice, so this is me giving it to you.'

I took a deep breath and sighed it hard out, thinking all the relaxing thoughts I could muster in that moment, but all

I could hear was my own heartbeat rushing in my ears. 'I'm listening.'

'Remember when you and Theo first sent me the manuscript for *Little Boy Lost*?' said Carla. 'I was blown away. I knew immediately that I wanted to be your agent and that I could sell this book. That editors at the big five publishing houses were going to be clambering over themselves to offer you a deal.'

I thought back to those heady days. My unfulfilling temp job in a dusty Victorian hospital with a pile of patient files on my desk so high that sometimes I couldn't see the other secretaries in the room. The thrill of taking my first writing course, of having the guts to actually turn up and – shocker – share my work. How surprised I'd been when the class's most talented (and undeniably popular) student wanted to team up with me to co-write a book.

'But we hate each other,' I said.

'Hate is a very strong word, Scarlett,' replied Carla.

OK, maybe it wasn't hate, exactly, but I couldn't even look at his book without having palpitations, never mind his photo! The only good thing about this whole saga was that we'd very successfully managed to avoid each other for six whole years. And now Carla wanted us to *work* together?!

'Why would publishers be interested in another book from the two of us, anyway, if our solo careers are supposedly flagging? Knowing my luck, we'd kill ourselves trying to write the thing and everyone would turn it down.'

Carla leaned forward, placing her hands on the table. She clearly meant business.

'Because you're stronger writers together than you are apart, and that's the truth of it.'

This was not what I wanted to hear. I didn't want to be my best self because of somebody else! And Carla saying that she thought our debut only worked because I was writing alongside *him* felt like a huge blow and one I could have done without after several other huge blows this afternoon. This was fast becoming a really, really shitty day.

'It makes perfect sense from a business perspective,' continued Carla. 'The press loved writing about you the first time around – two young, attractive authors writing together on a whim, selling their first book and having it be a massive sleeper hit.'

'We're not exactly young anymore, though, are we?'

'Scarlett. You're thirty-four.'

Which would make Theo thirty-two, I instantly worked out, annoyed with myself for remembering how much of an age difference there was between us. And that his birthday was on the tenth of August. Damn.

'Publishers could tout the story of your reunion,' banged on Carla, 'and the publicity would likely translate into book sales. In my opinion, they'd salivate at the chance to publish a book by the same phenomenal writing duo who wrote the bestselling *Little Boy Lost*.'

Oh, God. She was making an excellent case here, and I was trying my best to stay strong and stick to my guns. Perhaps she could re-train as a barrister if she ever got bored of agenting. I could totally imagine her annihilating some poor, unsuspecting witness on the stand.

'I've taken the liberty of running it past Theo and he's agreed to do it,' she said, bringing out the big guns.

Well. This was a shocking turn of events. He'd agreed to it? *Really?* I sat in silence for what felt like ages, twiddling the gold band I wore on the middle finger of my right hand. Mum's wedding ring. I never took it off.

'So what do you say?' asked Carla, calmly holding my gaze.

Every part of me was screaming in protest, but the advantages of her proposal were hard to refuse. I had to think about the money. My family. There were people relying on me to help them out and the cash from book one was long gone. So really, did I even have a choice?

'OK,' I said, forcing the words out of my mouth before I could change my mind. 'I *might* be prepared to give it a try. Or to have a conversation about it, at least. But I retain my rights to pull out immediately at any point if it all gets too much. Or if Theo starts acting like a knob again.'

Carla beamed at me. She had me and she knew it.

'You won't regret this, Scarlett, I promise you.'

Chapter Two

I pushed through the door of All Bar One Waterloo, which was not my first choice of venue, it had to be said, but it happened to sit midway between everyone's offices and my flat. Spotting Alexa and the others sitting in a corner booth, I waved, heading over, trying to put all the stuff whirling about in my head aside so that I could pretend to be my usual upbeat, sunny, interested self. The bar was dark to match my mood, and the music far too loud for my current disposition.

'Yay, Scarlett's here!' trilled Dan, my oldest friend Petra's husband.

Petra and I had met on our first day at school, a comprehensive in Reading that had seemed terrifyingly too big for us both on that first day, and I'd go so far as to say that entire first year. We'd been inseparable all the way through to sixth form, although we studied very different subjects in the end – I was the arty, creative one who spent my evenings reading novels instead of doing my actual homework, and Petra was strangely scientific. I say strangely, because I was of the misguided opinion that anyone who liked maths was a) weird and b) a genius. We lost touch a bit when she first met Dan and fell off the radar for a few months, but I'd never held it against her. I imagined I might have done the same thing if I'd met the love of my life when I was nineteen.

'Hello, hello,' I said, sliding off my jacket and unravelling my scarf, hugging first Petra and then Dan. It was March and there was the promise of warmer weather, but tonight felt like winter all over again.

'Cute pinafore,' said my other best friend, Alexa, standing up to hug me, too.

We'd met a bit later, when the two of us had worked on reception at a shabby yet hellishly over-priced hotel in the West End the summer before university. Like me, it had taken her a while to work out what she wanted to do with her life, but she'd got there in the end and was finally following her dream of becoming a doctor, although the training was much more stressful than she'd imagined. I clocked the bags under her eyes, the way her jeans and jumper looked a little too big for her, suddenly. Was she eating properly? I gave her an extra long hug, making a mental note to check in with her later.

'How was the meeting with your agent?' asked Petra, who was in the midst of IVF hell and therefore had recently been subjected to watching us chug wine while she sipped on sparkling mineral water. To be fair, she didn't appear to resent us for it – I supposed the end goal would be worth it, wouldn't it?

'Great,' I lied. 'I've actually agreed to write another book with Theo Winters.'

I clocked Petra and Dan giving each other a look.

'Blimey,' said Alexa, pouring me a glass of Pinot Grigio. 'I thought it all went tits up with you two once the book was done? And that you never wanted to see him again?'

I shrugged, playing it down. I hadn't told her, or anyone else, the whole story, so she wouldn't understand the full enormity of what I'd agreed to do, anyway. And I never wanted my friends to worry about me. Sometimes I imagined what it might be like to tell them how I was really feeling;

how underneath this cool, calm exterior I was sometimes an anxiety-fuelled, insecure wreck. But that was where it always ended: in a thought. And I never quite managed to vocalise what was in my head.

'It'll be fine,' I assured them. 'Once we've plotted out the story, we won't need to spend that much physical time together, anyway.'

Although the thought of having to see him at *all* still hadn't properly sunk in. I picked up a menu, glanced at it and threw it back down on the table. For some reason I'd lost my appetite.

Petra frowned at me. 'Are you sure that's what you want, Scar? Wasn't he always lording it around? Taking all the glory at your book signing events?'

I laughed it off. The publicity trail for *Little Boy Lost* had been challenging, to say the least. Because it had become a surprise hit, our publishers at the time, Rogers & Richardson, had sprung into action, organising signings galore and appearances at festivals and radio interviews all over the place. We'd had to pretend to be a team for the time it took to get through our event and then we'd gone our separate ways, not speaking or messaging each other until our presence was required at the next one. It had been exhausting.

'Talking of authors, I heard Jackson on the radio this morning,' said Dan, slinging his arm around Petra, who curled into him in the comfortable, cat-like way people did when they'd been happily married for years.

I recoiled slightly at the sound of my ex's name.

'I heard that, too. He was a bit full of himself towards the end of the interview, wasn't he?' said Alexa. 'I suppose it's because he writes "literary fiction".'

'He was always very supportive of my writing,' I insisted, still feeling the need to defend him.

Dan snorted.

'He was!' I said.

'Even though he told you commercial fiction was beneath him?' mused Alexa.

We'd been similar in so many ways, but at the end of the day, Jackson had been longlisted for literary prizes and I wrote books you could buy in supermarkets. But then I sold more copies than him, which to give him his due, never bothered him. He'd rather have prizes than a big pay cheque, he'd told me, which I sort of understood, but then he didn't need the money like I did.

'Is he still sleeping with that teenager?' asked Petra, her nose wrinkled in disgust.

'She's twenty-two,' I said, referring to the agent's assistant Jackson was now dating.

'Same thing,' said Petra.

Alexa patted my knee in sympathy. 'How are you feeling about it all?'

'I'm feeling like I'm better off without him,' I declared, hoping to shut this particular line of conversation down *tout de suite*.

In the end we'd felt more like friends than lovers, anyway, and instead of any grand romance, our lives together had felt like an extended co-writing session.

'I must say, you seem much more relaxed without him in your life,' said Petra.

Clearly my attempts to appear stress-free and totally fine, even when Jackson and I were literally in the throes of breaking up, had failed dismally. I was going to have to try harder next time I was upset about something. Like now, if I let myself think about my book and its dismal sales figures.

'Anyway, enough about me. Petra, what's the latest? Did

you get your test results back?' I asked, desperate to project the heat onto somebody else.

Also, I knew it helped Petra to share her journey with us and sure enough, she pulled her test results up on her phone, talking me through them in slightly unnecessary detail. Alexa got a phone call and excused herself and Dan went to the bar, so it was just me trying to keep up with her progesterone levels and what that meant for her cycle and whether or not she was ovulating. I would usually have been fully engaged, mainly because I knew how much it meant to her, but today I had this impending feeling of doom about not having a publishing deal and being back to square one and it was pecking away at the back of my mind, so much so that I couldn't seem to just listen and be in the moment. And I lost focus completely when Petra started talking about the positive effects of giving up meat when you were trying to get pregnant, regaling me with a particularly graphic account of animals being pumped with antibiotics that almost made me turn vegetarian on the spot.

I knew Alexa was having an anxiety attack the second she came back into the bar, clutching her phone tightly in her hand, her usually glowing brown skin looking decidedly grey. I immediately stood up, guiding her down into her seat.

'Breathe, Alexa. Remember your box breathing. In for four, hold for two, out for four. That's it.'

'Is she OK?' asked Petra.

I mouthed: panic attack.

Petra winced. 'They're happening a lot, lately. What's going on?'

'She'll be fine in a bit,' I said, in the soothing tone I knew Alexa responded well to, even through the fog of a panic attack. I'd been with her through many of them over the years and knew exactly what to do. 'I'll get us an Uber, OK?' I told her. 'We'll be back at yours in no time so that you can rest and relax.'

I ordered us a cab, repeating the box breathing mantra to Alexa as I thumbed through the Uber app, thankfully finding a car that was only two minutes away.

'In for four, hold for two, out for four, hold for two.'

Dan appeared at the table looking spooked. 'What's wrong with Alexa?'

'Another panic attack,' Petra whispered loudly to him.

'Jesus. Can I do anything?' he asked, depositing the wine we were all supposed to be sharing on the table.

'I'm taking her home,' I said. 'Is that OK, Alexa? Shall we go back to yours?'

A tearful Alexa nodded.

'Do you want us to come?' asked Petra, looking as though there were a million things she'd rather do.

'No, you two stay,' I said. 'Enjoy yourselves. These could be the last nine months of your life as a family of two. You won't be able to go out on a whim once you have a baby, will you?'

I knew it gave her a boost to talk about pregnancy as though it was definitely going to happen for her.

'If you're sure,' said Petra, looking at Alexa with concern. 'But call me if you need me.'

My phone beeped.

'Right,' I said, downing my drink with one hand and wrapping my scarf around my neck with the other. It felt as though I'd only just taken it off. Then I pulled on my coat and helped Alexa into hers. If I could just get her out of the bar and into the taxi, we'd be fine. I'd got this and I didn't want Dan and Petra to worry.

*

Half an hour later, Alexa was lying on her sofa with a blanket over her. She typically slept for hours after an attack, but I'd promised to stay the night regardless and was planning to give the place a good tidy. Her flatmate was away for a couple of weeks, and let's just say that housework wasn't Alexa's forte. I got it, she was busy with medical school and was struggling to keep on top of things – it wasn't surprising that cleaning her flat had been the last thing on her mind.

Instinctively I began to pick up used tea cups and dirty plates and carry them out to the kitchen. I opened the dishwasher, hoping to chuck everything inside, but it was full of dirty cutlery and crockery. *Why hadn't she just turned it on if she'd gone to the trouble of filling it?* I wondered. It was like living with my dad and siblings all over again. Speaking of familial responsibility, when I glanced at my phone, which I'd put on silent so as not to disturb Alexa, I saw that my younger sister, Kate, was calling. She needed me more than ever at the moment, what with her marriage being about to implode. I picked up the call without hesitation.

'Hey,' I said, wedging the phone between my shoulder and my ear while I ran a sink full of soapy water. I'd have to wash up by hand, and then in a minute I'd put the dishwasher on.

'Can you talk?' asked Kate, her speech slightly slurred, as though she'd had a couple of large wines. This was the case most nights at the moment – it was the only way she managed to get through an evening of simmering tension at home she informed me whenever I gently suggested she lay off the booze for a night or two.

'Sure. What's up?'

Kate sighed heavily. 'I tried to talk to Richard about divorce again and he threw it back in my face so that I felt like a terrible person. As though I'm the one ruining our marriage! I mean, how many times have I tried to sort things out? I have, haven't I?'

'Course you have,' I said, swirling my hand through the water. Now where did Alexa keep her sponge?

'So I decided to put the ball in his court again and suggested we get some outside help from a marriage counsellor, and do you know what he said?' said Kate.

'Let me guess,' I said, 'he doesn't want to talk to a stranger about his problems?'

'Exactly! How did you know?'

'That's what they all say.'

I wasn't sure who 'they' were, but in a way I sort of got it. I wouldn't want to talk to a professional about my problems either, in fact the idea of it made my stomach turn. This was just about the only point I agreed with Richard on. Much better to sort things out yourself in your own head, I always thought. Strong, contained and efficient, that was my mantra.

I listened as Kate lamented about her disintegrating relationship, getting angrier and angrier as the call went on. Because I didn't want to drop my phone in the sink, I put her on speaker and placed my phone on the side, washing dishes as quietly as I could so she didn't accuse me of only half-listening, which I wasn't, but I had Alexa to help as well and it was more time-effective to do the two tasks alongside each other.

'We'll make an appointment with that solicitor someone recommended to you, shall we?' I said to Kate.

She groaned. 'Why can't I be more like you, Scar? When things were going wrong with Jackson you dumped him, didn't you? You walked away, no questions asked. Why can't I do the same thing?'

'It did take me a while, to be fair,' I said. 'And it was

hardly no questions asked, I went back and forth over it for about a year before I actually did anything about it.'

'Did you? You never said anything.'

'Well I didn't want to worry you, did I?' I said, wishing I hadn't mentioned it at all.

Half an hour or so later I'd managed to calm Kate down by promising to catch up the following day, the dishes were done, the dishwasher was mid-cycle, the washing machine was on a wool wash and I was warming up some soup for Alexa. When my phone rang again, I almost didn't answer it – there was only so much I could deal with in one evening. But then I saw it was Carla and she rarely rang this late, and curiosity got the better of me. I took the call.

'Hello?'

'Scarlett? Me again.'

Like me, Carla never missed an opportunity to multi-task, and I could hear her tapping away on her MacBook. After a few seconds of me listening to her type, riveting as that was, I thought I'd better remind her that I was on the other end of the line and that *she'd* called *me*.

'Carla?'

'Hmmn-hmmn?'

'Did you need me?'

'Yes. Just hold on one ... second. There we go. All booked.'

'What's all booked?'

The microwave pinged. I opened it and poured Alexa's soup into a bowl, somehow managing not to spill half of it all over the work surface like I sometimes did when I tried to do too many things at once.

'I've done something a bit unconventional,' said Carla ominously, 'but I think you and Theo need a strong push in the right direction. Otherwise I fear this project will never get off the ground.'

I frowned, leaning against the counter for support. What had Carla done? Because I was absolutely not the sort of person you'd describe as 'unconventional'.

'What kind of strong push?' I asked, sliding open a drawer to find Alexa a spoon. Wasn't forcing us to work together in the first place enough of a huge shove in a direction neither of us – I assumed – wanted to go in?

'You're going to need to clear your diary for the next two weeks,' announced Carla in a gravelly, no-nonsense tone. 'Because I have just booked you and Theo onto a writers' re-treat in the South of France. You'll be leaving on Saturday.'

South of France? Writers' retreat? Me and Theo? Two weeks! The words ricocheted around my head, but for the life of me I couldn't get them to make any sense. 'Sorry, what?'

'Imagine, Scarlett … twelve nights in glamorous Cannes. The beach, the pool, the palm trees. You'll be able write to your heart's content with none of the distractions of every-day life. This will be the absolute best way for you and Theo to reconnect and get this book off to a flying start.'

My mouth was opening and shutting like a goldfish, al-though of course Carla couldn't see that, but I was pretty sure she could imagine my reaction if she tried. What exactly was I supposed to say, here? *No fucking way*, perhaps? I'd barely begun wrapping my head around the dreaded prospect of having to meet with Theo at all, and now Carla somehow thought we could handle two long weeks together in a foreign country? Theo's face popped into my head unbidden. There was no possible way I could do this.

'I think that's a really bad idea, Carla,' I stuttered.

'Well it's all booked now,' she said, 'so I guess the only thing to do is to go and find out.'

I tried the box breathing exercise for myself because not only did I not want to lose it with Carla, I also didn't want to startle Alexa, who was probably feeling fragile after the night she'd had.

'How does the retreat work, then?' I asked, my voice strained. Perhaps I'd give Carla the impression that I was considering her ridiculous suggestion before I vetoed it. 'Will there be other writers there at the same time?'

'Yes, exactly,' said Carla. 'There will be other people doing the exact same thing you are. Like-minded people. In a lovely setting. Did I say there was a pool?'

'You did.'

A pool in Cannes did sound nice. And other authors were good, I generally liked them.

'Will there be tasks and exercises to do and stuff like that, then?' I asked.

'That's right,' said Carla. 'There will be professional super-vision and guided activities, so your time will be structured. I thought that might work well for you both.'

She was trying to suck me in with all the nice things about writing retreats in the French Riviera, of which obviously there were many, but she was missing the point. I didn't want to do any of these lovely-sounding things with the not-so-lovely Theo Winters. Then something else occurred to me.

'Carla, there's my dad. I can't just go off for twelve days. Plus, I can't really afford flashy hotels and writing retreats at the moment, what with not having an actual publishing deal.'

'Oh, didn't I mention that it's all paid for?' said Carla. 'Courtesy of yours truly. Consider it a gift to my two favour-ite clients.'

I felt a bit hot all of a sudden. Nobody had ever bought me

a trip to anywhere. And I had never been anyone's favourite anything.

'I couldn't possibly let you pay for it,' I said, strangely flattered.

'You can repay me by writing another bestseller,' said Carla.

Fair enough, I supposed. She took authors on and kind of relied on them to keep producing work that people wanted to read, and that would make her a decent amount in commission. I hadn't exactly held up my side of the bargain recently, had I?

'And I'm sure you can find someone to help with your dad. It's about time your siblings stepped up, no?'

I mean, she had a point, and it was glaringly obvious to everyone else that that was exactly what needed to happen. But the actual implementing of it by me was where it all fell down. Because I'd always been the one to take the lead – I'd sort of had to be initially, and it had stuck. And I liked fixing things for people and I was good at it, so it was hard for me to relinquish control.

'Look, it's going to be divine out there,' gushed Carla. 'You told me you want to prioritise your career, Scarlett, and in order for you to do that, you need to physically remove yourself from the shackles of everyday life. Temporarily, of course. Otherwise you won't be able to focus on your novel, yes?'

Carla was very persuasive. And on the odd occasion I'd had to go away with work, my family had managed to cobble through, possibly because they knew they didn't have me to fall back on if things didn't quite go to plan. But twelve days? I'd never been gone for that long.

'Does it have to be the full two weeks?' I asked tentatively.

'It does. And it's all booked, and so are your flights. I'll get Lily to ping the details over to you first thing in the morning.'

'But—'

'Sorry, Scarlett, must dash, I've got an event. Let's touch base soon.'

The line went dead. I put my phone down and stared at it for quite a long time before picking up Alexa's soup and taking it through to the lounge. Could I really go off to Cannes on Saturday? Would Theo even agree to it – he might have people he didn't want to leave, too? The thought of that made me feel a bit queasy, so I quickly buried it, down in the deep, murky depths of my memory where other unpleasant things lurked.

I set the soup down on the coffee table next to Alexa, who had some colour back in her cheeks and looked altogether less terrible.

'Hungry?' I asked, kneeling on the floor next to her.

'Very,' she said, smiling weakly. 'Thanks for this, Scar.'

She sat up, using a scrunchie on her wrist to pull her dark curls off her face and into a bun.

'Smells good,' she said.

I shifted position, secretly longing to be in my cosy little flat, within a few feet of my own bed so that I could stagger there and lie in it and stew about my failing career and the upcoming horror of the retreat. But Alexa needed me and so I would be here, no questions asked.

'Would it help to talk about what triggered the panic attack?' I asked her gently as she slurped at her soup.

She shrugged.

'Same old. I read an email about my next placement. They've changed all my shifts around and they've put me on tons of nights. I got all worked up about how I'm going to fit in revising for my exams.'

I nodded. 'You'll find a way to manage. You've done loads of revision already, anyway, so hopefully it's just a matter of re-reading your notes whenever you get a chance. Why don't you make yourself a timetable? That always makes you feel more in control, doesn't it?'

'I suppose,' said Alexa, nodding. 'Maybe I'll do that this weekend. I think I'll feel better once I've got a plan.'

Alexa was generally far more organised than I was – her detailed plans and her ability to stick to them were basically all of my professional goals rolled into one. Every time I started a new book I would map out a chapter-by-chapter breakdown of what I was going to write and when. On average, I'd given up by day two.

'Who were you on the phone to out there, your dad?' asked Alexa.

'Carla,' I said.

'Oh?'

'She's only gone and booked me and Theo Winters on a writers' retreat in Cannes,' I said. 'We're supposed to be leaving the day after tomorrow.'

Alexa dipped some of the bread I'd cut for her into her soup.

'And you're sounding miserable about going on this delightful-sounding trip because …?'

'Because I've not spoken to him for years. And also, I don't want him thinking that I'm desperate to work with him again because my writing career has failed and his hasn't.'

'Yours hasn't failed, Scar,' said Alexa, reaching out to rub my arm reassuringly. 'You've just released a brilliant new book.'

I didn't think now was the time to tell her about the disappointing sales figures and the lack of faith from my publisher. She had enough on her plate without having to stress about my life, too.

'Anyway, you worked really well with Theo to begin with. I remember you telling me that you loved his enthusiasm. That it always felt like he dived into the depths of your mind and pulled out ideas for stories that you didn't even know were there.'

'Did I really say that?'

Theo was always full of ideas and was achingly confident about sharing them. And no doubt he'd be expecting me to have some of my own, the spark of something that we could start to work on. And I was still caught up with the story I'd been writing before Carla had told me to scrap that and start this new thing. What if I couldn't come up with anything else, and all I did was prove to Theo that I was indeed useless without him?

'Uh-huh,' said Alexa, chewing on a chunk of bread. 'And you also said that for the first time ever, you felt completely comfortable showing somebody else your work.'

'I cannot remember saying any of that,' I said, bristling. I must have been deluded.

'Oooh, I wonder if he's still smoking hot,' mused Alexa.

I tutted. 'No idea. And that's really not the point.'

'How long will you be away?' asked Alexa.

I groaned. 'Nearly two weeks.'

I was only just getting used to the idea of working with him again and now I had to spend a fortnight in the same hotel as the guy.

'That's doable though, right? Even if you don't get on that well anymore? I mean you managed that last year with Jackson when it was obvious that you two should probably split up and we were all waiting for you to come to that conclusion on your own.'

27

I swallowed hard.

'Why, what's everyone been saying about me?'

Alexa looked sheepish. 'Nothing bad. We were just concerned that you were in a relationship that clearly wasn't working.'

'And none of you thought to mention this to me directly instead of gossiping about it behind my back?' I said, crushingly disappointed in my friends. I hated the idea of them all feeling sorry for me and having secretive discussions about how unhappy I seemed. Anyway, it hadn't been that bad – Jackson was a nice person and I was glad that we'd taken the time to work out whether we were supposed to be together or not instead of rushing into a break-up that we might have lived to regret.

'We weren't gossiping,' said Alexa. 'But to be fair – and please don't take this the wrong way – you're not great at opening up to us about how you feel. Sometimes we have to guess.'

I went to protest, but stopped myself. She was right, of course.

'We hoped that when you were ready, you would talk to us about it. And you did.'

'Just not for about twelve months,' I said with a wry smile.

Alexa smiled back. 'Better late than never.'

I took a deep breath and rubbed at my temples. Maybe I could compartmentalise the way I felt about Theo in real life and the way I felt about collaborating with him on a novel. I didn't know, because I'd spent the last six years trying to put him out of my mind entirely, which was pretty hard when everyone you met at a book signing asked about bloody *Little Boy Lost*. And now this grand plan of Carla's was throwing all the hard work I'd done on myself (if you could call suppressing feelings hard work) out of the window.

'I think you should just go for it,' said Alexa. 'A trip to the South of France will do you the world of good.'

I wished I could tell her it wasn't a question of whether I *should*, but whether I *could*. Could I do this? Could I survive a couple of weeks of hell if it meant that I'd potentially have enough money to make my life – and my family's – easier? Perhaps Carla was right and something that forced Theo and me to be in close proximity to each other *was* actually what we needed – it would be a sort of immersion therapy, like how when you had a really intense phobia you had to stop avoiding the thing you were terrified of.

'Is the washing machine on?' asked Alexa, suddenly cocking her head as the machine rattled loudly in the kitchen.

'Uh-huh.'

Alexa put her spoon down, turning to face me, looking all earnest. 'You're the best, Scarlett. Thank you for being here when I need you. And for always knowing what to do.'

'Any time,' I said, meaning it, but also thinking that I almost never knew what to do, I just acted like I did.

Chapter Three

Heathrow Airport on a Saturday afternoon was not the best. All those snaking queues that went on forever and never seemed to move and groups so big it didn't seem possible that they could all fit on the same flight and the giant suitcases that looked as though they had someone's entire life packed inside of them. I stood patiently in line at the check-in desk for the 15:40 flight to Nice, mentally running the contents of my own reasonably sized suitcase through my mind. Had I got everything I needed? It had been a struggle to know what to pack, what with it being April. I was hoping for sun and blue skies, the kind that had soared over Grace Kelly's head in *To Catch a Thief*. But then it could be raining, couldn't it? Or cold (unlikely, Alexa had assured me, practically forcing a bikini into my hands).

The queue for check-in inched forwards and my stomach suddenly tensed so hard it felt like a rock had been dropped inside it. Because there at the desk, with only about ten people between us, stood Theo: the man I'd hoped never to see again. He was facing forwards, so I could only see glimpses of his profile as he handed over his ticket and took his passport out of his pocket, but it was definitely him. The previously piercing sounds of the airport were now strangely muffled, as though I was swimming deep under water and all the action was happening on the surface. I tried to centre myself. Perhaps if I looked at something else, focused on something that *wouldn't* make me feel as though my brain was about to explode. I zoned in on the loud American couple in the business class queue who were wearing matching Hawaiian shirts while still managing to look as though they had money. Within seconds, though, my eyes pinged back to Theo, taking in his dark hair, shaved short at the nape of the neck and then longer as it got closer to the crown. He had on one of the slim-fitting white T-shirts he always used to wear and the low-slung indigo jeans I'd seen him in a hundred times. His style hadn't changed, then, which didn't bode well for his personality. I watched him bend to haul his suitcase onto the conveyor belt, one of those sleek, business-like hard shell ones, which was different, because he was all about the rucksacks before. He had a jacket slung over his arm and a laptop bag over one shoulder. If I strained my ears I could hear his voice: deep, molten, his accent the perfect sweet spot between proper London and proper posh. All in all, things suddenly felt very real – I was going to have to talk to this man, who even from this distance was making me breathe far more rapidly than was good for me. I didn't think it was possible, but now that I'd seen him close-ish up, I was dreading this trip even more than before.

There was more movement in the queue and for a second I panicked that I was going to end up at the desk next to Theo and that I'd have to then make the most awkward of awkward small talk with him while simultaneously checking in for my flight and I wasn't ready for any of that, not yet. In fact, I'd been hoping I wouldn't see him until I got to Cannes. Once I was unpacked and wafting about in something summery and sweet, looking effortlessly chic (well OK, perhaps not effortlessly), I'd be better able to summon the inner-confidence required to get through our first interaction in over half a decade. I was intending to play it cool.

Be friendly and efficient. After all, we'd never had a proper conversation about what had happened before, so why start now? The past was the past, right?

Giving him another furtive glance to make sure he hadn't spotted me, too, I pulled my phone out of my bag. I knew nothing about him anymore, a conscious decision, but one I'd made when I'd thought I'd never see him again. Now I knew he was definitely coming to Cannes and wasn't going to bail at the last minute like I'd been tempted to, I realised I was going to have to face the unknown and check out his Instagram; that maybe it would help to be prepared so that I wouldn't be completely blindsided if he told me he was married with two beautiful children or something (and of course they'd be beautiful, with his hair, and those eyes). I searched his name and clicked into his handle – @winterswrites – bracing myself for an onslaught of self-congratulatory selfies and shots of him lying half-naked on the decks of yachts surrounded by model-esque children with high cheekbones and names like Milo and Allegra. Careful not to accidentally follow him or like any of his pictures, I began scrolling through, wincing each time I moved on to a new shot, as if expecting the worst, although I didn't really know what the worst would be. He wasn't the most prolific poster (but then neither was I) and I was surprised to note that these days he almost exclusively talked about his writing process. Perhaps he'd finally developed some humility, although given that the next shot was a layout of a pretentious article he'd featured in for a men's magazine with the headline *Why I Need To Be Alone When I Write*, perhaps not. Perhaps he wanted to give the impression he was a tortured artiste meandering solo along the mean streets of London. But if that was the case, why on earth had he agreed to team up with me again?

Still scrolling as the queue moved forward, I paused on a

photo of his desk – which was about ten times neater than mine had ever been – and a tantalising shot of the first page of the manuscript for his third solo book, which I seemed to remember was being published this coming autumn. In an unwise attempt to zoom in, my thumb slipped and I accidentally liked it. Complete and utter panic ensued as I frantically attempted to *unlike* it again.

By the time I looked up, feeling worse than I had before and wishing I'd trusted my instincts not to look, I was relieved to see Theo had turned and was striding purposefully off towards security. He didn't seem at all hesitant, which I supposed was good, but then that also told me that he had no qualms whatsoever about seeing me again. Why would he, I supposed, when I'd clearly meant nothing to him in the first place? I checked my ticket, suspecting that Carla would have booked us seats together. I didn't want to be strapped into a chair next to him for two hours – I wanted to feel as though I could escape and walk away if I needed to. Because it could go really, really badly, couldn't it, and somehow physical space felt like a necessary element to factor in.

I finally made it to the front of the queue and handed over my ticket and passport to the smartly dressed British Airways crew member who was managing to remain cheery despite probably having been at work since about 3 a.m.

'Is it possible to change seats at this point?' I asked as I lifted my suitcase onto the belt. I was already regretting packing four pairs of shoes – was it really necessary when I would be spending most of my time writing? But never one to be caught unawares when it came to my wardrobe, I'd brought the gamut of footwear with me so that all eventualities would be covered – trainers in case I decided to do some actual exercise (doubtful, although apparently there was a gym at the hotel), strappy sandals for evening, ankle boots in case it rained and flip-flops because the weather forecast said it was going to be twenty-two degrees tomorrow, which in my eyes was positively beach stroll weather. Oh, and the loafers I had on. Was that too much?

'Let me see what I can do,' said the woman. 'Anywhere in particular you'd like to sit?'

'Um, as far away from my current seat as possible?' I suggested.

I realised I was being a little irrational here – he might not even have the seat next to me, but I could hardly check, could I? It seemed safer to move regardless.

She tapped something into the computer with a wry smile and printed me out a new ticket. Clearly she knew the drill – the customer was always right, and ask no questions.

'There we go,' she said, handing it to me. 'Have a lovely trip to Nice.'

I took it from her gratefully and headed for security, hanging back so as not to accidentally catch Theo up. He might be rooting through his liquids or something, stalled by not being able to fit his designer skincare products into one, solitary plastic bag. After breezing through security I was silently thankful that Heathrow terminal five was so huge. I bought myself a coffee from Starbucks then found a spot in the corner from where I could surreptitiously keep an eye out for a dashing, egotistical author. I was only delaying the inevitable, but needs must.

When our flight was called and I made my way to the gate, I kept thinking I could see him but then it turned out to be a different man with dark hair and a dark beard and a white top. There seemed to be a lot of them at gate number 33. I was one of the last to board, having now been seated at the back of the plane. Unfortunately, I'd failed to compute that this would mean that my original seat was likely to be towards the front of the plane and therefore there was a good chance that I'd have to walk past … yep, and there he was. Sitting in the middle of row 11, shimmering in that annoying way he tended to. Ridiculously shiny hair, shorter at the sides than at the front. Brown eyes, a little narrowed as always, as though he was suspicious of something, or trying to work out what the hell you were talking about. Beard trimmed, moustache covering his top lip, bottom lip raspberry pink and full. My heart started hammering painfully against my ribcage, which annoyingly had always been my go-to reaction to seeing him face on. Next to him, in the aisle seat, was a teenaged girl wearing giant headphones and flicking manically through her phone; thankfully she seemed to be oblivious to the fact I was staring at her fellow passenger as though I was an axe murderer eyeing up my next victim. What should I do now? Shuffle past and pretend I hadn't seen him? If I dug around in my bag for a bit with my head down, he might not even notice me. Out of the corner of my eye I could see him fiddling with his seatbelt – if he could just keep doing that for another minute or so then I might just get away with it.

Of course, just as I lurched forward to scuttle past the end of his row, I made the mistake of glancing sideways at him and he looked up and caught my eye. He didn't seem remotely fazed, which was interesting, because my legs now felt as though they were made of melted butter and I was sure every single millilitre of blood had just drained out of my body. I wanted to look away but I was also frozen to the spot. He tried to smile, at least I thought that might be what he was aiming for, but instead it came out as a sort of grimace. I eyeballed him back, incapable of exuding any kind of fake emotion like a simple smile in return because I was overwhelmed with the suddenly very intense feelings coursing through my body – shock, regret, embarrassment, panic. All the bad things, basically.

We stared silently at each other for quite a few beats and I thought this might be hands-down the most mortifying situation of my life. Eventually I snapped myself out of it, aware that I was going to have to move on given that there were at least a couple of people looking for their seats behind me. I finally managed to give him the stiffest of stiff smiles and he nodded and said *Scarlett*. And I said *Hey*. Hardly cutting-edge conversation for two people who were supposed to write novels for a living. He unbuckled his seatbelt and started to get up.

'I assume you're in the window seat,' he said, his white, perfectly straight teeth dazzling, even in the dim artificial light of the cabin.

'I'm not, actually,' I said, taking a modicum of pleasure from watching the confusion on his face. 'See you in Nice,' I said casually, forcing myself to breeze past him.

I threw myself down in my seat in the farthest back corner of the plane, wiping the sweat that had literally sprouted from my forehead during our approximately twenty-second conversation onto the sleeve of my jumper. This was not a good start.

Eventually I recovered enough to do up my seatbelt and then I opened the bottle of sparkling water I'd bought in Boots – obviously it sprayed everywhere, because that was the kind of day I was having – and tried to act like a normal person doing normal things on a normal flight. I could do it, I knew I could. I would, once again, feel human. At some point. Probably once I was back in London. I realised I'd done a great job of burying any residual feelings I might have had for Theo, but I hadn't allowed for the fact that seeing him in the (tanned, glowing) flesh might unleash a certain type of emotion I appeared to have no control over.

As I settled down for take-off, I refused to let myself re-play the very short exchange with Theo over and over in my head, and panicked about the more familiar anxiety-provoking topic of my dad instead. Kate and my brother, Zach, hadn't sounded particularly confident when I'd sprung it on them that they'd be in charge for the next two weeks and that there was a good chance they were going to have to make decisions without me. I'd left them two A4 sides of instructions, but was it enough? Had I missed anything? I made the mistake of checking my messages before I put my phone on flight mode and there was already something from Kate.

What is Dad supposed to have for dinner? Or does the carer do it?

Damn. I was sure I'd explained to her about when the carer came and what they did, and also, why wasn't she just asking Dad what he wanted to eat? He hadn't lost the power of speech entirely, thankfully, so was quite capable of answering a simple question about his mealtime preferences.

It's on my note, I taped it to the fridge. Carer does it Monday to Friday. You'll have to feed him at the weekend. He'll tell you what he wants, just ask. Maybe try egg and chips, he's always happy with that?

And then I put my phone away and read a bit of my book and reminded myself about the parts of this trip I *was* looking forward to. Like having some headspace to myself. Walking alone on the beach for the first time in years. French food and chilled rosé wine. Starting a new writing project with a plot that potentially I wouldn't have to come up with all by myself.

When we landed and made our way into the terminal, I remembered how much I loved the feeling of arriving in a different country and Nice International Airport was no exception. Heat shimmered above the tarmac and it immediately felt heady and warm, even though I hadn't yet stepped foot outside of a Perspex airport tunnel. I turned on my phone and already had three messages – how could this be when I'd only been in the air for two hours?! One was from Carla wishing me bon voyage, and there was a similar message from Alexa. I'd had a missed call from Dad, plus a text asking if I'd landed yet.

I sighed, putting my phone back into my bag and joining my fellow passengers in the queue for security, keeping half an eye out for Theo so that I could avoid him if necessary. I passed the time by trying to read signs in French and picking out phrases I understood from the announcements piping out over the loudspeaker. The airport smelled like those part-baked baguettes I sometimes treated myself to when I was feeling sorry for myself and needed white carbs with lots of butter.

Once I'd collected my suitcase, which as usual seemed to be one of the last to appear on the conveyor belt, leaving me convinced it had been lost/left in London and that I would have to converse with Theo sporting the same jeans and roll-neck jumper combo I'd been wearing since the early hours of this morning, I headed outside to find a taxi and it was possibly the most glamorous exit from an airport I'd ever experienced. The weather was still and warm and I instantly pushed up the sleeves of my far-too-thick sweater. The Sheraton hotel shimmered in front of us, all glitz and glass, and palm trees sprung up alongside the roads leading out of the airport. I paused for a second, taking it all in, temporarily glad I'd come, before heading for the taxi queue, resigning myself to spending the best part of a hundred euros on a half-hour journey to the hotel (I'd googled it). Until

I stopped dead because there was Theo, leaning languidly against a row of luggage trolleys, staring right at me with his sunglasses on and looking all casual and smug about how attractive he thought he looked. He couldn't possibly be waiting for me, could he? He probably had a car pre-booked or something.

'Thought we might as well share a cab,' he said as I approached. 'If you want.'

I came to a stop next to him, willing myself to behave like a well-functioning adult and not a teenager who's just bumped headlong into her captain-of-the-football-team crush.

'Um, OK,' I heard myself saying, when every fibre of my being was screaming *No, no, no, don't do it!* This was going to be terrible: the two of us, in the confines of the back seat of a taxi, probably driving at top speed if I knew French cab drivers, and with absolutely no idea how to act with each other or what to say. On the other hand, it *would* save me fifty euros.

I followed him to the nearest taxi, which had already popped open its boot.

'*Cannes, s'il vous plait,*' I heard Theo say as the driver took my case and I slid into the back seat. '*Hôtel La Villa de L'Oliveraie.*'

'*Oui, bien sûr, Monsieur,*' said the driver.

'Oh, and is it possible to take the scenic route? No motorway?' said Theo with an upwards inflection I'd never heard him use before. I supposed we all did that to make ourselves understood when speaking to somebody whose first language wasn't English, but I'd always thought it was pretty pointless.

The driver grunted, and I was tempted to do the same myself. When Theo got in next to me, I couldn't help myself.

'Why the scenic route? Won't that take longer?'

He shrugged. 'There'll be more to see. The coastline is supposed to be spectacular.'

The thought of spending double the time that was strictly necessary in a car with Theo at this precise point in time was less than appealing, especially since he smelled unfairly good, like cloves that had been left out in a wood full of pine trees and baked in the sun, while I probably smelled like the inside of an aeroplane.

'I'd rather go the quicker way,' I said.

Theo slammed his door shut and put his seatbelt on. 'Please yourself. You'd better tell the driver, then.'

I tutted. 'Fine, I will. *Excusez-moi?*' I said to the driver, who was already pulling away from the kerb at about a million kilometres per hour. 'Can we go the quicker way, actually, please? The motorway?'

It wasn't like me to risk upsetting our driver, but the fear of spending more time alone with Theo had given me the courage to speak up.

The driver looked at me in the rear-view mirror, his expression unreadable.

'You want the motorway now? Not the coast road?'

'Yes, that's right,' I said, cringing. 'Sorry.'

He grunted again, which I took to be a yes. Theo wound down his window, turning his head away from me. It was just like him to take offense, just because I dared to have a different view on which route we should take to the hotel. He generally thought he knew best, which was one of the things that annoyed me – used to annoy me – about him. Actually, that wasn't strictly true. At first, I'd found it quite sexy that he knew what he wanted and was confident enough to tell everyone about it. It was only later – i.e. after we'd stopped talking – that I turned it into a negative. Now that I hadn't been hoodwinked into finding him phenomenally attractive, I could see him for what he really was – full of himself and far too opinionated for anyone's (well, my) liking.

Theo shifted in his seat, turning back to face me.

'Well this is weird.'

'Yep,' I said, still smarting from the exchange about which route to take.

'I wasn't sure what to make of Carla's suggestion at first, were you?'

I wound down my own window, then, needing a second to think. Two could play at that game. With its sweeping grey tarmac airport roads and American-style green road signs and the spindly palm trees popping against the darkening blue sky, Nice reminded me a little of LA, where Theo and I had once travelled to together. A bunch of producers had been interested in adapting *Little Boy Lost* into a screenplay and we'd had a whirlwind few days of meetings and trying to present a united front whilst hiding the fact that we couldn't stand each other.

'It took me a while to get my head around it,' I managed eventually.

'Not sure my head will ever be around it,' he said gruffly.

The fact he felt the same way as me was part insulting, because what had I ever done to him, and part a relief, because it meant that we'd probably both want to spend as little time together as possible. At least the view out of the window was a good distraction. As we passed a huge, glistening white block of tiered apartments that looked like a cruise ship from a distance, and Rome's Coloseum close up, the taxi driver explained that this was Marina Baie des Anges, a luxurious apartment complex built in the sixties. And soon after that, I could make out what I thought was the sea, a dark blue mass shimmering gently on the edge of my field of vision. As we rounded a hill just outside Cannes, the sky had turned orange and pink, and coupled with the shadowy hills in the distance the image reminded me of a beautiful Cézanne painting I'd once had Blu-Tacked to my bedroom wall. Our trip might not have got off to the easiest of starts, but if I had to write a book with Theo Winters anywhere, I thought I might be glad that it was here.

Chapter Four

For some reason the hotel reminded me of a smaller, cuter version of the Chateau Marmont in LA, all straw-coloured walls and green shutters and little wrought iron balconies. Theo and I had had one dinner there, with the producer who'd come closest to getting *Little Boy Lost* actually made. I'd spotted Ryan Reynolds at the bar.

Once I'd got out of the taxi and had properly taken in my surroundings, I realised *Hôtel La Villa de L'Oliveraie* looked altogether less ostentatious than its LA counterpart. The gardens flanking us on both sides of the winding stone pathway consisted of perfectly manicured grass lined with bushes that were bursting with flowers in the most gorgeous pinks and purples and whites, and I could immediately smell the roses curled around the entrance to the reception area, which was housed in a different building, a pale pink French cottage with a sloping roof and an arched doorway. I felt calmer than I had on the journey down here: there would be plenty of space for us both. I could write under one olive tree out in the garden, Theo under another.

'*Merci, Monsieur*,' said Theo, handing two fifty-euro notes to the driver. 'Keep the change.'

I pulled a fifty out of my bag and handed it to Theo, but he shook his head.

'Don't worry about it,' he said.

I put the note away. 'I suppose you can expense it, anyway,' I said.

I was very on-it with my tax return, about the only thing I was on-it with, actually, because I was so used to paying bills and looking after Dad's finances, and I religiously filed my receipts according to the accounting system I'd developed way back when I had time to create Excel spreadsheets. I had no idea whether Theo was like me in that regard or not. I knew that he was meticulous about planning when it came to his books and that he plotted absolutely everything out, or at least he used to, and that he stuck to it rigidly, even for the first draft, which we'd laughed about together once, because I was the complete opposite. I just had a vague idea and went for it, seeing what happened, discovering stuff along the way. I wondered if he'd changed. I had, a bit, over the years – I'd learned to at least come up with a synopsis for my books, otherwise they'd never have been signed off by my publisher in the first place. But I didn't like doing it, and I left as much wiggle room as possible – that was half the fun of writing for me, being free to take my characters' lives in whichever direction I – or sometimes *they* – fancied.

Theo held open the door for me as I shuffled my suitcase into the reception area, which instantly felt rustic and homely with a touch of French charm. The man behind the desk was in his fifties with shaggy grey hair and that undeniable French twinkle in his eyes and the sort of tanned complexion that came from living in the sunny hills of the Côte d'Azur.

'*Bonjour, Madame, Monsieur,*' he said, looking up from his computer screen as we approached the desk.

'*Bonsoir,*' I said, smiling at him.

I already felt a sort of sense of peace descending over me. There was definitely something to be said for physically removing myself from the day-to-day worries that usually weighed heavily on my mind. Knowing that I couldn't possibly visit my dad even if I wanted to helped, for starters. Usually I'd have this sort of internal crushing guilt about it all, because Cambridge was only an hour or so away from London and I could get on a train up there at pretty much any time, and therefore often felt bad if I fancied a weekend alone at home when I could/should be visiting him. But out here, in the beautiful surroundings of this little hotel, in the midst of rolling hills and enticing-looking vineyards, what could I do? As if on cue, a message pinged through on my phone. I went to read it and stopped myself: it could wait until I was settled in my room, surely.

'You are checking in?' asked the man behind the desk in his sexy French lilt. Mind you, the French language always sounded sexy, didn't it, no matter whose mouth it was coming out of? There were obviously some exceptions – the up-themselves, disinterested waiting staff I remembered from an ill-fated trip to Paris with Jackson, for example, during which he branded almost every single thing I wanted to do too touristy. It had felt like the beginning of the end; like we just didn't connect anymore.

'We are,' I said. 'I should have a room booked under the name Scarlett Green?'

He tapped away on his keyboard.

'Ah, *oui*,' he said. 'May I take your passport, Madame Green?' I rifled in my bag, handing it to him. 'And you must be Monsieur Winters?' he said, looking expectantly at Theo, who was standing next to me with his hands shoved in his pockets looking as though he'd rather be anywhere else but here. How could he not have been charmed by this place? Was the prospect of spending two weeks in close proximity to me really that distressing for him?

'That's right. But I'll check in after, don't worry.'

The Frenchman looked confused. 'Ah, but you are together, non?'

My eyes widened and I could only imagine the expression on Theo's face.

'No!' I said abruptly, forgetting to be my usual, polite self. I made a diligent attempt to soften my tone. 'We're not together.'

The manager furrowed his brow dramatically.

'But you are booked as a couple, *oui*? I have it here, Madame Green and Monsieur Winters.'

I flinched. Clearly there had been a misunderstanding.

'We're here for the writers' retreat, actually,' I told him, trying to hide the panic in my voice. 'Our agent handled the bookings for both of us, but we should have separate reservations. Sorry for any confusion.'

The manager was still looking at me. Shouldn't he have been saying *Oui, pas de problème*, and shifting our names around on his computer?

I became very aware of Theo's presence next to me. I'd forgotten how tall and perfectly lean he was, but now that we were shoulder to shoulder – or more accurately, my shoulder was parallel with the middle of his chest – I remembered how he'd always seemed larger than life. Wherever he was in a room, I could usually sense him, either by the rumble of his voice, or a glimpse of his profile out of the corner of my eye.

'Is everything all right?' asked Theo in the commanding tone I now also remembered.

The manager shifted uncomfortably. 'I am afraid to tell you that our writers' retreat is happening in one month's time. At the end of May, after *le festival du cinéma*. And this month, beginning tomorrow, we have our couples retreat.'

Theo took the words right out of my mouth. '*Couples* retreat?'

'That is correct, *Monsieur*. We have a world-famous psychotherapist here at the hotel who will be working with our couples – yourselves included – for the next ten days. It is the second year we have held this event and I can assure you that the feedback is very good. *Magnifique.*'

I was speechless. *Speechless.* Of all the things in the world to happen to Theo and me, who could barely tolerate each other's company, this was possibly the very worst thing I could imagine.

'But we're not a couple!' I screeched.

'This needs to be fixed. Now,' declared Theo.

I didn't dare look at him, but I could feel his thunderous aura from here. Ten days of therapy, as *if!* Alexa had been trying to get me to go for years and was always raving about a therapist she'd seen for her anxiety, but talking about my problems was not going to make them go away, so I'd never seen the point. Anyway, I was doing perfectly fine as I was – I sorted things out for everyone else, didn't I, and I wouldn't be able to do that unless I was totally on top of things.

The manager had the good grace to look mortified.

'You are not married? Partners?'

'No!' we both said at the same time, which would have been funny if we weren't in the midst of a crisis.

'Look,' said Theo, turning to me. 'Surely we can just stay here at the hotel and not participate in this ridiculous retreat.'

The hotel holds up a finger. '*Monsieur*, I'm afraid that is not possible. The rate you were given is for retreat guests only. The organisers are covering some of our hotel costs.'

'Well then we'll just pay the difference,' I said, frustrated now. 'How much extra would it be?'

The manager got out his calculator and began tapping numbers into it.

'If you wish to stay in the hotel but not participate in the retreat, you will need to pay an additional ...' he said, finishing his sum, 'six hundred and twenty-four euros each.'

'What?!' I said.

'Well we're not doing that,' said Theo, which was the most sensible thing he'd said all day.

I tried to think. What was the best way out of this? I looked around: it was a gorgeous hotel, but we were clearly going to have to move and find somewhere else with a more reasonable nightly rate.

'Can we just get a refund, then?' I asked, glancing at Theo. 'I'm sure it can't be that difficult to find another hotel.'

'Ah,' said the hotel manager ominously. 'I am afraid that your booking is non-refundable, as laid out in the hotel's booking policy and clearly listed on our website. We are forbidden to give refunds with less than forty-eight hours' notice.'

'Oh for God's sake,' hissed Theo. 'Can't you make an exception, just this once?'

'I am afraid not, *Monsieur*.'

Feeling like screaming myself, I tried to keep a clear head. There had to be some way out of this.

'Look, let me speak to the person who made the booking. Maybe she can tell us how to proceed,' I suggested to the manager. And then, because it felt weird to just ignore Theo: 'I'm going to call Carla.'

'Fine,' he grunted. 'But don't let her talk you into staying.'

I huffed at him. 'Do you honestly think I want to stay and take part in some sort of couples retreat? With you? Because I can assure you, that's absolutely the worst idea I've ever heard.'

Theo rolled his eyes. 'No need to be dramatic about it, Scarlett. I just meant that Carla can be very persuasive.'

'So you think I'm a pushover, do you?' I demanded to know. 'That I'll just roll over and say *fine, we'll stay?*'

'Oh for Christ's sake, did I say that?' he replied.

I caught the manager's eye, who was watching us with alarm, clearly realising the severity of the situation. Couples retreat indeed! I mean, who even went on those things?

I went back out into the garden to make the call, taking some deep breaths, hoping the fresh air would go some way towards making me feel as good as I had about five minutes ago, before the dreaded words *couples* and *retreat* had been uttered in the same terrifying sentence. Ugh, the mere idea of it made me shudder. I could just imagine the naff activities we'd be forced to take part in: icebreaker games! Role-plays! Couples bingo! And presumably these things were meant for people who were actually in a committed relationship with each other and wanted to work things out, not two writers who hadn't said a single word to each other in six years and had never even been a couple in the first place. Not that it hadn't felt possible at one stage – I supposed you couldn't spend that amount of time alone with someone and not feel close to them. But ultimately, what I was feeling couldn't have been what Theo was feeling otherwise things would never have panned out the way they did.

I checked the time: 7.15 p.m. I knew we were an hour ahead here, but Carla sometimes turned her work phone off in the evenings, particularly if she was at a book launch or something. I let it ring, metaphorically crossing my fingers that she'd answer the phone and that a simple and efficient solution to this fuck-up would roll right off her tongue.

'Hello?' barked Carla, just as I was about to hang up and fling my phone into a bush, a prime example of what being in close proximity to Theo Winters could do to me. 'Is that you, Scarlett?'

'Yes,' I said, sounding more measured than I felt. 'It's me, calling you from Cannes. I've ... we've just arrived.'

'Good, good. So is it gorgeous there, or what? Didn't I tell you that the change of scenery was exactly what you needed!'

Fucking hardly.

'There's a bit of a problem, actually,' I told her, bracing myself. She was amazing at the business side of things but I didn't find it particularly easy to talk to her about my personal life. Which was why I'd never told her what had happened between Theo and me, despite her having tried to drag it out of me on several occasions. And because she didn't know, it would be difficult for her to understand the gravitas of just how awkward this all was, and I wasn't about to get into it now because ... well, he could probably hear me for one thing.

'Oh yes?' she said.

I could hear the clinking of glasses, some schmoozy chatter. She was at a book event, I could tell, and therefore I imagined her with a glass of champagne in one hand and only one ear tuned in to what I was saying.

'You've accidentally booked us on a couples retreat,' I said, trying to keep the judgement out of my voice, even though I really wanted to yell: *How could you???!!* 'Run by some kind of world-famous psychotherapist, apparently. The writers' retreat is next month.'

Carla was uncharacteristically silent for a moment or two. 'Well, that's unfortunate,' she said eventually.

'To put it mildly. And now they're saying that if we want to stay here and not do the retreat we'd have to pay another twelve hundred euros. Or we can find a different hotel but they wouldn't be able to refund the money you've already paid.'

'Oh dear,' said Carla. 'Well obviously I can't cover any of that, Scarlett. I don't do this sort of thing for my other clients, you understand.'

I glanced nervously around at Theo, who was looking expectantly at me through the glass. He was going to kick off, big time if I didn't return with positive news.

'So what do you suggest, then?' I asked her, the last vestiges of optimism draining out of me. Obviously I couldn't expect her to cover those extra booking charges, but I couldn't cover them myself either, and it didn't seem like Theo was willing to. But there had to be something we could do. Please let Carla have some grand plan to get us the hell out of here, I thought. She was an excellent trouble-shooter, it was part of her job; surely she could think of something?

'Look. You and Theo were friends before, am I right?' said Carla.

I didn't like where this was going, not one bit. 'Briefly.'

'And you wrote well together. Brilliantly, in fact. Six weeks on the *New York Times* bestseller-list brilliant. Bidding war for movie rights brilliant.'

I shrugged, even though shrugs didn't transmit over phone lines.

'I know you've already agreed to try writing together again, but would it also be worth trying to rekindle the friendship, do you think? And could you – and hear me out with this one, Scarlett, because I can hear you huffing and puffing from here—'

I promptly huffed again because I couldn't help myself. There seemed to be no other way to express how I felt about the idea of being friends with Theo again. I had enough on my plate making sure my family were fully functioning without entertaining a friendship that was doomed from the start.

'I'm listening,' I said through gritted teeth.

'You mentioned there will be a therapist at this retreat, yes? What if a bit of therapy together might help you have an actual conversation with Theo about what happened before? What if the issue could be resolved? What if hearing one another's point of view, in a sort of controlled way, with a professional guiding you, actually helped sort out whatever went wrong between you in the first place?'

'That's impossible. The damage is done now.'

I knew I sounded belligerent, but honestly, Carla had no idea how hard it was for me to even be here. I'd spent the last six years trying not to think about the past and the last thing I wanted to do was rehash it now, especially in front of Theo!

'Think about it,' said Carla, using the slightly controlling fake-sympathetic tone I'd heard her deploy whenever she wanted to persuade someone to do something they clearly didn't want to do. 'You need this book to be a hit. And the writing process would be so much easier if you could just get along.'

'But—'

'Now, I really must go. You two might be my favourite clients, but alas, you're not my only ones. Let me know what you decide, yes?'

And with that she was gone. Back to the familiar territory of another bookish event where all she had to do was schmooze with a few publishing folk and drink warm white wine. I, on the other hand, now had to work out how the hell I was going to tell Theo that we were essentially stuck here.

I took a deep breath, pushed open the door to the reception area and steeled myself.

Theo looked at me like an eager puppy. 'What did she say?'

I took a deep breath, silently cursing Carla for leaving me to explain. I was just going to have to tell him straight.

'She's not prepared to pay extra for us to stay here.'

His dark expression said it all. 'Right.'

'Or for us to move hotels.'

He raised his eyebrows, seemingly speechless.

'She thinks it might do us good to have some therapy to see if we can rebuild our ... friendship.'

Theo shook his head, as though he couldn't believe what he was hearing. 'She said what?'

'Do you really want me to repeat it?' I said, irritated. He should have called her himself if he wanted all the details.

'*Madame*, what did you decide?' asked the manager, looking as though he wanted this situation to be resolved as quickly as we did. We were probably ruining the chilled mojo of his hotel foyer with our bad vibes and our pacing around and our weird non-relationship that he probably couldn't work out for the life of him.

'I think we'll ... well, I can only speak for myself,' I said, glancing nervously at Theo and wondering why I kept referring to us as a 'we' as if we were in this together when we clearly weren't. 'If there's no way you're prepared to waive the fee for us to stay here and not do the retreat, then I think we're going to have to stay and ... take part.'

I winced. Theo stiffened next to me.

'*Très bien*,' said the manager, palpably relieved. He plucked a key from a hook behind him before we could change our minds and shot round to the front of the desk. 'Follow me,' he said.

I stalked off after him, looking over my shoulder at Theo,

whose jaw was clenched tight. If he could have shot flaming arrows through his eyes at me, he totally would have done.

'I'll wait here,' he mumbled, more to himself than anything.

'No, no. Come, *Monsieur*!' said the manager, strutting off.

Oh God. I bet our rooms were opposite each other or something. It was a small boutique hotel and I suddenly longed for one of those huge, characterless Ramadas, where I could be housed in a completely different wing of the building and never have to see him. Mind you, there was still the small matter of the therapy business, but we could cross that bridge when we came to it. They couldn't force us to join in, could they?

As I trailed up the wooden stairs behind the manager who was picking up speed as though he couldn't wait to get us checked in and out of his sight, I thought how charming the place was with its pictures of film stars enjoying the French Riviera flanking the walls and the shabby chic lampshades above our heads. If it wasn't for the retreat thing, or for Theo being here, simmering away behind me like a frustrated Hulk, this could actually be a delightful place to write.

We reached the second floor and the manager stopped outside door number twelve. He unlocked it and ushered me inside.

'*Madame, Monsieur*, your room.'

I followed him inside, not catching what he'd said at first, until Theo piped up.

'This isn't for both of us, I hope?' he said.

I laughed nervously. No. Definitely not. That couldn't have been what he'd meant?

'Yes, which one of us is staying here?' I asked brightly.

It would all be cleared up in a second. Theo's room would

54

be across the hall or something. But to my horror, the manager looked panicked again.

'*Madame*, *Monsieur*, you only have one room booked. You do not wish to stay together?'

'No we do not!' I said, horrified.

A king-sized bed with plump pillows and a lilac satin bedspread on it sat in the centre of the room and I was transported straight back to six years ago, to another bedroom and a morning I badly wanted to forget. Now all I could picture were Theo's high-thread-count sheets all tangled up on the floor; my black, lace bra flung over the back of his desk chair; his muscular, naked thighs wrapped around mine. I shook the deeply uncomfortable memory from my mind's eye.

'Tell me you have another room free?' I said to the manager, still flustered and dispensing with basic courtesy. If it came to it I'd have to fork out the money for another hotel myself, although that would mean eating into the miniscule amount of savings I had left and which I'd earmarked for family emergencies only. It wasn't like they weren't a regular occurrence.

'I am very sorry, *Madame*, but the hotel is fully booked and we do not have any other rooms available. Sadly there is nothing I can do.'

I put my fingers to my temples feeling as though I was going to lose the plot again.

'We cannot stay in the same room,' said Theo, sounding as weary of all this as I was. '*C'est pas possible*.'

The manager sighed deeply, as though he was the one being forced to share a bed with someone he couldn't stand. Empathy clearly wasn't his strong point.

'There is *one* room available,' he said, looking troubled.

'But we do not usually place our adult guests inside it. It is not as nice as this one.'

'It's fine, I'll take it,' I said, relieved.

I didn't care what the room looked like at this point, it could be a converted broom cupboard for all I cared, as long as it was far, far away from Theo.

'No, you stay in this room,' said Theo, in a rare display of chivalry. 'I'll take the other one.'

'Fine,' I said. I wasn't about to argue about it, and this room *was* lovely.

'OK,' said the hotel manager in a tone that suggested things were anything but. He removed a bunch of keys from his belt loop. 'Follow me, please, *Monsieur*.'

I stood back, fully expecting him and Theo to leave through the door we'd just entered by, but instead he lurched at an arched doorway carved into the left-hand wall which I'd assumed was my bathroom, inserted a key and turned it. I watched in ever-increasing horror as the door swung open revealing a smaller room with twin beds and not much else on the other side.

I gasped. 'Is this an inter-connecting family suite?'

'Yes, *Madame*, and it is the only room available,' said the manager, ushering Theo through before either of us could complain again. 'Usually it is for our … smaller guests. But there is an en-suite bathroom and a balcony.'

And not much else, I thought, looking at it, thankful that Theo had let me stay in this part of the room. If I was essentially trapped here for the next fortnight, I at least wanted to be comfortable. Theo caught my eye for a second as he closed the inter-connecting door behind him, no doubt already regretting his generosity.

'I hope this door locks?!' I called out.

A few seconds later I heard the clunking of the key

turning on the other side, although I could still hear the murmur of their voices as they talked. Great, there would be no escaping Theo now, with only paper-thin walls and a shared door between us. Huffily, I swung my suitcase up onto my bed and began to unpack, giving up halfway through and stuffing the whole thing under the bed instead. I checked out the bathroom, which was invitingly shiny and new with a black-and-white chequered floor and a bathtub that would be big enough for two, should it need to be. I took the plastic off one of the glasses and stood it next to the sink, ready to put my toothbrush in. Four fluffy white towels hung enticingly on the heated rail and I was tempted to strip off and wrap myself up in one immediately.

Twenty minutes or so later, I was feeling settled already and had thrown open the French doors leading out to a balcony overlooking the pool, which was more beautiful, even, than the photos I'd seen on the website. That felt like a rare thing, for a hotel to be nicer in real life. But it was, it was perfect. I was already inspired to write, even if I didn't exactly know what. And I was relieved to note that you couldn't see through to the other balconies on this side of the building (e.g. Theo's), with sage green shutters dividing up the balcony space at each end, meaning I could spend a lot of time out here enjoying the peace and quiet of the surrounding countryside without fear of bumping into *him*.

When I went back into the room to get my book, I thought I could make out the hiss of water from his room. Tentatively I crept towards the internal door, placing my ear carefully against its cool wood. Yes, there was definitely running water coming from somewhere. Perhaps he was in the shower, a thought I instantly wished I hadn't had because it brought back a whole host of memories, not all of them good. I crept away as silently as I could, shaking my head at my own patheticness. What on earth was I doing listening at his door? I couldn't be doing this for twelve nights straight, and why would I want to be? What was I hoping to achieve? I sat on the edge of my huge bed with its soft, slippery sheets, deciding I ought to check my phone – I hadn't looked at it for at least an hour, which was unheard of, and anything could have happened in that time frame. True to form, there were three texts from my dad, a ranty WhatsApp from my sister about how much she hated Richard and a message from Alexa.

How's the reconciliation going? Give me all the deets immediately!

I messaged straight back.

Other than the fact that our agent booked us on a couples retreat instead of a writers' retreat, it's going swimmingly.

Alexa sent three laughing face emojis. I sent three angry faces back.

I lay down on the bed, wondering how long I could feasibly leave it before I had to ring Kate back. All I wanted to do was lie on my back and breathe in the scent of the French Riviera. To see if I could hear the sounds of the sea from here. To think about anything other than a potentially naked Theo next door and the fact that if this trip continued to go as badly as it had so far, we were in for a rocky ride.

Chapter Five

The following morning I attempted to micro-manage breakfast time so that I wouldn't have to bump into you-know-who. I'd thought I'd heard Theo's door – the one leading out to the corridor – open and close at 7.30, so presumably he'd gone down to eat then. I left it until 8.30 to be on the safe side, hoping to avoid him altogether – I was all for a breakfast buffet, but surely you couldn't eke it out for an hour.

I'd drunk two coffees already this morning, and had sat out on the balcony, listening to the sounds of the Côte d'Azur waking up – the flap of a bird's wings; a car reversing out of the hotel's driveway; the hum of a lawn mower somewhere in the distance. In front of me were undulating hills covered in deep green trees and what looked like huge white villas and luxury apartment blocks. Down by the pool a member of the hotel staff was sweeping away leaves, and the air smelled fresh and pure in a way it definitely didn't in Ealing. It was like a different world and I loved it already – even from my bed I'd been able to see the giant pine tree that towered over the pool, giving the water some much-needed shade in the summer, I presumed. After breakfast, perhaps I'd have a swim. For the moment I was putting off the inevitable, i.e. having to talk to Theo about whether we could actually do this writing a book thing. And I was *completely* burying the other thing, the retreat that shall not be named.

There was no sign of Theo in the pretty dining room, which had tables and chairs set out in little clusters and tablecloths and napkins in the same colour scheme as my room – lilacs and purples and pale silver. They'd opened up the doors out to the courtyard and a warm breeze swirled pleasantly around the room. I was wearing jeans and a jumper again and thought I should probably go and change at some point because, give it an hour, and I was clearly going to be far too hot. Why did I have to keep reminding myself that I wasn't in rainy London, I was in the glorious French Riviera?!

Taking a plate, I began to fill it with some of the delicious-looking breakfast items laid out in glass cabinets. I plucked tiny little glazed croissants out of a basket and popped them on my plate alongside creamy scrambled eggs and a pile of green salad leaves; a hunk of unidentifiable crumbly cheese was the *pièce de résistance*.

'Morning.'

I turned to see Theo standing behind me. Great. So much for my grand plan for a peaceful breakfast. This was what happened when I tried to control something to within an inch of its life, it sometimes went completely the other way. I'd been so keen to avoid him that I'd over-thought it and had ended up being perfectly in sync with his schedule. Brilliant.

'Hi,' I said, smiling tightly at him.

'Nice spread,' said Theo, picking up a plate himself. He was positively glowing of course, his hair damp from the shower, smelling of limes and sea air. His T-shirt this morning was racing green, but his jeans were the same as they had been yesterday.

'Very,' I said.

I grabbed a yoghurt and headed to a table for two out in the courtyard. This was excruciatingly uncomfortable, but at least if I sat down first, he'd have to make the decision about whether to join *me* or not. Part of me wanted him to stay inside and sit at the table farthest away from me, preferably out of my eyeline altogether, but I also suspected that I'd be a little bit put out if he did, so basically, it was a lose-lose situation. We had to face each other sometime, but at no point did it feel like the right time. Irritated by the way I had to complicate everything by rolling every scenario over and over in my head and going back and forth over it, I pretended to be very interested in the contents of my plate, carefully slicing open the croissant and delicately inserting a teaspoon of apricot jam inside. I swallowed hard when a shadow fell over my plate.

'Mind if I join you?'

It was, of course, Theo, sounding more sure of himself than I felt. But then, lack of confidence had never been his problem. Quite the opposite, one might say.

'Fine by me,' I said, making myself glance up to prove that I could look at him without spontaneously combusting.

He slid into the seat opposite and despite being determined to keep my cool, for a second I was thrown. I'd forgotten about his luminous brown eyes with flecks of what seemed like gold if you caught them in the right light, and how it felt when he looked at you close up. Like your insides were being turned into hot maple syrup, basically, which *could* be pleasurable, but definitely wasn't in this scenario. I pulled the end off my croissant and shoved it in my mouth, trying to remember how to chew normally and instead feeling all ungainly, like a cow chewing the cud. Flustered, I poured myself a glass of water from a jug, spilling some on the tablecloth because it came out about ten times faster than I'd expected.

'Shit,' I said, frantically mopping it with a napkin.

Theo raised his eyebrows at me. Trust him to try to make me feel as embarrassed as possible.

'Water?' I asked breezily.

'Sure,' he said. 'Preferably in my glass.'

I scowled at him and poured some into his tumbler, more successfully this time, but it took extreme concentration.

'Carla called me this morning,' he said, cutting into his own croissant.

His legs were so long that when he leaned forward to pick up the pot of butter, his knee brushed against mine under the table. I scraped my chair back an inch or two. That couldn't happen again.

'Let me guess,' I said, 'she wanted to reiterate that the couples retreat could be good for our writing careers?'

'I told her she was wrong, of course,' said Theo.

'Obviously,' I said.

'Doesn't seem like we've got much of a choice, though, does it?' he said.

I hid my surprise. 'So you're saying we should do it?'

He shrugged. 'I suppose we could see how it goes. And at the same time we can start hashing out the beginnings of our story idea. If you're up for doing that, still,' he said.

'Doing what? Writing a book together?'

'What else would I be talking about?'

'Just checking,' I said, my cheeks beginning to redden.

Honestly, why was I acting like this? I tried to channel how I'd conducted myself when I'd first met him. It had been seven years ago, on the first evening of our creative writing for beginners class. I'd come straight from typing up medical letters about people's failing kidneys. My life was not going well, although possibly better than it was for the aforementioned renal patients whose notes I'd been filing. I'd graduated from university with a pretty useless media degree four years earlier and had struggled to find a job that I was passionate enough about to compete with a hundred other graduates for. I'd kidded myself that if I temped for a bit, just to make ends meet, at some point the penny would drop and I'd know exactly what I wanted to do with my life, and my real career would begin. But the only thing I kept going back to was that I wanted to be a writer, and that hardly seemed realistic. I wasn't the sort of person who wrote a novel and got it published, I was far too ordinary and unglamorous and unlucky. But I'd finally got so fed up with being stuck in an office typing letters all day that on a whim I'd booked myself a place on the course, in July, so September had seemed far enough away, but suddenly it was about to start and I felt utterly unprepared and a bit of an imposter. I'd been good at English at school, and had loved writing essays and dissertations at uni (much better than having to give presentations or speak up in class) but this felt different. Creative writing ... was I even a creative person?

The class had been small, with twelve of us altogether, plus the tutor, and Theo had been the last to arrive. I remembered nervously getting out my pad and pen, poised to write extensive notes because I knew I would be way too overwhelmed to take everything in. I was one of the first to look up when Theo breezed into the class and so I observed everyone sort of stopping what they were doing and brazenly staring. Whereas I *wasn't* the type of person to write a book, he was everything you'd imagine a novelist to be: tall and beautiful and a little bit cocksure, with a twinkle in his eye and a trendy rucksack on his back and wearing black jeans with a black roll-neck jumper, already looking like an author in the making. I knew immediately that he'd be a good writer, and I also knew that I was not going to fawn all over him like all the other women (and some of the men) in the group were clearly going to. I generally found it was much safer to focus on things I could control, rather than let my head be turned by good-looking men who had the capacity to throw me off track in a second. I was here to learn how to write a book and I would not be distracted by this annoyingly handsome guy and his luscious head of shiny hair and his ludicrously perfect eyebrows that looked as though they'd been professionally shaped. That evening, I caught him looking at me a couple of times with a sort of confused look on his face. Presumably, he couldn't understand why I wasn't as desperate for his attention as everyone else.

I watched Theo now, still as handsome as he was then, more so if anything. He hadn't even had the decency to grow the beginnings of a beer belly in the years since I'd seen him last, and he didn't have a single grey hair. I pushed my hair behind my ears, wondering how I looked to him. Whether he thought I'd aged. Whether it mattered if he did.

We ate our breakfast in silence for what felt like far too long before I decided to make some attempt to break the ice.

'What have you been up to, then?' I came up with. I was nothing if not original.

'What, for the last six years?' he replied.

What was with the little digs? Anyway, it was his fault that we hadn't seen each other, not mine. I swallowed it. I thought back to something my friend's mum had said to me once, when we'd all gone to the park and I'd taken Kate and Zach and they'd run me ragged, refusing to do a single thing I'd asked them to. *Pick your battles*, she'd said, and it had stayed with me. Nothing like being given parenting advice at eleven years old.

'Your books are doing well,' I said, sticking to safe territory.

'They're not, and you know it, otherwise I wouldn't be here.'

I popped a cherry tomato into my mouth. That was me told.

'You were Waterstones Book of the Month,' I said, remembering how insanely jealous I'd been when I'd walked into my local branch and had seen an entire table dedicated to him.

That particular accolade had felt like something I could only ever dream of and it meant thousands of sales pretty much guaranteed. Plus it signalled that his publisher was backing his book, going all out to make it a success. It had been his first solo offering after *Little Boy Lost*. I was certain it would have sold well, but perhaps his second hadn't.

'What about you?' he asked. 'Your second solo book has just come out, right?'

He knew how many books I'd written.

I, on the other hand, had pretty much stuck to my vow never to google him or his novels, although sometimes information about his career was thrust upon me without me even looking for it. And very occasionally, my fingers hovered over the *buy now* button when I happened to be on Amazon and one of his books popped up as a suggestion – it would have been so easy to download a copy to my Kindle, secretly, as you could with ebooks, so that nobody ever had to know what I was reading. But I'd have known and I'd have been annoyed at myself, so I avoided his glossy, manly covers, and had never even looked at his Instagram feed until yesterday (OK, I had once or twice, ages ago, and had instantly regretted it because I'd seen a gorgeous black-and-white shot of him walking through Washington Square Park and had imagined him in New York with his latest stunning, successful and highly intelligent girlfriend and it had nearly killed me).

'My second – *The Mother-in-Law* – hasn't sold as well as they thought it would,' I admitted, instantly regretting being so upfront. I was supposed to be giving him the impression that he was lucky to be working with me again. 'I actually thought it was my best one yet,' I said, attempting to redeem myself.

Theo raised a perfectly manicured eyebrow. 'Better than *Little Boy Lost*?'

I knew he was teasing me, but two could play that game. 'By a mile.'

The truth was, there was something about the novel we'd written together that had resonated with readers all over the globe. Perhaps it was just a case of right story, right time: *A newly employed au pair drops her three-year-old charge at nursery. At collection time, the school denies all knowledge of his existence. Can she find him before his high-flying parents discover he's missing?* The reviews had pretty much all been four or five stars. People had said they 'couldn't put it down'. I'd even seen a few people reading it on the Tube, which was one of the things I'd thought happened automatically when you were a published author, but clearly not, since none of my other books had ever made an impromptu appearance on public transport. In my darker moments, when I began to doubt whether I could write at all, I'd think that maybe it was Theo who had made *Little Boy Lost* work. We'd done a lot of press; he was very photogenic. His fan base was almost 70 per cent women, Carla told me once, and of course my imagination had gone wild after that. Was he sleeping with his fans? Did he pick up women at book signings? Probably. I knew he'd been on three dates with Gayle from our writing course and, after we were published, I'd once seen him leave an event with Lilian Rich, the insanely beautiful books editor at the *Observer*. I'd assumed he was going home to shag her. Not that it was any of my business if he was, but still. It kind of hurt.

Just as I took my first delicious bite of the jam-filled croissant, one of the most dazzling women I'd ever seen walked into the room. It was like she'd been blown in on the breeze, with her wispy, barely there maxi dress, thong sandals and mane of curly blonde hair framing an elfin face, and sporting the sort of perfectly even deep tan that indicated she spent her year hugging the sun – Ibiza, probably. Bali next. She was mid-forties, perhaps, but it was difficult to tell because she exuded health and happiness and youth – it didn't matter how she looked on the outside because I could tell that on the inside she was in the best condition of her life. I returned my pastry to my plate, instantly feeling bad. If I wanted to look like that in a dress, I should probably be eating fruit and yoghurt, not buttery white carbs.

Theo glanced at her, too. No doubt he'd have tried to chat her up if I wasn't here. I bet he used the 'I'm a bestselling author' line to perfection when it came to making small talk with women at a bar or a party. For some reason it worked better that way round, I reckoned – women were impressed by stuff like that. Because he was an author, they'd no doubt assume that he had a certain ability to empathise, to get into somebody else's head, to use evocative words to perfection. And he could, because he was a brilliant writer. Which made me think that maybe I needed him more than I cared to admit. If we could collaborate on this new book without killing each other, writing together was potentially the perfect solution – whatever our own work lacked, the other would hopefully fill.

The goddess wafted around the restaurant, chiffon billowing in the breeze, her face lit up with a huge smile showing off her perfect teeth.

'Do I have a Scarlett Green and a Theo Winters out here?' she called out in one of those weird but quite nice transatlantic accents, her voice louder and less fairy-like than I'd have imagined. I was so caught up in watching her, mesmerised by her ethereal presence, that it took me a second or two to register what she'd said. Had she just called my name?

I glanced at Theo. For a second we were united in fear. Who was she and what did she want with us?

He grimaced. 'Should we just ignore her, or what?'

We couldn't do that. What if the hotel manager pointed us out? We'd look ridiculous.

'Maybe she's the owner come to apologise about the mix-up yesterday,' I suggested.

'Oh good point,' said Theo. 'Over here!' he called out, waving his hand in the air.

The goddess wafted in our direction and I wondered what had possessed me to wear jeans, an albeit cashmere jumper and trainers to breakfast in the French Riviera? I had nicer things in my suitcase and now desperately wished I'd had the foresight to put them bloody well on. This – *this* – is how I should be dressed, I thought to myself as this stunning woman appeared at our table, smelling every bit as good as she looked.

'Hi,' I said, deciding to act less like a lamb to the slaughter and more like an adult human being. 'I'm Scarlett.'

She grinned at me. 'Lovely to meet you, Scarlett. And you must be Theo?'

She turned to him and he shifted in his seat. I watched carefully, knowing that any second now he'd turn on the flirtatious charm.

'That's me,' he said, the familiar twinkle reaching his eyes. 'What can we do for you?'

There it was. He hadn't lost it, then.

She looked at her watch and then beamed at us as though she was expecting us to do something, but I couldn't for the life of me think what. 'I'm Melissa. We're down at the pool waiting for you guys. Perhaps you didn't realise it was a nine o'clock start this morning?'

'I'm ... um, who is waiting for us exactly?' I managed to stutter. It was slowly beginning to dawn on me that Melissa looked suspiciously how I imagined a world-renowned psychotherapist might look. And there could be only one reason she was trying to find us.

'You're on the couples retreat, right?' she said.

My heart started hammering in my chest for some reason I couldn't explain. In hindsight, perhaps I'd thought that I could just pretend to take part in the retreat but then not actually do any of it, or at least that I'd be able to pick and choose what I wanted to join in with. Theo and I hadn't discussed it yet, of course, but I imagined we were in agreement on this.

'We were actually expecting to be on a writers' retreat,' said Theo, saying the exact same thing I'd been about to. 'We're not a couple,' he added.

'Fabulous!' said Melissa. 'So you're friends?'

Theo and I looked at each other. How to describe it? I shook my head.

'Colleagues?' suggested Melissa.

'Not exactly,' I mumbled.

'Ah. I sense there's something quite challenging going on here,' said Melissa enigmatically.

'We're authors,' said Theo. 'And we're supposed to be writing a novel together but we haven't seen each other for ... quite a few years, now.'

'Mind if I sit down?' asked Melissa, not waiting for an answer and pulling across a chair from a neighbouring table.

69

She perched on it, clasping her hands in her lap and looking at us with interest.

'What I'm sensing is that the two of you are struggling to communicate. You have to write this book together but you're not sure where to begin. And both of you are holding something back.'

Blimey. How did she know all of this? Was she a therapist or a psychic?

'Have either of you had therapy before?'

'No!' we said in unison. Funny how we kept doing that.

'Well there's a first time for everything, right?' she said enthusiastically. 'And it seems a shame not to participate when you're all paid up for the workshop. I'm only in Europe for a few months of the year. The rest of the time I'm mostly in California. I usually head over to Bali in the winter.'

Knew it.

'So what I'm saying is, I encourage you to come and join us for our introductory session this morning. It's nowhere near as scary as you might think, I promise.'

'As it happens, we haven't exactly got a choice,' said Theo. 'We're being forced into it by our literary agent.'

'And the hotel manager,' I added.

'I see,' said Melissa, looking disproportionately pleased about all of this.

I decided to try another angle.

'If everyone else is in a proper couple, won't it be weird that we're not?' I asked hopefully.

'Not at all,' said Melissa, waving my suggestion away with a waft of her hand. 'I often have clients in my workshops whose friendships have broken down. It's the same premise – connection, getting to know each other on a deeper level. Being honest about our feelings.'

'Ah,' said Theo wryly. 'You've lost me there.'

I laughed a little bit, I couldn't help it. Theo hated talking about feelings, I remembered that now. Not that I was much better at it.

'Come,' said Melissa, holding out her arm, which was tinkling with about twenty gold bangles. 'Join in for today and see how you get on. Where's the harm?'

I looked at Theo, willing him to come up with a reason why we shouldn't, why we couldn't possibly.

'I'm not sure—' he began, before Melissa swiftly cut him off.

'Only one way to *be* sure. Come on, guys. Take a risk. Do something differently. Embrace this opportunity!'

It was Theo's turn to laugh this time. He looked completely different when he wasn't wearing his trademark scowl. Almost approachable. Even more handsome. Damn him.

'What do you say?' he said to me. 'Do you think you could tolerate my presence for a few more hours this morning?'

I bit my lip, hating that I was being put in this position. I supposed I just had to keep the goal in mind: we had a book to write. And not just any book, a brilliant one that would make me enough money to do the stuff I needed to do for my dad and the others. If this stupid couples retreat thing could in any way help – not that I could imagine how it could at this precise moment – then I supposed it was worth a try.

'I can if you can,' I said with fake conviction.

Would we be expected to do the whole group therapy thing I'd only ever seen on TV, I wondered? It was funny that this was what was prompting me to go into therapy for the first time. If anything, I should probably have done it years ago, but nobody had suggested it, probably because I'd done such a good job of convincing them all that I was absolutely fine.

'Perfect,' said Melissa, scraping back her chair. 'Follow me. And bring your coffee!'

I took one defiant bite of my croissant, picked up my cup and followed her out into the garden with Theo close behind. What in God's name were we letting ourselves in for?

Chapter Six

Melissa led us out into the garden, past the cute baby orange tree and the fragile-looking summer house. In all honesty, it would have been a whole lot nicer out here if I hadn't had to join the group of couples sitting in a circle – I *knew* there'd be a circle involved! – around the white cast iron table past the far end of the pool.

'Everyone, this is Scarlett and Theo!' announced Melissa as we approached the group.

I wanted to add the addendum *and we are not a couple*.

'Take a seat, guys,' said Melissa, pointing to two empty chairs. I took the one next to a beautiful, bohemian-looking mixed-race woman in her forties, who was giving off intimidatingly beautiful Zoe Kravitz vibes. Again, I cursed myself for my frumpy housewife outfit choice.

'Hi,' I said to her, perching awkwardly on the chair next to her.

'Good to meet you, I'm Harmony,' she purred in a soft American drawl.

Of course she would have a name like that. This was exactly the sort of person who would fly halfway around the world to do group couples therapy. I suddenly felt out of my depth and terrified that I was going to be forced to reveal my deepest, darkest secrets to this group of strangers (and Theo!). I hadn't even set foot into the centre of Cannes yet and I wanted to see the beach close up and I wanted to think about book ideas because that was what I was actually here for. I did not want to be doing any of this other stuff.

Theo took a seat next to me and I noticed Harmony's eyes flickering across to him appreciatively. *Here we go*, I thought. People couldn't *not* notice him, even when their actual partners were sitting right next to them. I scooted closer to Harmony to avoid coming into physical contact with Theo in any way, shape or form. Theo being Theo, and a virtual paragon of manliness, seemed to have no such qualms and relaxed back in his chair with his legs spread so wide that if I hadn't had the foresight to move, our knees would definitely have been pressing up against each other's.

'Right,' said Melissa. 'We're all here. Let me introduce myself. My name is Melissa Smart and I am a psychotherapist and life coach. My speciality is couples work, and when I say couples, I mean any form that that might take,' she said, looking pointedly in Theo's and my direction. 'I use a combination of exercises, group exploration and one-on-one therapy to really get to the heart of what each of you would like to change in your partner, but – more importantly – yourselves, and to help you move your marriage, your relationship or your friendship into a new realm. We have ten days to do this and I am confident that by the end, you will all feel very differently about each other. So why don't we start there.'

Start where? I thought?

'I'm going to go around the table and I want you to tell me your name, where you're from, how long you've known your partner and what you would like to be different about them at the end of our journey together. Let's start with you, Paul,' she said, turning to Harmony's older but equally well-groomed and attractive partner.

God, this was already unbearable. What on earth was

I going to say? The only other person who was probably feeling the same way was Theo, but I didn't want to give him the satisfaction of thinking I couldn't handle it. The thing was, Carla was expecting us to get her money's worth out of the retreat – she'd made it clear that she was doing this as a special favour, and I didn't want to let her down. But at the same time, it was hard to focus on what I did or didn't like (there were far more of the latter, obviously) about Theo when really it didn't matter anymore and what we really needed to do was sit down together, come up with a killer plot and start writing so that this whole process could be over with as quickly and painlessly as possible.

I tried to concentrate on listening to Paul, who was telling us that he was from San Diego originally but now lived in Orange County and that he and Harmony had been together for three years.

'And what brought you on this retreat, Paul?' asked Melissa, a pad and pencil poised in her hands.

'Honestly? I didn't want to come at first,' he said.

Oh good, glad I wasn't the only one to find the idea of therapy repellent. See, it was normal not to want to do it!

'He flat out refused,' piped up Harmony.

'Let Paul finish, Harmony,' said Melissa gently. 'What was it that was putting you off, Paul?'

He laced his hands behind his head in a sort of cocky, masculine stance. I reckoned he worked in the film industry. I bet he was an agent, or something, and although he was wearing shorts and a polo shirt today, I decided he was probably the sort of guy who felt more at home in a suit. I could imagine him doing kick-ass deals in loud, expensive LA restaurants.

'I personally thought our relationship was in a pretty good

place,' he said. 'But Harmony gave me an ultimatum: come to Cannes, or she'll leave me.'

Blimey. Harmony did not mess around.

Melissa nodded sympathetically. 'And how did that make you feel?'

'Angry?' he said.

I heard Harmony tut.

'And so what you'd like to be different about Harmony is...?' asked Melissa.

'I want her to not leave,' said Paul, his cockiness sliding for a second.

Melissa scribbled some notes. 'Great start, Paul. Harmony, you're up.'

Harmony, of course, was brilliant at this. She took to the floor with aplomb, waxing lyrical about being about to turn forty-five and realising life was passing her by and that her relationship had become stagnant. She wanted to feel desired and Paul didn't make her feel like that anymore. His career as a producer took him all over the world (I *knew* he was in the movie business!) and it had always been the most important thing to him but *she* wanted to be somebody's most important thing. Something about that resonated with me, somewhere deep down, in all the stuff I'd buried. That was kind of what I wanted, too, but it was a distant thought that I didn't give much lip service to. I pushed up the sleeves of my jumper, enjoying feeling the sun on my forearms. The skies above our heads were clear and blue and I reckoned it was twenty degrees or so already and presumably it was only going to get hotter this afternoon. I would like to be walking along the beachfront with my toes in the water by that point, if that wasn't too much to ask.

'Scarlett. Let's hear from you,' said Melissa.

I shifted nervously in my seat. There was no way I was

going to be able to be as coherent as Harmony and Paul, but then they were probably used to this – didn't they all have therapists in the US? Especially in California, I imagined.

Theo turned to me, whispering in my ear, his breath disconcertingly warm on my neck.

'Good luck.'

I nodded a thanks. My mouth felt so dry that I wasn't sure whether I'd be able to speak, full stop. I looked around the circle, taking in the other two couples properly for the first time. Would they be as articulate as Paul and Harmony? Or was this as new to them as it was to me? At least, presumably, they had the advantage of actually being a couple. Oh, and of having knowingly signed up for this thing.

I cleared my throat. *Here goes nothing*, I thought.

'I'm Scarlett,' I said, wondering whether I could leave it at that. Melissa gave me an encouraging nod. Guess not. 'I'm an author. I write psychological thrillers. And I'm here because my agent booked me on the couples retreat by mistake. We thought it was a writers' retreat,' I said, laughing lightly.

Thankfully the others joined in, except Harmony, who furrowed her brow in confusion.

'You said "we"?' said Melissa. 'What's the nature of your relationship with Theo?'

God, this was awful. I couldn't even get what we'd *once* been straight in my head, let alone what I felt about him now. Which was nothing. Obviously.

'We're writing partners,' I said. 'Or at least we were. We wrote one novel together and then we …' I faltered. Whatever I said, Melissa was going to push me on it, so I had to be careful. 'We went our separate ways.'

That was one way of putting it. I could see Theo rubbing his jaw in my peripheral vision.

'Tell me more,' said Melissa. 'How long ago was that?'

'Six years,' I said. 'And we haven't really spoken since then.'

Melissa looked surprised. 'So why now?'

'As I said, our agent forced us to come,' I said, deciding to blame Carla because I felt extremely fucked off with her right about now. 'She thinks it will help us write together again.'

Melissa nodded and did some umming and aahing as she mysteriously wrote some notes.

'Thank you, Scarlett, that's a very good start.'

Phew, I could relax for a second.

'One more question, though,' said Melissa.

Or maybe not.

'What would you like to be different about Theo?' she asked.

I couldn't even look at him, never mind work out what I wanted to change about him. I mean, nothing. Everything. I didn't know.

'I suppose if we're going to write a book together, I'd like us to be on friendly terms again,' I reluctantly imparted, not sure if I really meant that or not, but I had to say something, didn't I?

And then I instantly wished I'd thought of something else because Melissa was on it like a dog with a bone. 'Ah, so you had a solid friendship once and then something went wrong and now you haven't spoken for six years but you have to write a book together and it would be a much smoother process if you were friends again?'

'Basically,' I mumbled, hating that my cheeks were growing hotter by the second. 'Can we move on?'

I was literally squirming here, couldn't she see this was all too much? I hadn't imagined therapy to be this full-on.

Wasn't it supposed to be all gentle questions and interminable silences?

'Theo, let's hear from you. How do you feel about what Scarlett just told us?'

Ha, now it was his turn. Let's see how he fared. I waited for him to answer but silence hung over the group like a storm cloud and it went on. And on. I flipped my eyes to the right, hoping to give him the signal that he was going to have to speak, it was only fair. Why wasn't he talking?!

'Theo?' prompted Melissa.

He sat forward in his seat, hanging his head. A lock of dark hair fell over his eyes. 'Sorry, this is really not what I ... this is really quite difficult ...'

For a second I felt a shot of something like sympathy. He'd told me once that expressing himself in writing was the only way he'd got through his teenage years. He found it much harder to actually talk about emotional stuff, he'd said, and I'd told him that I felt the same, but that perhaps we dealt with it in different ways; while Theo kept everyone at a distance, I focused on fixing everybody else's problems instead. I didn't know which approach was healthier, but it was what it was. Except here was Melissa talking about it being possible for things to change, which honestly, I'd sort of never considered.

'How would you like your relationship with Scarlett to be different?' asked Melissa, going for the jugular.

I waited for Theo's answer, irritated with myself for feeling a pang of nerves about what he might be about to say. Or would he throw in the towel and refuse to take part? After all, Carla's mistake had put us in this position – she was always in such a rush, trying to do three things at once, it was no wonder she'd booked us on the wrong retreat.

'I'd like us to be able to write together again,' said Theo after a while.

Melissa nodded earnestly and there were some rumblings from the rest of the group. I tried to nod along encouragingly, but it jarred with me that all he seemed to care about was the writing. Clearly, resurrecting our friendship was not a priority for him.

'That's a great start, Theo. Let's leave it at that for now and move on. Rob? Claire? Can you introduce yourselves to the group?'

Rob and Claire, the couple in their late thirties to Theo's right, were from London and had been together for fifteen years but married for only two of those. Claire was rocking a shocking pink jumpsuit and Rob was wearing a zipped-up tracksuit top and looked like he worked in media. They seemed nice, and normal. She wanted to bring some excitement back to their lives. Rob wanted Claire to be happy, like she used to be.

The final couple to make up the group were Renee and Justin from Denver, Colorado, who were in their late twenties. Having moved in together two years earlier, they'd recently discovered that life together wasn't the bed of roses they'd imagined it to be. They'd met at college and had enjoyed a whirlwind romance which turned into something more solid over time, but the thrill of those early years was long gone. I could imagine how that might have been a shock to the system – Renee looked delicate and a little lost, with the kind of blonde curls you read about in children's books and a fragility that made me wonder how she was going to stand up to Melissa's scrutiny. Justin, who gave off distinctly Ivy League vibes (in a nice way), was baby-faced handsome.

Once we'd all done our talky bit, the atmosphere lifted

a little. The whole introducing myself to a group thing had always filled me with dread, and while some people took the floor and ran with it, I could never wait for it to be somebody else's turn. Melissa reassured us that we'd all done a great job. But just as I thought she was about to release us from this frankly hellish situation, she had one more thing to say.

'Before I let you go, I just wanted to circle back to Scarlett and Theo.'

Theo, who was already on his feet, sat back down again in slow motion and I smiled brightly, wondering what the flip she was going to say next.

'Sure,' I said, as though I didn't have a care in the world.

Melissa, of course, could see straight through me. 'No need to put a brave face on it, Scarlett, I know this can't be easy for you guys. As you've told us, you're writing partners rather than a romantic couple. And to complicate matters, you haven't spoken for several years. But I really do think you've got an opportunity here to shake things up. You need to write a book together, yes?'

I nodded dutifully.

'That's the plan,' said Theo.

'And how high are the stakes?' asked Melissa.

'Pretty high,' I said, thinking of my dad.

'We need to make this work,' added Theo, who of course was being all mysterious about exactly why he needed this project so badly.

'Then can I ask you both to commit to this couples retreat and to do it with an open mind? I'm guessing you've got nothing to lose ...' said Melissa.

'And everything to gain, dudes,' said Paul, who was irritating me already.

'Just to say, though,' piped up Harmony, 'and no offence, you guys ...' she added.

I braced myself.

'It's just that I'm not comfortable with there being members of the group who aren't willing to open up,' said Harmony. 'Melissa, you're asking all of us to bare our souls, but in my opinion, everyone has to be all in, or else it won't feel right and it won't be fair.'

Bloody Harmony, just because she'd probably been in therapy since she was about five years old. It clearly hadn't helped her empathise with others.

'Good point, Harmony,' said Melissa. 'Scarlett and Theo, how do you feel about this? Are you willing to throw yourselves into the task at hand and get involved in the exercises I set for you?'

I chewed on my bottom lip, not wanting to commit to something I wouldn't then be able to deliver. If I said I was going to do something, I meant it, even if I often immediately regretted agreeing to it. I wanted to take a second this time. And I wasn't going to let therapy-queen Harmony push me into something I wasn't comfortable with.

'Can we come back to you on that?' asked Theo, as if reading my mind.

'Don't overthink it. Go with your heart, guys,' said Melissa. 'Does this feel like something you can commit to?'

Theo and I looked cautiously at each other. At least he was going to find this as hard as I was, and Claire and Rob seemed nice and Justin and Renee were sweet. Perhaps we could muddle through. The word 'stakes' was in the forefront of my mind – I had to do whatever it took to make this book work. Even if what Harmony wanted was basically something I might not ever be able to give. I was all for talking about feelings – other people's! I could get emotional myself, of course I could. Good emotions, that was, like joy and excitement. Sad, even, if I was watching a film or something. And thinking about the book world, I was completely au fait with rejection, disappointment and envy. But I knew what this lot wanted, especially Harmony and probably Melissa, too – they wanted me to tap into the stuff I'd long ago buried, to show raw, unadulterated emotion. I mean, I might be being a bit dramatic here, but they wanted tears, I knew they did. Again, my experience of therapy was loosely based on what I'd read in books and seen on TV, but from what I gathered, unless someone started sobbing uncontrollably, it wasn't a proper group therapy session.

'Are we really doing this?' Theo asked dubiously, looking at me as though he was hoping I'd say *No, of course we're not*.

But if we didn't do the retreat, we'd have to find a different way to muddle through, involving us forking out over six hundred pounds each to stay on at the hotel.

'I think we're going to have to give it a go,' I said bravely.

He gave me a little nod in return and then true to TV-dramedy form, a couple of people (Melissa and Harmony) clapped and whooped. I glanced back at Theo who was now wearing the sort of confused expression that indicated that he wasn't sure why any of this was cause for celebration.

'Excellent, both of you, great decision,' said Melissa. 'And I'd like to remind the group that everything we say will be confidential. We have to have complete trust in each other for this dynamic to work. Understood?'

Everyone nodded and agreed, even Theo, and when everyone stood up to high-five each other, Theo laughed in surprise and promptly joined in, his soft, sexy, rumble of a laugh impossible to miss, even when everyone else was guffawing away beside him. It was like his voice was on a different frequency, and I wondered whether it was just me who could pick it out.

'So guys,' said Melissa, 'before I let you go, I wanted to let you know what to expect from the next ten days. There will of course be lots of opportunities for you to talk and share within the group, like we have this morning.'

Great, I thought.

'But we'll also be getting out of the hotel and taking part in some activities in the surrounding area. And I've got games and exercises up my sleeve that I hope will guide you and help you set intentions for yourself and your relationship. On which note, I'll see you this evening for our first session – a sunset walk along the famous La Croisette!'

To be fair, this didn't sound too bad. At least I'd finally get to be by the sea. One by one everyone got up and wandered off with promises to see each other later in the day, and I followed suit, picking up my coffee cup and heading back inside. Realising that Theo was still standing where I'd left him, looking out at the hills, I hesitated and turned back to face him.

'See you later,' I called to him. 'Unless you wanted to talk. About the book, I mean?'

Theo glanced over his shoulder at me, the laughter of a few moments ago gone as quickly as it had appeared. 'Can we take a raincheck? I'm not sure I'd be able come up with anything useful.'

'Sure,' I said, feeling irrationally put out. 'Whatever.'

Smarting a little from his brush-off, I headed back up the garden. There was no way I was putting myself on the line again if he was going to knock me back every time, a sensation that felt achingly familiar. Surely he could have managed a quick coffee? After all, the sooner we started, the sooner all of this could end. Nope, from here in, the ball was well and truly in his court.

Chapter Seven

Having spent the afternoon on my balcony stressing over plot ideas and fending off calls from my siblings, I was the last of the group to arrive at La Croisette, which didn't particularly faze me because I was pretty much late for everything. Not out of a sense of arrogance or not respecting people's time or anything like that, but because I always seemed to have a plethora of tasks to complete before I could successfully set foot outside of my front door. Either that or my dad would call just as I was about to leave and I didn't like talking to him while I was out because he spoke softly when he wasn't feeling great and I couldn't hear him properly with the roar of London traffic to compete with.

It was glorious out, exactly what you'd expect from a late-April evening in Cannes. The sky was streaked through with the most beautiful peachy pinks and golds and palm trees were silhouetted against the sky like graffiti. Light reflected off the pale-coloured buildings, many of which looked like mini chateaus painted in shades of blush pink and pale lemon. Flash cars crawled up La Croisette – Aston Martins and Porsches and Ferraris, making sure that we all noticed them, which of course you couldn't not. I wondered what sort of person drove a yellow Lamborghini up a street and then revved their engine completely unnecessarily so that everyone looked at them. It could actually make for an interesting character trait.

Melissa, who was wearing a tie-dye maxi dress and pulling it off with style, waved me over. I caught Theo's eye – he was hanging towards the back of the group wearing a checked short-sleeved shirt tucked into black jeans and desert boots, which I was beginning to think was the only footwear he'd brought with him. His hair seemed more voluminous and shiny than ever – talk about hair envy on my part. I'd done my best to curl mine this evening, wanting beachy waves that hung just below my jawline and that I could toss around enigmatically when Theo asked me a question about my book idea (what book idea?! I still didn't have one and I was dreading him asking me). His skin was a light bronze and from this distance so flawless that I wondered whether it would be as smooth to the touch as it looked like it would be, and then I berated myself for having such an outrageous thought. I would not be touching Theo's face or indeed any other part of his body.

Melissa informed us that this evening's task would be to stroll along the promenade in our couples with a particular goal in mind: to tell each other at least one of our earliest memories. I didn't quite get why we needed to be walking to do this, or why it needed to be sunset, but I supposed if I was going to subject myself to abject torture (i.e. talking about my past) I may as well do it in beautiful surroundings and in gorgeous light. Saying that, La Croisette was more touristy and considerably busier than I'd imagined, and was full of people wanting to lap up some of the glamour of the upcoming festival, or of days gone by when stars like Brigitte Bardot and Cary Grant might have taken an evening stroll along the palm-tree-lined boulevard before heading back to the Carlton Hotel for a night of gambling and partying.

I made a beeline for Theo but then the two of us stood together in silence not sure what to do next, as the other couples strolled off one by one. Harmony and Paul were holding hands, Renee and Justin had their cameras out and seemed more interested in taking nice photos for their Instagram than following Melissa's instructions and Claire grimaced over her shoulder at me as she followed Rob down the street in the direction of Antibes, the next town along and one I had every intention of visiting while I was here if I had time. It was just a short walk along the coastline, following the curve of the cliffs and round the headland, out of sight.

Melissa gave us an encouraging look.

'You two good?'

'Hmmmn!' I said, fake enthusiastically.

'Is this something we really need to do?' asked Theo. 'Because it feels like a task that might be better suited to actual couples.'

That stung. Not sure why, because he was right, but also did he have to find the idea of being in a couple with me *quite* so repulsive?

'Just take it easy,' said Melissa. 'Be gentle with each other. You don't have to share your entire life stories, but try to open up a little bit if you can – after all, it's all there inside you, waiting to be discovered.'

'Or not,' I quipped.

Theo raised an eyebrow at me. 'Do you have secrets you don't want me to find out about, Scarlett?'

I gave him my best mysterious glance in response. 'Wouldn't you like to know.'

'Oooooh,' said Melissa clapping. 'I can feel the ice melting already. I knew this exercise would open the two of you up. Off you go,' she said, shooing us off and turning to walk away. 'Before the sun sets.'

I called after her. 'How long are we supposed to be doing this for?'

87

She waved over her shoulder without turning round.

'Great,' I said. 'That would be how long?'

'Bloody Carla,' said Theo.

I wrapped my cardigan tighter around myself as a cool breeze rippled under my dress and up my spine. It was the sort of evening-by-the-Med weather that was nice enough that you wanted to wear dresses and sandals and sunglasses but cool enough that when you did, you wished you'd been sensible and worn something more substantial. Mind you, after my disastrous outfit earlier when I'd felt like the least-chic person ever to sit around a hotel pool, I was determined to exude Gallic charm, chilly or not. I'd noticed that Theo, annoyingly, seemed to be doing it effortlessly: tonight he was all casual and tanned, like Romain Duris when he wooed Vanessa Paradis in *Heartbreaker*, fitting in perfectly with the vibe of the French Riviera. I wondered if maybe he just fitted in with all vibes, everywhere. Certainly the London press seemed to love him, a sore point for me given how things had gone down with the *Little Boy Lost* coverage. Let's just say that although we wrote the whole thing together, it managed to feel as though Theo was the lead writer and I was his second in command.

'Shall we walk along the beachfront?' asked Theo gruffly, nodding to the promenade and the sea beyond.

'Sure,' I said, following him across the road and heading for the smooth concrete walkway running alongside the beach, which was wider and more beautiful than I'd thought it would be. The white sand looked as though it would be warm and powdery, perfect to sink your feet into on a warm day. Perhaps I'd do that tomorrow, come down here on my own, slip off my flip-flops, take a walk in either direction to see what I could find.

The beach bars were already hotting up, their doors

thrown open for sundowner cocktails and dinner, many of them housing cool DJs spinning tunes and revving up the hedonistic atmosphere.

'We should probably start thinking about the book, shouldn't we?' said Theo.

I resisted the urge to point out that I'd said the exact same thing earlier that day. His mood had clearly improved since this morning.

'Well that is why we're here,' I said, lest he thought I'd got so caught up in couples retreat shenanigans that I'd forgotten that we were supposed to be working. Hardly.

'What have you come up with so far?' he asked, glancing sideways at me.

That would be nothing. I dredged the back of my mind for something useful to say.

'Maybe we need to work out what it was about *Little Boy Lost* that captured readers' imaginations,' I offered. 'I mean, it wasn't like we were the first people to write a novel about a child going missing, was it?'

The reviews I had been brave enough to read seemed to like the multiple points of view. The fact that we'd shown them what was inside the killer's head as well as other characters who were caught up in it all. Carla had always said that it was a case of right place, right time plus excellent writing.

'From what I remember, we worked really hard to show readers that even bad people have good bits, and vice versa,' said Theo, sliding his sunglasses out of his back pocket and slipping them on, instantly looking even more like an A-list film star than before. I even saw a couple of tourists sneaking a furtive peek in his direction.

'That's definitely something we can do again' I said. 'Come at the story from several different angles and then somehow link them all together by the end.'

In hindsight, I should have followed that format for both my solo books and then perhaps they would have sold half as well. Naively, I'd assumed that I could write whatever I wanted within reason, and that readers would follow me from book to book, but that hadn't really been the case and my sales figures had got progressively worse. Also, plotting multiple viewpoints on my own was something I'd avoided doing. It wasn't that I couldn't do it, it was just that without Theo there to push me, I stuck to what came more naturally – a single point of view I could really get behind. I supposed that was the beauty of writing with a partner. What did I push *him* to do, I wondered? He'd never said.

'Now all we need is a starting point,' said Theo. 'I don't know about you, but getting going is the most difficult part for me.'

'Same, I'm afraid,' I said.

We walked in silence for a little while. I looked enviously across at the designer shops, wanting to go inside but also knowing that I hated the feeling of browsing in a store that I already knew was way out of my price range. What was the point? But if money *had* been no obstacle, I would have been in my element here: Gucci, Prada, Dior and Balenciaga jostled for attention, and to the other side, I excitedly noticed some of the plush beach bars I'd read about in gossip magazines: The Carlton Beach Club, La Plage du Festival.

'Are we going to do this task, then?' asked Theo. He wasn't wearing a tie, but if he had been, it would have been undone and hanging loosely around his neck. Or was I fantasising about Romain Duris again?

'Do we have to?' I said.

I didn't like to dwell on the past because what was the point when I couldn't do anything to change it, even though I'd longed and longed for things to be different when I was younger. That was probably where my desire to write started – I liked visualising myself living a different kind of life. I'd been able to picture every detail, to imagine what it would have been like if things had played out differently. In my daydreams I was a relaxed, happy child pursuing her great loves outside of school: drama and dance and netball. I had loads of friends and all we did all day was laugh and play. And my mum would be there, waiting for me when I got home from school, a batch of those delicious flapjacks she used to make in the oven. My dad would be at work but when he came home he'd joke around and tease us and make time for us. And I'd play with my brother and sister sometimes but at other times I'd read in my room or have playdates and it wouldn't matter. I'd spent hours living in this fantasy life, which I'd eventually decided was probably unhelpful. It wasn't until years later that I realised that my imagination had saved me, in a way, and that it had shaped the person I'd become. And now, through becoming an author, I got to do that for other people – transport them to different worlds, take them out of their own problematic lives for a split second. It was something I didn't take lightly. I always kept my readers in the forefront of my mind, dwindling numbers or not. I wasn't sure other writers felt the same. I'd never asked him, but it felt as though Theo probably wrote books to heal something inside of himself, although I'd no idea what because we'd never got to know each other that well. All our energy had been focused on finishing our novel around our day jobs, getting an agent, getting a deal, getting it to sell. And then nothing. Well, not nothing, but nothing together. That part of our lives had been over long ago.

'What made you say yes to coming on this thing in the first place?' I asked him, as two or three seagulls sailed over our heads looking for their last meal of the day. 'Carla was quick to tell me that you were already on board.'

'Well, I thought it was a writers' retreat, obviously. I'd never have come if I'd known it was this.'

'Obviously,' I said, turning my head towards the shore-line so that he couldn't see me roll my eyes. Did he have to hammer the point home every other second? 'But why agree to that? With me, after all this time?'

He sighed. 'Fear, I think. That my writing career is about to go down the pan. That I need to do something to claw my way back up, because the alternative is down, and that's not somewhere I want to be again.'

I nodded. I got it. His reasons were much like mine, then.

'What about you?' asked Theo.

I watched people walking their mostly small and fluffy dogs; the super-svelte runners in expensive workout gear. A couple and a little boy skimming stones out into the water.

'Family stuff,' I said. 'Things haven't been great over the last couple of years. And I need to support them and that requires me to have a certain amount of income that if I'm not careful, I'm not going to be able to sustain.'

He didn't say anything for a bit, which I liked. I'd always liked, actually. He never bowled in with an answer without having considered it thoroughly. Sometimes it meant that you thought he wasn't going to answer you at all and you were about to repeat yourself and then suddenly he'd have this really astute thing to say and you'd realise that he'd been thinking about what you said and actually giving it impor-tance. That was something I rarely felt with other people.

'Let's not pretend money isn't an issue,' said Theo.

'Exactly, no matter how much I wish it wasn't,' I agreed.

'But know that if you're finding it too hard to write with me, if we're not gelling or whatever, then you'll find another way. It doesn't have to be this. You have to do what's right for you.'

There. He'd listened. He'd somehow tapped into the very thing I tried to remind myself of daily but never quite managed to believe: what I wanted mattered, too. Except often it didn't feel like it, and it hadn't for years now.

'Are we going to do this thing about earliest memories, then?' I said, wincing.

'I'd rather stick pins in my eyes, but yeah, sure,' he said.

I sighed. 'Bloody Carla. I'm literally just going to keep saying that on repeat.'

'I'm with you. And if we ever get this book written, I reckon we should name one of the victims after her as a form of revenge.'

We shared a smile.

'I like that idea,' I said.

Up ahead, I caught sight of Rob and Claire, deep in conversation.

'Do you want to go first?' I asked.

'Oh, ladies first. I insist.'

Fantastic. Memories, especially the older ones, were not something I tended to dwell on. Too painful, perhaps. Too visceral. Just the thought of it made me feel a bit shaky and as though I needed to get into the probably freezing cold waters of the Mediterranean and swim far, far away. What *was* my earliest memory? There was the obvious, but I'd been nine then, so I could definitely go earlier if I tried. There was one image that popped into my mind. I went to say it but my throat contracted and I had to breathe a bit before I could feasibly get the words out.

'I was five or six. I don't remember my brother being around, so maybe five.'

'You're really doing this?' asked Theo, looking panicked. He'd have to go next, after all.

'I'm a stickler for doing what I'm told,' I said.

'I remember,' he said, and for a second our eyes met, and the only memories I could think of were the ones I'd made with him. I forced myself to look away, out to sea, bringing my mind back to where it was supposed to be.

'So yeah, I was five years old and I was reading a book. Sitting cross-legged on the bed with my mum. She was smiling at me, telling me how to pronounce words I didn't know how to pronounce. When the book was finished she asked me if I liked the ending and I said no, and she asked me to tell her how I would have done it differently and I did and she said it was much better than the original.'

It was a bit rushed, even I could see that, but that was about as much as I could share without getting all maudlin. I glanced across at him, waiting for his reaction. When I saw the tiniest shake of his head, his dismissive expression, I couldn't believe it.

'Why are you looking at me like that?' I asked him, not sure whether I really wanted to know the answer, but also not prepared to let him off the hook.

'Like what?' he said, immediately on the defensive.

'Don't try and pretend it was all in my head, because I saw you. Something I said seems to have touched a nerve.'

He groaned. 'Sorry. I didn't actually mean to do it. It was sort of an involuntary action.'

Was Theo for real? It had taken me a lot to share that stuff and *this* was how he made me feel afterwards?

'Why?' I asked, incredulous. To give him his due, he didn't know the full story and so he couldn't possibly know how things had panned out. But still. Even he wasn't usually this insensitive.

'Look, can we just forget it ever happened?' he said.

'Not until you explain yourself,' I replied.

He ran his hands through his hair. 'You really want to know?'

'I just said, didn't I?'

'Do me one favour, though. Can we not argue about it?' he asked, holding his hands out to quieten me.

'Who's arguing? I'm simply asking you to explain yourself.' I was not going to let him fob me off. 'Go on,' I prompted, tempted to put my hands on my hips like a disgruntled school marm.

'OK.' He took a sharp intake of breath. 'It's just that I could have guessed that about you.'

It was harder to make out his features now that the sun was sinking below the horizon and the sky was fast turning an inky blue. I looked for the stars and saw them twinkling into view, more and more of them as my eyes became accustomed to the lack of sunlight.

'Guessed what?' I asked.

I was sure I'd never talked to him about my childhood before, and knew for a fact I'd never mentioned my mum.

'That you had this perfect, cozy childhood with perfect, loving, interested parents. It's kind of … obvious.'

I stopped for a second, actually shocked. I was going to take back everything I'd said about him answering things thoughtfully and intuitively. There was nothing thoughtful about what he'd just said. He had no idea what my childhood had been like, no idea at all.

'Is that really what you think?' I asked him.

'Well you've just described the idyllic mother/daughter scene. So yeah. I suppose.'

Maybe I should tell him how completely un-idyllic my

childhood *had* actually been, but now I didn't feel like sharing anything with him at all.

'You're wrong about that, for your information,' I said. 'And don't bother asking me any questions about it because I'm done with this task. I've got nothing more to say.'

I quickened my step, lengthening my stride. I didn't care if he caught me up or not, in fact I'd rather he didn't. Realising there was no point in me carrying on in this direction when the hotel was the other way, I stopped, swivelled and, giving him a wide berth, headed for the hotel and the safety of my room. I didn't make eye contact with him but I could feel him watching me as I strutted past. Baffled, probably, but I didn't care and also that was what happened when you were an arsehole to people. Idyllic indeed!

Of course his stride was twice as long as mine and he caught me up within seconds.

'I didn't mean to upset you, Scarlett,' he said. 'I'm sorry, I shouldn't have assumed. I know nothing about your childhood, you've never talked about it.'

I walked faster, my breath coming in short, sharp bursts.

'Exactly! So you've got no right to comment on it. That isn't what we're supposed to be doing here. You've made me feel really crap.'

'Can we just rewind and start over?' he asked hopefully.

I tutted. 'You can't un-say what you said.'

'No, but I can explain.'

I slowed my pace a little, mainly because I couldn't keep it up for much longer.

'Go on, then,' I said. 'And this had better be good.'

Seriously, I was done with this guy. How could I put my heart and soul on the line to write a book with this person who clearly couldn't read people because if he could, he would have known that I hadn't had one of those relatively

96

easy upbringings that you heard about a lot in our industry: grammar schools, English Lit at a swanky uni, parents who paid for you to rent a flat in London while you pursued your dream of becoming an author. If he thought I was that, then he'd clearly never really got me at all.

'My earliest memory is my mum and dad screaming at each other,' said Theo, looking at the ground rather than at me. 'Then Mum storming off to her room and slamming the door and Dad going out and not coming back until the following day. And me in my room on my own too scared to go out there in case I made whatever it was they were arguing about this time worse. So I read books. That's what I did, I escaped into somebody else's life.'

Other people had done this, then?

'Right,' I said.

'And the reason I was so ... snappy was because I feel kind of jealous, sometimes, when I hear how close people are with their parents and I realise that I never was and never will be.'

I nodded.

'Did they get divorced then, in the end?'

Theo ran his hand through his hair. 'They did. And then there was a custody battle from hell, which, honestly, felt like it was all about them getting one up on each other and not really about them both wanting me to live with them.'

OK, I had to admit, I felt a tiny bit bad for him. I'd made assumptions of my own and had imagined him cruising through life looking the way he did, when actually it sounded like he'd had a difficult start. Maybe that explained why he gave romantic relationships a wide berth. Anyway, he might have struggled more than I thought, but that didn't mean he could treat people however he liked.

I slowed my pace right down so that I was walking at a

normal speed again, with Theo falling into step beside me. We passed a couple dumping their bags and towels on the beach. Both of them had swimsuits on and I admired them for braving the water, which looked dark and cold, and also thought they were crazy. It was much too dangerous to go in, if you asked me, but nobody *was* asking, and perhaps it was different if you lived here and knew the tides or whatever. But then, as they approached the water, I noticed they seemed to be arguing about something. She was hurling her arms about in huge gestures and he was pacing up and down by the water's edge. I thought that the only thing that could possibly make having a row with your partner worse was to have it while in your swimsuit in the dark. I couldn't tear my eyes away from them. That was the thing about being a writer, or maybe it was the other way round, the thing that had made me want to be a writer in the first place – I liked observing other people. I was nosy, basically, but also I liked trying to work out what was going on under the surface. It was difficult to see clearly, but from what I could tell, she wore the trousers in this relationship. He seemed to be pleading with her. She was using dismissive body language and I could practically see the rage boiling away inside her. I nudged Theo, who was looking a little uncomfortable but, like me, couldn't seem to tear his eyes away. The two of us watched as the man strode into the water, wading in up to his waist and then throwing himself in the rest of the way, his arms curling into an angry front crawl. The woman grabbed her stuff and stomped past us, muttering under her breath in French. Wrapping a towel around her shoulders, she carried on up the beach without so much as a backwards glance.

Theo and I looked at each other.

'Could that be a starting point for our book?' I tentatively suggested, raising my eyebrows. 'A couple arguing on a beach. A married couple. We don't know what they're rowing about but it's something serious. He goes into the water and she storms off.'

Theo crossed his arms looking pensive and I could practically hear his brain ticking over.

'Imagine if he never comes back,' he said, looking out in the direction of the man, who was now so far out he was barely visible.

'And imagine if their marriage has been unravelling and he's been keeping all these secrets from her. And she from him,' I suggested.

Theo nodded. 'We could be on to something here, you know.'

Relief surged through my body, possibly a little prematurely. After all, we might not be able to take the story any further. It might turn out to be too clichéd, or too predictable, or another of the phrases that was routinely bandied about by people on Goodreads, which I never went on anymore because some of the reviews of my books on there were savage and would make me cry and I hardly ever cried.

'Shall we both go away and have a bit of a brainstorm?' he suggested.

I shivered. It was probably time to head back anyway, and I wanted to get some of my thoughts down on paper while it was fresh in my mind.

'Let's do that,' I agreed. 'And don't take this the wrong way, but do you think it's best if we spend as little time together as possible? After all, once we've got our storyline, we can go off and work on it individually, can't we? We don't need to be in each other's pockets. It's probably best if we aren't.'

I had to protect myself here – if we were really going to

do this, it was important that we continued to be civil to one another. Which might prove difficult if we encroached on each other's space – it was bad enough that we had to see each other at Melissa's retreat activities.

Theo did his trademark loaded pause and I as usual began to overthink what I'd said. Did he think me callous? Cold-hearted? Difficult, for suggesting such a thing? Given his track record – i.e. women throwing themselves at him at every turn – he was probably finding it very hard to grasp the concept that I didn't particularly want to spend time with him. Not for the first time I wondered about his relationship history since we'd seen each other last. Had he had something long-term, like I'd had with Jackson? Or had he, true to form, kept it casual? Maintained his reputation as a free spirit, a serial dater who you'd better not fall for because if he got wind that you had, he'd be off like a shot?

'I think that's probably for the best, yeah,' he said after a minute.

'Great,' I replied.

'Perfect,' he said.

'Head back?' I suggested.

'Yep,' he said, striding ahead.

I scuttled along, struggling to keep up but secretly thrilled that we had the nugget of something. Up until now our book had been an abstract thought lurking at the back of my mind: could we come up with a killer idea? Would it work? And it still might not, but we had a starting point and we were on the same page with keeping our distance. So far this was working out better than I'd expected.

Back in my room, I opened my computer and wrote down everything that came into my head about the potential new story. As I was reading it through deciding if there was anything I could add, my phone rang. I picked it up, aware suddenly that Theo must be at his computer next door because I could hear the muffled clacking of his fingers on the keyboard.

'Hey, Dad.'

'The carer hasn't turned up.'

I pinched the top of my nose. What were they playing at? I'd double and triple checked that everything had been in place so that I could be assured that nothing like this would happen.

'Sorry about that, Dad, they must have got in a muddle over timings.'

'Well I'm starving. What am I supposed to eat?'

'I'll see if Kate can pop round if I can't sort it out.'

My dad snorted. 'That would be too much trouble for her, you watch. Anyway, I prefer your cooking.'

'You're the only one who does.'

For a start, I was always in a rush so I cut corners a lot, meaning I often didn't bother measuring things, or whacked the oven up to piping hot when the recipe required a gentler approach. As a result, my food was often a little burned on top, or worst-case scenario, not properly cooked in the middle. Dad had never minded, but Zach had complained about it constantly when he was a kid. He'd moaned that his friends' mums all cooked succulent roast chicken and squidgy homemade cookies and I'd tell him that I wasn't his mum and that he was stuck with my cooking unless he'd like to have a go at doing it himself. That had usually shut him up.

I closed my laptop. My writing stint was clearly over.

'Let me go and ring the agency. I'll let you know what they say,' I reassured Dad.

Over the years, I'd made it my mission to make him feel better about life, but sometimes I couldn't quite work out what it was he thought I could do about it all. I'd even asked him directly on more than one occasion: What could we do to make things easier for you? Is there anything you'd like to do? To see? To read? But when he was in one of his low moods, nothing helped, which didn't stop me feeling the need to keep trying.

While I was looking for the number for the care service, my phone pinged in my hand, making me jump. It was my sister, now. What did she want?

I can't stand this anymore. Please can you contact that solicitor for me, you're better at explaining it all?

This was nothing new. Kate and her husband fell out quite badly at least once a week. Apparently Richard never helped around the house because he said he was out at work all day and why should he? And he hogged the remote control and never let her watch *Love Island*. And he left her to do all the running around after the kids. I felt bad for my niece and nephew, having to live in the marital equivalent of a war zone, and I thought briefly of Theo and wondered if they would grow up with similar memories of living in a tension-filled house. I really hoped not, and all I could do was keep encouraging Kate to leave. I hated to see her unhappy like this and Richard wasn't a bad person, but they were clearly bad together.

Can it wait until I get back? All a bit intense on the retreat. Got to write a book asap.

Within seconds she messaged back.

OK, but please do it soon, I'm dying here!

She'd been threatening to leave Richard for the last three years, so I was pretty sure it could wait another ten days?

I'll look into it in the morning. Oh, and please can you go and see Dad? The carer's not turned up – I'm ringing them now. But he needs to eat!!

After a certain amount of grumbling and back and forth she made it clear that she did not possibly have time to go and see Dad but that she would pop in tomorrow if she could.

You have to go. You can't let him starve! I typed out, beyond annoyed now. Was it really that difficult for her to walk the twenty minutes to Dad's and make him beans on toast?

After what felt like ages – she'd probably gone and made a cup of tea or something on purpose to stall for time and make herself look important – she replied.

Sorry, Scar, I really can't. Ask Zach. Promise I'll go round first thing in the morning.

I clutched the phone in my hand in disbelief, trying to calm the swirl of stress, and feeling overwhelmed about not having enough hours in the day to do everything everyone expected of me. And then I pulled myself together and made some calls.

Having sorted out a carer for that evening, which Dad moaned about because they probably wouldn't get to him until late, he said, and he was hungry, I went back to my work, reading through the ideas I'd sketched out. Something sparked an idea for a character and I had the sudden urge to knock on Theo's door and tell him. I put my ear to the communal door, my fist poised to rap softly on it, but then I realised it was all quiet on the other side now. He was probably asleep, given it was gone eleven, or reading in bed like anybody might do while on a retreat in the South of France. Anyway, we'd just agreed to give each other space, and me barging into his room – great character development idea or not – was not sticking to the rules. And rules felt important for us. Because bad things happened if we didn't keep to them, I had actual evidence of that.

Chapter Eight

I woke up feeling a little groggy the following morning after sitting up late to think about the book. Rather than going down to breakfast and having to make actual conversation with anyone, I skulked into the restaurant, grabbed a black coffee and a croissant and went back up to my room. Out on the balcony, the metal chair not yet warmed by the sun, was ice-cold on the backs of my legs. It really was a glorious view, all lush green mountains dotted with houses and the glittering turquoise pool and giant firs and pines that surged out of the earth like flames. I could smell the flowers in the garden even from this height and I breathed in their scent and the fresh mountain air that I hoped would clear my head enough to get through another day of hideous couples retreat activities. I wondered how we were supposed to navigate this next bit: how to go from typing a few notes on a screen to beginning to write a fully formed book together. It had been fine last time – we'd run everything past each other, had had brainstorming sessions (usually in the pub) and had shown each other our work at every single stage. It felt different now. We were supposed to be professionals. Theo had high expectations of himself and others, and what if I didn't live up to them? I'd become more confident about my writing skills as time went on, but the stuff with *The Mother-in-Law* had really rocked me and if my sales were so bad, perhaps I wasn't actually capable of writing a very good novel anymore. Perhaps *Little Boy Lost* was a never-to-be repeated fluke. Or perhaps Theo had carried me and maybe that was what he thought, too, which was why he'd taken the lead on the publicity. I wondered whether this would be a lesson in humility, whether I was going to have to accept that Theo was the stronger writer. I convinced myself that even if that was the case, I should be able to contribute something useful, surely.

By nine o'clock I was dressed in black gym leggings and a white vest and was picking my way across the garden, stalling because, honestly, the last thing I felt like doing was a couples yoga session. Melissa had put a note under my door last night with instructions about when and where to meet, and I could only assume the other retreat participants had received the same invitation. And there had been no way to complain or to say that no, I didn't want to do that, and if I didn't rock up Melissa would only make a scene and come and look for me. So here I was, the most inflexible woman on earth, heading off to an ominous-sounding yoga class with 'couples' in the title.

For once I was one of the first to arrive, after Renee and Justin, who were wearing matching varsity tracksuits and looking as sceptical as I was. I went to join them, feeling that they could be my reluctant allies for this particular task.

'I don't know about you, but I'm crap at yoga,' I whispered to them.

'Oh, me, too,' admitted Renee. 'I can't even touch my toes.'

Harmony and Paul glided across the grass as though they were professional yogis (was that even a word?) and in the time it took for me to say *good morning* to them both and yank up my leggings because the elastic was going at the waist, they'd pulled two mats from the pile under the olive tree and were sitting cross-legged on them with their eyes closed. Could you get any more pretentious, I thought, and then as I caught sight of Melissa wafting up the pathway tinkling a tiny brass bell, it was confirmed that you absolutely could. Before I could stop her, she came closer and shook it loudly in my ear. I winced. What on earth was this supposed to achieve?

'This will be good for you, Scarlett,' she purred, shaking it next to the other ear. 'You look very tense.'

The bell wasn't helping, I wanted to say.

I spotted Claire and Rob making their way over to join the group and widened my eyes at Claire, alluding to the fact that I needed urgent help. She marched straight over.

'What is couples yoga?' I hissed to her.

'Fuck knows,' she said. 'But I can tell you one thing, I won't be very good at it and neither will Rob. He's as stiff as a board.'

And then the two of us snickered, which was childish but we were probably both nervous and so had reverted to acting like teenage girls on heat. There was also a streak of horror as I realised that maybe the class would have some sort of sexual element to it. What was it that Sting and his wife did? Tantric sex? Was that something to do with yoga? Surely Melissa wouldn't subject us to anything like that. In any case, Theo wasn't even here, although he'd better make an appearance soon because if he left me to suffer the humiliation of doing the class on my own, I'd kill him.

'For those of you who haven't already, please take a blanket and a bolster and lie or sit on your mats.'

I did as I was told, working out what a bolster was by following Harmony's lead, moving as slowly as was humanly possible, as if that was going to put off the inevitable. When I glanced towards the hotel I saw Theo striding out into the garden looking all sleepy and as though he'd literally just rolled out of bed. His usually perfectly coiffed hair was a bit shaggy at the front and I was delighted to see he was also capable of having bad hair days. It was clearly irritating him, though, because in the space of time it took him to join the group he must have brushed it out of his eyes about ten times. He was wearing black football shorts and a white T-shirt and running trainers and I thought he'd probably struggled to work out what the hell to wear. He wasn't the only one. For the first time – in a long time, at least – I noticed how muscular his legs were, all sculpted calves and thick, powerful thighs. He never went to the gym when I'd known him before, but he'd been in his twenties then and I guessed things changed when you hit thirty and the abs you'd had once began to mysteriously disappear. Not that I'd know how that felt – visible abs had sadly eluded me my entire life and I'd never had any desire to put in the amount of hard work and dedication required to get them.

'Theo, take a mat and sit next to Scarlett,' said Melissa, who looked as though she was born for this kind of thing with her expensive-looking vest bearing the slogan *Eat More Greens* and her curly hair piled up in one of those topknots that somehow looked effortless and perfect at the same time.

I smiled awkwardly at Theo as he threw his mat on the ground and sort of folded down onto it. He glanced across at me.

'Overslept,' he explained.

As somebody who was perennially late, it always made me feel much better about myself when other people were, too.

'I was beginning to think you'd bailed on me,' I said.

'Tempting as it was, I couldn't do that to you,' mumbled Theo, prising his knees into an awkward cross-legged position.

'Right,' said Melissa. 'Let's warm up our bodies and our minds.'

After a set of relatively easy exercises and some sun salutations which were about a hundred times more challenging than I'd imagined, I was feeling marginally better about the whole thing. While my body didn't always go into the elegant shapes that Melissa and Harmony were eliciting, the rest of us were as bad as each other and I didn't feel self-conscious about stopping if I couldn't manage something, or retreating into child's pose for a few seconds, which Melissa had told us we could do if we needed a few moments of rest and rejuvenation. I wished I could stay in child's pose for the entire session, to be honest, not least because with my forehead resting on the backs of my hands and my eyes closed, I could block Theo from my sight altogether. For some reason I was finding him quite difficult to ignore, what with his six-foot body lunging and downward-dogging next to me. It didn't help that I'd glimpsed the full magnificence of his sculpted back muscles when his T-shirt had fallen forward over his head during one of the more challenging poses. My mind had immediately flashed back to that morning again; that bed. I remembered how raw attraction had hit me like a wall of heat one night, after a late writing session. The realisation that I'd wanted to rip his clothes off there and then had been devastating because up until that point, I'd prided myself on being highly pragmatic when it came to romance, calculating when I could and couldn't let myself fall for somebody based on how much I was at risk of getting hurt. But this had been different; these had been guttural feelings I could *not* seem to control. And it had been both terrifying and electrifying all at the same time.

'OK,' said Melissa. 'Now our bodies are nice and warmed

108

up, let's get together in our couples. Please stand up with your backs to each other.'

I caught Theo's eye. He raised one eyebrow and I tried to smile as though this was no big deal, but it didn't feel remotely authentic because, truly, this felt like a very bad thing for us to be doing. Reluctantly, we stood with our backs to each other, putting as much space between us as possible. I could already feel the heat of him permeating my leggings and my shoulder blades and, worst of all, the back of my neck, where it felt most intense. I tried to focus on the others. Claire and Rob were bickering about how close to each other to stand, Harmony and Paul were kind of melded into each other and Justin and Renee looked a little bit wobbly but were taking it very seriously. It felt serious to me, too – seriously mortifying. Surely Melissa had enough empathy to cut us some slack. Give us some less 'intimate' poses if it all got a bit much.

'Scarlett, Theo, I want your bodies pressed together in as many different places as possible.'

OK, scrap that.

'I don't think—' I gulped before Melissa cut me short.

'Just try it, guys. See how it feels.'

I groaned inwardly and although Theo was silent, I could practically feel the tension emanating off him, too. At least I couldn't actually see his face. It could be anyone standing behind me, couldn't it, the point was, supposedly, to focus on my own body and mind. I took a step backwards and felt the tops of my thighs bump against his. A thousand sparks flew up along up my spine and I closed my eyes for a second to stop myself gasping out loud. OK, focusing on my bodily sensations was clearly not a good idea. I tried to distract myself by thinking about plot points for the new book, but not even that could stop my heart from hammering against my chest.

'Buttocks touching, shoulders touching, heads touching, feet touching. I want you making a connection at as many points as possible,' said Melissa, parading around us all with an eagle eye.

'Is this really happening?' mumbled Theo, clearly about as in to this ridiculous exercise as I was.

He shifted position and I felt a gentle pressure on the base of my spine; his skin would be touching mine if it wasn't for a piece of thin cotton legging. It felt so inexplicably good I could barely breathe. I tried to rationalise it: it was because nobody had touched me for months. Even before that, Jackson and I hadn't done much more than hug each other occasionally for the last year or so of our relationship. It was just an involuntary reaction, it wasn't Theo specifically. As I forced myself to straighten up so that almost every part of me was making contact with some part of him, a fizzing sensation worked its way down my arms, pooling in the tips of my fingers. I clenched and unclenched my fists several times to get rid of it.

'Rotate your shoulders, Scarlett. And Theo, lift your head,' instructed Melissa.

My shoulders folded into the fleshy part of his back and I let my head sink back into the top of his spine. Looking up at the sky, hoping that would calm my anxiety, I noticed how the rhythm of our breathing was different, mine fast and shallow, his deeper, longer, until slowly we began to find a middle ground. I could feel every sensation, every inhale as air flooded into his chest, every exhale as he released it again. I instinctively filled my lungs harder, matching him breath for breath.

'Now I want you to fold forwards, like we did before, so that your fingers are lightly touching your toes,' said Melissa.

'Jesus,' I heard Claire grumble.

Trying not to overthink it, I bent at the waist and Theo must have followed suit because suddenly his coccyx was pushing against mine and I had to force my bodyweight backwards to avoid falling forwards and landing flat on my face on the grass. As I tried desperately to stay upright, it felt as though I was having to engage every single muscle possible.

'Now I want you to put your arms behind you and catch each other's hands,' said Melissa.

No.

'Um ...' I gurgled, because my head was basically hanging upside down.

And then I felt Theo's arms brushing against my shins. In my peripheral vision I could see his hands. Outstretched. Neat, square nails. Comforting, fleshy palms. I liked that he'd done it first, that he'd come over to my side rather than the other way round. Tentatively, I took one of his hands and then the other. It felt strange at first as fingers found fingers, completely unnatural. Clunky. It was like every nerve in my body was on high alert. Wasn't yoga supposed to be relaxing?!

'Now pull slightly away from each other, leaning forwards so that your arms are taking the strain. Trust each other that you won't fall,' said Melissa in soothing tones that belied the presumably advanced yoga pose she was asking us to contort ourselves into.

I leaned forwards first because selfishly I wanted Theo to be solid and upright and ready to steady me if I started pitching. But he must have had the same idea because all of a sudden there was tension in our arms and my biceps were burning as we pulled away from each other so that we were almost suspended in time and space. Theo's hands were wrapped around mine and I was gripping his fingers so hard that I knew it must hurt, but I was too scared to loosen my hold.

'Now close your eyes and breathe ...' said Melissa.

Breathe? All I could think about was how much I was going to ache tomorrow. Even Harmony and Paul were making strange groaning noises next to us, which wasn't helping. I squeezed my eyes shut hoping that might signal to my body that I should relax. It was fine, Theo wasn't going to drop me, that he could be trusted with. Everything else, not so much.

Melissa's melodic instructions filtered into my ears.

'Now rock back on your heels. Release your hands and curl up to standing, very slowly, one vertebrae at a time.'

My eyes remained closed as I returned to standing, relieved to have not embarrassed myself completely but also strangely exhilarated at having pulled it off. I dropped one of Theo's hands immediately. The other one took longer to disengage – was it my imagination, or did his thumb stroke my wrist as I pulled my left hand out of his right one? If it did, it would have been an accident, obviously.

'Now turn to look at your partner. Really look at them. And then I would like you to tell them in one word how that exercise made you feel,' said Melissa.

Oh, come on. This was going too far, now. Doing stuff with my back to Theo had been bad enough but if I looked him in the eye, I was going to have to face every unwanted thought I'd had over the course of this disastrous yoga class; every bubble of heat, every tingle, every breath I couldn't quite catch. I knew it didn't mean anything, that anyone would have felt the same if they'd had a relatively (OK, hugely) attractive man pressed up against them for the best part of fifteen minutes. But once this class was over, I very much wanted to forget that any of this had ever happened.

Sighing inwardly, I turned. It took me a second or two to find my focus, for us to make eye contact again. He looked flustered and a little red-faced, and I felt a jolt of embarrassment, because was it that I'd been too heavy? Because he'd taken the strain on that last exercise and I hadn't been doing it right? But then I felt a bead of sweat rolling down my own temple and was reassured that yoga was clearly far more strenuous than I'd realised – I was one hundred per cent sure I looked hot and shiny, too.

When our eyes finally met, I realised this was the longest I'd looked at him for years. I held his gaze, even though my stomach was flipping about like one of those plastic fish you get in Christmas crackers that you watch curl and turn on your palm. It was his eyelashes I noticed first, how they were unbelievably long, framing the oval of his brown eyes, their tips touching the bottom arch of his brow.

He cleared his throat. 'What's your word?'

I chewed on my lip as I thought about it, not taking my eyes off him, wondering whether I might be able to think more clearly if I did.

'Relieved,' I said. That it was over, of course, but I presumed he knew what I meant.

He nodded earnestly.

'And yours?' I asked him, pleased that my part in this was done.

He furrowed his brow, looking directly at me with the trace of a smile. 'Challenged,' he said.

'Sorry if I was putting too much strain on you. Or if I hurt you, or something,' I mumbled begrudgingly. After all, I'd tried my best.

'I didn't mean physically, Scarlett,' he said quietly.

'Oh.'

What *had* he meant, then?

Melissa rang her bell again, bringing an end to whatever it was this had been. The nine of us came together as a group – a more chilled group, I couldn't help but notice – and did some stretching and then sat cross-legged in a circle and chanted Namaste several times. I had to admit, I reckoned that with a bit more practice I could get into this. Relaxation and exercise had fallen by the wayside over the last few years and I beat myself up about it constantly because I knew it was important, but every time I put a meditation app on or tried to go for a run I'd get a phone call from my dad or my sister or my brother or Alexa or Carla and the whole thing would be abandoned. Perhaps when I got home, I might try, somehow, to find some space for myself now and again.

Chapter Nine

We were silent on the walk back to the hotel. I wasn't sure how to start a normal conversation after we'd just been touching each other in places I'd never imagined us to be touching ever again.

'So we should probably catch up about the book,' I said finally, as if my fingers hadn't just been curled through his. As though I hadn't secretly liked the way it had felt when Theo held me.

'About that,' he said. 'I've been thinking about what worked for us last time.'

'Yeah?' I said, shuddering internally. 'Last time' was not something I chose to think about if I could help it.

'Sharing our work early on was good,' said Theo, holding the front door of the hotel open for me.

'Did we do that?' I asked, pretending I couldn't remember. Of course I could remember. We'd spent almost every night together, shared every sentence, every character trait, every plot twist (he'd always been better at that than I had, but still).

'You'd forgotten?' he asked.

I thought I detected the tiniest nugget of disappointment, which was interesting. Had he imagined me pining for him, then? Had he thought I'd be raking over the details of the time we'd spent together, remembering every single moment of our writing journey?

'Must have done,' I lied.

We walked through the reception area, nodding a hello to the hotel manager as we went. The poor man had had his work cut out for himself the other night, what with the mix-up over retreats and then rooms. I must remember to leave the hotel a glowing review on Tripadvisor.

'As I was saying ... I thought that maybe we could share whatever we did last night. You were working, right? Only I thought I heard you on your laptop,' said Theo.

I was not going to give him the satisfaction of admitting that I'd heard him typing away, too. And actually, I'd had to press my ear up against the door to be sure, so had he done the same thing? What else had he heard?

I followed him upstairs to the first floor and our weird intertwined rooms.

'Mine's not really shareable yet,' I said, hoping to put him off. 'It's just notes. I doubt it would even make sense.'

Things had been different when we were fresh out of the writing course, full of hope and optimism, excited at the prospect of writing anything at all, let alone a whole novel, which had seemed impossible: all those words! I was an actual, proper author, now, even if hardly anyone was buying my books anymore, and for some reason Theo asking to see my 'work' was putting the sort of pressure on me that I didn't feel when Carla asked to read something, or my editor at Saturn House. I had this sense that Theo would be expecting something I couldn't deliver. A fully formed idea. A clue as to what was actually going to happen once our male protagonist went into the sea after the row with his wife.

Theo hesitated outside his door.

'Look, whatever we've been doing on our own since *Little Boy Lost* clearly isn't working for us. Is it? There's something missing and, tough as that is to admit, it's reflected in our sales.'

'You don't know anything about my sales figures,' I protested. He was making a lot of assumptions here.

'You literally told me that your publisher wasn't happy with them.'

Damn. Why had I done that, again?

Theo pulled his key out of his pocket.

'Unless of course you're reluctant to share because you're worried that your ideas won't be quite as good as mine ...' he suggested with a glint in his eye.

'Don't flatter yourself,' I said, rising to the challenge.

'Oh dear, have I hit a nerve?' he asked, raising one eyebrow at me.

'Hardly,' I said, struggling to get my key in the lock and having to bend down to peer more closely at it because the bloody thing just wouldn't turn. 'I'll have them over to you in the next half an hour.'

As much as my notes were in a complete mess, there was no way on earth I was going to let him think he had the upper hand.

'Can't wait,' he said, grinning at me and then effortlessly turning his key and gliding into his room leaving me steaming with indignation in the hallway.

Once I was finally back in the safety of my room, smarting about our exchange, I threw myself down at my desk, combing through the notes I'd made the night before. I'd worked through until two in the morning and they'd become progressively less coherent as they went along, even if I *was* used to working late. But it was a starting point, wasn't it, and I wasn't going to let Theo make me feel bad about my process. There was value in hashing things out on the page, in not being sure, in questioning yourself and your work.

Just as I was giving the document a final read-through, an email from Carla to both Theo and me slid into my inbox, sitting there ominously in bold at the top of the page. I braced myself and clicked on it.

Guys, I wanted to share some exciting news with you. I've taken the liberty of getting the word out with editors and publishers both here and in New York, and I cannot tell you how excited they are about your collaboration. Several of them have already requested a first look. I've got a very good feeling about this, so get writing and when you have some chapters to share, ping them over asap. I'm feeling an auction coming on, which will hugely bump up your advances not to mention the marketing budget.
Happy writing, both of you!
Carla
PS hope the couples therapy is proving useful ...

I read it again and then one more time for good measure, trying to ignore her comment about the couples therapy because no, it wasn't proving useful, and focusing on the point of the email which was altogether more positive. For the last couple of years I'd sent my book proposals and my first drafts and my final drafts off to my publishers with trepidation, not entirely sure that they were going to love them as much as I did. And now there was supposedly this buzz about a novel that we hadn't even started writing yet. I was a little bit put out, because it basically played into the narrative that I needed Theo to be a success, but I was excited, too, obviously, because the more editors who were interested, the more likely we'd be to get an offer, potentially a very good one. I replied to Carla, keeping it short and copying Theo in.

That's brilliant news, Carla. We'll let you know as soon as we have something to share.

S x

Then I opened up my notes from the night before again, shifting them around and putting them under headings so that it would be easier for Theo to understand where I was going with it: Hook Ideas; Character; Plot (this category was the sparsest); Themes. And then I pressed send. I imagined Theo at his laptop, opening my message, skimming through it, probably being judgemental about the lack of actual content. I could picture him frowning, taking it all in. Perhaps he was out on his balcony. Had he changed out of his yoga shorts? Was he in his towelling robe? In his pants? In the shower? The thought of that gave me butterflies in my stomach again which I instantly dismissed, annoyed with myself for entertaining the idea that I was in any way interested in Theo's attire or lack thereof. I made myself a cup of too-weak English Breakfast tea and as I was trying to decide whether it would taste better or worse with UHT cream in it, my laptop pinged and I nonchalantly wafted over, checking my inbox casually.

I opened the message.

Thanks for this. Looking forward to reading. Here's mine.

Theo

I stared at the document he'd attached, wondering how it would feel to read his words again after so long. I picked up my laptop, opened my French doors and stepped out onto the balcony. I thought about all the writers the French Riviera had inspired over the years. Perhaps I would be able to embody the words of F. Scott Fitzgerald or Somerset

Maugham. I could write about the glittering sea, the lush green mountains dotted with houses and pools; the palm trees along La Croisette. And then I sat down and opened up Theo's pages and began to read. His notes were much more structured than mine, written like a synopsis and about three times as long. I raced through it as his ideas for plots and twists and conflict unfolded in front of my eyes. He had something already, after only a day, and annoyingly I loved it.

Chapter Ten

The next morning my alarm went off at seven, which having had a relatively early night after an evening group therapy session followed by a couple of drinks at the bar, was just about bearable. I'd kept my distance from Theo as much as was humanly possible and had enjoyed getting to know the others better – Claire, especially, who I was starting to feel close to already.

I prised myself out of bed and put on some leggings and a T-shirt, determined to hit the tiny gym I'd passed several times but had not yet found the energy to venture into. I may as well take advantage of having it right there, metres from my room, meaning it was impossible to talk myself out of doing a workout by persuading myself that I didn't have the time. Plus, wasn't exercise supposed to be good for focus? And now, more than ever, I needed to be able to do that. Theo had set the bar very high, which made sense, because I'd hardly want to write a novel with someone who wasn't brilliant, but he was just so 'on it' when it came to plot and no matter how hard I tried, my storylines seemed to fall ever-so-slightly short.

It was empty in the gym, so I put my headphones on and did some lunges and squats to warm up, gearing myself up for the treadmill, a piece of equipment I despised and yet never felt as though I'd really pushed myself without. It was a necessary evil, although I wasn't sure what good ten minutes of huffing and puffing across a perfectly flat fake terrain actually did anyone. And so when somebody tapped me on the shoulder I felt a rush of horror followed swiftly by relief – horror that it would be Theo, in which case working out in front of him would be impossible and I'd have to pretend I was warming down, not warming up – and relief when I realised it was Claire, who looked as unenthused about the prospect of an hour in the gym as I was.

'Morning,' she said, looking suspiciously at the rowing machine.

'Hey,' I said. 'We had the same idea.'

'What, you mean forcing ourselves to do a modicum of exercise so that we don't feel guilty about the copious amounts of French wine we plan to drink later?'

'You took the words right out of my mouth,' I said, eyeing the treadmill. 'Right. I'm going in.'

'You're brave,' she said. 'I think I'll start with a gentle cycle.'

We pounded/cycled along in companionable silence for a few minutes before Claire, who was already out of breath, stopped, slid off her saddle and came over to me, draping herself over the arm of my treadmill.

'That's quite enough for one day,' she said.

'You're literally making me look good here,' I said, 'and that's saying something.'

'Talking about not looking good, what the fuck was that yoga class about yesterday?' said Claire. 'Rob can barely move this morning. Hardly conducive to sexy romance that, is it?'

I laughed. 'Well how do you think I felt? Theo and I aren't even a couple and next minute he's got his coccyx rammed against mine.'

Claire snorted. ' I thought it might get you two all worked up. You know, get the inevitable over with.'

I felt myself flush, which I hoped Claire would put down to the running.

'What inevitable?' I asked.

'I just thought maybe you two found it more of a turn-on than we did,' said Claire.

'Absolutely not,' I said emphatically.

I was pretty certain I could speak for Theo on this one – I didn't imagine seeing me swaying about in a poor-man's downward dog wearing thinning Primark leggings was in any way arousing for him.

'Plus, let's be serious,' said Claire conspiratorially, 'there's no way you can have a strictly platonic writing partnership with a guy who looks like that.'

I spluttered an answer: 'Looks aren't everything!'

Claire waved my protestations away, as though I was being ridiculous even trying to pretend that I didn't want to get naked with him. It would have been much easier, I sometimes thought, if I'd chosen to write a debut novel with somebody else from my writing course. Anybody else. But then, Theo had been the best writer by a mile, so swings and roundabouts.

'I wish couples yoga had got Rob all fired up,' lamented Claire. 'I'm prepared to try anything at this point.'

I looked at her, instantly regretting turning my head while running and having to grab hold of the arm rest to stop myself from stacking it off the back of the machine.

'Is everything OK with you two? I mean, I'm guessing that you're on this retreat for a reason. What made you sign up?' I asked.

Claire rested her chin in the palm of her hand looking fed up.

'It feels like our last chance, to be honest.'

'Don't say that,' I said. 'You two look great together.'

'On the outside, maybe. I think we both thought that getting married would give us a new lease of life. That it would be a new start. Silly, really. As if having a piece of paper declaring us husband and wife was going to miraculously eradicate the things that annoyed us about each other. If anything, it's pulled us further apart. He doesn't want to do anything together anymore and would be perfectly content falling asleep in front of Netflix on his own every night. We don't talk about anything, ever.'

'I can't imagine being with someone for fifteen years,' I admitted. 'My longest relationship has been five and it felt a bit like that for us.'

'Exactly. And shall I tell you what weddings do for you?' said Claire. 'They put you in massive debt, that's what. Ten grand it cost us. Which is partly why I'm determined not to get divorced. All that wasted money! All those gifts our guests spent their hard-earned cash on.'

'That's certainly one reason to try everything you can to stay together,' I agreed, prodding at a button to slow the treadmill down. It was official, I could not run and talk at the same time.

'So I had the bright idea that couples therapy and a trip to the French Riviera might put a bit of sparkle back into our marriage. Big mistake. Rob's an accountant and keeps banging on about how over-priced everything is. Last night he even got his Excel spreadsheet out!'

The treadmill ground to a halt, thankfully, and I stepped off it, relieved that that particular form of torture was over.

'Mission accomplished,' I said, wiping my mildly sweaty forehead with the sleeve of my hoodie.

'Fancy a coffee?' suggested Claire.

With zero qualms about having spent a total of fifteen minutes in the gym between us, we headed out to the garden, grabbing a cappuccino each from the machine on the way through the dining room. None of our lot were around, except for Justin and Renee who seemed to be hell-bent on working their way through a plate of croissants. We gave them a wave and carried on outside, where the sun was already beating down on the grass and the air smelled fresh, like lemons and sea.

'It's gorgeous here, isn't it, that's one good thing,' said Claire, plonking herself down in a chair and stretching out her legs. 'If nothing else, we've had a nice holiday. Nothing lost, I suppose. Except I'm not really sure where to go from here if this doesn't work. How to make things better.'

My instinct to fix things for everybody was instantly activated and despite me trying to rationalise the situation (i.e. it was Melissa's job to help them, not mine; I had enough problems of my own with a book to write and Theo in the room next door etc.) I couldn't help myself.

'Can I do anything?' I asked, a question I found myself asking at least three times a day on average. I'd discovered, over the years, that I felt compelled to put other people first, which was actually quite satisfying, it turned out. People needed me, and in a way that validated me. It was nice to assume that people couldn't possibly live without me. I mean, they probably could, but at the very least, I took it upon myself to make life a little easier for them. They usually (but not always) appreciated it.

Claire sighed dramatically. 'I can't imagine what. Although any help would be very gratefully received. Don't tell me you were a marriage counsellor before you were a writer?'

It wasn't a bad idea, actually, in fact I'd surprised myself by not going into a caring profession. When I was little I'd wanted to be a nurse until I'd seen sense and realised that since I was scared of blood and couldn't deal with bodily fluids full stop, I would make an absolutely terrible one. There were some aspects of the job I thought I would have enjoyed. Imagine making people's lives better (or trying to at least) every single day. Although I'd convinced myself I was doing that with my books, anyway: distracting people from their real lives. Cracking them up with a funny line or two when they felt sad, or making them feel seen when they read a storyline that resonated with them. It was why I'd started writing in the first place, to entertain other people. I used to make up stories for my siblings when they were little and I'd been quite good at it. Except that the success of *Little Boy Lost* notwithstanding, being a published author was harder and more stressful than I ever could have imagined.

'So tell me,' I said. 'What's your main issue with Rob? What are you hoping he'll change?'

'Easy,' said Claire. 'I want him to give the therapy thing a go, that's all. He's so defensive and resistant, constantly moaning that he doesn't need it and that the whole thing is a placebo and who needs to talk about every single feeling they have? He says it's no fun.'

'I mean, he's not wrong,' I said.

Claire gave me a look.

'But it's different for me,' I added hastily. 'I didn't sign up for this. But I totally would have done if I was in a relationship that wasn't quite working.'

'You are in a relationship that isn't quite working,' said Claire.

I shook my head. 'Friendships don't count.'

'Says who?'

'Anyway,' I said. 'We were talking about you and Rob. I think we need to show him that couples retreats aren't all about therapy. We're in the South of France, there's loads to do.'

'Such as ...?'

'Drinking,' I said, plucking something out of mid-air. 'Walks on the beach. Or is he into sports, because I saw a tennis club not far from here when I went out for a walk yesterday morning.'

Claire perked up. 'He used to love tennis. Joined a club and everything.'

'There we go. Let's organise a friendly mixed doubles match. Get our juices flowing. Show him how much fun Cannes can be.'

Claire looked at me with concern. 'Do you think Theo would be up for it, though? Does he even like tennis?'

I shrugged. 'Don't ask me. But even if he doesn't play, what could be nicer than a casual knockabout in the sun?'

'Hmmmn,' said Claire, 'I'm not sure the words "casual" and "knockabout" go together in Rob's vocabulary. He's ridiculously competitive.'

I thought about Theo. I supposed that, in a way, his career choice indicated that he was ambitious, which usually – not always, presumably – came hand in hand with being competitive. Even I was secretly more competitive than I wanted to admit. And I didn't like that part of myself. And while I was mostly happy for other authors who were hitting bestseller lists and getting picked for the Richard and Judy Book Club, and I certainly wouldn't want to take anything away from them, I wanted it, too. Desperately. And I wasn't entirely comfortable with myself for feeling that way.

'Look, I'm sure it'll be fine,' I said, trying to reassure myself as well as Claire. 'And the main thing is, we're doing this to help you. If Rob realises that he can actually have a good time out here, he might relax enough to get something out of it.'

Claire held up her fingers and crossed them.

'Anyway, I'd better go and write for a couple of hours before lunch,' I said, picking up my water bottle. 'Theo wants us to share our work, so the pressure's on.'

Claire shook her head. 'I don't know how you two do it. I was crap at creative writing at school.'

'Ah, but I bet you were brilliant at lots of other things,' I said, smiling at her.

She was the type of person I'd always wished I could be. Outspoken. Funny. Carefree. Could speak in front of a crowd without going crimson.

'See you at this afternoon's task,' I said to Claire as I started back to my room.

'Let's hope there's no sexual yoga poses involved,' Claire called after me.

On my way in I passed Harmony and Paul who had pitched up on a towel on the grass; Harmony was reading a pretentious-looking self-help book and I noticed that Paul had his nose in Jackson's latest, a reminder I didn't need of another relationship gone wrong

At 2 p.m. we all gathered in our usual spot at the far end of the pool, where Melissa had laid out something akin to a kindergarten's art table adorned with scissors, glue, glitter and piles of magazines and postcards. My instinct was to turn and walk the other way. Whatever she had in mind, it didn't seem as though it was going to be a particularly productive use of my time.

'Welcome to our next task, everyone. Something I hope that you'll find rewarding and insightful,' said Melissa.

Theo and I made eye contact for the first time that day. We'd been in our rooms writing separately and although I hadn't seen him, I'd heard him once or twice, moving around, going out onto his balcony, the scraping of chair legs on his lino floor.

'Afternoon,' he said, his deep rumble tapping into an old memory.

I used to love the way he sounded confident and unfazed in even the most uncomfortable of situations. He was the sort of guy who walked into a room and commanded attention, an ability I'd always quietly envied.

'I want you guys to make yourselves a beautiful vision board,' announced Melissa, holding up an A3-sized piece of white card.

There were some positive ooohs and aaahs (mostly from Harmony).

'And I specifically want you to focus on how you want your life to look in five years' time,' added Melissa.

I gave Claire a disgruntled look. Harmony and Paul were, of course, nodding along worthily as though there was nothing in this world they'd rather spend their afternoon doing. Seriously, the whole of the French Riviera was out there, sparkling enticingly, just down the road. Did I really want to be stuck here cutting pictures out of magazines?

'What exactly are we supposed to be putting on this vision board?' asked Renee, trying to pretend she was up for it.

'Let me explain,' said Melissa. 'This task is all about thinking ahead. I want you to consider your hopes and dreams as individuals – your careers, your families, your hobbies, your friendships et cetera. And also what you want to achieve together, as a couple. How would you like your relationship to be different in five years' time? What are you hoping that this retreat is the start of? What changes do you want the ten days we have together to ignite?'

I sighed inwardly. Yet another task that wasn't relevant to me and Theo. If I had my way, I wouldn't have anything to do with him in five years' time. In my fantasy, we'd write this book together and the sales would be excellent (let's try to stay optimistic here), but I hadn't thought beyond that. To my mind, this would never be a permanent partnership. Perhaps we'd dip our toes in once a decade: write something together, tolerate each other for the six months it took us to complete, and then go back to writing on our own, just as we liked it.

Melissa encouraged us all to grab a pile of magazines from the table.

'I want you to find a place in the garden, nowhere near your partners,' she said.

Theo took a step closer to me, bending to whisper in my ear. His breath tingled on my neck.

'I really feel like we should be writing,' he said. 'I was getting into a flow upstairs and now I've interrupted it for some sort of toddler's playtime task.'

'I know, I feel the same way,' I said, keeping my voice low, too. 'But I don't think we can walk off now, can we? I'd feel bad for Melissa.'

He shook his head, standing upright again. 'We should never have got involved in all of this in the first place. This is vital writing time we're wasting and I don't know about you, but I want to get this thing done and dusted as quickly as possible.'

So that he didn't have to spend any more time with me than was strictly necessary, I supposed. I mean, I got that it was awkward, but couldn't he be a bit more tactful about it?

'Heard anything more from Carla?' I asked, ignoring the rumblings of something in my chest, a reminder of how rejected by him I'd felt and was dangerously close to feeling again. See, this was what I hated about relationships: you had to open yourself up to the possibility of getting hurt.

That's what had worked so perfectly with me and Jackson (even if that was the only thing that had worked perfectly) – in hindsight, neither of us had thrown ourselves into the relationship fully. We were friends with benefits who ended up living together. I didn't think either of us had truly imagined it as a forever thing.

'Not since her email the other day. Sounds promising, though, doesn't it?' he said, his face softening a little.

I nodded. 'At least we're not enduring all of this for nothing.'

He laughed, and so did I. This was the closest we'd got to being nice to each other and it was good to see him do something other than glower at me. He used to smile a lot when he was younger – let's just say our creative writing tutor had taken teaching *extremely* seriously and the two of us had snickered like school children whenever he'd said something particularly wanky. Was Theo really less laid-back now, or had age simply beaten some of the unbridled joy out of both of us? Was it possible to change that much in six years? I supposed things had become more difficult for me, especially recently. Splitting up with Jackson, my diminishing finances, my dad's deteriorating health. Perhaps it was the same with Theo. And although I'd been determined to keep him at arm's length, I slowly found myself wanting to know what he'd been doing since I'd seen him last, to hear about the experiences he'd had, what he was hoping for now. And I didn't know what that meant, but from a logical point of view it made sense – if things went well with the book, would we really be able to see it through without knowing a single thing about each other's lives?

'Right, off you go to find your spots,' instructed Melissa.

A grumbling Claire and Rob picked up some scissors and glue and Justin and Renee dithered about which magazines to choose, picking one up, flicking through it and then throwing it back down on the table as though it was a hot coal. I hung back with Theo, thinking that if I went last I'd have less choice, which suited me. My life revolved around making decisions, and so when I got the chance to not make any, I positively revelled in it.

'I don't think I'm going to be able to do this. Thinking about the future really isn't my thing,' said Theo, looking worriedly at the craft table. I glimpsed his pearly white teeth as he bit his lip, the pink of it paling a little.

This task seemed to be making him anxious, which was strange – it was only supposed to be a bit of fun, surely. And it was his life, it wasn't like he could get it wrong.

'How come?' I asked before I could stop myself. I really wanted to know. Perhaps this was one of those changes Melissa was talking about. I'd just stepped out of my comfort zone and so far, Theo hadn't told me to mind my own business. I reached for a magazine, flicking through it, not sure what kind of reaction to expect.

'It feels difficult enough to stay in the present sometimes. To focus on the things I have to do now, to give it my all. To not look back. I can't imagine trying to look forward as well,' he said.

I looked at him, thinking that this was the most open with me he'd been. Ought I to give him my honest response to what he'd just said, or should I cut the conversation dead? Stick to safer topics, as per the plan I'd come up with before I'd even set foot in France.

'Like, it's overwhelming for you, you mean?'

He shook his head. 'Not exactly. I mean that when I try to think about what my life might be like in five years' time, I can't picture it. At all. I've got no clue, my brain just sort of shuts down.'

I tried not to look surprised, but I was. How did he keep going as a writer, then, if he wasn't forward-thinking? Because the industry was all about trying to second-guess the next best thing. Come up with a hook that might still be relevant in eighteen months when the actual book came out.

'You weren't expecting that, I presume,' said Theo, reluctantly picking up a pair of scissors and peering at them as though he had no idea what he was expected to do with them.

I turned to face him. 'I'm the opposite, I suppose – all about the future, scared to let my mind pull me back to the past.'

On a gust of wind I could smell his aftershave again. He was standing dangerously close, so close I could see the solitary crease in his black T-shirt, noticed that his beard was already longer than it had been when we'd shared the taxi together. The breeze was warm and I could hear the rustle of the palm trees all around me. It was perfect. Perfect for what, I didn't know.

'Scarlett? Theo? Everything all right?' called Melissa, looking over at us, one delicate hand shielding her eyes from the sun.

I gave her a thumbs-up. 'Yep! Just choosing our bits!'

Theo moved closer to the table, bending to peer at the magazines on offer.

'Well. Guess there's no avoiding this,' he said.

'Doesn't look like it,' I replied, grabbing a Pritt Stick and a copy of French *Vogue*. I smiled to myself as out of the corner of my eye I watched Theo pick up a pot of gold glitter, frown at it and put it back. He didn't strike me as the type to put glitter on his vision board, although I was intrigued to see what he did come up with.

'Have fun,' I called over my shoulder to him before turning and heading for a lounger by the pool.

An hour or so later, Melissa, who had been wafting around checking our work and making soothing, encouraging comments about our burgeoning boards, made us all get back into our pairs to talk through our creations. Theo joined me by the pool, pulling up a lounger next to mine. My shoulders were hot from the sun and I looked longingly at the water, desperately wanting to go for a swim but knowing that once we were done with this I'd have to head back to my room to write. We were supposed to be sharing our first two chapters later and mine needed a considerable amount of revising before I did.

'Was it as bad as you thought?' I asked, looking pointedly at the back of his vision board which he'd put face down on the ground as though he was going to do a big reveal of what was on the other side.

'Affirmative,' he said.

'Shall I go first, then?'

'Be my guest.'

I pushed my vision board in his direction, swivelling it round so that it was upside down for me but the right way up for him. It wasn't the most impressive bit of artwork I'd ever produced, but I'd put some effort into it, and it looked about as aesthetically appealing as I could hope for in an hour and with limited materials.

Theo nodded approvingly.

'Nice,' he said.

'So this person in the middle represents me,' I told him, pointing to a tiny picture I'd found of a woman slumped at her laptop.

'Is she supposed to look exhausted?' asked Theo, peering at it.

'Um, she's just writing,' I said. 'Typing. Look.'

I made him look at it again.

'OK,' he said. 'Not tired, then.'

'No. Vibrant. Passionate. A zest for life.'

He smirked.

'What?' I demanded to know.

'Nothing. Carry on,' he said.

I gave him a look. He was on dangerous ground here. If he was just going to ridicule my hard work, then I was going to stop participating in the task.

'And then around me is my family. And my friends here. Well, all over, really,' I said. 'These kids are my nephew and niece. I spend a lot of time with them when I can.'

Theo looks surprised. 'Your brother had kids?'

I shook my head. 'My sister. They're eight and six. She'd tell you they were a handful, but they're usually good as gold when they're with me. We go to bookshops together and hang out there for hours and then I treat them to something new. Kate gets annoyed with me because she says she hasn't got space for all these books.'

Theo laughed. 'They have a way of lightening the mood, children, don't they?'

I swallowed hard. Is this where he told me he had kids of his own? I braced myself. I could be cool about it, I totally could be.

Theo narrowed his eyes at me. 'I can see your mind ticking over. You're wondering if I have children, aren't you?'

I laughed, a tinkling sound that felt like it came from somewhere outside of my body. 'Not at all,' I said. And then: 'Do you?'

He shook his head. 'No, Scarlett.'

Annoyingly, I felt a visceral rush of relief, which I desperately tried to cover up.

'Oh right. Because it would be cool if you did. Obviously.'

135

A beat.

'Would it?' he said.

I nodded, not trusting myself to speak.

'I have a younger half-sister,' he said, his voice low. 'On my mum's side. She's … funny. Full of life. We get along pretty well, considering.'

'Considering what?' I asked.

'Considering I don't get along with our mum.'

'Ah,' I said. 'How old is your sister?'

'Sixteen. So weird to think she'll be an adult soon. To me she's still a little girl. Sometimes I think I need to adjust the way I treat her. Stop mollycoddling her.'

'She probably loves it that way,' I said.

'Maybe.'

I looked back at my board. What more was there to say about it? I'd found some random pictures of people of different ages, lots of them, representing my dad, my siblings and my friends. I'd cut out some hearts and flowers to illustrate how important they were to me, which I realised was a bit childish in hindsight, but it was too late now, because Theo was staring at it, his head cocked to one side.

'That's a whole lot of other people on your board,' he said, peering at it again.

That was a good thing, wasn't it?

'But where are you in all of this?' he asked.

'I told you. There in the middle,' I said, my voice faltering, because now that I had some distance from it and I was having to explain it to someone else, it was clear that other people were totally dominating my board. 'There's some books here. And look, there's a computer screen with some writing on it, and a pile of notebooks. And a bookshop table because I always want to be on the front table but never seem to be. And see here, there's New York, because I dream of being a *New York Times* bestseller.'

'Again,' said Theo, looking up at me. 'A *New York Times* bestseller *again*. Don't ever forget what we achieved, Scarlett.'

God, I really wished he would go back to being all cold and detached and *not* giving me sexy, smouldering stares.

'And how does your writing connect with all of these other people?' he went on. 'Because it feels kind of separate.'

I shook my head. 'It's not. I partly write *for* these people. So that I can support them and help them.'

Theo looked confused. 'You write for other people?'

Was he serious?

'Of course. For my family and for my readers. So that I can give something back. Isn't that what it's all about?'

He still looked baffled. 'I'm sorry, but I just don't get it.'

I snatched up my mood board, moving it out of his sightline. I'd had quite enough of his feedback for one day.

'And I don't get why the idea of doing things for other people feels so alien to you,' I said, a little snippily. I realised, too late, that I was basically accusing him of being self-centred. Which he was, a bit, if you asked me.

'Because you have to think about yourself, too, Scarlett,' he said, pulling my vision board closer to him again. I watched his fingers curl around the corner of the card.

'I don't see Jackson Clark represented on here. Do you not see him in your five-year-plan?'

He knew I'd been with Jackson, but he thought I was still with him. It hit me like a bolt because I'd thought he hadn't given me a second thought after I'd left his flat for the last time that morning. So he wasn't like me, then. He hadn't avoided reading anything about me because he couldn't bear it. He could bear it, because he didn't care, I supposed.

'We broke up,' I said.

He looked surprised. 'When?'

Did it matter? 'A couple of months ago.'

Theo went to say something but it was as if he stopped himself and changed tack. I desperately wanted to know what he'd originally been going to say. Did he have a secret hatred of Jackson, or something? Had they had a run-in at some high-profile book event that I hadn't been invited to? I'd made the mistake of telling Jackson the bare bones of what had happened between us and I suspected he'd always harboured a deep-seated grudge.

'Sorry to hear that,' said Theo, sounding a little bit as though he wasn't sorry in the slightest.

'Thanks. But enough about my life. Show me your board,' I said, holding his gaze.

But all I could think was: he knew about Jackson. He'd read stuff about me, or he'd spoken about me to someone and somehow that changed things because I thought he'd shut every part of me out, like I'd done with him. And I didn't know whether it made me feel better or worse that he hadn't. Because it had been much easier to paint him as the villain – not good enough for me, anyway; more trouble than he was worth. But the more time I spent with him, the more I was beginning to think that he wasn't as one-dimensional as I'd made him out to be. That I'd never really considered that maybe I was at fault too, somehow. I mean, I hated to be wrong, but that didn't mean I never was.

Reluctantly, Theo plucked his vision board off the ground, holding it between his thumb and middle finger as though it was something he didn't particularly want to have to touch, and dropped it face-up in front of me.

'There,' he mumbled. 'It's not very good. As I said, I don't do thinking about the future.'

'Hmmmn,' I said, taking in his design which was – to say the least – sparse.

There were seven pictures on there in total, all spaced out with what felt like acres of white card in between. Whereas mine had been bustling and full and colourful, his felt bleak and monochrome and empty. How had it taken him an hour to put this together?!

'Talk me through it,' I said, trying to be kind.

Mind you, I wasn't going to let him off lightly after the grilling he'd given me.

He coughed. Picking up his reusable coffee mug, he drank almost manically from it, wincing.

'Ugh. Cold coffee,' he said, his face contorting in disgust.

I laughed. 'Go on, then. I'm waiting,' I insisted, nodding my head towards his board.

He put his cup down and sat bolt upright, as though he was in a really uncomfortable job interview.

'There's not much to say, as you can see. That's me, in the middle. My books. Dogs, because I really want a dog. A Peloton, because in five years' time I want to be the sort of person who can justify buying a Peloton because they will use said Peloton and not leave it gathering dust in the corner. There's a clapperboard because I'd like to write a film one day, although I've no idea where to start. Um, that's it, I think?'

I took it all in. Not that it took long.

'It's not exactly fun-filled,' I said. 'Where's the mess? The joy? Where's the colour?'

'I have colour,' he said, pointing at the one photo that wasn't in black and white. 'Also, I hate mess, so why would I make a messy board?'

I thought back. It was true, his room in the house he'd shared with his writer friend, Jake, and a girl who I seemed to remember did something in the city, had always been very tidy. His draft chapters were tidy. Even the notes he'd written in the margins for me had been neat and precise and clear.

'But where's everyone else?' I asked, staring at it, wondering if I'd missed something, if perhaps he'd added a symbol to hint at family and friends and lovers (not that I wanted to think about that, particularly).

He crossed his arms defensively. 'This is my vision board. Why would I fill it with pictures of other people?'

I squinted at him. 'But this is supposed to depict how you want your future to look. Don't you want other people in it? You know, friends around you? Family? Marriage? Kids?'

He baulked. 'I don't know. Not really.'

Admittedly, I hadn't been able to imagine kids and marriage, either. I hoped it would happen at some point, but I'd never allowed the thought to take over because it might *not* happen, and I'd managed to reassure myself that if it didn't I'd be fine because I had all these other people to care about and spend time with and that was enough. I had a niece and a nephew. I could get a cat. That would be more than enough.

'It feels a bit sad that you haven't put anyone else on your board,' I continued, wondering if I was being too pushy. But wasn't that the point of this exercise, to make us think hard about our choices, and about what we might be missing out on because of the way our lives were currently set up?

'Well, I think it feels sad that you worry more about everyone else than you do about yourself,' he said defiantly.

OK, then.

'Look, I'm sorry if—'

'Why do you care so much about other people, anyway?' he asked. He couldn't look less tense if he tried and he'd completely missed the point of the exercise – surely it was supposed to be a bit of fun!

'Why *don't* you care?' I countered, up for the challenge.

As we sat looking at each other, daring each other to say something that would turn this into a full-blown row, which was something we'd never done and maybe, in hindsight, what we'd needed, Melissa tinkled her bell. I let out a little sigh of relief. We were different, that was all, this exercise had proved it. In fact, our differences were probably what made our writing collaboration possible – if we had the same ideas, the same perspective on life, we might as well write the book by ourselves.

We got up, retrieving our boards, our cups, my sunglasses. As Theo walked off ahead, I called after him.

'By the way, are you OK to play tennis with Claire and Rob tomorrow morning at ten? We'll meet in the foyer?'

This was probably the worst timing ever because he probably hated me more than ever right at this moment, but I had to ask because it was all arranged and if he stormed off to his room, I might not see him again until breakfast.

He threw me a look over his shoulder that indicated that he probably couldn't think of a single thing worse than spending additional time with me. I held my nerve. He was going to have to come, because I'd promised Claire.

'It's all arranged,' I said, smiling as sweetly at him as was possible under the circumstances. 'Hope you don't mind?'

He shook his head, turned away and carried on walking over to Melissa and the others. Good. That wasn't a no, was it?

Chapter Eleven

Today was going to be the hottest since we'd arrived, I could feel it in the air, even though it was only ten in the morning. In my white vest and navy city shorts combo, which was the closest thing to tennis whites I could throw together, the sun was warming my skin and I thought I might have to pop my sunglasses on if there was to be any hope of me seeing the ball and subsequently hitting it. Theo was limbering up next to me, stretching his hamstrings, which I thought was a bit much for the kind of laid-back rallying I had in mind.

The court felt very professional and I didn't know what you'd officially call the surface, but it looked like a sort of red clay, and it felt very 'South of France' with an achingly attractive couple who looked like they were warming up for the French Open playing next to us, grunting every time they slammed the ball over the net. Off in the distance was a huge hotel with a cute red awning over every window and expansive gardens housing the huge pine trees that were obviously native to this part of the world, plus a slew of impressive palms. A chalk scoreboard was hanging on the netting to one side, which Theo was looking ominously at.

'You do know this is just a friendly game, right?' I said, approaching him with concern. He seemed to be taking this very seriously and was all kitted out in actual tennis whites, like a slightly more beardy Roger Federer, which wasn't an unpleasant look.

'Is it?' he said, feigning innocence and plunging into a series of inter-connecting lunges and squats.

Oh God, this was not what I was expecting at all. I bet he was a member of one of those swanky tennis clubs that were as pretentious as hell and where everyone was secretly ruthlessly competitive.

I glanced nervously at Claire and Rob who were warming up on the other side of the net. Rob was wearing board shorts and a tie-dye T-shirt, which was a sign that he didn't take tennis anywhere near as seriously as Theo clearly did.

'Let's just have fun, yeah?' I said, feeling the need to re-iterate the point. We were doing this for Claire and Rob, not so that Theo could dazzle everyone with his ball skills.

'I'm afraid I can't promise that,' he said, worryingly launching into a set of star jumps.

Aaaargh, what had I done? I should have checked that Theo was happy to throw the game before I arranged all of this. My only hope was that Rob was a better player than his garish attire suggested. Perhaps he had his own set of pristine tennis whites at home but had decided, quite sensibly, not to bring them on a couples retreat.

'Right,' I said, not wanting to keep the anticipation going any longer. 'Shall we get going?'

Theo took charge, working out who was starting at which end and then telling me where to stand, and that as we'd won the toss, he would be serving first. I had a very bad feeling about this, which was quickly justified when Theo smashed a serve over the net that Rob made a feeble failed attempt to hit back. I caught Claire's eye and mouthed: *Sorry*. She grimaced at me with good humour. I had clearly made a mistake in assuming that Theo was as crap at tennis as I was.

The game progressed, with Theo dominating and Rob getting the occasional winning shot back, which seemed to spur him on. I heard him giving Claire a pep talk although to be honest, it felt like the two of us were pretty much redundant, crouching poised at the net while the guys flew about the remaining three quarters of the court. It felt a little sexist, if the truth be told, because I would have liked to have tried hitting it from the back of the court – not to say I'd have done it successfully, but it was a game, and games were supposed to be fun. Although, on the other hand, I had to admit there was something quite sexy about hearing Theo thundering about behind me, grunting as he hit a particularly hard shot. I looked over my shoulder a couple of times and felt bad that he was so red-faced and determined while I was wafting about barely breaking a sweat, but he only had himself to blame.

At one point, while he was handing me the ball because it was my turn to serve, which I could tell pained him, I whispered to him to take it easy.

'We're supposed to be making sure Rob has a good time,' I hissed at him.

'What?' he said, looking at me confused.

'Let them win, OK?' I said in what I hoped was a stern manner.

Theo looked me directly in the eye. 'Scarlett, there is absolutely no way that is going to happen.'

For fuck's sake. If I'd known he'd be this determined to win, I'd never have come up with any of this. And I felt terrible because now Rob was going to feel all emasculated instead of us showing him what a lovely time he could be having in Cannes and that it was worth them spending all that money he'd logged on his spreadsheet.

We played on, with me messing up as many shots as I could without being too obvious – not that I had to try that hard, to be honest – so that it gave Claire and Rob a fighting chance to catch us up. And I noticed that as time went on, Rob's confidence was building, so that towards the end of the match – and Theo had, of course, insisted on playing three sets as though we were in some kind of professional tournament – the scores were pretty even. I could see Theo glaring at me every time I missed a shot and chose to ignore him as he and Rob engaged in a sort of frat-boy-style battle and Claire and I ducked and scooted out of the way to avoid getting a ball smacked in our faces. As we started the final game, the decider, I lurched so far out of the way that I slammed to the ground, scuffing the entire left side of my thigh. I rubbed at it, wincing. Theo, to his credit, came bounding over.

'Are you OK?' he asked, crouching down next to me.

He was breathless, I noticed, his chest heaving and falling, because he'd really been going for it a second or two before. His forehead was rippled with concern as I examined my thigh, which was burning painfully the way it tends to when you've just dragged it across a gravelly surface.

'I'll be fine,' I said, attempting to stand up.

'Here,' he said, holding out his hand.

I looked warily at it, as though it was something alien and frightening that I shouldn't go near. I had the distinct feeling that if I took his hand, something would change between us. Which was completely irrational, obviously. What could possibly happen in the split second it would take him to haul me off the tarmac? So I took it. And as his fingers wrapped around mine and his bicep tensed underneath his sweat-soaked T-shirt, I felt a powerful rush run up my arm and into my chest and down into an area that it probably shouldn't be travelling to. Dropping his hand instantly, I muttered a 'Thanks' and limped back onto court. See? I should have trusted my gut. This was bad, bad, bad.

We won, obviously, because Theo wasn't going to let us not, even though I was next to useless due to my leg (who was I kidding – the guys may as well have played a singles match for all the input Claire and I'd had). We all shook hands, with Rob and Theo patting each other on the back, both looking as though they were about to keel over.

'Great game, man,' said Rob.

'It was a close call,' said Theo. 'You really gave me the run around.'

Claire and I gathered our things together as they dissected the match, complimenting each other for that serve, or that shot. I felt terrible that Theo didn't do what I asked and throw the match. Maybe I should have been clearer about my motivation for wanting to help Claire and Rob, but I hadn't really had a chance and also I hadn't wanted to break Claire's trust by telling Theo about the issues they were having with their marriage. Perhaps if I'd spelled it out to him, though, he'd have been more likely to comply. Then again, I couldn't imagine it. Tennis was clearly his thing. I wondered what else was his thing and simultaneously tried not to watch as he bent over to pull his tracksuit bottoms over his shorts.

I snapped my head round to focus on Claire.

'I'm so sorry,' I said to her, keeping my voice low. 'I had no idea Theo was going to approach our friendly knockabout like a bloody Wimbledon semi-final. I hope Rob isn't too pissed off.'

'What are you talking about?' she shrieked. 'He loved it! When we swapped ends before the final set, he told me he was going to rejoin our local tennis club. He said sparring with Theo had really got his juices flowing.'

'But you said he hated losing,' I said, looking over at them. He and Theo were laughing about something and so admittedly he didn't seem too fed up, but I still felt as though I'd let Claire down.

'Well tough, you can't win them all,' said Claire. 'And maybe he should have let me have a shot or two. That might have swung it for us for all he knows,' she said all seriously, before dissolving into laughter.

'We didn't get a flipping look-in!' I said, cracking up, too.

'Still, it's more exercise than I usually get in a week, so all good in my eyes,' said Claire. 'Now let's go and have a drink. I need cold white wine pronto.'

That afternoon we were forced to endure yet another group therapy session which, luckily for me, had been mostly focused on Justin and Renee, who Melissa felt needed a little more encouragement than the rest of us (I didn't think she could have been including Theo and me in that analogy). And then in the evening, the eight of us plus Melissa had dinner together at a little bistro a short walk from the hotel. I'd spent a worrying amount of time wondering whether to nip down to Rue d'Antibes beforehand to buy myself something new to wear. Suddenly nothing I owned seemed chic enough for a night out in Cannes. Part of me also thought I owned nothing nice enough for a night out with Theo, who always looked as though he'd just stepped out of the pages of *Vogue Hommes*, but I squashed that thought pretty quickly. This was about me and how I felt about myself. In no way was I doing any of this for him.

At dinner, Theo sat to one side of me, Claire the other.

'I love your jumpsuit,' said Claire, referring to the one thing I'd packed that I didn't feel like a suburban housewife in. 'I wish I could wear stuff like that, but I just don't think I've got the waist for it.'

'Nonsense, you always look amazing,' I told her.

Her style had a modern vintage vibe, all bright colours and scarves in her hair and big hoop earrings. Like Theo, when she walked into a room she made an impact, which I loved and which I wished I could emulate. I'd had a couple of awkward incidents at book events where I'd introduced myself to booksellers to explain that I was one of the authors there for the event and they'd given me a look to suggest that they'd never have had me down as an author in a million years.

'By the way, I need to thank you and Theo for putting a rocket up Rob's arse. He's even talking about the four of us doing a round of golf before we leave,' said Claire.

'I'm not sure if I can deal with any more not-so-friendly competition,' I said, glancing at Theo who was chatting to Harmony on the other side of him, about books, interestingly enough. She was cooing all over him and was now bending his ear about the book that she wanted to write and assumed she'd get published the second she sent it out on submission. In fact, I heard her say, she was already pre-empting a movie deal. As if sensing that I was watching and also – possibly – desperate to break away from Harmony, who was now proceeding to give him a chapter-by-chapter breakdown of the book she hadn't even started writing yet, Theo swivelled to face me.

'Having a good evening?' he asked, his shoulder brushing against mine. I should probably move my chair so that it didn't happen again, but I somehow felt rooted to the spot. Perhaps I'd stay where I was for now.

'Definitely,' I enthused. 'Delicious food.'

I'd gone for a salad *Niçoise*, a speciality of nearby Nice, plus nigh-on half a basket of breads and olive oils. Theo topped up my wine, then his own.

'How's your leg?' he asked.

I appreciated his concern. Perhaps he felt bad about the way he'd bulldozed his way through proceedings.

'I'd forgotten all about it, to be honest,' I said. 'Still pumped up from winning the match, are you? You seemed pretty keen to come out on top.'

He smiled, picking up his wine to take a large sip.

'You think I was too much,' he said, his eyes boring into me.

I hesitated, wondering how much he'd been able to pick up on.

'I feel you missed the point of the game.'

'Which was …?' he asked.

'It doesn't matter,' I said, bottling it. The game was over now, wasn't it?

'You need to tell me about this point I missed, Scarlett. Otherwise I might inadvertently miss it again,' he insisted softly.

I checked on Claire, who was deep in conversation with Rob. Would she mind, I wondered, if I gave him the bare bones of what was going on?

'OK, but keep this on the down low,' I said, shuffling closer to him so that there was no denying the fact that our shoulders were pressed together now. Needs must, because nobody else could hear this. Mind you, they all seemed pretty caught up in conversations of their own, anyway, and it wasn't exactly quiet in here with the chatter and the clink of glasses and loud voices in forceful French and a smattering of English.

'You're making me very anxious,' said Theo.

'Am I?' I asked, genuinely surprised.

'No.'

I tutted. 'Haha. This is actually quite serious.'

'The suspense is killing me,' said Theo.

I lowered my voice so it was little more than a whisper. 'Rob isn't too happy about being on the couples retreat. He thinks it's too expensive and that there's too much wanky group therapy.'

'I knew I liked him,' said Theo.

'And I told Claire I'd help show him a good time. So that he relaxes a bit and, you know, makes a bit more of an effort with the other stuff.'

Theo looked confused. 'And you're getting involved in this why?'

It was a reasonable question.

'I'm simply trying to help Claire out.'

'But it's their relationship, isn't it?' he said, leaning into my thigh while he speared one of the olives he'd ordered for the table to share. 'It's for them to sort out. So why are you meddling in it?'

I was taken aback by that. Was that really how he saw it? 'Meddling?!' I said.

'Yes. Not everyone needs to be fixed, you know.'

'I think it's extremely rude of you to say that when I'm only trying to help,' I said. There were lots of things I could do to make things better for people. And so why on earth wouldn't I try?

'Genuine question: Do you like people interfering in your business when you're having relationship issues?' he asked.

'I've ... yes! If it helps.'

Saying that, I'd never really talked about my relationships with anyone. Possibly a little bit with Alexa on occasion, but I tended not to. I'd never felt the need. What good would involving other people do?

'And does it usually? Help?' asked Theo, like a dog with a bone.

I sighed, exasperated. 'We're not talking about my

relationships. We're talking about me helping other people.'

Theo looked sideways at me with an expression I couldn't quite read. 'I have to say, if nothing else, I admire your tenacity. The fact that you wade headlong into somebody else's war zone without a second thought.'

He pulled away then, his shoulder detaching from mine, his knee moving an inch the other way. The mood had shifted and I didn't quite know why. Although it was probably a good thing. I didn't like it when he was being nice because it was much easier to not be able to stand him.

'By the way, not every bit of conflict has to feel like a war zone,' I said, because it didn't. Sometimes things just needed a little push in the right direction. For someone to approach things from a different angle. 'And even if it did,' I admitted, 'I'd probably throw myself in there anyway.'

Theo clinked my glass as though we were celebrating something.

'I applaud your bravery,' he said.

'Are you drunk?' I asked him in all seriousness.

'Not yet.'

I watched the others for a bit. How Justin and Renee were choosing a dessert, all earnest and thoughtful as though it was the most important decision in the world. How Paul clearly fancied Melissa and how Harmony was so self-assured she didn't bat an eyelid. How Claire and Rob sporadically made each other laugh out loud.

'We should probably exchange chapters tonight,' said Theo. 'If you want.'

My stomach flipped. I knew this was what we had to do in order to move forward with the novel, but it still felt terrifying. He'd written chapters one and three, leaving me to do two and four. Four had been particularly hard because by then we'd established that the husband was missing and that their marriage hadn't been as idyllic as it seemed, but we needed the story to change direction again, to push the narrative forward.

'Sure,' I said. 'I'll ping them over when I get back to my room.'

Theo nodded in a way that felt reassuring for about a second. There was no going back now.

Chapter Twelve

The following morning I lay in bed with the windows thrown open reading through the chapters Theo had sent over. I was gripped from the off. He'd set up everything so well: the deserted beach, the marital row, the husband disappearing into the water for a swim, his wife beginning to worry when he doesn't arrive back at their hotel room. I'd picked it up from there and had sent my chapters off late last night, after I'd tweaked and tweaked them, anxious that they weren't quite right, that he'd find fault and I'd take it personally (which I didn't ever when it came to notes but I felt like maybe I would with him this time) and then it would be difficult to come back from because I'd be second-guessing every single thing I wrote. Anyway, in the end I'd had to send something off because I'd promised to and I wasn't one to miss a deadline. Carla's words were ringing in my ears: she needed sample chapters as soon as possible. I knew how fast publishing changed, how one minute they couldn't wait to read your work and the next the genre was out of favour and they were on to the next big thing. If we wanted to take advantage of the interest, we had to act quickly.

Theo's chapter three was equally as good and I read it with a mixture of admiration and envy, flicking through the pages on my phone at the speed of light because his pacing was just so good and he kept setting up all these questions that I was desperate to know the answer to but knew that even he probably didn't know what they were at this point, because that was something we would have to work out together. But he was planting seeds all over the place and it was phenomenally effective.

I jotted some notes down on my pad, lines of dialogue I'd particularly liked, and plot points I thought were spot on. Our main characters needed some developing, in my opinion, and that's what I liked best about writing, fleshing them out to make them three-dimensional and (always) flawed. Perhaps this was an area I could excel in, a place where I could actually give Theo some helpful feedback in the same way that he was clearly going to have to give me some on plotting and pace. Sometimes I wondered whether I was even cut out to be a thriller writer, although what else would I do? My prose had never been beautiful enough for literary fiction, and pacy psychological thrillers were what I loved to read, and so why wouldn't I want to write them?

I checked the time: 7.45 a.m. The calm before the storm. I forced myself out of bed, determined to check out the hotel spa, which Claire had told me was mega relaxing and involved a rooftop hot tub with sea views. And if I got up there early enough, I might have my favourite all to myself: the sauna. Jacuzzis were amazing, but a hot bath with bubbles and one of my aromatherapy oils had almost the same effect. But I could never recreate the dry heat, the sweat, the way my skin glowed with health after twenty minutes in a sauna.

I pinged Alexa a quick message.

How's your course? Hope things are a bit less stressful?

I saw she was online and waited for her reply.

Never mind that, are you and Theo Winters an actual couple yet?!

I tutted loudly to myself.

That will NEVER happen.

She sent three hearts-in-your eyes emojis in return. I knew she was only winding me up, but still.

After a wasted ten minutes spent looking for my swim-suit, which I was almost sure I'd packed but now couldn't find anywhere, I had no choice but to put on the black-and-white polka dot string bikini Alexa had forced me to buy when we were out shopping last summer. I'd never had the opportunity to wear it and had stuffed it in my suitcase alongside the much plainer racing green swimsuit I now couldn't find thinking that maybe – if the South of France happened to have an April heatwave, which didn't appear to be the case thus far – I'd have an opportunity to wear it. It felt very Hollywood glam, although I would have preferred a slightly more substantial cut. When I looked at myself in the mirror I didn't hate what I saw, but I also felt very exposed, or at least I thought I would feel that way wearing it in public. But I was only going to the hotel sauna and it was so early I doubted anyone from our party would be up, especially after the myriad bottles of wine we'd polished off between us last night. I grabbed my robe from the back of the bathroom door, slid into my flip-flops and headed up to the spa on the fifth floor.

I thought I'd do the sauna first because afterwards I could shower and jump in the jacuzzi and then I'd slip my robe back on and head back to my room for another shower and to get dressed for breakfast. There wasn't a soul around, which was good, as it would mean I could completely relax and zone out and try not to think about Theo or Dad or how hot it was in there and how I wasn't feeling as confident as I'd have liked about the chapters I'd written.

I opened the blackened glass door and was faced with a wall of burning heat that curled straight into my nostrils.

And then I spotted Theo, silently sitting on the top tier wearing what I can only describe as a flannel. OK, it was a towel, but it was *tiny*. Of course it would have to be him. Out of the sixty or so guests staying at the hotel, I had to bump into the one person I really did not want to share a boiling hot wooden cabin with.

'Morning,' said Theo, who looked all languid and relaxed like he'd been in there for about an hour and was slightly delirious with heat stroke.

'Hello,' I said cautiously, wondering whether it would be rude to back up, close the door again and go out to the hot tub instead.

Deciding it would be, I stepped inside, closing the door behind me. The silence engulfed me almost as much as the heat. I tentatively sat as far away from Theo as I could, keeping my robe firmly wrapped around my body.

'Aren't you going to be too hot in that dressing gown?' asked Theo, rather untactfully, I thought. Just because he was happy wearing a postage-stamped size piece of towelling, didn't mean we all had to be.

'I'm not staying long,' I said breezily. 'I want to check out the jacuzzi.'

'It's lovely,' he said. 'Beautiful views.'

'So I've heard.'

I tried to relax, sinking my back into the wooden bench behind me which was so hot that I sort of ricocheted straight back off it again. I could see Theo in my peripheral vision, which made him pretty difficult to ignore. I took some deep breaths, letting the hot air fill my lungs. Sweat began to prickle at my brow line.

'So I read your chapters,' I said, thinking that if I stayed on topics we were familiar with, all would be well. 'They're great. I'll pop some notes over to you later on today.'

Theo was silent for a few seconds, which was disconcerting. Had I said something wrong?

'Why not tell me what you thought right now?' he said.

How strange, I thought, to have a conversation about our mutual book in the hot and the dark and to not be looking at each other. Strange and also quite nice. I felt as though I was in a confessional box and that I could say things I wouldn't normally say. Which is probably what gave me the confidence to tell him what I really thought.

'I loved the set-up in chapter one,' I said. 'You're raising questions immediately about who these people are and what's gone wrong. Scene-setting is good, although I think we can probably add some more description once we've spent more time at the beach. Same with my chapters.'

'I usually add that in later,' said Theo. 'But yes, I completely agree.'

'Character-wise, I think both protagonists need more developing from the off. I don't really get a sense of their relationship and I think that could make it even more intriguing when things go wrong. The opening pages are prickling with tension, but it would be great to see their differences; how they each respond to their argument.'

'Hmmmn,' said Theo. 'Funny, I really thought I'd nailed the character work this time. But then I go and get the same note I always get.'

I was surprised. 'You get notes about character?'

'Every. Single. Time.'

I laughed softly. 'You always get there eventually though, right? In later drafts, I mean. Like it's the last layer to go on.'

'I'm not sure it does go on,' said Theo. 'Or so my Goodreads "fans" would have me believe.'

I turned to face him, swivelling on my bench, resting my elbow behind me, my chin in the palm of my hand. I could barely make out his features and only the white of his towel popped in the dark. 'Did I just hear that right? You go on *Goodreads*?'

'Of course,' he said. 'Don't you?'

'Don't be ridiculous.'

Theo leaned forwards so that a bit more light fell on his face. 'Please explain.'

'There's nothing to explain. Goodreads is brutal. And my fragile disposition simply can't take it.'

Theo made a show of being mock-shocked. 'Wow.'

'Wow what?'

'I thought you were made of stronger stuff.'

'Ah, well. That's the impression I like to give people.'

'You're very convincing,' he said.

Was it me, or was it about twenty degrees hotter in here now than it had been when I first sat down? I pressed the back of one hand against my cheeks, but that did little to cool them down. I was going to have to either leave or take my robe off. And I didn't see why I should rush off just because Theo was here. Really, etiquette dictated that he should go first so that I could enjoy the peace and tranquillity of being here by myself.

Without thinking too hard about it, I undid the belt of my robe and let it slip off my shoulders, wriggling out of it. But then I was still sitting on it and even that felt too hot, so I stood up to hang it on the hook just inside the door, hoping it was too dark for Theo to notice what I was wearing, or, more realistically, that he didn't care enough to look. I fumbled with the hook, and when I turned to sit back down his eyes were burning into me. My breath caught in my throat for a second, and then I carried on back to my seat, my heart suddenly hammering against my chest. I was being ridiculous. Men were programmed to look at women in bikinis, weren't they? It didn't mean a thing.

'Would you like your notes?' said Theo, his voice softer than usual.

Ugh. No? I wanted him to send them to me in written form so that I didn't have to pretend to be fine if he hated every single word I'd written.

'Later?' I said, closing my eyes. 'I'm trying to relax.'

'You're scared, aren't you?' said Theo, his voice light and teasing, a reminder of the easiness that used to exist between us.

'I most certainly am not.'

I could almost hear him smirking. God, he knew what he was doing. There was no way I could let him have the upper hand now.

'Fine, give me your notes. But be kind,' I said.

'I'm not a monster, Scarlett.'

I snorted. 'If you say so.'

I heard him shift. The bench creaked. I kept my eyes firmly closed, as though that was going to help.

'So I liked your chapters,' he said, his voice piercing the hot, dead air.

Great. 'Like' was a pointless word that never felt enough. I thought I'd said I'd loved his. Even if I hadn't said it, I *had* loved them and so it would have come across that way. He'd only 'liked' mine.

'Praise indeed,' I said.

'Your character interactions are phenomenal,' he said. 'The dialogue sparkles and pops off the page.'

My pulse quickened. This was better.

'There's a but, isn't there?' I said, hoping I was wrong, but protecting myself just in case. As in, whatever he said now

159

would be fine because I'd casually insinuated that I knew he couldn't 'like' everything about it.

'The plot is a bit laboured,' he said. 'And slow.'

'Ouch.'

'Easily fixed.'

'For you, maybe.'

I mulled over what he'd said. To be fair, he was probably right. And in the same way his reviews criticised his characterisation, mine (the occasional ones I let myself read, anyway) sometimes alluded to the plot being thin. Which hurt, of course it did, but it felt like something I could improve on. I just hadn't yet, no matter how hard I'd tried.

'So I was thinking …' said Theo.

'Your brain is really working overtime here,' I said. 'Is it the heat, do you think?'

'Possibly.'

'Go on, then. What's this grand thought of yours?'

'I reckon that instead of writing separately, in different rooms, as though we're a thousand miles apart, we should write together.'

Luckily he couldn't see my face, which was contorted into a mixture of horror, fear and downright panic. No, no, no, this was not what we agreed.

'How would that help?' I asked, trying not to sound as though I'd written his stupid suggestion off already. Which I had, obviously.

'Well, I'm good at plot but terrible at character and you're sort of the opposite.'

'Oh, so I'm terrible at plot now, am I?'

'I've read worse.'

He was saying some not very nice things about my work, although, to be fair, it wasn't anything I didn't already know myself. And yet at the same time, my eyes – now open – kept flickering up to his naked torso, the smattering of dark hair across his chest, the slick sheen of sweat on his shoulders, the taut skin between his belly button and the start of the towel ...

'You really are a charmer,' I said, dragging my mind back to what felt safe and familiar, i.e. hating him.

'Not so much these days,' he said.

It was so quiet you could have heard a pin drop.

'Are you referring to your former Lothario status?' I asked, wandering into unchartered territory. The heat must be going to my head, too. 'I meant to ask what you've been up to for the last six years. Whether you've had any actual relationships, or whether you've still got three women on the go at once.'

I heard a faint huff. 'I was in my twenties when we met,' he said. 'Isn't that what you're supposed to do? Try things out? Have fun? Work out what it is that you want and don't want?'

I turned to face him. 'That's fine if you're not hurting people in the process.'

He rubbed his jaw. I was making him uncomfortable – good.

'That was never my intention,' he said. 'And for your information, I don't do that anymore.'

I swallowed hard.

'So there's someone special?' I asked, shifting again so that I wasn't looking directly at him when I heard the answer.

'No. Not really. I start seeing someone with the best intentions. Sometimes it's great for a while. But it feels like there's always something missing. You know?'

'Not really,' I said.

'But there was something missing with Jackson?'

He had me there.

161

'Shall we get back to talking about the book?' I said, wishing I'd never started this particular line of questioning. Although I supposed I had gleaned some interesting information about his romantic life, even if I did feel annoyingly relieved that he hadn't found anyone he wanted to spend the rest of his life with. It made it feel less personal that he hadn't wanted to spend it with me.

'How would you see this "writing together" thing working?' I asked, trying to get back to sounding remotely professional when really all I could think about was him, sitting behind me, half-naked in the dark.

'We'd pitch up somewhere. Down by the beach, maybe, why not, since our book begins there? And we write together and critique our work as we go along. Plot it all out before we start,' he said.

'I don't do plotting,' I said.

'How's that been working out for you?'

'Good point,' I conceded.

'Look,' he said, and I could sense that he was leaning forward even if I suddenly couldn't bring myself to look at him, 'if we plot it out together, chapter by chapter, scene by scene, then we'll know exactly where we're headed. And most importantly, we'll both be heading in the same direction. The last thing we want is one of us going off on one tangent and the other one going a different way and then none of it makes sense. The strands all have to come together in the end, don't they, with a proper, satisfying conclusion? If we have that clear in our heads, it will also be clear for our readers.'

Maybe, but it also sounded like the opposite of fun. I liked to almost improvise and to let my characters take over and show me how they wanted to react to a certain situation and what they wanted to do about it. It was what I loved about writing books, being able to behave and think like somebody who was nothing like me. If we planned it all out like a military operation, I thought it would take that joy away. Plus, it would mean spending more time with Theo, whose near-perfect abs I was finding it harder not to think about with each long minute that passed.

'Can I think about it?' I said, knowing I ought to compromise. I was usually excellent at putting other people's needs first, but there was something about Theo that made me want to dig my heels in. I desperately didn't want him to have the upper hand, a dynamic I felt I could easily fall into with him, but which I knew I could resist if I put my mind to it.

'Sure,' he said. 'If you need to.'

I was far too hot and I needed fresh air. As Theo seemed happy as Larry up there, it was clearly me who was going to have to leave first. I bolted up, darting for my robe to cover myself up before he realised what was happening.

'Don't leave on my account,' he said. I could hear the amusement in his voice.

I tutted. 'I did say I'd be going to the hot tub.'

'I might come with you, actually,' he said, making a move to get up.

I must have looked horrified.

'I'm joking, Scarlett,' he said. 'Enjoy some quiet time in the jacuzzi. And I'll see you at breakfast.'

I did not enjoy the jacuzzi because before I'd even climbed the few steps out to the roof, I decided to check my phone (bad idea) and there were six missed calls from my dad. With panic flooding my body as it always did when I saw he'd been trying to get hold of me and I hadn't answered, I called him, not caring that I was standing right by the entrance to the sauna. Theo came through the door at the worst possible time, of course, still in that ridiculous towel. He clocked me, hesitated and then started out in the direction of the men's changing rooms.

'Dad?' I said, my tone thick and urgent. 'Is everything all right? I'm sorry I missed your calls.'

Theo looked over his shoulder at me and I caught his eye for a second before turning my back on him, focusing on Dad who at least was alive or else presumably he wouldn't have been able to answer his phone.

'When are you coming back?' said Dad. 'Nobody is cooking for me like you do. Kate refused to send an email I asked her to do because she said she was too busy, but busy with what, I ask you? She's only got to do the school run.'

'I'm sure she'll do it at some point, Dad,' I said, silently thinking that rather than refusing Dad's request, perhaps it was more that Kate didn't just wade in and do what he'd asked the second he clicked his fingers. And it dawned on me that perhaps, without even realising, I'd sabotaged my siblings' efforts by diving on things and fixing them before anyone had even realised they needed fixing. It was a strange and new realisation that I wasn't the only one capable of looking after Dad, and that I didn't need to be.

Chapter Thirteen

That evening I made an extra effort to look nice for a drinks reception Melissa had organised. It was being in France that had sparked this newfound need to be the chicest version of myself possible, I told myself. Cannes was a particularly fashion-conscious town. So what if I wanted to wear little dresses and heels instead of my usual jeans and cardigan combo? I was adaptable. I read the room. The French Riviera demanded style and an element of panache, even from those of us who were fundamentally not stylish in the least but who occasionally gave it a go. And things were hotting up for the film festival – earlier, on a walk down to the beach, I'd noticed a crowd were taking photos of themselves on the steps leading up to the Palais des Festivals, which had a fake-looking red carpet draped over them, and railings were stacked up on the kerbside, presumably to be used to control the crowds who would soon be gathering to see some of the biggest movie stars on earth.

I secretly loved awards season. I say secretly, because it was something Jackson had despised because he said he was fed up with people in the movie industry patting each other on the back and who was interested, anyway? When I'd pointed out that he'd seemed to quite enjoy all the pomp and ceremony around being a Booker Prize longlistee – twice! – he shut me down, branding it completely different.

I mean, how? It was exactly the same! Except that everyone was about a thousand times better dressed at the Oscars.

I was one of the last to arrive in the hotel bar, a room to the left of the dining room which housed an upright piano, several tables and chairs and a giant TV screen, which I guessed meant this room was also used for meetings and small conferences. Theo was already there, standing over at the far side of the room wearing black jeans and a pale blue shirt with the sleeves rolled up. My stomach flipped when he looked across and smiled at me, warming me from the inside out. It was nice to see him like this, relaxed again, like before. Except that it was becoming increasingly difficult to keep on hating him, which felt much safer, if less productive writing-wise. He was holding a glass of wine in each hand and had been chatting to Paul until he saw me and now we were sort of beaming at each other as though everyone else in the room could fade away and we wouldn't notice. I forced myself to pull it together and walked breezily over to him, otherwise other people were going to notice how weirdly we were acting around each other.

'Hey,' I said, approaching him and Paul, who didn't seem to have clocked that Theo was now only half-listening; he was waxing lyrical about a team spending millions on somebody and them not playing well. Football, I presumed. Or soccer, as Paul called it.

'Ah, here she is,' announced Paul as though everyone had been waiting with bated breath for my arrival.

I loved this group, I decided there and then. Despite entering the retreat under duress and without being in an actual couple, they'd all welcomed me and Theo with open arms. I felt properly seen for the first time in ages. Part of something. Cared about, which was strange since I'd only known them all for only a matter of days. I felt a pang of sadness at the thought of leaving all of this and going home to my real life, where I had no time and space to think about myself and life seemed to be made up of a series of tasks, as though I was ticking things off a list before writing a whole new list and then starting all over again. It was exhausting. And here, in this little hotel in Cannes, I felt energised and grounded and like I shone in a different way, i.e. not just because I was giving everything of myself to others.

'I got you a glass of red,' said Theo, passing it to me. 'I hope that's OK? Only I remember it's what you used to drink?'

'Thanks,' I said, touched that he hadn't forgotten. 'Just what I fancied.'

I took a sip: he'd picked a good one. I wondered whether wine appreciation was something that he now indulged in. Like tennis. And saunas.

'I'm just going to go and say hi to Claire,' I said, as Paul started up with the football chat again. Theo nodded at me, a sort of casual no problem. Like an *I'll be here if you need me*. I didn't know whether I was imagining it but suddenly Theo felt like a bit of a wing man after all. The kind of secure base that I'd always tried to be for everyone else. Perhaps getting hot and sweaty in the sauna together had been good for us, despite it feeling mortifying at the time.

Claire was pleased to see me, she said, because Rob was in one of his grumpy moods after she'd persuaded him to go for lunch at one of the beach bars and the bill had come to ninety-five euros. Then to add insult to injury they'd had a one-on-one session with Melissa, something we were all apparently going to have to endure.

'Was it like those therapy sessions you see on TV dramas, with one person revealing a long-held grudge and the other getting mad and then a huge row breaking out and one person saying they don't want to do this anymore and storming off?' I asked, wanting to prepare myself for what was to come and also genuinely intrigued by Melissa's process. I didn't know how she did it, but that woman seemed to be able to read people's minds – she could even read the stuff you'd buried somewhere because you didn't *want* it on your mind.

'Ha. Sort of, yeah,' said Claire, downing the remains of her drink. 'It's my own stupid fault for signing us up to this when my husband is the least therapeutic person on earth.'

I put my hand lightly on her arm. 'You were trying something different. That's a good thing, isn't it?'

Claire sighed. 'Maybe. Anyway, why are you and Theo suddenly giving each other smouldering looks across the room?'

I took a too-big sip of wine and promptly coughed and spluttered so loudly that the entire room – including Theo – looked over. Great, just what I'd been hoping to achieve. I looked down in a panic to check I hadn't sprayed red wine all over my white linen mini dress, which somehow I'd managed not to.

Claire was looking at me with amusement.

'Went down the wrong way,' I croaked, covering my tracks.

'Uh-huh,' said Claire, giving me a knowing look.

'Smouldering is definitely not an accurate description,' I pointed out.

'If you say so,' said Claire, smirking at me.

Honestly! I mean, I'd looked at him once – or maybe twice – in the last few minutes, but I was simply trying to figure out what had changed between us, that was all. Why it suddenly felt a tiny bit more comfortable than it had done previously and how I could keep it that way.

'I think we've both figured out that if we want to write this bloody book, we're going to have to communicate with each other,' I said, trying to make sense of it as I went along.

'How successful was the first novel you wrote together, exactly?' asked Claire. 'I looked you up on Amazon, and you've got, like, 40,000 reviews.'

'I know,' I said wistfully. 'Did you happen to notice the four hundred or so I've got for my second book? I mean, until I became an author I'd literally never noticed how many reviews any book had anywhere, nor did I care, nor did I read any. And yet now here I am obsessed with them.'

'Sounds like a whole load of pressure you don't need,' said Claire.

Paul cackled loudly and I was forced to look in their direction again. Had Theo said something funny? I guessed so, since they were now both bent double with laughter. I smiled to myself. It was lovely to see Theo so happy. Perhaps the French Riviera was rubbing off on him, too.

'And what, did you win a prize or something?' asked Claire.

'No, our books are too commercial for that. We hit number two on *The Sunday Times* bestseller list, though,' I said.

'You didn't!' said an impressed Claire.

I supposed it was quite an accolade. Perhaps I should throw it into conversation more often, although it had always been tinged with regret about Theo, so I'd tended to avoid mentioning it altogether.

'And we were on the *New York Times* bestseller list for six weeks,' I added.

'Fucking hell,' she said. 'The two of you are actually proper writers, aren't you?'

I looked over at Theo and smiled despite myself. We

were. I was. And I had to remind myself of that when things weren't going so well career-wise because no matter what happened going forward, there were two and a half books out in the world that I'd written. And I'd never have thought that possible when I was scrabbling to find time to do my homework as a teenager because there was so much housework to do and my only escape had been getting into bed at the end of the evening, exhausted, and longing to lose myself in a book.

'So are you like famous, then, or what?' asked Claire.

I laughed. 'Well, have *you* heard of us?'

'That doesn't mean anything, I'm not a big reader and I'm also very unobservant. Once I walked straight past Kate Winslet in the street and had no idea until I noticed Rob was hyperventilating next to me and I asked him what was wrong.'

Rob, who had just joined us confirmed the story.

'She's useless at celebrity spotting,' he said.

'We all have our talents,' said Claire, winking at Rob, who then threw his arm around her, pulling her closer to him with affection.

Perhaps that tennis match had helped after all. I caught Theo's eye over Rob's shoulder and he seemed to notice that I was kind of gatecrashing Claire and Rob's moment and came straight over.

'Hey,' he said, standing so close to me that when I took a sip of my wine, my elbow knocked against his. 'How did the writing go today?'

'Good,' I said, trying not to acknowledge the smell of him, that woody pine again. 'I pitched up in the garden. Wrote another chapter and a half.'

He nodded pensively. 'Did you give any more thought to us plotting the story out together?'

'I'm coming round to the idea,' I admitted. 'When did you have in mind?'

As if on cue, Melissa clapped her hands, gathering the group together. I really hoped she wasn't expecting us to do one of her tasks because for once I was properly enjoying myself. The blanket of tension that I'd felt wrapped around me since I'd seen Theo again had all but disappeared this evening and standing here now, next to him, felt safe and familiar in a way that it hadn't before. And I didn't want to risk setting things back a step, which I was pretty sure would happen if we were made to talk about our 'relationship' or – worse – in any way touch each other.

'I wanted to let you know about a very exciting day I've got planned for you tomorrow,' said a tinkly voiced Melissa, who somehow managed to sound enthusiastic about absolutely everything.

'We'll meet at 9.30 in the foyer,' said Melissa, 'when I've arranged for taxis to take us up to the beautiful medieval village of Mougins. We'll spend a couple of hours there, exclusively in your pairings, and I will be giving you something specific to focus on while you explore.'

This was more like it. I'd read about the pretty villages dotted around Provence and the Côte d'Azur and was looking forward to wandering through its narrow cobbled streets and taking some nice shots for my Instagram page, which I'd neglected of late. When I'd first become an author, social media hadn't felt quite so pressing, and it was mostly about Facebook plus my author newsletter, which was relatively fun to write as long as I actually had stuff to say. Sometimes my life had been as mundane as hell and the newsletter would be particularly short that month. At least when I got home I could pepper my next instalment with pretty shots of the French Riviera. I might even tease the collaboration with Theo, although maybe that was tempting fate; there was still a huge chance it might not work out.

'I wonder what this mysterious task is,' Theo said to me.

I shrugged. 'Dread to think. Something excruciatingly awkward, probably.'

'Still thinking about that couple's yoga?' said Theo in a teasing tone.

'I wasn't, but I am now,' I said, having an instantaneous flashback of myself and Theo pressed against each other, my head cradled in the curve of his shoulder blades. Heat rushed through my body at the memory and I buried my nose in my wine while my heartbeat returned to normal. Which it didn't seem to be. I was going to have to extract myself from this situation pronto.

'Think I'll take a glass of wine back to my room and do some writing out on the balcony,' I said, making as little eye contact with him as possible.

He nodded. 'Same. We should probably check in with Carla tomorrow. Let her know we haven't killed each other yet.'

'Yet being the operative word,' I said.

He laughed lightly.

As we said goodnight to the others, Claire raised her eyebrows at me at the sight of us leaving together and I shook my head at her. Her imagination knew no bounds – perhaps she should try writing a novel sometime. My phone buzzed in my pocket and I swiped it out, checking it wasn't anything urgent. It was a voice note from my brother and I assessed whether it was urgent or whether it could wait, deciding on the latter.

'Everything all right?' asked Theo, as we headed up the stairs towards our rooms.

I nodded. 'Family stuff.'

'Ah,' he said.

We reached Theo's room first and he stopped, fumbling to find his key in his jeans pocket.

'Happy writing,' I said, pulling mine easily out of my bag.

'Let's catch up tomorrow. See where we're both at with chapters,' he said.

'Sure. And we'll try the plotting thing, maybe. It's a different way of working for me, that's all. But as you say, something needs to change, so ...'

He grinned at me.

'I knew I could bring you around to the not-so-dark side.'

'I'm still a pantser at heart, you understand.'

And then we laughed. Genuinely laughed, like we used to, not as some attempt to act as though things were fine between us when they weren't. It felt natural, easy. And as I turned my key I couldn't resist one more look at him as he pushed open the door to his room. He must have had the same idea because our eyes met in the middle, stopping me in my tracks for a couple of seconds before I refocused and carried on because I could literally lose myself in his eyes if I let myself. I closed the door behind me and leaned against it, my stomach flipping left, right and centre. Theo's lovely face was burning bright in my mind's eye, which was highly disturbing. Perhaps if I thought about it objectively: he was handsome and authorly in a way I admired. It didn't mean any more than that. I remembered the queues of giggling women at book signings, who couldn't wait to move past me so that they could get to the main spectacle: Theo, in all his polished, charming glory. I was not alone in finding him attractive, which should have made me feel better but didn't. It was fine. I was fine. So fine that I felt strong enough to listen to my brother's message.

Hey, sis. Hope France is cool. Think that's where you are?

173

Anyway, wondered if you could help me find some cheap accom-modation near uni at some point? Know you're great at all that stuff. Let me know.

I went to respond straight away and then stopped myself, throwing my phone on the side, reassuring myself that it was fine not to think about it tonight. But then I didn't want to think about the other thing, either (Theo) so I opened up the French doors, grabbed my laptop and went out onto the balcony, hoping that losing myself in the world of our novel would be just the distraction I needed.

Chapter Fourteen

The taxi dropped us off at the edge of Mougins, next to the very plush-looking tourist office, and we spent a few minutes doing nothing but look at the view and take selfies that didn't do our beautiful backdrop justice. It felt like we were literally in the centre of Provence, with green hills on all sides, as far as the eye could see. Delicate clusters of white buildings were dotted about here and there, villages and towns. Grasse, famous for its perfume production was on my must-see list, but at this rate, I wouldn't make it over there this time. I'd already vowed to come back when I could take life at a slower pace and explore the Côte d'Azur properly. Between the retreat and the writing, I'd barely had time to see any of it.

Once we were all photographed out, we walked into the heart of the pedestrianised village, which was like something out of a film set, and almost perfectly preserved. Melissa, Theo, Justin, Harmony and Paul went striding off ahead with me, Renee and Claire bringing up the rear because we kept stopping to look in the windows of chic, summery boutiques and poking our heads into rickety little candle shops and cool art galleries that I made a mental note to come back to with Theo since we had two hours to kill.

When we arrived in a pretty, cobbled square, Melissa stopped by the clock tower, which I assumed must be hundreds of years old. I closed my eyes for a few seconds, letting myself imagine what it would have been like to live here in the Middle Ages with the sun beating down on our heads, marooned on this hilltop, Cannes and the coast an hour or more's walk away.

'Right, guys,' announced Melissa, who was looking floatier and more sylph-like than ever today in her floor-sweeping maxi skirt and crop-top combo with a scarf tied loosely around her neck and gladiator sandals. It went without saying that I'd played it safe, with jeans and a lemon-coloured peasant top, my own very subtle nod to floaty and bohemian. 'Let me set you your task for the day. I want you to go off in your couples and explore this stunning village. There's plenty to see, whether you're into Michelin-star dining or art galleries. Take your pick. All I ask is that by the time we meet back here at 1 p.m., you have discovered three things about your partner that you didn't know before.'

I heard Claire tut next to me and stifled my laughter.

'I know everything I want to know about my husband, thank you very much,' she grumbled under her breath.

I nodded in alliance. 'And I couldn't care less about getting to know Theo. In fact, the less I know about him, the better.'

Fearful of being caught slagging off the task, I retrained my focus on Melissa, pretending to give it my full attention.

'I'll see you back here in two hours' time,' trilled Melissa. 'Have fun, guys!'

And with that, she sent us on our way with a jaunty wave and the noisy jangle of her massive drop-earrings that looked more like wind chimes than jewellery. Theo and I shuffled closer to each other. I wondered if he was thinking the same thing I was: that this might be a good opportunity to pitch up somewhere and write. I might not have my laptop with me, but I had my notebook so I could write longhand and type it up later. And Melissa would never know. It wasn't like she was going to ask us to spill each other's secrets in the bar later. As if reading my mind, Melissa approached us, touching me lightly on the arm.

'An additional note for you two. No shop talk. No writing, no talking about writing, no planning your writing. I want you to engage with each other and really dig deep. I guarantee you, getting to know each other better will only improve your creative process. Yes?'

I nodded obediently. 'OK, sure,' I said brightly, as if I wasn't dreading every single second of this. I'd partly lied to Claire, which I felt bad about now, but it was a turn of phrase more than anything. It wasn't true that I 'couldn't care less' about getting to know Theo. It was more that I was afraid that if I did, I wouldn't be able to convince myself that he was the terrible person I'd made him out to be. It suited me to paint him as the villain, after what had happened before. If I found out some other truth, I'd feel rocked and confused and – most terrifyingly of all – there was a danger I might start liking him – really liking him – all over again.

As we watched Melissa gliding away, we stood alone in the square, both of us seemingly unsure where to start.

'Which way shall we go?' he asked. 'Should I pull up a map?'

'Let's just wander,' I said. 'See where it takes us. It's only a village, we can't get that lost.'

Famous last words, of course, but I'd looked it up on Google maps last night and it was miniscule, so I was pretty confident that we could find our way back to what was clearly the main village square.

I strutted off into one of the streets that looked most appealing, although we were spoilt for choice. The sweet stone buildings on either side of the cobbled lane were swathed in ivy and there were pops of colour from hanging baskets bearing tiny cerise flowers, and the ubiquitous shutters on the upstairs windows, pale blue with little heart-shaped cut-outs. It was achingly atmospheric and romantic and, frankly, the sort of place you could easily get carried away and spill your most closely guarded secrets to someone. I'd have to keep my wits about me, and not drink too much, although I was already craving an ice-cold glass of rosé, it was that kind of day, with the blue sky stretching crisp and clear above our heads. We passed a glass-roofed restaurant with a huge tree sprouting out of it, as though they'd built their business around it using nature as a centrepiece. Every other shop was a sweet little gallery housing paintings and sculptures that I found interesting but had no idea if Theo did. I glanced at him out of the corner of my eye, gauging whether or not I should suggest going in. He happened to be looking at me, too, and I got momentarily caught up in his gaze all over again.

'Another day, another task,' said Theo, smiling wryly, and maddeningly still looking at me in a way that made me feel all lightheaded.

'Let's give it a go,' I suggested boldly. Not that I particularly wanted to either, but it felt like we ought to at least try. The further into the retreat we got, the more invested in it I was trying to be. And I wasn't necessarily thinking about me and Theo – God, no – but about myself and my relationships and how I might like to navigate them in the future. After all, Melissa had a world-class reputation – if anyone could turn me into the bold, confident resilient woman I strived to be, she could.

Theo frowned. 'What kind of things does she want us to reveal?'

'Just say whatever comes into your head,' I insisted.

'My God,' said Theo. 'You're really into this, aren't you?'

'I'm not,' I protested.

'You're acting like there's nothing you'd rather do!' he declared. 'You wouldn't rather be off getting drunk on French wine with Claire?'

'Well, when you put it like that.'

That got a smile out of him.

And then just as I was thinking of what to say next, whether to just get on with it and put something innocuous about myself out there so that I'd followed Melissa's instructions but had swerved having to get to the stuff I really *didn't* want to talk about, my phone rang. I'd actually been hoping I wouldn't have any reception up here in the hills so that I could have had a couple of hours off from worrying about what was going on at home, but clearly that was not to be. Despite the centuries-old buildings, Wi-Fi up here didn't appear to be a problem.

Theo watched me as I answered. I indicated we could carry on walking while I took the call.

'Hey, Dad,' I said. 'Everything all right?'

'I've seen something in the diary about an appointment. In the morning. But I've got no idea what it's for.'

'It's a doctor's appointment, Dad. Just a check-up. Kate's taking you.'

'How are we going to get there, then? Will Kate take her car?'

I glanced at Theo who was pretending not to listen in.

'Yes, she'll have to drive, Dad. And she'll take your wheelchair in case the disabled parking bay's taken and you have to park on one of the side streets.'

I made a mental note to remind Kate about all of this. She'd complained to high heaven when I'd told her about the appointment, and I'd purposely left it until I was on my way to the airport to tell her because I'd have a legitimate reason to cut the call short. She couldn't handle Dad being in a wheelchair. She felt like everyone was looking at them, she said; pitying them. Kate hated being pitied, which I thought was a trait that might run in the family because I couldn't stand it, either. But on the other hand, I also did what I had to do, and if that involved a tussle with a wheelchair in the GP's car park, so be it.

I managed to end the call with Dad pretty swiftly by telling him I was in a beautiful French village and needed to take some photos and that I'd send him some.

Theo fell back into step beside me with his hands in his pockets. I thought he'd probably be all coy and pretend he hadn't ear-wigged on my entire conversation, because that's what I would have done, but he surprised me almost instantly.

'What's happening with your dad?' he asked, looking at me with concern.

Well this was new. No edging around the topic, just straight in there. And it was an open question, too, so I couldn't fob him off with a 'yes' or a 'no'. I hesitated, unsure how much to tell him. I so rarely talked about it that a well-practised explanation didn't roll off my tongue and I'd usually stutter and skirt around the issue and the person who'd asked would usually end up wishing they hadn't bothered in the first place. I thought I might try something different, in the spirit of Melissa's task. This could be one of the three things about myself that Theo didn't know, I supposed.

'He had a stroke,' I told him. 'A couple of years ago. He's paralysed on the left side of his body so he needs quite a lot a care.'

Strangely, I felt a wave of emotion that I wasn't expecting.

I never let myself get maudlin about Dad. What would be the point? It had happened and that was that and I went to great lengths to avoid the outpouring of sympathy I assumed I'd get if I told people how difficult things really were. Theo wasn't giving me sympathy, exactly; he was listening. Which somehow felt worse.

'Sorry to hear that,' he said, his voice low and soft. 'That must be hard for you.'

To give myself a chance to compose myself, I paused to look at a painting propped up on an easel outside a gallery. It was of a beautiful woman wearing an oriental-style gown. Theo looked at it, too, but I could sense he was more interested in hearing what I had to say.

'It's fine,' I said, because it was what I always said. 'You just have to get on with these things, don't you? We've got it all under control. It's just that I do most of the organising and taking him to appointments, usually. I don't like my siblings having to do it, they've got busy enough lives as it is.'

I could see Theo was watching me, taking it all in, even though I'd made a concerted effort to keep my annoyingly watery eyes peeled on the painting. I was hard-wired to cope with anything, or to at least look like I was. But for some reason, it felt difficult to be that way in front of Theo.

'So it mostly falls to you?' he said. 'Even though you're busy, too?'

'Uh-huh.' For some reason I couldn't actually speak, it was like a lump had formed in my throat. This was very unusual indeed.

'What about your mum?' asked Theo, pointing to a doorway that looked like the gateway to Narnia. I followed him inside, immediately finding myself in the tiniest church, hidden from the outside, but glorious inside. I tipped my head back, taking in the small but impressive nave; the central aisle had only two rows of benches. The stained glass windows were made up of gorgeous colours depicting scenes from the Bible – fuchsia pinks, electric blues and emerald greens. To our right was a vestry with a stand holding twenty or thirty candles pressed into coloured glass jars and above their flickering light, Christ on the cross. I got a couple of euros out of my bag, popped them into the donation tin and lit a candle, adding it to the ones already on the stand. I found it a comfort that there were other grieving people, always, even in this miniscule place. Being here, in this little church that we'd stumbled upon by chance, and the fact we had it all to ourselves, just Theo and me, looking up at the beautiful curved roof of the church, with the only sound the faint hiss of flames, I felt brave enough to tell him.

'My mum died,' I said, getting it out there before I could run for the hills, or the nearby Alps, perhaps. 'When I was nine. She had cancer and they caught it too late.'

Cue dramatic reaction. At least, that was what usually happened when I revealed the tragic turn of events that had rendered me motherless before I'd turned ten. People would pull me in for hugs, and gush about how sorry they were and how awful it must have been and poor me, poor little nine-year-old Scarlett. It made me cringe, to be honest, and I avoided it at all costs. I had nightmares about having to go into school in the days afterwards, how my teacher had moved me to the front of the class so she could keep an eye on me, how the other parents had whispered and cried at home time.

'That's very young to lose your mother,' said Theo quietly.

Oh. This was different. He wasn't being particularly over the top. He was calm and measured without being dismissive or acting like he couldn't handle talking about somebody dying (another common reaction, resulting in people moving on to another topic as quickly as was humanly possible).

'There's no good time, really, is there?' I said.

'No, but there's definitely a bad one,' he said.

Perhaps I should stop making such a big deal out of telling people, because this actually didn't feel too bad. And I most definitely was not alone when it came to experiencing bereavement. Sometimes it had felt like it before, but less so now I was in my thirties. Some of my friends had joined me in having lost a parent and I always felt bad for them, because I knew exactly how awful it was going to be, for a while, at least. Forever, really.

'Just checking, this definitely counts towards my task,' right?' I said, hoping to lighten the mood and also because this meant I only had one more thing to divulge about myself. It would be his turn next and I could grill him if I wanted to – I wasn't going to let him get away with superficial stuff about books and loving dogs, the trivia that I could easily have read on his Amazon author page. Not that I'd looked at it, I hasten to add.

'Of course,' he said, wincing. 'I mean, I have to say, you've set the bar for big reveals pretty high.'

That made me smile. He'd made me smile when I'd just talked about my mum, and the two things never usually went together. I quietly appreciated his lack of fuss. It was as though he'd sensed that I neither needed nor wanted his sympathy, nor did I want an in-depth conversation about the whys or wherefores. He'd seen me and he'd understood, which was a surprisingly rare thing. Jackson had had a morbid obsession with death (that was literary authors, for you) and had asked me about my dead mother at every single fucking opportunity. I'd always responded by being sort of robotic with my answer. Going through the motions of telling him what he wanted to know, but not allowing myself to feel, to connect emotion to my story. And he'd got the details he'd needed, so all had been good. For him.

We left the darkness of the church and stepped back out into the sunlight, stopping briefly so that I could take a photo of a bronze statue of a naked woman that I liked.

'I wish I'd known about your mum,' he said. 'Before, I mean.'

I fished my sunglasses out of my bag, putting them on. It felt too bright out here now.

'It wouldn't have changed anything, though, would it?' I said, shocking myself, because it was the last thing I had expected to come out of my mouth.

'Scarlett ...'

Aaaaargh! Why had I said anything?!

'Is there something you want to talk about?' he asked, still being annoyingly calm.

I tucked my hair behind my ears, I put my phone back in my bag and then I dipped into it again to find my water bottle which I glugged at like a maniac. Anything to avoid looking at him, basically. Because the thing was, if I brought it up now, told him how hurt I'd been, there would be no going back. It would be out there in the universe. How I'd misread the signals and had got too invested – it would be utterly humiliating.

'That came out wrong,' I said.

He looked at me dubiously. 'What did you mean, then?'

Oh, so now he wanted to probe. Not that morning, when it had actually been happening in real time and he hadn't reached out to me. At all. But now, six years later, here he was, just gagging to have a conversation about it.

'Look, can we please forget I said anything and focus on the task?'

He let out a sigh of exasperation, which in my opinion, he had no right to feel.

'If it's ... difficult for you to work with me, why did you agree to it in the first place?' he asked.

I crossed my arms defensively. 'I've told you why already. I need the money to help my family. I'm the oldest, so when my mum died and my dad basically fell apart, I was the one who had to step up and carry everyone else. And even though they're grown adults now, nothing much has changed.'

I swallowed, suddenly feeling a rush of sadness at having talked about something I'd barely admitted to anyone, ever. That it was a struggle to keep going sometimes. That I was a tiny bit resentful that I was stuck in this caring role and couldn't seem to get out of it.

'But you wish that all of that didn't mean you had to write with me again?' asked Theo, with a sprinkling of what sounded like disappointment but was probably just his ego shattering into a million pieces. I wondered if he thought it was partly the idea of writing alongside somebody as talented and successful as him again that had lured me over the channel to France.

'Yes,' I said, defiantly. 'I'm sorry, but that's how I feel.'

He nodded. I felt bad, even though I shouldn't. After all, it didn't need to be like this. If he'd behaved differently all those years ago, we could have carried on writing together in the first place and wouldn't be standing here now, desperately searching for the right words to say. Honest words, but not too honest, because we still had a book to write and if the truth all came spilling out, as it was threatening to do, then maybe we wouldn't be able to manage it after all.

We stood in silence for what felt like far too long. It was like I was rooted to the spot. I needed to move, to change the mood. To get back to safer ground. Even Melissa's task felt easy in comparison to this, although I supposed it was her instructions that had got us into this dangerous territory in the first place.

'By the way, I hope you're going to tell Melissa I deserve a gold star for all those earth-shattering revelations I just shared,' I said, laughing lightly, desperate to get back to the easiness we'd had before. I should have trusted my instincts – hashing up the past was bad, and pointless. It was the future we should be thinking about.

'Fancy grabbing a glass of wine while I attempt to keep up?' asked Theo.

He pointed to a cute wine bar carved into a centuries-old brick building, with a couple of rickety looking chairs outside and a wine list chalked onto a piece of slate on the wall.

'Absolutely,' I said.

Alcohol. Alcohol was what was needed in this moment. A refreshing glass of something to cool the heat that seemed to be rushing to every part of my body.

But then he put his hand on my right side to guide me into the bar, pressing his palm into my waist, just for a second or two, but long enough for me to feel the aftermath of it pooling deep inside me as we sat down and I picked up the menu and I couldn't focus on a single word.

Chapter Fifteen

I ordered a glass of chilled local rosé, the name of which I couldn't entirely pronounce but which sounded romantic and floral and, well, pink. Theo went for a heady red. I thought that if I was going to describe him as a drink, it would be that: bold, spicy, robust. Impossible to ignore. Fills your mouth with – OK, I was taking this *way* too far!

'Feel free to crack on with your task,' I said, flustered.

For want of something to do, I scraped my hair back into the tiniest of ponytails, pulling a couple of strands loose around my temples.

'Your hair looks nice like that,' Theo observed.

I cleared my throat. 'Really?'

I'd never been good at taking compliments.

'Really,' he said. His fingers were covering his mouth, but I could see traces of a smile through his fingers.

'You're just trying to stall for time,' I said.

For some bizarre reason, my brain was going to places I didn't want it to. Like how my skin was burning where he'd touched it just now; how part of me wanted him to put his hands on me again.

'Hmmn,' said Theo, looking pensive. 'Where do I start?'

A waiter delivered our wine to the table, the condensation on my pink-hued glass shimmering in the afternoon sun. I watched Theo's throat constrict and relax as he took a mouthful of his red and swallowed.

'Wherever you like,' I said.

He nodded.

'OK, well my first thing involves a teacher at my senior school. Mrs Mackenzie. I was one of her favourite pupils, or so I thought. Because she taught English, which of course I loved. I was that guy who was always putting his hand up and volunteering to read the text and handing in relatively well-crafted essays on the themes of *Macbeth*, or whatever.'

I ran my fingertip around the rim of my glass.

'So you were a teacher's pet, essentially?' I teased.

'Basically.'

'Go on.'

He rubbed at his jaw with his hand. 'This is hard.'

'Oh, I know.'

Theo put his glass down very slowly.

'I've done a pretty good job of burying all of this. Feels weird to talk about it.'

'Well don't stop now,' I said.

'So fast forward to sixth form,' said Theo, looking increasingly uncomfortable.

'Yes ...'

'And we're chatting about careers. Most people in my class didn't have a clue. Lots wanted to go to uni, but only because they wanted to get as far away from home as possible and had heard that there wasn't actually that much work to do. Somebody wanted to go into the army, which none of us could believe because he was ... well, not the sort of person you'd imagine would want to put himself on the front line.'

'And what did you say you wanted to do?'

He looked up at the sky, as though he was going to find the answer up there. 'This is where it gets tough. It's like, as I'm telling you, I'm there all over again. And it still hurts, weirdly enough, all these years later.'

This was intriguing. How could a relatively innocuous group chat about careers have had such a profound effect on him? I wanted to tell him to hurry up and tell me but thought I ought to appear patient, even if I definitely wasn't feeling it on the inside.

'I told her – in front of the whole class, I might add – that I wanted to be a writer. An author, specifically, and that I wanted to write novels and for that to be my job.'

'OK.'

'And she laughed,' he said, his voice breaking a little.

I frowned, utterly affronted for him.

'She didn't.'

'Yep,' he said. 'She did.'

'That's outrageous,' I said, feeling a surge of anger, as if I'd been there with him. As if it had been me. 'Why on earth did she react like that if you were her star pupil?'

He shook his head, sighing heavily. 'I've no idea. Why would she want to shatter someone's dreams like that, but mine specifically, when she'd always encouraged me before? It was such a crashing disappointment.'

'What did you say to her?'

He shrugged. 'I didn't say anything. Not a thing. In case you hadn't noticed, I'm not big on conflict.'

'I had picked up on that, yeah,' I said, emboldened by the fact I'd spilled some dark stuff about myself. There had to be a reason for it, and I suspected that it was something to do with his parents, who he'd mentioned were always fighting.

'It was my way of coping. Of not annoying anyone, mainly my parents, because that would always make things ten times worse. If one of them told me off, for example, the other one would wade in with all guns blazing, sticking up for me as though they were parent of the year. But I never wanted that. What I wanted was for them to be united in something. To be a couple, a team, but it never felt that way.'

I could see in his eyes that he meant every word.

'Did they know you wanted to be writer?' I asked.

Now it was his turn to laugh. 'They knew. And they thought it was a ridiculous idea, too. My dad told me you had to have real talent to be an author and that writing a few half-decent stories at school hardly qualified. Apparently I was living in a "dream world". And so I think that when Mrs Mackenzie basically said the same thing, it reinforced the belief I'd had about myself all along: that I wasn't good enough. That I was never going to be a successful writer, or actually, a successful anything.'

Melissa had been very astute to make us do this task. I thought that understanding where somebody came from, the secrets they were keeping from themselves and others, was possibly the key to feeling connected to someone. I realised that what we'd had before had been superficial. A friendship with the hint of something more. But we'd never known the more difficult parts of each other, because we'd never been open about them. For me, other people knowing I was struggling felt all kinds of wrong, so I hid it well, and I could hardly complain, then, could I, when nobody noticed it was all getting a bit much?

'You should go waltzing back into the school now. Have an *I told you so moment*, even if stupid Mrs Mackenzie isn't still teaching there.'

Theo smiled weakly. 'I've actually fantasised about that.'

'You do know they were all wrong,' I said, watching as he drank his wine twice as fast as me, as though he was trying to drown out the memory. Did he really think he wasn't good enough? Because if so, the picture I'd painted of him in my head – full of himself, narcissistic, cocksure – was a figment of my imagination. Something I'd created to make myself feel better about the fact he hadn't wanted me, not properly.

'It's a work in progress,' he said. 'If people tell you you're useless enough times, it kind of sticks.'

'Who did that? Who said that to you?'

'My dad, mainly. If he couldn't get at my mum, he'd lash out at me instead, calling me all the names under the sun.'

It wasn't fair, I thought, that there were all these terrible parents in the world, who had a chance to care for their kids and watch them grow and be part of their lives and they messed it all up. And then my mum, who was brilliant and loving and funny and kind, didn't get to see us become teenagers, even. Zach had only been three when she died, and Kate five, so how come Theo's crap dad got to still be here and my mum didn't?

'You have all of these books and all of this success. You should be proud of yourself,' I said, worried that none of what I was saying was actually going in.

'But not successful enough for my publishers to give me another deal. They don't believe in me either, do they, so I'm back to square one,' Theo said dryly.

'But your readers love you,' I said, realising immediately that this must mean that I'd seen the odd review and that I'd read them. This was information I hadn't wanted him to have, and actually hadn't even wanted to admit to myself, but it was out there now. 'And you get all of this great press that I'm totally jealous of.'

He was always featuring in magazine articles, and 'Best of' pieces and appearing on podcasts. I'd done a few of those things but had never got much traction. It had always been that way: when *Little Boy Lost* had come out, he had felt like the star, the one everyone wanted to talk to. The final straw in our already disintegrating relationship had been when he did an interview for a prestigious magazine and had barely mentioned me at all. There had been a double-page spread of glossy shots of him looking all moody and gorgeous with the tiniest thumbnail photo of the two of us together on the last page, as though I was some sort of afterthought. I'd felt so frozen out, and watching someone else shine while I put my own needs and desires on the backburner had felt painfully familiar.

'I guess we just keep going,' he said, raising his glass to me. 'Do our best work and carry on.'

I followed suit, clinking my glass against his in a show of solidarity.

'To friendship,' he said.

I mulled his words over in my head. Were we friends again? We were certainly the closest we'd been to it for years. Things weren't exactly free and easy between us, but the hatred I'd felt for him was slowly dissipating over time, replaced with … I wasn't sure what. I knew what it absolutely couldn't be replaced with, and my reaction to him touching me was distinctly worrying.

'To a … working friendship,' I said eventually, tapping his glass again.

If us getting along was what was best for our writing partnership, then unexpected as it was, I was going to try to go with it for the good of the book, my career and everything else that came with it.

Chapter Sixteen

That night, we gathered in the hotel bar for one of the sessions I always desperately wanted to avoid: group therapy. There weren't the tears I was expecting, not generally – Renee had teared up once, but other than that nobody had really said anything devastating enough to cause full on hysterics, although there was a first time for everything. And the hugging I'd dreaded hadn't really materialised, either. The couples had been tactile with each other of course, but nobody had tried to hug or comfort me, which was just how I liked it; crying in public was something I literally went to the ends of the earth to avoid. In fact, I'd pulled Melissa aside when I'd first got there to see if she could let me off the hook when it came to the group sessions, suggesting that it wasn't appropriate for me and Theo to hear about the other couples' relationship issues when we had nothing to comment on ourselves. Melissa had chirpily informed me that we wouldn't be left out, and that she had plenty of questions to ask us and then persuaded me that this was the most valuable task of all and that if anything was going to help move our partnership forward, this would be it. I very much doubted it, but it had been clear that she wasn't going to take no for an answer.

It seemed Theo had arrived just before me and was laughing away with Paul and Rob as though we weren't about to have our souls stripped bare in front of each other. I steeled myself and took a seat between him and Claire.

'What are we letting ourselves in for?' I hissed.

'Don't ask me,' she said, 'but if Melissa can get Rob to connect to one of his actual feelings, I'm all for it.'

Great, even she was up for this. Claire was usually my only ally in this mad journey we were all on. And Theo, I supposed, but then we didn't really talk about it openly. I thought we were probably both trying to pretend it wasn't happening.

'Right,' said Melissa, clapping her hands. At least she didn't have her bell out. 'I want you to sit in a circle facing inwards. That's right,' she said, dragging a chair for herself into the mix. 'Move back a tiny bit, Scarlett, let Theo shuffle closer to you.'

I sighed inwardly. Him being closer to me was not something I wanted to entertain right now, although at least I could avoid eye contact if I just kept staring straight ahead. Theo dragged his chair closer, his arm brushing against mine as he settled into the tight space. I tried to relax, as though it wasn't a big deal that we were essentially pressed up against each other, but my mind wasn't playing ball and I was acutely aware of his tall, manly frame shimmering away in my peripheral vision. A surreptitious sideways glance confirmed how rock hard his biceps were (as if I hadn't already imagined them a hundred times) and it took extreme effort to stop myself drifing off into a daydream about running my hands over them, up and under the sleeve of his T-shirt, undoing the jumper he had tied round his shoulders, Riviera-style. I shifted in my seat, needing to change the dynamic here. I was being ridiculous: it was just Theo. Annoying, know-it-all, will-ghost-you-at-the-drop-of-a-hat Theo. So what if he was also devastatingly handsome and if when he listened to you, his eyes went all intense and liquidy so that you forgot what you were talking about in the first place? He did that to all women, which was why he was a serial shagger and why I absolutely could not start fancying him again. It would be a recipe for disaster and if I didn't pull myself together, I was going to struggle to give my all to this book.

'Why don't we start with Scarlett and Theo tonight?' said Melissa, spouting the *exact* words I was hoping not to hear.

'I actually find it helpful to hear other people go first,' I said, attempting to regain control over proceedings. 'So that I know what I'm supposed to be doing.'

Melissa looked at me earnestly. 'There's no right and wrong here, Scarlett. Just say whatever comes into your head, no judgement. Right guys?'

A chorus of *yeses* and *absolutelys* punctured the night air drifting in through the open windows. Thanks for having my back, guys, I thought, although I noticed both Claire and Theo had stayed quiet.

'So ...' said Melissa, striking the fear of God right through me. I could feel Theo tense, too, so perhaps we were more in tune with each other than I thought. At the very least, I knew that both of us would rather be holed up in our rooms working on our book than stuck here talking about feelings. 'We're going to think a little bit about attachment theory this evening. Theo, is that a term you're familiar with?'

He gave a small nod. 'I've heard of it.'

'It's about our way of relating to others based on the bond – or lack thereof – we had with our parents or carers as a young child,' explained Melissa. 'Depending on our past histories, we might be securely attached or various forms of insecurely attached.'

'Right,' said Theo, sounding confused as to what any of this had to do with him. I was vaguely aware of the theory, having read about it in magazine articles over the years, but I'd also given it very little thought beyond that.

'Let's think about what your own personal attachment style might be,' said Melissa, sitting back in her chair, all louche and laid back as though making people squirm was par for the course in Melissa's world.

I dared to glance at Theo again, noticing how I could physically see his jaw set tight, as though he was clenching his teeth together.

'I don't think I have an attachment problem, if that's what you're getting at,' he said.

'Hmmmn,' said Melissa, clearly not believing him. 'So what you're saying is that you're securely attached? That you can enter into relationships without the fear that they're going to end? Without pushing people away for reasons you can't quite explain?'

There was a beat. A few beats, all of them excruciating.

'Yes,' he said, his voice low and gravelly as though it was an effort to speak at all.

Part of me wanted to protest, to tell Melissa she'd hit the nail on the head, that that was exactly what he did. But I couldn't do that to him, and also, it would be my turn next and I didn't want him going for the jugular to get back at me.

'And you don't find yourself clinging to relationships, desperate to make them work at all costs, even though you know they're wrong? Feeling as though you can't live without that person and panicking that they're going to leave you at any second?'

'Absolutely not,' said Theo with confidence.

That was true. It definitely didn't feel like he did that.

'And what would you have to say about all of this, Scarlett?' she asked, directing her gaze at me. 'Because am I right in thinking that the friendship you had – or the writing partnership as you might prefer to call it – came to rather an abrupt end? What are your thoughts on what happened there?'

Bloody hell, she was going for it tonight. How was I supposed to answer honestly with Theo next to me and our forearms practically welded together? I was torn between being completely honest and letting it all out, and sweeping in to save Theo from Melissa's unfairly intrusive line of questioning.

'I've got no idea what Theo's attachment style is,' I said, in a rare display of boundary-setting. I didn't need to do anything extreme, here. 'And I don't think I'm really in a position to guess.'

Claire nudged me in the ribs. I was being quite impressive for once, even if I did say so myself. I wasn't going to let Melissa push me into sharing more than I felt comfortable with – she was always banging on about the therapeutic circle being 'our space', so here I was, drawing a line around it.

'Did you experience Theo as being difficult to pin down? Kind of elusive, like you didn't know what he was thinking? Was he giving you mixed signals?'

Fucking hell, she wasn't messing about, was she? It was like she'd seen it first-hand and was somehow tapping into the memories I'd stored neatly away for the last six years. Because that was exactly how I'd felt – one minute he blew hot, the next he blew cold. By the end, I'd had no idea whether he was falling madly in love with me or couldn't care less about whether we were more than friends or not. Given how it had panned out, I'd assumed the latter.

'Sort of?' I admitted, sensing Theo stiffen next to me. I could feel myself crumbling under the pressure of everyone waiting for an answer, and I felt really bad about throwing him under the bus like this, but Melissa was relentless. I'd held her off for as long as I could, but truly, it was like I imagined I'd feel if I was ever on trial. 'It's hard to tell, because we were only … working together,' I added, hoping that would shut her up.

'Yes, but often our attachment style affects our relationships across the board, with friends, colleagues, lovers and family members. Theo, can I ask about your mother? What is your relationship like with her?'

I winced, imagining what his face must look like right about now. There probably wasn't a more devastating question she could have asked.

'Can we not talk about that?' said Theo, his voice strained.

'Stay with that feeling, Theo,' said Melissa, her voice dropping an octave and going all soft and gooey. 'Tell me about her.'

'There's nothing to tell. I barely speak to her. I might see her at Christmas for a day or two if I'm lucky. Otherwise she does her own thing with her new family and I do mine.'

'New family?' said Melissa, not missing a beat.

'She re-married,' said Theo simply. 'A couple of years after she left my dad. I have a half-sister, Violet. She's about to turn seventeen. Once she came along, my mother barely bothered to make contact.'

I had the urge to scoop Theo into my arms and hold him tight and tell him that everything was going to be all right, like I used to do with Kate and Zach, even when everything blatantly wasn't going to be all right. Difficult as my family could be, I couldn't imagine not having them in my life. Without them, things would be quiet and lonely and kind of meaningless. Which sounded quite appealing when I had a writing deadline and needed to focus, but I wouldn't want it like that all of the time.

'Are you scared of getting close to people, Theo?' asked

Melissa, leaning forward in her seat to emphasise her point.

Claire raised her eyebrows at me and I quickly grimaced at her. This was horrendous.

'Not particularly,' said Theo.

It was no good, I was going to have to save him.

'It's interesting because I lost my mum when I was nine and so she wasn't around at all, but I still don't feel like I avoid getting close to people again,' I blurted out.

Paul let out a soft whistle and the entire circle went silent, and of course Harmony was giving me the sort of pouty, sympathetic look I hated. But I'd had to say something quite shocking and big to pull the attention away from Theo because he couldn't bear it and I probably could, just about.

Theo gave me a weird look, clearly wondering what in God's name had possessed me to bring that up.

'Thank you for sharing that, Scarlett,' cooed Melissa. 'That must have been a very difficult time for you.'

I nodded, desperately willing myself not to get choked up. I didn't want to save Theo at my own expense, that would be the ultimate humiliation. I must be strong, I must not let them see how awful it was. Still was sometimes, if the truth be told. Hold it together, Scarlett, I told myself.

I took a deep breath, keeping my voice steady. 'It was – challenging. She was a wonderful mother. But you get over things, don't you?'

Melissa gave me one of her disbelieving looks. 'Grief affects us in all sorts of ways,' she said. 'I wonder whether you find it quite hard to give everything of yourself to someone, Scarlett? Because being able to have relationships is one thing, but truly showing somebody your heart and soul is quite another. After all, what if they leave you, like your mother did?'

Now it was my turn to want to push my chair back and

strop off into the garden and dive into the pool, never to resurface. Why had I subjected myself to this, again? Theo probably hadn't even wanted my help.

'I also noticed you were very quick to jump in and rescue Theo,' said Melissa, really going to town. Seriously, could I just leave?!

'That wasn't my intention,' I lied.

'Have you two ever been romantically involved?' she asked, looking from one of us to the other.

'No!' we said in unison. I attempted to put a trace of disgust in my voice to demonstrate what a ridiculous concept that was. 'We're writing partners!' I added for emphasis.

'Physically intimate?' asked Melissa.

Theo made a sort of yelping sound. 'Oh, come on!'

I looked at Claire who had her hand over her mouth in shock, probably wondering what fate was to befall her and Rob when it was their turn. So far Melissa had been quite gentle with us, but it was day six of the retreat – halfway through, in fact – and things were clearly hotting up. And it was too much for Theo and it was on the cusp of being too much for me, too.

'Theo, let's talk about it. Can you vocalise how you're feeling right now?' asked Melissa.

'Like I'm going to go back to my room and drink the entire contents of the mini bar?' he said, raking his hands through his hair.

'You've had quite an extreme reaction to my question,' pointed out Melissa. I mean, she wasn't wrong. 'Is there something the two of you want to share with the group? Something that might be stopping you from moving forward with your relationship, whatever that might look like?'

'There's nothing to tell,' I said under my breath, but loudly enough that I caught Paul and Harmony giving each other a knowing look. I hoped when it was their turn some dark secret would be pulled out of them so that they were one iota less smug about the whole thing.

I shot up and out of my seat. It felt like a stand had to be made, but against what I wasn't quite sure, because Melissa was only asking a perfectly reasonable question, one that I already felt bad about lying about. I desperately tried to convince myself that I'd told a version of the truth. There was nothing romantic about what had happened between us, not outside of the fairytale that had momentarily played out in my head, anyway. It felt like all eyes were on me, even Theo's, and my skin was burning up under the gaze of all these people who had actual, proper relationships and OK, they clearly weren't perfect otherwise they wouldn't be here, but what if Melissa was right? What if I was incapable of truly being in a loving relationship; what if I was too scared to be, and that what had happened before hadn't been all about Theo being an arsehole, it had been about me not being able to give him what he needed, too?

'I'm just going to get a glass of water,' I said, waiting for approval and then deciding I was a grown adult and didn't need it. 'Back in a sec.'

As I stalked out to the bar in reception, trying to gather my thoughts, I imagined what they were all saying, or if not saying, thinking. That I was hiding something. That I wasn't engaging in the process, just as Harmony had predicted on day one. I slid onto a bar stool and waited for the barman, who was making a row of margaritas for a group of giggling women. It was somebody's big birthday, I reckoned. The big 4-o, perhaps. In any case, the hold-up at the bar would buy me some time and that suited me fine because I was already wishing that the night had gone differently and that I'd been able to brazen it out, laugh Melissa's insights off. Theo and I had done such a good job of pretending that nothing had happened between us to anyone who ever asked – why couldn't we have done it one more time? That was therapy for you, Alexa would have said.

I did rejoin the group eventually, attempting to slip into my seat unnoticed, which was pretty much impossible when I'd just made a massive spectacle of myself. Theo, who I was half-expecting to have stomped off to his room, was still here, albeit looking moody with his arms tightly crossed. Our arms weren't touching this time and instead there seemed to be a sort of gulf between us again, like there had been in the taxi from the airport. Bloody couples therapy. And to add to the nightmare, just as I'd thought we were off the hook, Melissa had honed in on me and told me in front of everyone that I spent too much time checking my phone and that this retreat was supposed to be about me working on myself, not working to sort everyone else's problems out for them.

'I challenge you to leave your phone in your room at all times, Scarlett. Let's see how it feels for you to focus on you and only you.'

I'd spluttered and protested over her ground rules (no bringing my phone with me anywhere; no checking messages until bedtime), but to no avail, and somehow I'd found myself agreeing to give her stupid challenge a go.

Afterwards we all went for a drink at the bar which I would have skipped if I hadn't had the feeling that I had to over-compensate for my rather dramatic behaviour earlier. I hadn't been able to do what Melissa had asked of me: I hadn't felt able to dig deep and really think about what had gone wrong before, and why I'd felt the way I'd felt, and I hadn't been able to think about how my mum's death might have affected every relationship I'd ever had. It was different for the other couples, they wanted to spend a lifetime together, it was important that they hashed things out. But Theo and I just needed to get through the next few days and then we could go our separate ways again. OK, there might be a bit of to-ing and fro-ing with the book, but there was always Zoom. I thought things might be easier if we weren't physically in the same room.

'Hey,' said Claire, elbowing Rob out of the way to rush up to me. 'That was pretty intense. Are you OK?'

I nodded. 'Bit embarrassing, but I'll get over it.'

'Oh, don't worry, Paul and Harmony didn't get off scot-free either,' disclosed Claire. 'While you were getting your glass of water, Melissa asked Harmony why she'd threatened to leave Paul if she hadn't meant it. You could have heard a pin drop it was so tense.'

I shuddered. 'Hardcore.'

'I know. And not to alarm you, but Theo keeps looking at you.'

I looked over my shoulder and caught his eye for a second, feeling a tug in my gut, as though there was an invisible line from him to me, connecting us together.

'*Is* there something you're finding difficult to share with us all?' asked Claire, lowering her voice. 'Because you could just talk it through with me if that would help. Did something happen between the two of you when you wrote the book before? Is that why you fell out?'

I trusted Claire, and in the spirit of being on this retreat, I did want to explore my feelings about Theo and how our working relationship had basically imploded. Melissa was always going on about change being difficult, which I couldn't argue with. If I wanted to move forward and live my life to the full and potentially have another relationship one day, get married even (although annoyingly Theo popped into my mind's eye, as though I would ever be marrying *him*), then I was going to have to take a risk and do something differently.

I sighed. 'It's hard for me to think about, that's all, because I expended so much energy on blocking the whole thing out.'

'Blocking what out?' asked Claire, clearly intrigued.

'God, where to start?'

Claire smiled at me and her face was so warm and open that it was impossible not to tell her literally everything. 'It's good to be brave. Go on, start at the beginning. I know you met at an evening class. How did you end up writing a book together?'

'On the last day of our course, he approached me in the pub and asked me if I wanted to try writing something together. I'd loved the extracts he'd shared with the group and we both wanted to write a thriller, so I thought: *Why not?* We began to meet up regularly after that, maybe twice or three times a week. Usually after work, but sometimes at weekends. We'd write together and then share our work and critique each other's. The usual.'

'And then what, you started to get closer?' asked Claire.

'Yeah,' I said, cringing. What on earth had possessed me? 'Which was stupid of me, because I'd seen first-hand how he kept people at arm's length, especially women. When we were writing together, he'd usually get at least one message from someone he was planning to meet that evening. And I never got to meet any of them because after about three dates he'd stop mentioning them and I'd ask him what happened and he'd give some feeble excuse about him just "not feeling it". I used to joke with him that I was glad we were just friends.'

Claire frowned. 'I couldn't imagine him being like that now.'

I shrugged.

'What happened next?' asked Claire.

I took a breath, giving myself permission to really think about it.

'The more time I spent with him, the more difficult it was to ignore the fact that I'd started to really like him,' I admitted. 'And even though the rational part of my brain knew that he wouldn't be able to give me what I wanted, I thought that maybe the connection we had was special enough to change him.'

'Of course. We've all been there, you mustn't beat yourself up about it,' said Claire. 'Plus, let's be real here, he is *very* cute.'

I groaned. 'I know, but developing actual feelings for him was a huge mistake.'

'So what? Making mistakes is a normal part of life.'

'I don't usually, that's the thing.'

Claire reached out to touch my arm. 'You're being too hard on yourself. I mean, how bad was it? Did you sleep with him, or something?' she asked and then out of nowhere I felt Theo behind me. I could sense him, weirdly, and then there was the scent that trailed subtly after him and followed him everywhere, wood and amber and crackling fires.

'Hey,' he said, his breath tickling the back of my neck.

'Hello,' I said, flushing beetroot red. Had he heard any of that?

'Hope I haven't interrupted anything ...?' he asked, looking at Claire and then back at me again. I made space for him to join us. Did he know we'd been talking about him?

'Course not,' I said.

I couldn't even look at Claire, but out of the corner of my

eye I could see her trying not to crack up. This was not, in my opinion, a laughing matter.

'Everything all right, Claire?' asked Theo, probably wondering why her shoulders were shaking and why she had her nose buried in her drink.

'Mmmmn,' she said, looking up. 'Sorry. Just hoovering up my wine after that horrendous couples therapy session. Brutal, or what?'

Theo laughed hollowly. 'That's a nice way of putting it.'

'Are you ... you know, OK?' I asked tentatively, not wanting to bring it all flooding back if he was trying desperately to forget about it.

He nodded. 'You?'

'Oh, I'm fine,' I said dismissively. This wasn't about me. I'd only shared that stuff about my mum to help him out, so it hadn't really had any affect on me at all. I mean, I had a bit of a tension headache between my eyebrows, but that was probably more to do with the book stuff looming over my head.

'I wondered whether you fancied a late-night writing session by the pool this evening?' Theo asked me. 'Only I've noticed you do tend to work quite late. I can hear you tapping on your keys sometimes, when I wake up in the middle of the night. I can never believe you're still up.'

'Ah. Well, 3 a.m. tends to be optimum writing time for me. Nobody else is awake so they can't disturb me, can they? I can get on with some work without any distractions.'

Claire was watching with interest. 'A late-night writing session sounds very romantic,' she said.

I narrowed my eyes at her, but she was clearly enjoying playing devil's advocate.

'Sounds like just the thing to get your creative juices flowing,' she added with a smirk.

'So what do you say?' asked Theo, seemingly oblivious to Claire's not-very-subtle innuendo. 'Shall we get our word count up? Grab a table by the pool?'

'Sure,' I said, thinking it wouldn't hurt. The sooner we could send Carla our chapters, the better. If she liked them, it would mean this whole dreadful set-up had been worth it. 'Let me pop up to my room to grab a jumper. The temperature will probably drop in a bit.'

'Good idea,' he said. 'Let's meet down here in twenty minutes?'

Claire looked on, impressed. 'This feels like progress, guys. Maybe that group therapy session did you both more good than you realise.'

'No, it did not!' I insisted, looking nervously at Theo. I didn't want to set him off again. But I couldn't stop thinking about what Claire had said – that maybe I did need to talk about what had happened in order to move on. But how would I even start a conversation like that with Theo? And when would ever be a good time?

Chapter Seventeen

We were the only two people out by the pool that evening. When I'd arrived, Theo had been there already, a bottle of red and two glasses waiting for us on the table. His laptop was out, plus a notebook, a pen and a cup of coffee.

'Need the caffeine, do you?' I teased, sitting down opposite him, the chair legs scraping on the marble-like flagstones of the pool surround as I made myself comfortable. This could be a long old night.

'Some of us need a bit of medicinal assistance if we're required to work past 7 p.m.,' he declared.

I reached down to get my own laptop out of my bag. 'My friends joke that I'm like Margaret Thatcher: four hours of sleep a night and I'm good to go.'

'I trust that's the only similarity,' he replied, looking horrified.

The vibe was friendly but professional. Earlier, during the group therapy session, it had felt as though lines had been blurred, but things seemed to have gone back to our version of 'normal'.

'Thanks for what you did earlier, by the way,' said Theo.

Or possibly not.

'Why, what *did* I do?' I asked, playing dumb.

'You noticed that I was struggling with Melissa's barrage of questions. And you stepped in,' he said, taking a sip of his coffee. 'To help me.'

I went to answer but didn't quite know how immediately, so instead I busied myself with setting up my screen, logging in and pulling up my manuscript. I could feel his eyes boring into me and it was both uncomfortable and thrilling for reasons I couldn't quite put my finger on. Eventually I managed to respond, although I was acutely aware that I was in dangerous over-thinking territory.

'I like helping people,' I said, because I didn't want him to think it was about him. I would have done the same for anybody.

'I'd noticed,' he said.

As if on cue, my phone pinged in my bag. I ignored it for about five seconds hoping Theo hadn't heard it.

'Thought you were supposed to be leaving that in your room?' he said with the trace of a smile.

'Challenge starts tomorrow,' I said, before casually glancing at the screen. It was my brother. In the spirit of what I'd agreed to do about an hour ago, I made the executive decision to ignore him for now. It couldn't be anything that urgent or he would have called. As much as it pained me to say it, Melissa did have a point: Theo and I were here to write, to focus on the story we were trying to create. It was hard to do that if I let stuff from home filter in, clouding my vision. When I was in one of my anxious moods, if something had happened with Dad, for example, I'd try to push on and write, but when I read my work back, my words would sound clunky and cold with no flow to the story. I didn't want that to happen tonight, so I closed my bag, hoping that would muffle the sound of any further messages.

'Any of that wine going?' I asked.

'Sure,' said Theo, picking up the bottle and pouring me a glass first and then one for himself.

'Everything OK?' he asked.

I nodded. 'Let's get started. How do you think we should work this?'

Theo hesitated then sat back in his chair, looking far more relaxed than I felt. I noticed he'd dressed up a bit tonight, and was wearing black jeans and a black-and-white checked shirt. Light and cool, perfect for a warmish spring evening on the French Riviera.

'I wanted to broach the subject of plotting again,' he said. 'I know you explained that you prefer to discover the story as you go along, but when there's two of us working on the same thing, I'm not sure that's the best way to go about it.'

I'd been mulling his suggestion over for the last few days, and I'd decided that he had a point. So far we'd roughly mapped out our chapters verbally and then we'd gone off and written them, but questions needed to be asked and answered, plot twists needed to happen (not my forte, just getting it out there) and most importantly we needed to keep up the pace so that the reader didn't get bored. I had the sneaking suspicion that my first solo book had lagged a bit in the middle and I suspected that didn't happen with Theo's writing – judging by what I'd read (namely *Little Boy Lost* and what he'd produced so far on this trip), he had the ability to take you on a sort of breathless ride from beginning to end.

'I think you might be right,' I said. 'We need to play to our strengths, don't we, and complicated storylines don't appear to be mine.'

'That Goodreads crowd has really got to you, hasn't it?' he said, grinning at me.

'How could they not?'

'Are you saying that my plotting technique is better than yours?' he asked, clearly looking for a reaction.

'Fishing for compliments again, are you?' I said.

'Maybe I just like that you like my work.'

Oh. I felt like I looked as flustered as I felt, but luckily I didn't think he'd notice because there was barely any light other than the warm glow from the hotel and the moon and the fig-scented candle flickering away between us. Before I could stop myself, the question I'd been dying to ask since I'd seen him at the taxi rank at Nice airport a week ago slid out of my mouth.

'Do you ever think about what happened before?' I asked him.

Aaaargh, this was desperately dangerous territory. One wrong move and it could ruin everything, just as we were setting up for a pleasant night of co-writing. So much for keeping the vibe professional. Wishing I could backtrack and keep my mouth firmly shut, I waited for his answer, which was more delayed than it might have been because the woman from behind the bar came padding out to bring us some crisps and olives, laying them out on our table in pretty little terracotta dishes. I'd never wanted snacks less.

'*Merci*,' said Theo.

'*Bonne nuit*,' she said, smiling at us both before circum-navigating the pool and walking back in the direction of the bar.

Perhaps he'd forgotten my question in the interim, that would be the best thing. But there was something about the heady Mediterranean air that made me feel like I'd swallowed a truth bomb; as though it was safe to say whatever came into my head without the fear of repercussions. Which was ridiculous, because our whole working relationship this time around had been based on the fact that there was stuff that had been left unsaid and was probably better left that way. Now I'd gone and rocked the massive, stupid boat.

I picked up an olive between my thumb and forefinger,

sliding it into my mouth and sneaking a glance at Theo. Instead of looking put out or closed off, like I'd expected, he was watching me with interest.

'Care to elaborate?' he said.

No, no I wouldn't. In fact, I wanted to take back every single thing I'd just said.

'You know what? Don't worry about it,' I said, making a show of typing a flurry of meaningless words on my keyboard and then opening up a document and scrolling through it for no reason other than to give myself something to do that didn't involve looking at him. He wasn't reacting in the arsey, closed-off way I'd expected and that had thrown me. Or had he always been this way and rather than being afraid of upsetting him all of this time, it was actually more that I was afraid of getting hurt myself if we rehashed the past?

'We can talk about it if you like?' he offered.

Why, oh why, had I started this?

'I think we should stick to our plan,' I said. 'We're here to write. And I'm even open to talking about plot, how's that?'

He looked at me intently for a beat or two, as though he was deciding whether or not to let it slide. Luckily for me, he saw sense and didn't push the point.

'I knew I'd win you round eventually,' he said, smiling softly. 'Which is why I happened to bring an extremely effective plotting tool with me. Just in case.'

He dipped into his laptop bag and pulled out a pack of lined index cards, presenting them to me like a magician pulling a rabbit out of a hat. 'Ta-da!'

'Do you always get this excited about stationery?' I asked.

He nodded. 'This is actually the most exciting part of writing a book for me. Working out what's going to happen and where. Moving things around to see where scenes fit best.'

He fanned the index cards out on the table and handed me a pen.

'Let's jot down what we've got so far. If you can, sum up your chapter in a couple of sentences and write it on the card. One index card for every chapter you've completed,' he said.

I took the pen from him, wishing I could drum up half of his enthusiasm. See, this was my *least* favourite part of the writing process, working out what the hell was supposed to happen. I reluctantly took a card and wrote out the second chapter: *wife realises husband hasn't come back from his swim. Goes to look for him* and then chapter four: *wife finds husband's phone. Hint that he is having an affair. She tries to log on to his laptop but can't work out the passcode.* And finally, the chapter I finished this morning, chapter six: *flashback: three years earlier. Husband and wife are at a party. Husband says something that upsets her, they argue, she pushes him, causes a scene. The embarrassed party host takes her to one side to cool off – wife pretends everything is fine.*

When I looked up, Theo was still scribbling away.

'I'm not sure I've done this right,' I said, doubting myself now. Perhaps I should have written more detail, but he said a sentence for each chapter, didn't he?

'As Melissa would say, there's no right or wrong,' said Theo.

'Melissa says a lot of things,' I grumbled.

'Right, let's see what we've got so far,' said Theo, finishing with a flourish and flinging his pen dramatically on the table.

He laid out the six chapters we'd finished and I could immediately see something that didn't look right.

'I think that flashback chapter should come later, don't you?' I said, peering closely at it. 'Otherwise we're revealing too much about their marriage too soon.'

Theo nodded. 'Yep, hard agree. We need to drip feed their marriage problems, so that the reader *eventually* begins to suspect the wife has murdered him but not until later. Meanwhile, the real murderer is skulking around in the background unnoticed until we decide to reveal them at, say, three quarters of the way in? End of act two?'

I rested my chin in the palm of my hand. 'Do we actually know who the murderer is? And I suppose the other question would be, do we need to, at this stage?'

Theo gave me one of his intense looks, which almost threw me off. I was on a creative roll and wanted to keep it that way, which would be much easier if he didn't look so bloody good this evening. 'I think we need to, yeah. Because if *we* don't know where it's going, I don't think the plot would be tight enough. It needs to be so finely tuned that readers almost have to give it a second read to pick up on all the clues. Don't you think?'

I put my head in my hands. 'I'm terrible at this.'

'You're not,' said Theo reassuringly. 'I get that some writers hate this part. And that's exactly why we're doing this together.'

'If you say so,' I groaned.

'So, the murderer ... who did you have in mind?' asked Theo, topping up my wine.

I'd had a couple of thoughts, more than a couple. For the last few days I'd been in that place I always got to when I was writing a book where everything became about that. Whatever I was doing, wherever I was, it would be there, festering in the back of my mind. Character traits would be lurking, hazy scenes that had something but needed developing further would pop up out of nowhere, usually in the middle of the night when I couldn't actually be bothered to get up and write them down. It was exhausting in a way, but it was also fun and exciting; a rush.

'One thought I had was that our main protagonist could have a sister,' I ventured. I hadn't been planning to share my idea until it was clearer in my own head, but we were here now and needs must. 'Maybe they're even twins. And they've always been a bit competitive in the way twins are, but they are also really close and tell each other everything. Except for one thing – the twin has been sleeping with her sister's husband. And he's refusing to leave his wife. What if the dominant twin sister wants this one final triumph over the sister who is standing in the way of her one true love?'

'Yes!' said Theo, sitting forward on the edge of his chair. 'So she's there being all supportive and helping with the search for her brother-in-law, taking over like she always does. And nobody would ever suspect it was her. We'll drop in a few subtle clues as we go along, but we want the reader to be shocked, ultimately, don't we?'

I added a couple of notes to my document, smiling to myself.

'You know, I'm actually quite enjoying this,' I said.

'I don't want to say I told you so, but ...'

I held up my hand, laughing. 'Please don't.'

My phone buzzed again. It was like I was fine-tuned to hear it, even if I'd buried it in the darkest depths of my bag. And if I ever did switch it off I'd be panicking the whole time that when I turned it back on there would be a slew of emergency messages involving the worst possible things happening to my entire family. In a way, it was less stressful to check it every few minutes so that I could be sure that tragedy hadn't yet occurred. Although funnily enough, I hadn't felt like that at all this evening. I'd been enjoying getting immersed in our plot. And Theo had been far better company than I'd imagined he could be.

'Sounds like you've got another message,' said Theo. 'Is it your dad, do you think?'

'Not sure. As you reminded me, I'm not supposed to be looking at it until bedtime. Whoever it is will have to wait until then.'

Theo looked impressed. 'You're really taking this seriously.'

'No point doing half a job,' I said, even though I was itching to check my phone.

'It'll be my brother again, anyway,' I said, as much to myself as to Theo. 'I'm funding him through a Masters and now he needs me to help him sort accommodation,' I said, although I wasn't quite sure what had made me share that information. Sometimes the (often self-imposed) demands on my time and money stacked up until the pressure was so immense I had to literally scream into my pillow. I supposed that Theo was the equivalent of my pillow, for tonight at least, and I was tempted to vent.

'What's he studying?' asked Theo.

'Computer science,' I said.

Theo winced.

'Your worst nightmare, too?' I asked.

'I can't even use Excel properly,' he admitted.

'Zach was always into all of that, even when he went off the rails a bit when he was in his teens. Nearly messed up his GCSEs. I felt crushingly guilty, because it all happened when I was at uni myself.'

'Did you move away?' asked Theo.

I shook my head. 'I commuted in to London. But I had lectures, obviously, and I wasn't always at home to micro-manage every single thing Zach did – or as it transpired, didn't do.'

'Where was your dad?' asked Theo.

I shrugged. 'Working mostly. Around. I don't know, he's never been good at that sort of stuff.'

'What stuff?'

'Keeping tabs on his kids. Making people do their homework.'

Theo was chewing lightly on his lip, teeth pressing into plump raspberry flesh. It was very distracting.

'You seem under quite a lot of pressure to be a mother figure for your entire family,' said Theo after a while. 'You have a sister as well, right?'

'Yeah,' I said. 'She's great, but she does tend to get caught up in her own problems, of which there are a LOT. And she has two kids, which means she hasn't really got the time to help out with Dad.'

'That's on you,' said Theo.

'Always has been.'

We sat in silence for a moment or two and it felt good, as though Theo understood that things could be difficult for me. It also made me wonder how he could see through me in a way that lots of other people couldn't. Usually, other than when I was with Alexa, I could pretty much pretend I was fine 100 per cent of the time and nobody would question it. But with Theo it was like the protective armour I drew around myself became transparent. I wasn't sure if it had always felt like that between us, or if it was a new thing.

'And you?' I asked. 'Who's your go-to person when things get tough?'

'Ah, well. As you may remember, I don't often admit to struggling with something. But if I did … if I *had* to, it would be Jake.'

'You're still friends with Jake Thorn?'

Jake was a very successful crime writer, a sort of lovable

rogue who was hugely talented and annoyingly cocky and full of himself, but who you couldn't help but like despite all of that.

'You seem surprised,' said Theo.

'Not at all. I just ...'

'Didn't think I was capable of sustaining a friendship?'

I tutted. 'That wasn't what I meant. It's just that the two of you are very different.'

'What, because he's an extrovert and I'm not?'

'He's just so loud.'

Theo laughed. 'A lot of it's bravado. Plus he makes me laugh. A lot. Not sure if you've noticed, but I can be quite serious,' he said, with a twinkle in his eye.

I covered my mouth with my fingers to stop me smiling. 'Really?'

Theo rolled his eyes and went back to his laptop. I imagined his cheeks might be a little red; his eyes bright and amused. I thought that underneath finding this funny he might also be embarrassed at having shown me what he thought other people's perception of him might be.

'Look at us,' I said. ' We're talking about emotions unprompted and without Melissa ruling over us with an iron rod.'

He stopped typing and looked at me.

'You should take care of yourself, you know,' he said, suddenly sitting back in his chair again. 'And feel free to ignore me, because as I said, I've got no idea what it's like. I have my half-sister, who's great, actually. We see a lot of each other, but she's quite self-sufficient. And I rarely see my parents – they don't require anything of me other than a phone call every couple of months. But what I'm thinking is, you should put yourself first. Sometimes. Maybe.'

'I can handle it,' I said.

The fear that he was about to start pitying me was kicking in hard and fast. It made it so that it was impossible to really listen to what he was saying because there was this booming voice on my shoulder yelling at me that I should be able to cope and that I must not show vulnerability to anyone, ever.

'Or maybe it's more that you're so used to living with such high levels of stress that you don't even notice it anymore. When was the last time you really switched off? Relaxed and went for a swim or read a book? Not a proof, or your own book, but a purely for pleasure book?'

'Ummm …' I said, wanting to contradict him but literally not even able to remember when I'd last picked up a romcom, the not-so-guilty pleasure I allowed myself on the rare occasion I did take a break. Which hadn't happened for … ages.

'Just a thought,' he said.

As if reading my mind, he filled our glasses, finishing off the bottle. I liked watching his forearms as he tipped and poured. The air around us smelled sweet, like lavender mixed with honey. He placed the bottle back down on the table, brushing his fingers against mine and leaving them there, the tip of his little finger touching the tip of mine. Surprisingly, neither of us made any attempt to pull away. A gust of wind blew strands of hair across my face but I was kind of frozen to the spot, not wanting to break the moment, whatever this was. Then Theo reached out, slowly at first, then confidently, gently brushing it out of my eyes for me, tucking it behind my ear. He let his fingers trail down my neck, skimming them across my collar bone. My breath caught in my throat as he leaned towards me, and I towards him, his hand cupping my shoulder, my hand resting lightly on his waist. Touching him again felt electric and I closed my eyes for a second, wanting to feel it even more intensely.

And then he'd released me, and my eyes popped open and he sat back in his chair. My heart was racing. Had he been about to kiss me? I hadn't imagined the whole thing, had I? His expression was unreadable so no clues there, and instead I tried to focus on my laptop, my eyes burning into the screen without taking in a single word I'd written on there, my mind whirring with what might have been.

Theo cleared his throat. 'Right. Back to plotting,' he said.

OK. So we were pretending nothing had happened.

'Let's hash out as much of the story as we can, then divide up the chapters. I reckon once we've written a couple more chapters each, we should polish them up and send them over to Carla,' he said. I could hear the tiniest hint of self-doubt in his voice, but it was only because I was extra tuned into these things, especially now.

'She'll want a synopsis, too, I expect,' I said, the words feeling hard to form.

'And our hook,' he said. 'Although I think we've already got one of those.'

He glanced at me, as though checking I was going along with his pretence.

'A couple argue on a beach on the French Riviera,' he said, reading from his screen. 'He wades angrily into the water to cool off but never makes it back to their hotel room. Where is he? Did he drown, or did somebody want him gone?'

'It's not bad,' I said. 'We can refine it a bit.'

'If you're any good at refining hooks, be my guest. As you can see, brevity isn't my forte,' he said, pointing to his index cards which had mini essays written on each one.

I laughed lightly. 'You said a sentence or two. Not a sentence or six.'

For the next couple of hours we plotted hard, drank coffee, got up occasionally to stretch our legs. Did not mention how

220

good his fingers had felt on my neck. At one point tiredness got the better of me and my eyes started to close, much as I didn't want them to, and annoyingly Theo must have noticed, because he tactfully suggested we bring the night to an end. What was wrong with me, I was usually up to 2 a.m., no problem?

'I don't know about you, but I think I'm done,' he said, snapping his laptop shut.

I didn't even bother to protest – he'd clearly seen me almost nodding off.

'Fine, but let's get back on it tomorrow morning. In fact, I cordially invite you to a masterclass in character at ten sharp. Are you in?'

'And who will be running this masterclass exactly …?' teased Theo, packing everything back into his bag.

'Hahaha,' I said sarcastically, making him smile.

As we made our way back to our rooms, the hotel was silent, except for the gentle movement of the night manager on duty at reception as we passed through. When Theo held the door open for me up on our floor, it dawned on me that for the first time in years, I was beginning to remember what I'd liked about him in the first place. But then, this was what he did, wasn't it? He was charm personified at first; a good listener, easy to talk to and looked – well – amazing. But if you showed any sign of actually liking him back, he ran for the hills. I wondered if our almost-kiss out by the pool had been enough to make him want to run again.

Chapter Eighteen

The beach bar we decided to hole up in for our 'masterclass' was everything I imagined Cannes to be – achingly cool and chic with white sand beneath our feet and the turquoise waters of the Mediterranean lapping at the shore metres from our table. Attractive French staff with impeccable tans brought us bottles of sparkling water that I didn't dare look at the price of, plush posh crisps that looked positively good for you and plump, green olives.

We wrote for a bit, not really talking, just tapping away next to each other which felt much more motivating than trying to write on my own in my room. I always worked best when there were other people around – in a library, for example (although they couldn't be too quiet or else I'd worry about disturbing somebody as I bashed my fingers over the keyboard) or in a coffee shop or on a train or a plane. Anywhere, really, it was how I'd always been, snatching moments of time, not having the luxury of being able to wait for inspiration to come. It was a process and I always got there in the end. But I had to admit, working with someone else was *lovely*. It was something I'd thought about off and on since starting the retreat. We'd done a lot of thinking about ourselves, something I usually avoided. And it had become crystal clear that what I wanted had always taken a back seat. What I hadn't realised until now was that in some ways that was a choice. It might not feel like it, and it might not have been when I was nine, but it was now I was the grand old age of thirty-four. And if there was something that made things easier for me, why *wouldn't* I grab hold of it with both hands?

'Shall we stop and grab some lunch?' I suggested, my stomach rumbling with hunger, even though I'd stuffed it with croissants and bread and fruit this morning at the hotel buffet. Why was it that everything in France tasted so good? I could probably live on their crispy baguettes and salty butter.

'I thought you'd never ask,' said Theo, snapping his laptop shut.

'Actually, I've got a challenge for you,' I said, suppressing a smile. I knew he was going to hate this and I knew I was going to relish every second of his discomfort.

'Why do I get the feeling that I'm not going to like whatever it is you have in mind?' he said.

'You're going to like it about as much as I liked your index cards.'

He grimaced. 'That bad? Is this the start of the character masterclass you promised me?'

'Bet you thought I'd forgotten about that,' I said, grinning at him. 'But oh no. We are about to get under the skin of our two main protagonists with a little game I like to indulge in.'

'Oh God. OK. Tell me.'

'Are you any good at role play?'

'I'd literally rather do group therapy.'

'So you're going to play the role of our husband – Ethan,' I said, ignoring Theo's protestations, 'and I'll be the wife – Caroline. And we're going to imagine that Ethan and Caroline are having lunch together at a beach bar in Cannes, just like we are at this one. The day before they argue and Ethan goes missing. And we're going to order lunch as if we are Ethan and Caroline.'

He was looking at me as though I was mad and I thought I probably was a little bit, but this exercise had helped me in the past, if I was struggling to find a character's voice, and therefore I thought it might be fun to give it a go. For all of Theo's plotting expertise, I could tell he was finding it difficult to truly understand why our characters were behaving in the way they were. This might just free something up in us both.

'I keep waiting for you to tell me that this is a joke,' said Theo.

'Afraid not. Ready?' I said.

'No!' he replied, looking absolutely terrified. 'I'm terrible at this kind of thing, Scarlett. Seriously, I really don't think I can do this.'

'Excuse me!' I said as a waitress rushed past, getting the ball rolling before Theo had a chance to pull out. She doubled back, arriving at our table.

'My husband and I need to order,' I told her.

Our main character, Caroline, was mid-thirties, like me, but had had a very different childhood. She'd come from privilege – her parents were both alive and well, both she and her twin sister went to private schools followed by top universities where other privileged young people went to study and she now worked at a pretentious art gallery in Central London. She was confident, sassy, someone people were often slightly on edge around. I wondered whether, if she actually existed, she would be the sort of woman Theo would use his authorly chat-up lines on?

'Of course, *Madame*. What can I get you?' asked the waitress.

'I'll have a glass of the Sauvignon Blanc. Large. And to start, the tabbouleh. Followed by the whole fish of the day.'

It felt strange not saying *please* or *thank you*, but I went with it.

'Would you like anything on the side, *Madame*?' asked the French girl, who couldn't have been more than twenty-one. I didn't envy her this job, although perhaps the tips were good enough to make up for all the crap she probably had to take from the pompous yachting crowd.

'Hmmmn,' I said, flicking to the sides section, not caring how long I took, or worrying about taking up too much of the waitress's time. It was actually very freeing. 'I'll take the seasonal salad.'

I flipped the menu shut and thrust it at her rudely. I thought that might be a step too far, but Caroline was kind of taking over so I let her. Finally looking up at Theo, who I was sure was a shade or two paler than he had been a few minutes before, I gave him the nod.

'What are you having, darling?' I asked, making my own generic estuary accent sound as RP as I could manage. The fact I never missed an episode of *Made in Chelsea* was clearly paying off.

'Um ...' said Theo, faltering. 'I'm not sure. I ...'

'Hurry up, *Ethan*,' I said, rolling my eyes at the waitress as if to indicate how pathetic my husband was. She humoured me with a trace of a smile, even though she clearly thought I was a complete bitch. Mission accomplished. That was exactly how we wanted Caroline to appear: somebody so unlikeable, she could potentially be capable of murder.

'I'll take a beer, please,' said Theo, sounding like a politer version of himself rather than Ethan, who was more world-weary than that, and pretty much hating on his wife.

'And to start, *Monsieur*?'

'The falafael. Thanks.'

'Certainly. And for your main?'

I watched Theo, his eyes flicking back to the menu. He

was doing his best, bless him, and I had sort of thrown him in at the deep end.

'I'll have a burger, please. With a side of frites.'

'Honestly!' I said, deciding to give Caroline one last bitch fest. 'Darling, we're in France. You can get a burger anywhere!'

'Does it *really* matter to you what I have to eat, *darling?*' he said. This was better. Ethan might be fed up in his marriage, but we didn't want him to be a complete pushover. 'Why don't you concentrate on yourself? You're usually very good at that.'

Ha! I knew he'd get into it.

'And what's that supposed to mean?' I asked, pretending to grit my teeth.

'Is that everything?' asked the waitress, clearly desperate to get away.

'Yes, yes, that's all,' I said dismissively.

Once she was out of earshot, I broke out into a big smile. Theo put his head in his hands, groaning loudly.

'That was horrendous!' he moaned. 'I don't think I acted like Ethan at all.'

'You did towards the end,' I reassured him. 'I feel a bit bad, actually. I've never been that horrible to anyone in my life. I'm going to have to leave that poor waitress a massive tip now to make up for my terrible behaviour.'

He leaned forward in his seat. 'You were brilliant, though. It was like sitting opposite the Caroline I'd created in my head. Utter cow. Confident. Sexy,' he said, sounding a little breathless.

'Is she the kind of woman you're in to, then?' I asked, teasing him.

'What, self-obsessed and obnoxious? Yep, totally my type.'

I grimaced. 'Only thing is, I'm not sure it would work to have two such massive egos in one relationship ...'

'Touché,' he said, smiling at me and holding my gaze.

As the waitress delivered our drinks, I reverted to my snippy, Carloline-esque tone, thankful that she'd forced me to look away from Theo at least.

'Are you sure that's a large?' I demanded to know.

'*Oui, Madame.*'

Theo shook his head and stifled a laugh as the waitress walked away. 'I think you're enjoying being Caroline a little bit too much.'

'It felt very weird, to be honest. Is this really how people operate?'

'Probably,' said Theo. 'Although we have to keep in mind that we don't want Caroline to be one-dimensional. She's awful and controlling and bossy and all of those things, but she's got to have another side to her. Otherwise we won't care that her husband is missing, or that her sister has been sleeping with him.'

The sun had come out, breaking through the clouds. I popped my sunglasses on so that I didn't have to squint at him. It dawned on me that if I'd kissed him as part of the task, I could have written it off as being nothing more than improv. If I'd wanted to, that was. Just to see whether I'd imagined the spark I'd felt between us last night. Personally, I was convinced I must have been sleep-deprived from years of late nights and that my mind had been playing cruel tricks on me.

'Nice to see you thinking about character layers,' I said.

He winked at me and my stomach gave a totally-uncalled-for flutter.

'If we carry on like this, we'll have a decent first draft in a couple of months' time,' I said, pulling it back to what we knew. The work. The book. I reached for my glass.

'Cool, but can we give mortifying role-play exercises a

miss?' he asked, putting his hands together in the prayer position.

I laughed. This was exactly where we needed to be – I was tolerating Theo's company and we were bouncing ideas off of each other but I was absolutely not feeling anything for him. Nothing romantic, anyway. Maybe the odd rush of attraction, but otherwise not a thing. We were writing partners – possibly quite good ones. And as we worked alongside each other, stopping only to eat delicious food and drink more wine, my fingers flew across the keys of my laptop and the words were tumbling out of me so fast I could barely keep up. I put this down to the location: the Mediterranean sea in my eyeline, warm sand under my feet, palm trees swaying in the breeze. As writing spots went, it was perfection. It had nothing whatsoever to do with the fact that Theo was sitting next to me with his arms bronzed by the sun and his sparkly brown eyes squinting at his laptop and his brow all cute and wrinkled as he concentrated on his work.

We made our way back to the hotel late-afternoon, mainly because Melissa had booked us an ominous-sounding couples massage. If I could have got out of it, I would have done because there was absolutely no way I was going to be able to relax with Theo lying half-naked next to me, not after last night, and then our really quite pleasant day together. Perhaps the candles and the heady aromatherapy oils and the meditative music piping out of speakers on the ceiling would help put me in the zone. Except that when I saw the massage couches lined up next to each other and there wasn't as much of a gap between them as I thought there would be, I assumed it was doubtful.

We were instructed to change into white towelling robes, leaving just our underwear on. For some reason the mere mention of the word underwear made me break out in a cold sweat. Why on earth had we agreed to this?! I'd spent ages in the changing room, hoping that by some miracle they'd forget I was here so I could sneak away while Theo was being suitably pummelled. But then the beauty therapist popped her head around the door to see if I was all right and I realised I'd made things worse, because now I'd have to walk into the treatment room last, with Theo lying there watching my every move.

Thankfully the room was dimly lit and smelt divine and would have been lovely if I could have ignored the fact that Theo was lying face down on one of the couches with a white towel barely covering a thing and his glistening back and shoulders tantalisingly on show. I felt an involuntary jolt run through my body. He really was in excellent shape. Which was not what I was supposed to be thinking, not ever, but especially not now when I had to lie down next to him wearing nothing but my bra and knickers.

'*Madame*, please take off your robe and lie down on the bed. I will use a towel to cover your body for you.'

Oh. My God. How was I going to do this without Theo getting a bird's eye view of, well, everything? It was bad enough that he'd seen me in my bikini in the sauna, but somehow this felt even more intimate. I felt as self-conscious as hell, as you would if you had to strip off in front of someone who had muscles you hadn't even known existed. As if reading my mind, Theo turned his head so that he was looking at the far wall. Taking advantage of this gentlemanly gesture, and unsure how long I had before he turned back the other way again, I threw off the robe, flicked it over the back of a chair and dived on the bed so clunkily that the whole thing rocked.

It seemed to take the masseuse absolutely ages to arrange

the towel over me and meanwhile I was panicking that Theo was going to turn back round. Thank goodness I'd put my most substantial pair of knickers on. I closed my eyes, hoping that would take some of the embarrassment out of the situation, like a child putting its hands over its eyes to play hide and seek. If I couldn't see him, I could use my writerly imagination to convince myself that I was here by myself, having a relaxing solo massage like I'd had myriad times before. That seemed to work. I took some deep breaths in and out, feeling my stomach melt into the couch.

The massage was great, once I'd successfully managed to not look at Theo for fifteen whole minutes. I could sense him next to me, and if I thought about it too hard it would send shivers down my spine, but he was very quiet. Once or twice I heard the low rumble of his voice, when the masseuse asked him if he wanted more pressure or less; if he wanted de-stressing or re-energising (he chose de-stressing). His voice rippled right through me, lulling me into a soothing half-sleep until I heard the familiar ring tone of my phone blasting out from the pocket of my robe. Aaargh. I'd meant to leave it in my room, but had obviously picked it up on auto-pilot.

'Sorry,' I whispered, wincing.

'I just jumped out of my skin,' said Theo, rearing up and clutching his hand to his chest. 'I must have been dropping off to sleep or something.'

My phone rang off and then started up again almost immediately.

'Would you like me to pass it to you, *Madame*?' asked the masseuse.

I wanted to say no, but what if it was important?

'OK, yes please, if you don't mind. I'd better just check it's not my dad. He's not very well, you see, so ...'

'Scarlett,' said Theo.

'Yes?'

'You're not supposed to be checking messages until bed-time. It can't be good for you to constantly be on high alert.'

I knew he was right but his tone felt judgemental, something I was very sensitive to. The masseuse passed me my phone and I checked it quickly, realising I'd missed two calls from my sister. She'd texted, too.

Call me. Need to ask you something urgently.

Nothing to do with Dad, then, otherwise she would have said. It would be about Richard and that could easily have waited, except that Kate never saw it that way.

'Anything wrong?' asked Theo.

'Nope.'

'Disaster averted?'

It was all right for him, wasn't it? He didn't worry about his parents at all because he never saw them, meaning he was living a life in which he could do what he wanted, when he wanted and with whom he wanted. He had *no* idea what it felt like to feel as though you had to carry the whole family's successes and failures on your shoulders and sure, I'd set this dynamic up for myself, but I'd been so young and I hadn't known what else to do and now how was I supposed to change it?

'Unfortunately I'm not like you, Theo. I can't switch off my feelings when it suits me to avoid dealing with the difficult stuff.'

That was a bit harsh, I realised that immediately, but I didn't think me having my phone on me was the big deal he was making it out to be. It was hardly a relaxing situation in the first place with both of us lying here all oiled up with hardly any clothes on.

'Thank you for your observations, Scarlett,' said Theo, his

voice muffled because, as I could see out of the corner of my eye, he was face down on the bed while his masseuse pummelled his neck. 'But what *you* clearly don't understand is that burying emotions is what some people do to protect themselves. And on the odd occasions that one does allow themselves to feel connected to someone, they generally let you down, in my limited experience.'

He turned his head an inch or two to the right and caught my eye. Surely he wasn't talking about me, because how had I let him down? I also felt bad for the massage therapists who were probably thinking this was the most unromantic couples massage they had ever administered. But I couldn't let it go. It felt as though there was some truth bubbling around here, some resentment from him that I couldn't get my head around. And given what had happened in the past that was pretty rich, to be honest.

'Can I ask what you meant by that?' I said. 'Because presumably you're talking about me letting you down and, I'm sorry, but I just don't get why you'd say that.'

'It's fine, Scarlett. Just leave it,' he said huffily. 'Why don't you try to relax, that's what we're here for, after all?'

I could hardly relax now, could I? In fact, I couldn't wait for this to be over. I lay back down on my couch, bubbling with frustration and counting the minutes until I could get up and leave.

Chapter Nineteen

Still riled up after the world's most awkward massage, I decided to go and cool off in the pool. I was stewing on his ridiculous insinuations. If it was true that he thought I'd hurt him then his version of events must be the opposite of everything I believed had happened.

I eased myself into the warm turquoise pool, which thankfully I had to myself. Other than a couple of guests I didn't know who were sitting on sun loungers at the far end, it was blissfully quiet and I swam a couple of lengths and then floated on my back, looking up at the blue sky dotted with the odd fluffy cloud, enjoying the way I was creating a mini-current as my fingers combed back and forth through the water. Until someone thundered past me doing an exceptionally splashy front crawl that was, sending a tidal wave of water over my face so that I had to stand upright, gulping for air. Surely they'd seen me floating there! I swam to the side, watching with irritation as the man – of course it had to be a man – turned at the other end and powered back towards me. As he got closer and turned his head to take a breath, I saw that it was Theo. He caught my eye, slowed down and swam in my direction.

'Thanks for nearly drowning me,' I said, low-level raging.

'Sorry,' he said, 'I didn't notice how close you were until it was too late to stop.'

'How could you not see a full-sized human lying flat-out in the middle of the pool?'

He stood up in the water, slicking his hair back, droplets of water running over his face and neck and chest. It was like something out of a Diet Coke ad, and not in a bad way.

'I was miles away,' he said. 'To be honest, I was thinking about what I said to you while we were having our massages. I feel a bit bad about it, actually.'

Well this was a turnaround. I'd never known him to feel bad about *anything*, because that would require him to have actual connections with people and also to be able to name his feelings (in this case guilt, which I'd never heard him express before, either). I smugly prepared to accept his apology for trying to make out that I'd wronged him. As if!

'I'm all ears,' I said, leaning my elbows on the side of the pool and tipping my head back so that the remnants of the day's sun hit my face.

Theo bobbed down into the water again so that I could only properly see him from the chin up. 'I didn't mean to sound as though I was telling you off for bringing your phone. Sorry. I was only trying to help.'

Oh. He wasn't feeling bad about what I'd thought he was feeling bad about. I took a beat or two to change tack.

'I don't need your advice, as you well know,' I said. It was the best I could do when I was still confused about what he'd meant about the other thing, but now suddenly didn't want to ask when he was here in front of me looking all fresh and glowy and half-smiling at me in the way that sent my insides soaring. Why spoil the moment, I thought?

'Understood,' he said, pushing a stray strand of dark hair out of his eyes. I wondered how it was that it looked just as lovely wet as it did dry. 'But needing help now and again isn't the weakness you seem to think it is.'

I was suddenly finding it very hard to look at him and his broad shoulders and his skin tinted golden by the Riviera sun and the little mole on his right shoulder that once I'd pressed my mouth against. He shifted in the water, sending ripples travelling across the surface from him to me. A cool breeze whipped against my cheek and I dipped my shoulders back into the water, too, trying to stay warm. And then I found myself drifting off into a daydream: I imagined what would happen if I were to take the two or three watery steps to meet him. If I hooked my hands around his neck and lifted my feet off the ground, wrapping my legs around his waist. And then what if he put his hands under me, pulling me into him so our bodies were pressing hard up against each other's. And as I was thinking these totally inappropriate things, it was almost as though he could see inside my head because he was staring hard at me, too, doing that thing he used to do, where he'd look at me so intensely that I was almost paralysed with a combination of fear and (I supposed) lust and I had to remind myself to keep beathing.

'Scarlett?' he said, not breaking eye contact.

I swallowed. 'Yes?'

'I'm really enjoying working with you again.'

Warmth rushed through my body, starting in my toes and working its way up out of the water and into the apples of my cheeks. He took a step towards me. My heart leaped in my chest so hard that I felt dizzy for a second.

'It's so much better than I expected,' he said, his deep voice resonating so that I could feel the vibrations of it in the water. 'You're bringing out something in my writing, a side of myself I've not been able to tap into on my own.'

Still thrown by my unfortunate yet thrilling daydream, I couldn't seem to come up with a suitable response other than: *Please kiss me right now.* I looked over his shoulder, searching for something solid and grounded, something to bring me back down to earth and to stop myself thinking about how much I wanted to press myself up against his wet, toned body. Then I spotted a pissed-off Justin and Renee opening the gate to the pool.

'You don't make any effort whatsoever,' hissed Renee. 'It doesn't matter what I do or what I wear or if I cook you a meal, all you want to do is watch movies or basketball. It feels like you don't care if I'm there or not.'

'Bullshit, Renee,' bit back Justin. 'Maybe if you spent less time drinking margaritas with your friends we'd actually be *able* to spend more time together.'

Theo grimaced at me, almost physically recoiling. 'Come on, let's get out. Leave them to it.'

I watched Justin and Renee dumping their bags on a sun lounger. She was standing with her hands on her hips, he was sitting, yanking off his trainers.

'Don't you think we ought to do something?' I asked.

'Like what, for God's sake?' asked Theo.

I ignored him, pushing off the wall with my feet and swimming in their direction. I indicated for Theo to follow me, but as I passed him he looked horrified.

'What are you doing?' he said out of the side of his mouth.

Confused, I swam back to explain.

'When people are arguing, sometimes all they need is a re-set,' I said under my breath. 'Someone to come in and change the atmosphere and stop them from saying things that they'll most likely regret.'

'And let me guess, that person is you?' said Theo.

'Exactly.'

'Stay out of it, Scarlett,' said Theo, visibly shuddering. 'If they keep arguing that badly, maybe they shouldn't be together, anyway?'

'I'm not sure they *keep* arguing,' I said. 'And anyway, they clearly want to make their relationship work, otherwise they wouldn't be here.'

I thought he was being very over-dramatic. It was just Justin and Renee bickering.

'All couples argue,' I carried on, although who was I to say? My general rule was to cave in and give people what they wanted and then there'd be nothing to argue about, would there?

'Oh, I know that all couples clash,' whispered Theo. 'Why do you think I don't want to be in one?'

I sighed, looking over at Justin and Renee again who were now jabbing their fingers at each other, their voices even louder than before.

'I'm going to have to do something,' I said, not able to let it go.

'Please don't,' said Theo, sounding annoyed.

I promptly ignored him. 'Justin! Renee!' I called out, waving jauntily as though I'd only just spotted them and hadn't heard them screaming at each other about ten seconds ago. I could practically feel Theo glowering in my direction as I glided towards them.

'Scarlett!' he hissed after me.

I pretended I hadn't heard him and swam over to the side nearest to Justin and Renee. They were looking a tiny bit embarrassed, but at least they'd stopped arguing.

'Everything OK?' I asked brightly. 'The water's lovely if you're thinking of coming in for a swim.'

'Good idea,' said Renee, pulling off her shorts and jumping into the water.

'You coming, Justin?' I asked, as though I was totally oblivious to what had just been unfolding in front of our eyes.

He shuffled about a bit and then picked up his bag and trainers. 'You know what? On second thoughts, I think I'll head up to the room instead,' he said.

I gave him a thumbs-up, looking at Renee who was shaking her head, irritated. Once he'd disappeared down the path, I turned to her.

'Hope I didn't interrupt?' I said. 'I thought you could do with a hand, that was all. Things seemed to be getting a bit heated.'

Theo chose that precise moment to wade over and throw me another dark look.

'Renee, I'm so sorry if we stepped out of line,' he said, looking pointedly at me. 'It wasn't our intention to listen in on your ... conversation. Or to interfere,' he said, his eyes flickering to me again.

I tutted, annoyed. I didn't need him apologising for me as though I'd done something wrong. People needed me to step in sometimes and that was a fact. Just because he was too scared of conflict to help out anyone, ever.

'Trust me, it's totally fine,' said Renee. 'I actually really appreciate you coming over, Scarlett. We were arguing about the same shit we always argue about and it was going nowhere fast.'

I nodded empathetically. 'I know what you mean,' I said, giving Theo a look of my own.

'Justin finds it super hard to be romantic,' said Renee. 'Even a little bit. Twenty-seven years old and zero clue about how to make his wife feel good about herself. I don't understand why he can't put himself out there and try, for me.'

'That's men for you,' I said, sympathetically.

'Excuse me,' said Theo, 'but men are capable of romance, too, you know.'

'I hope you're not talking about yourself?' I quipped.

'Obviously not,' he said, smiling at me with a tight mouth.

Renee, perhaps realising that she had a chance to consider the situation from another perspective, rounded on Theo.

'You're an author, right?' she said.

'Yes ...' said Theo with trepidation, as though there were going to be some horrible repercussions to admitting it.

'So you must be good at tapping into your own emotions, then?'

I resisted the urge to snort out loud.

'Um ...' said Theo.

'Is there any chance you could have a word with Justin?' said Renee earnestly, her blonde curls turning darker and more tightly coiled in the water. 'Show him that it's not emasculating for men to be romantic, too?'

I laughed out loud at that point, I couldn't help myself. As if Theo was capable of showing other men how to express romantic feelings. If anything, it should be the other way round. Justin might not be particularly demonstrative when it came to hearts and flowers, but at least he was feeling *something*.

'What's so funny?' asked Theo, turning to me.

'Nothing?' I said hopefully.

'Well clearly there's something, Scarlett,' said Theo, not letting me off the hook. 'Do share.'

Renee was looking at me quizzically, too. Fuck.

'Sorry,' I said. 'I shouldn't have laughed, that was rude of me.'

'It was, a bit,' said Theo, looking all affronted. Was this guy for real? He surely couldn't think that stringing multiple women along at once and then ghosting them when things got 'serious' made him an expert in romance?

'It's just that Theo doesn't really do feelings either, Renee,' I explained. 'Or at least, that's how it comes across. Obviously I can't profess to know what goes on in his head,'

I added, even though I thought I was one hundred per cent right on this. 'He's sworn off relationships altogether, in fact. And I reckon he'd be hard-pressed to come up with a single romantic gesture if his life depended on it.'

I thought I'd probably gone a bit far with that last statement, but in for a penny, in for a pound.

'Renee, if it will help, I'm happy to have a chat with Justin,' he said, looking at me defiantly. 'And no, perhaps I'm not the most emotionally literate person, but I like to think I've learned something in the thirty-two years I've been on this planet, despite what Scarlett might think.'

'You're actually offering to do this?' I said, incredulous.

'Absolutely,' he said. 'Consider me at your service, Renee,' he said with a mock half-bow.

'That is very nice of you, Theo,' said Renee. 'And honestly, anything you can do has to be an improvement.'

A look crossed Theo's face that I couldn't quite work out. Like he'd had a memory of something, or as if he realised what he'd agreed to do and was wondering what he'd let himself in for.

'On that note, I think I'll head back to my room. Enjoy the rest of your afternoon, ladies,' he said, nodding at me and then swimming over to the steps and getting out as Renee and I watched him appreciatively. I mean, you couldn't not. It was like Daniel Craig emerging from the water in those pale blue trunks in *Casino Royale*.

'You two make a beautiful couple,' said Renee, unashamedly following him with her eyes.

'We're just writing partners, Renee,' I mumbled.

'Scarlett, we can all see what's really going on here,' she said.

'I have no idea what you're talking about,' I said. Had everyone been gossiping behind our backs or something?

'Oh, I think you do,' said Renee, smiling to herself.

I wondered if Renee had somehow picked up on the highly inappropriate fantasies I'd been having lately. And if she could, could Theo? Well, there would be no more of that, I vowed to myself as I mumbled a goodbye to Renee and swam for the steps. I'd just have to summon all the acting skills I had for the rest of this trip and pretend like I still hated Theo as much as I had when I'd touched down in Nice a week ago. Which was pretty hard when he was in the next room with nothing but a flimsy wall between us and a door that could lock and unlock from both sides.

Chapter Twenty

Having spent the rest of the afternoon chained to my laptop, finishing off the chapters we planned to send to Carla the following day, it had felt good to meet up with the others for dinner. Except that now Melissa had organised after-dinner drinks, and I was pretty sure there was going to be a task involved.

'Tonight, we're doing an anti-speed-dating exercise,' Melissa announced, directing us each to a particular table.

I was wearing the white linen shorts I'd bought from Zara on Rue d'Antibes earlier in the week and had paired them with a navy-and-white knitted vest I'd had for years and my go-to pair of black strappy sandals. For the first time since I'd arrived I felt polished and chic in a way that Theo had appeared to effortlessly embody every single evening.

'An anti-what?' asked Claire, looking worried. 'Please tell me we're not going to be speed-dating our own husbands?'

'Actually, you'll be *anti*-speed-dating somebody else's husband,' said Melissa.

'Huh?' I said, confused, and also getting a very brief thrill out of the thought that Theo was effectively – for one night only – my sort of husband.

Melissa pointed me in the direction of a table where Paul was ominously waiting for me and a baffled-looking Theo (who I had to say was looking particularly good in a blue jeans and white shirt combo) to a different table, with Claire following closely behind.

Once we were all seated, Melissa gave us our instructions.

'In a second, the lovely hotel staff will serve you all a cocktail – a signature blend epitomising the verve and beauty of Cannes.'

'Great,' I said, meaning it. Alcohol was clearly key with a task like this.

'I can get a mocktail, right?' asked Paul.

Great, a sober Paul was going to be even less fun.

Melissa waved his question away and carried on. 'I want you to spend the next half hour or so discussing with your partner everything you've observed about their relationship so far. So Claire, you tell Theo what you've noticed about him and Scarlett. Any thoughts you have, any suggestions, anything that resonates with you in terms of your own relationship that it might be helpful to share. And then you swap. Does that make sense?'

There was a collective mumble/groan. It made sense, essentially, but I also didn't particularly care what Paul had to say about me. He was probably the person in the group I felt least connected to – we'd literally had one conversation about California weather and that was it. What great insights into my not-a-relationship could he possibly impart? I glanced over at Theo, who was already deep in conversation with Claire. I supposed that at the very least, something useful might come out of that. Claire was easy to talk to in a way that maybe I wasn't (not for Theo, at least) and she was already a good friend – she had my back, and I didn't think she would hold back when it came to getting the truth out of him.

'Who wants to start?' asked Paul, his smooth standard-American accent gliding across the space between us.

'I'll do you first,' I said, delaying the inevitable. Paul and Harmony had been pretty vocal about not wanting Theo and me in the group from the start and I wanted to put his acerbic opinions off for as long as possible. Not that I cared, I reminded myself.

A cocktail was delivered at the perfect time and after a few sips I felt brave enough to start.

'So I know you're a movie producer and that Harmony runs a yoga studio,' I said. 'And it feels like the two of you really complement each other. She grounds you and you energise her.'

'Guess so,' said Paul, sitting back in his chair and chugging on his syrupy-looking mocktail.

'And I noticed there's a lot of kindness in your relationship,' I said, treading carefully now. Because I was determined to be honest, that was the whole point of the exercise. 'But I wonder whether perhaps you're masking some of your more difficult feelings?'

There, I'd said it. It might not go down well, but it was true. I was fed up with Paul dominating our group sessions with his insights about everyone else. Time for him to face the music.

'How so?' asked Paul.

'Well, you and Harmony haven't been getting along. Or at least, I'm presuming you haven't been, otherwise she wouldn't have got to the point of giving you an ultimatum, would she?'

Paul looked put out, just as I knew he would be.

'She said it in the heat of the moment. She didn't mean it,' he insisted.

Didn't she, though? I thought. To be fair to Paul, he did seem to be taking in what I was saying, even though I could see it was difficult for him.

'OK, you got me,' he admitted. 'I can be kinda gloomy and difficult to be around when work gets tough. She'd had enough and I couldn't blame her.'

'We're all snappy sometimes,' I said gently.

He nodded. 'Yeah, and you know what? When I do open up to Harmony and let her in instead of starting a row just so I can release some of the tension building up, it feels good. I feel better for getting it out there, you know?'

'I do.'

Paul squirmed in his seat and then leaned forward to put his head in his hands. For one terrifying moment I thought I'd made him cry, but then thankfully he sat up and looked at me with a sort of wan smile.

'You're pretty good at this,' he said.

'Thank you,' I said, disproportionately chuffed. I knew how to talk to people about their feelings, that was true. It came easily. I found it interesting and also reassuring to see that not everyone had it as sussed as I'd thought they did. But talking about myself? That was another matter entirely.

'Your turn,' said Paul.

'Already?' I said, looking at my imaginary watch and playing for time. Melissa had said we had half an hour so if we spent twenty minutes on Paul, my 'session' would fly by.

Paul stayed silent for a bit, as though he was pondering some really important question that only he had the answer to. Mind you, at least it was another time-waster.

'OK,' he said eventually, huffing dramatically. 'I think you're showing the world what you want people to see.'

'Oh, yeah?' I said, feeling my defences rise. I was very good at denial, and very persuasive when it came to blind-siding other people into thinking that there was nothing to worry about.

245

Paul crossed his arms in the self-satisfied way that drove me mad.

'Yeah. You want people to think you're strong and invincible and can cope with anything. And maybe you can, some of the time. But I reckon that underneath all of that, you want love and affection as much as the next person.'

His statement hung in the air. I wanted to think of a suitably quippy reply, but of course my ability to banter had to go and abandon me just when I needed it most, and instead I was left staring at him, wondering who he thought he was but also thinking that he could – *could* – be right.

'Can we stop now?' I said, laughing it off. I even looked over at Theo hoping he might save me, just as I had him at the couples therapy session, but oh no, he seemed to be having a whale of a time with Claire. The two of them were absolutely cracking up. Trust me to get stuck with the least easy-going member of the group.

'You're trying to defend your way out of this,' said Paul, smirking at me annoyingly. 'I can see it, clear as day.'

'I'm not!' I protested. But that was my defences talking, wasn't it? I took a few beats to let what he'd said sink in. 'OK, maybe I am. But as you know, we didn't sign up for this. I thought I was on a writing retreat!'

'Ah, but you could have walked away at any time,' said Paul. 'You could have checked into another hotel.'

'I couldn't! It would have cost us a fortune.'

'You know what I think?' said Paul.

I wanted to say no and that I didn't care to know, but I bit my tongue.

'I think that subconsciously, both of you wanted to stay and work through your shit. And you can tell yourself it's just about your book, but in my opinion, it's about you wanting to work things out with Theo, whatever the hell that looks like.'

What did he know, he wasn't a therapist, was he? But then, I also knew, deep down, that he had a point. If I'd *really* wanted to leave, I could have sucked up the financial losses and dealt with the consequences later. Something had made me stay. It was the book, I told myself. That was all it was.

'I'll give that some thought,' I lied, unless thinking about how *not* to think about it counted.

Thankfully, Melissa chose that moment to tinkle her bell and we all came together again as a group. What we'd discussed was to stay between the two of us, Melissa informed us and I was grateful for small mercies – this way there would be no de-brief and Theo would not have to hear Paul's skewed theory about why we hadn't walked away from the retreat on day one.

We all hung around, with another round of cocktails handed out, much to our delight. Paul still insisted on sticking to mocktails and he was unnecessarily holier-than-thou about it, even though I'd seen him chug enough wine to sink a ship over the last few days. A big round moon was lighting up the courtyard and I savoured the feeling of being outside having drinks in April, of the burst of sweetness coming from the wisteria lining the fence running alongside us and of feeling warm enough to roll up my sleeves despite it being nearly 10 p.m.

'That was actually much easier than I thought,' said Claire, making a beeline for me. I was desperate to know how things had gone with Theo but I couldn't expect Claire to break the confidentiality clause Melissa had quite rightly imposed on us.

'Yeah, well you didn't have Paul to contend with. We

weren't the best match – for a start, we're probably the two most highly defensive people here,' I said.

'Did anything useful come out of it?' asked Claire.

I took a second to think about it. 'OK, yeah, it did. A bit.'

In my head, I recounted what he'd said, about how he thought I wanted people to see me. And how this was at odds with the yearning for affection I had underneath all of that bravado. But even if he was right, what was I supposed to do about it? Start spewing out all the stuff that scared me and made me angry and upset me on a daily basis? Nobody would know what had hit them.

'How did you get on?' I asked Claire casually.

'You're dying to know, aren't you?' she said, on to me immediately.

I winced. 'Was it bad?'

'You know we're supposed to keep everything confidential ...' said Claire in a mock-scolding voice (or at least I hoped it was 'mock').

'Definitely don't say anything you don't feel comfortable with,' I assured her, playing it cool.

'You want to know, though. Right?' teased Claire. Clearly my version of cool was way off the mark.

'Aaaargh,' I said. 'OK, I want to know! But I get that we're not supposed to share, so ...'

Claire looked over her shoulder at Theo, who was deep in conversation with Justin. I'd spotted them, too, and wondered if he was giving Justin his mysterious and surely useless romantic advice. I couldn't, for a second, imagine what words of wisdom he was hoping to impart, given his own relationship history.

'I can tell you one thing and one thing only,' said Claire, turning back to me.

My stomach turned. Was this going to make my night or

ruin it? And what would this 'making of my night' even look like? Did I want Theo to like me romantically, was that what my heart was getting at? And if so, was it because I wanted some sort of redemption for what had happened before? To know I could have him if I wanted to? Or was it more to do with the here and now, and how well we'd been getting along recently and – yes – how incredibly gorgeous he looked every single time he set foot outside of his tantalisingly close bedroom.

'Go on, then, let's get it over with,' I said, preparing myself for the worst.

Claire bit her lip and leaned in, whispering into my ear. 'I think Theo has a thing for you.'

I felt like the ground had opened up and I'd fallen about ten foot into it.

'He hasn't,' I spluttered.

'He didn't exactly say as much. We talked about … other things, mainly.'

What 'other things'? I wanted to scream.

'What makes you think that he likes me, then? Do you mean as a friend?'

'No!' said Claire. 'Not as a friend. And it's just a feeling I have. But I can't say any more so please don't make me. I'm finding it really hard not to spill my guts as it is.'

This was excruciating!

'Got it,' I said through gritted teeth. 'Thank you for telling me that much.'

What I really wanted to say was: please *do* spill your guts. Please tell me every single thing he said, every breath he took, every facial expression he made. Because I didn't quite trust Claire's opinion. Not because she wasn't a good judge of character, because she seemed very astute, but because Theo could turn on the charm whenever he wanted to and most people fell for it hook, line and sinker. And she had no idea what he'd been like before, how he'd treated me last time. And even though I felt all heady and excitable now at the thought that he might like me in a way that I was desperately trying not to like him, I wasn't sure how genuine it was from his end. Six years had gone by and he hadn't once tried to contact me, so he could hardly have been pining for me all this time, could he?

And then of course, as I looked up, the first person whose eye I caught was Theo's, as if he'd been searching for me. And I felt a bit dizzy immediately, sort of wild and bubbly, and my emotions were not flat like I preferred them to be, but all over the place: I liked him, I didn't; he wanted me, but then he didn't. God, I was driving myself mad. Placing my still-full cocktail glass on a nearby table, I told Claire I was getting an early night.

'I didn't freak you out, did I?' she said, laying a hand on my arm, concerned.

'Course not,' I reassured her. 'I've got a ton of writing to do, that's all. We're sending what we've done so far to our agent tomorrow.'

'Ah,' said Claire. 'Well, good luck getting it finished.'

Forcing myself not to give Theo a longing look as I passed him and keeping my eyes straight ahead, I went inside the hotel and made my way through the reception area and up the stairs. I was nearly at the top when I became aware of Theo thundering up behind me.

'Hey,' he said, leaning against the wall, catching his breath.

'Hi,' I said. Had he just chased after me?

'Just wondered if you fancied another late-night writing session? I don't know about you, but I've got some editing to do and I seem to find it easier when I'm working alongside you.'

He'd meant it, then, when he'd told me he was enjoying writing together again. And I was, too, it was just that every time I glanced up from my screen and he was right there looking all earnest, concentrating on the next beat of his story, it would throw me for a minute or two. I repeatedly found myself mesmerised by his sculpted arms and the fact he was always so engaged in whatever I was saying and his semi-surprised expression as he plucked brilliant book ideas out of thin air.

'Think I'm too tired to write, actually,' I said, which wasn't a lie. 'And I'm pretty happy with my chapters. As happy as I can be, anyway.'

He smiled. 'All that writing through the night has paid off.'

'I know how to get those extra hours in.'

He hung his head, looking at the floor, then looked up to meet my eye, nodding towards his door. 'How about a nightcap then? Just a quick one. I could do with running an idea for our mid-point twist past you.'

'Who, me? Queen of plotting? Why, of course,' I said, making a joke, but also feeling giddy with anticipation. I'd imagined him in his room so many times and now I was going to see it for myself. I followed him inside. It was small and sparse and nothing like mine, and I felt a pang of guilt, but also relief. Instead of a lilac colour scheme, his was burgundy and grey, and instead of a king-sized double, there were two narrow single beds housing the flattest mattresses I'd ever seen in my life. And whereas my suitcase was still lying on the floor only half unpacked, or else shoved out of sight under the bed, his room was neat and tidy, with everything put away in its proper place. Jake Thorn's latest book was open on his bedside table, alongside his wallet and keys. I glanced into his bathroom, where manly, expensive products were symmetrically lined up next to the basin.

'Wine OK?' he asked, going over to the desk, where a bottle of red was already open.

'Sure.'

I watched as he poured us each a glass.

'Shall we sit out on the balcony?'

I nodded, stepping through the French doors behind him.

I sat down first, wrapping my cardigan tightly around myself, chilly now I was up higher and more exposed.

'Shall I get you a blanket?' asked Theo, concerned.

I shook my head. 'I'm fine. So what's this twist, then?'

He sat down next to me, leaning back in his chair and propping his left foot up on his right knee.

'So the wife, Caroline … what if she has a problem with alcohol? You know how judgemental people can be around addiction. How suddenly she's not just the wife of the missing man, she's the potentially drunk wife of the missing man.'

I thought it through. 'I like it. As long as we tackle her mental health with integrity, then I think it's a brilliant idea. We want our readers to think they've worked it all out, don't we, and then we'll roll out the big guns? Make our narrator unreliable so they don't know who to believe.'

Theo held his hand out for a high-five. I laughed, tapping my palm lightly against his.

'What's that for?' I asked.

'We have our killer twist. Deserves a celebration, don't you think?'

'*Your* killer twist,' I said.

'Scarlett,' he said, reaching out to touch my arm. My heart instantly skipped a beat and I really wished he'd stop touching me, innocently or not. 'You do know we're in this together, don't you? That as far as I'm concerned, I could not have done any of this without you. Why do you think I asked you if you wanted to write a novel with me all those years ago?'

I laughed lightly. 'I know why. Because we were the only two who wanted to write a thriller.'

'We weren't,' he insisted. 'There were a few of us. I wanted to team up with you because I'd admired your work from the beginning. You were by far the strongest writer in the class and I felt nervous about asking you because I wasn't sure if you'd say yes to co-writing with someone else, let alone me.'

Surprised, I looked down at the gardens and the pool, quiet now except for the faint hum of conversation and laughter from the courtyard, where our fellow retreaters must still be enjoying themselves and trying to keep quiet about what their spouses had been saying about them in the anti-speed-dating task. Perhaps it would have been safer to stay down there, surrounded by all of them, instead of thinking it was a good idea to sit up here alone with Theo and his unexpectedly sweet revelations.

'Thanks for saying that,' I said. 'And ditto. Obviously.'

'It's a shame we left it so long to do it again,' said Theo, stretching out his legs, crossing them at the ankle, now.

I let that fully sink in. It was a shame.

'How's it going with Justin, by the way?' I asked, changing the subject. 'Teaching him the nuances of conducting a romance, are you?'

'You'll see,' he replied mysteriously.

'Tell me everything, immediately,' I said.

'I will not.'

I pouted playfully.

'How are you finding the retreat on the whole?' he asked me.

'More fun than I thought it would be when we rocked up from the airport and realised the full extent of Carla's cock-up. And I've never done any sort of therapy before, but it's interesting what you start to discover about yourself, isn't it? I suddenly feel much clearer about a lot of things, mainly to do with my family, but other stuff, too.'

He was going to think I meant him. Did I mean him?

'I feel the same way,' he said. 'Despite convincing myself, quite successfully, that I'm not capable of having a serious relationship, I've realised that maybe it *is* something I want. But there's this block that makes it feel impossible; that I'd have to work out how to break down first. My parents' relationship was just so fucking bad and there was always so much tension in the house. I'd never want that, and I'd especially never want to inflict it on my children.'

I thought this might be the most honest about himself I'd ever heard him be. And I'd never have imagined him to want children, but perhaps that was because I still wasn't sure if I wanted them myself.

'I get why conflict would make you feel unsafe,' I said. 'And it might feel like I'm not scared of it in the same way you are, but what I do is, I wade in and I manically diffuse the situation. Like it's my role, as though it's my job to single-handedly sort everybody else's problems out.'

'It sounds exhausting,' said Theo.

I nodded. 'Yep. Can be.'

'At least you can have relationships, though,' said Theo, sitting up and leaning his forearms on the balcony. 'You were with Jackson for years.'

'Yeah, well. In the end I was with him out of a sense of loyalty rather than because I loved him in that deep, all-consuming way we all dream of loving someone.'

Theo grimaced. 'Can I tell you something?'

'Is it going to make me feel better or worse?'

'Better? I hope,' he said.

'Go for it.'

'I've met Jackson a few times, at launches and festivals and suchlike. And he's fine. A nice guy. But I could never imagine him with you.' He looked at me, as though expecting me to disagree.

'It's strange, with relationships, how you can just fall into spending years of your life with the wrong person,' I said, watching the wind pick up, the way it whirled leaves around the garden. 'There was something very familiar about the dynamic between me and Jackson. It felt like he needed me – and as you know, I like to be needed – but as it turns out, he didn't need me, it had just been easier for him to sit back and let me organise his life for him. It took me a while to work out the difference.'

'So you ended things?'

I nodded. 'It was hard. I thought I'd be letting him down, that he wouldn't be able to cope.'

'And could he?'

I smiled wryly. 'He hooked up with his agency's assistant the week after we broke up, so I'd say so.'

Theo looked across at me. 'Is it wrong that I'm glad you're not with him anymore?' he said softly.

I swallowed hard. When I looked down, I noticed that our knees were pressed against each other's. The after-effects of the cocktails plus the wine were kicking in and I felt woozy and happy and relaxed and all the things that were dangerous when it came to Theo and I being in such close proximity. I slid off my shoes, wiggling my toes, closing my eyes. I never wanted this feeling, of sitting next to him, of feeling properly understood by somebody for once, to end. And then my foot brushed against his, and the top of his arm nudged my shoulder. When I opened my eyes again I could see his eyelashes in my peripheral vision, could tell that he was looking at me. My chest was rising and falling, rising and falling and I turned to meet his gaze. I was spiralling deep into something that I didn't know if I was going to be able to get out of. Part of me wanted to stop and the other part wanted to melt into him immediately, to give everything of myself to him, just for tonight, just once more. Because when you looked at Theo like that, you were pretty much undone, I knew that from experience.

And then the inch or two between us seemed to get smaller and smaller and I couldn't stop it. He was moving closer, never breaking eye contact and as if in slow motion, and then suddenly a shot of pleasure jolted through me as he put his mouth over mine, gently at first, then more urgently. I leaned into him, tugging at the hem of his shirt to bring him closer to me and then working my hands over his chest so that they were in his hair – that hair! – and I was running my fingers through it and it felt every bit as delicious as I'd remembered. His hand was on my back and I gasped as he ran his palm up my spine tantalisingly slowly and then finally he cradled my head in both hands so that I felt safer than I ever had and held by him in a way that felt so reassuring, as if I'd been waiting for him all my life. Then he stood, pulling me up with him, turning me round so that my back was pressed up against the balcony. I let out a gasp of pleasure, because now when we kissed I could feel every part of him rocking against me and it felt as though my entire body was on fire. When his hand found the space between my bare thighs, slipping it under the hem of my dress, I moaned, putting my fingers on top of his, lacing them together, stopping him from going any higher. I knew where it would lead if he did and I couldn't. I wanted to, more than anything, but I couldn't.

He stopped and for a second or two we stood very still, locked together, our breathing coming in heavy bursts.

'We shouldn't be doing this, should we?' he whispered into my ear.

I shook my head, not trusting myself to speak.

'Shall we stop?' he asked, resting his forehead against mine so that I couldn't look at him properly with perspective any more, it was like we were one person. I wanted to taste him on my tongue, like I had a second ago, and almost grabbed the back of his head and made him kiss me again.

'Absolutely,' I said, sounding more certain than I felt.

He took his time releasing me from his grasp, running his hands down the sides of my body and then taking a step back. I felt instantly cold and alone again and wanted to say forget it, let's go for it and drag him into the bedroom and have the night of our lives. Because it would be, I knew it, and it wasn't my imagination playing tricks on me. But I'd felt similarly last time – less guarded, perhaps, but with the same desire and recognition that I was happier when I was with him than I was when I was with anybody else. And then it had fallen apart and I didn't want that to happen again, not when we were in such a good place, and Carla was relying on us, and my whole family were relying on me.

'I should get some sleep,' I said, fumbling to find my shoes, my heart still pumping blood around my body at a rate of knots, wondering how we'd got here when this time last week we hated each other.

'Do you have to go?' he asked, reaching out to take my hand, tugging me gently towards him again. I made myself pull in the opposite direction, my hand slipping out of his.

'See you in the morning, OK? We'll email Carla then.'

He nodded. 'OK.'

I looked over my shoulder at him as I left his room. He

was still on the balcony, facing me and I almost ran straight back into his arms. Of course it would be amazing to stay with him all night long, to throw caution to the wind, to do something just because I wanted to and to hell with what happened after that. To be with someone who didn't need anything from me, except perhaps for me to write half a book. But it was too much of a risk and there was too much at stake and when I was back in the safety of my room, I knew I'd made the right decision.

Except that that night I had the worst sleep of my life. I kept thinking about how there was just a door between us, aware of how my body ached for him, tossing and turning, tossing and turning, imagining him naked under his covers until I almost gave in and got up and knocked on his door. It would be so easy, a few steps, the turn of a handle. I thought about that for what felt like hours until eventually, exhausted, I fell asleep.

Chapter Twenty-One

I was pacing around my room wondering whether I dared go down for breakfast and what the hell I was going to do about my (frankly phenomenal) kiss with Theo when a white piece of paper slid under my door. I looked at it for a beat or two, my heart in my throat. For all the listening at our interconnecting door I'd done, all the pressing my ear up against it and trying to work out what he was doing, what he was watching on TV, whether or not he was writing, I'd never considered slipping him a note. Perhaps it was something bad and he thought it best to do it in writing. Maybe yesterday had finished him off and he'd booked himself an early flight home. I approached it tentatively, bending to pick it up. On the hotel's headed notepaper he'd simply written:

Breakfast? Fifteen minutes?

I smiled to myself. He wasn't blanking me, that was something. We weren't going to have another six years of silence, we were going to face this like the mature, emotionally intelligent adults I assumed we were. So what if we'd kissed? We'd stopped before we'd gone too far. It had been nice (an understatement) and really, no harm had been done. I didn't feel any differently about him today than I had yesterday. Or if I did, I wasn't going to let myself go there.

I went over to my desk, grabbed a pen and scribbled a reply.

See you down there.

*

Just as I sat down to tuck into what had become my usual breakfast – scrambled eggs, crusty French bread and a slice of Comté cheese followed by yoghurt with berries – Theo joined me at my table, his hair still wet from the shower. I tried not to think about how, if I'd made a different decision, I could have been showering with him this morning. How that would have felt. Great, probably. I pulled myself back to the present. For now, my plan of action was to act like nothing had changed, even though I could hear Melissa's voice in my head telling me to communicate, to stop being afraid of telling people how I felt.

'Been for a run?' I asked.

'Gym,' he said, scraping his chair back, throwing himself into it. 'Rowing machine.'

'Very impressive,' I said. As was everything about him.

I envied the fact that Theo seemed to be able to focus on anything he set his mind to, whereas for me that level of focus and ambition seemed only to apply to writing books. Which I supposed was something. Lots of people said they wanted to write a book but never did. I regularly reminded myself that the success of *Little Boy Lost* had been an experience most authors could only dream of, especially when my bi-annual royalty statement had revealed distinctly mediocre sales of late. I desperately wanted to achieve everything we achieved back then all over again. I considered what it would mean to get another *New York Times* bestseller. Money, for sure, but also recognition, prestige, reassurance. Security. And if we could experience the highs of it together rather than being in a state of pretending the other didn't exist, that would make it even more special than the first time around.

'I got your chapters,' I told Theo. 'I've combined them

with mine and I've tidied the manuscript up, added page numbers and so on. Are you happy for me to send them over to Carla?'

'Hmmmn,' he said, keeping his mouth firmly closed over a mouthful of black coffee. He swallowed. 'Let's do it.'

I got my phone out, opened the document I'd emailed to myself, looked at it as though it held the key to my future, good or bad, and then forwarded it to Carla with a short note. When I'd laid in bed this morning reading through all eight of our chapters, I'd thought it might have been the best work we'd ever done together, and it was certainly tighter and pacier than anything I'd managed on my own.

'Sent,' I said.

Theo held two fingers out, crossing them in front of me.

I crossed my fingers back.

'I have to say, this whole experience has been far less painful than I thought it was going to be,' he said with a teasing smile.

I laughed. 'It could never have been as bad as I'd imagined.'

My phone pinged. And so began my obsession with checking my emails every ten minutes to see if there was any news. I was always like that when a book was out on submission – when I was waiting for someone to read it and give feedback. It was like a compulsion: refresh, refresh, refresh. I couldn't do anything else, focus on anything else, it was like my whole life hinged on one person's opinion on whatever it was I'd handed in.

'Carla,' I said, scanning her message. 'Acknowledging my email. She's keen to read it asap and is going to clear her schedule for the day.'

'We should be honoured,' he said. 'She never cancels meetings.'

The weight of what this must mean felt overwhelming, suddenly. It dawned on me that Carla was counting on this working out almost as much as we were – after all, she only made a living if we made a living, and although she was taking a percentage from all her other clients, too, that didn't add up to much unless at least some of them were making big money. The fact that she was promising to get back to us by the end of the day was testament to how much she believed in us. I hoped we hadn't let her down. It didn't feel like we had, but until somebody had read it with fresh eyes, you never knew how it was going to be received.

'Scarlett?' said Theo.

I'd got caught up with re-scanning Carla's email, trying to read between the lines, wondering whether she literally meant she'd email us back by the end of the day, or whether that was publishing speak for she'd get back to us when she was ready (which could be a week, a month, anything, who knew)?

'Hmmmn?' I said, looking up.

'Do we need to talk about last night?' he said with a gleam in his eye, challenging me to take him up on the offer.

'Not sure that's necessary,' I said, feeling the all-too-familiar walls going up.

'So we both know where we stand, then?'

'Course,' I said convincingly, although the truth was I had no idea what he was feeling, or even what I was feeling. At least he'd made an attempt to acknowledge that *something* had happened, which was a definite improvement on last time. But then I'd shut him down, so what did that say about me? Melissa would have been very disappointed if she'd overheard this particular exchange.

'Still up for joining the others in the balneotherapy pool later?' asked Theo.

'Definitely,' I said, watching as he downed the last of his coffee. 'By the way, what *is* balneotherapy?'

'I guess we'll find out,' he said, reaching for a delicious-looking croissant.

The balneotherapy pool was easily big enough for the six of us – Theo and me, Justin and Renee and Claire and Rob. Paul and Harmony were off on their one-to-one with Melissa. We'd each had to choose an area of Cannes or the surrounding area to explore, with the idea being that we would walk and talk about our experiences so far and what they'd thrown up for us. I was obviously dreading ours, which was scheduled for that afternoon, especially after last night, every single second of which was still playing over and over in my mind, despite acting like it hadn't been to Theo.

'What is balneotherapy?' asked Renee.

'That's what I just asked,' I said.

'I think it's basically a hot tub with some therapeutic properties,' said Rob. 'Minerals or something.'

'It's really good for relaxation, apparently,' added Claire, who was floating on her back in a star shape.

'This is so cool,' said Justin, submerging his body in the water, which was as warm as a medium-hot bath. On three sides we had beautiful views of the hills surrounding Cannes and the millionaires' houses dotted through the lush green of the trees like sprinkles on a cake. And beyond, behind the rooftops and grand hotels, glimpses of the sea.

'Who's next with Melissa, then?' asked Rob.

'We are,' said Theo, indicating the two of us. I liked that he'd referred to us as a 'we'. We were a team now, it was official.

'Where are you guys headed?' asked Claire.

263

'Le Suquet,' I said. 'The old town. There's a church up there, apparently, and stunning views.'

I wasn't sure if pretty surroundings were going to make the whole thing any easier, but it felt as though it might. Would Melissa pull the truth out of us, I wondered? Would she help us talk about what had happened instead of squashing it, like I'd blatantly just done? Theo had offered to talk about last night and I'd shut him down. Did that mean he was investing in this process more than I was? That he was trying to change when I wasn't? Why couldn't I just be vulnerable for once – were the feelings I kept hidden from everyone really so terrible? I dived under the water to drown out the dialogue in my own head, listening to the gurgle of the pool's motor instead, and the shifting of water as somebody swam a couple of lengths above me, their legs sending a cascade of froth across the surface. I could stay here forever, I thought, in this warm paradise of a pool, secure in the knowledge I'd done, or at least I'd started doing, the thing I came here to do. And I was proud of what we'd achieved so far. And I may have shared a kiss with Theo, but at least we were both on the same page with avoiding it going any further. We'd handled the morning after like a pair of professional writing partners who'd had a little blip and were now moving on and focusing on the task at hand. Except that as I broke through the surface of the water, Theo's was the first face I saw and he was smiling at me and I felt confused all over again.

As we approached the base of Le Suquet at the far end of Rue d'Antibes, where we were due to meet Melissa, I nudged Theo in the ribs. She was there already, pacing up and down the street with the phone clamped to her ear. I hesitated, glancing at Theo, who looked as surprised as I was to see Melissa looking anything other than serene.

'I'm telling you, I'm not putting up with it anymore. So either sort your shit out immediately, or we're done!' she hissed into the handset before ending the call and chucking her phone angrily into her shoulder bag.

'This is awkward,' I said.

'It's actually making me feel much better to see that even Melissa's relationships don't run smoothly all of the time,' said Theo, keeping his voice low as we approached her.

'Hi!' I said, extra cheerily.

'Hi, guys,' said Melissa, looking a little wearier than usual, but still about ten times more chilled than I could ever hope to appear after a row like that. 'Let's get walking. And talking!'

The three of us began winding our way up a narrow, pedestrianised street flanked by cute little shops selling jams and herbes de Provence and white cheesecloth dresses. Restaurant tables spilled out onto the cobbles, and disco bars that looked as though they might properly get going in high-summer showed little sign of life, although it was only late-afternoon.

'Thank you for joining me, guys,' said Melissa, wafting ahead in her psychedelic-print maxi dress and the requisite straw hat. I felt decidedly ordinary in comparison in my denim cut offs and a white vest. I did have the hat, though, purchased on a whim on the walk here. Theo had found it hilarious and I'd offered to buy him one, too, and when he'd refused, I'd joked that he hadn't wanted to mess up his near-perfect hair.

'It should be … interesting?' I said, struggling for something more positive to say.

Theo looked even less enthusiastic. I'd got into the swing of this therapy thing now, but I could see Theo was still finding it a grind, although judging by this morning, it was having more of an effect on him than he'd realised. I wondered if he was worried what would come up now that it was just the three of us and he couldn't use his reluctance to share in front of the group as an excuse for staying silent.

Melissa eyed us with suspicion as we turned to walk up a flight of red-bricked steps nestling between buildings. It was dark and shady in the shadows, and the staircase curved up and round a steep hill, past people's front doors and windows, some of them thrown open to let in the cooler air. They mostly had shutters painted in shades of lime, sage, olive and emerald. Some windows were flanked by gingham curtains, red-and-white, like a tablecloth. Others had plant pots of colourful flowers outside their doors, or window boxes bursting with tropical plants – mini palm trees, cacti and bushes sprouting tiny buttercup yellow flowers.

'Something has changed between the two of you,' Melissa quite rightly observed.

The memory of the kiss came flooding back. His lips, his tongue, the way he'd pinned me against the balcony wall and I had wanted to give everything of myself to him. I hung back a few steps to compose myself. It had been … spectacular.

'Is there anything you'd like to talk about?' enquired Melissa.

'Don't think so,' said Theo breezily.

'Maybe?' I said, countering him. He looked at me, surprised. As he would be when I'd been so reluctant to face the truth at breakfast.

It was just that we were here in beautiful Cannes with a world-class psychotherapist giving us her undivided attention. It would be an opportunity missed, surely, if I didn't try to push myself out of my comfort zone. And not talking about it didn't work last time, did it? Perhaps opening up to

Melissa would ease any uncertainty between us and allow us to keep working together as the friends I wanted us to be. I didn't think suppressed passion was a good idea, not with us, anyway. It tended to consume my every thought, whereas my thoughts needed to be elsewhere, on the book we were writing. And on my dad, who was begging me to come home soon, and on Alexa, who had had another panic attack and who had called me in the middle of the night so that I could help calm her down. These were the things that mattered, not residual feelings I held for a man who hadn't wanted me then and presumably didn't really want me now, either. He'd said it himself, he was probably incapable of having romantic relationships, and I in turn seemed to be incapable of keeping it casual, at least where he was concerned.

'Scarlett, can you elaborate?' asked Melissa.

We turned another corner where the steps widened out. At the top of the hill, I could see an ancient clock tower and the tops of giant fir trees.

I glanced at Theo, steeling myself. 'We kissed,' I said. 'Last night.'

Melissa let this hang in the air. Theo frowned, no doubt wondering why I was telling Melissa this when hours ago I'd agreed that it wasn't worth talking about.

'Theo, how does it feel to hear Scarlett say that?'

'Surprising,' he said, a little stiffly. 'It happened. But we've both agreed that it shouldn't happen again.'

'I see. And is that what you want?' she asked me, as we reached the stone archway of the clock tower. We followed Melissa through it, arriving in a serene courtyard. In one corner was the Musée des Explorations du Monde, which I'd read about and wished I had time to visit. But the writing was becoming all-consuming and we only had a few days left in Cannes, which was now spread out below us, all pale biscuit buildings with orange terracotta roofs, reminding me of my favourite French dessert: crème brûlée. To the right was the harbour, and the start of La Croisette, and the glittering dark, blue waters of the Med, curving into the distance, round to Antibes and beyond, to Nice.

'It feels really difficult to talk about,' I admitted, following Melissa over to a set of benches looking out over the Vieux-Port. To distract myself, I counted the boats – five rows of small vessels and then the giant mega-yachts in a row behind.

'Can you articulate why that is?' asked Melissa. 'Why you're holding back from telling Theo how you feel?'

God, we were really getting to this. The dangerous territory we'd done so well to avoid thus far was about to hit us head on and I didn't think I could stop it even if I wanted to.

'I guess it stems from the beginning,' I said tentatively.

'Can you tell me about it?' asked Melissa in such a soothing voice that I knew it was all about to come spilling out. It felt like the perfect place to reach into the depths of my memory, several hundred metres above Cannes, a calming sea view laid out in front of us.

'When we met on the writing course we did together, I was all smug at first, because although I found him attractive, I was able to kind of ignore that and focus on our friendship instead. And on our writing.' I said.

Theo shifted uncomfortably next to me. I made a concerted effort not to worry about whether I was saying something out of line. This was my therapy session, too, and I was only revealing all of this to Melissa because I thought it might be better for us in the long run.

'What made you scared of entering into something more with him?' asked Melissa.

'Feel free to interrupt me, if I get any of the details wrong, or whatever,' I said to Theo, making eye contact, just for a beat.

'Will do,' he said, although his voice sounded strained. As usual, I had no idea what he was thinking.

'So we we'd more or less finished work on our novel – *Little Boy Lost*. We'd secured ourselves a literary agent and a publishing deal, and it suddenly felt as though things were happening at breakneck speed. I'd given up my day job, so the stakes felt high.'

'Same,' said Theo. 'I felt the same.'

'I guess things started going wrong the day we heard from our agent, Carla, that the book had sold in America. That it was going to be published there the following summer and that the advance was even bigger than our UK one had been. We went out to celebrate and as the night went on, I began to realise I'd developed feelings for him.'

'Love?' asked Melissa.

'Not quite love. The beginnings of it, maybe. But I also knew that he had major commitment issues. It had been a running joke between us, something we'd laughed about together. Except that now the defences I'd put up to stop myself getting hurt were crumbling in front of my eyes. And stupidly I went with it.'

'What did that "going with it" look like?' she asked.

'It looked like us sleeping together,' said Theo gruffly.

I felt a pang at the memory of how perfect it had felt at the time. The culmination of months and months of friendship turning to passion. I remembered the exact moment things changed: we'd been in his kitchen, opening a bottle of champagne. He'd given me a celebratory hug and we'd looked at each other and that was all it took. It escalated very quickly from there and we'd spent the night together, tangled up in each other's arms, not able to believe what was finally happening between us.

'And what were you thinking at this point, Theo?' asked Melissa, standing up. 'Shall we walk? Sometimes it's easier.'

Theo and I stood up, following Melissa past the giant umbrella pine tree in the centre of Place de la Castre and taking a left, towards the church.

'I remember thinking how I'd been refreshingly open with Scarlett and that it felt great. I prided myself on being honest with all the women I dated, but even more so with her.'

'All the women?' clarified Melissa.

'There were a few at that time,' he said. 'And they all knew I wasn't looking for anything serious.'

As we walked down some steps into what felt like a secret garden, I was regretting what I'd started. It was difficult, even after all this time, to hear the details relayed to me. To have it spelled out like this.

'But you found something serious,' said Melissa. 'Without meaning to. With Scarlett. And perhaps you were scared of what might happen if you *did* actually let yourself fall for someone. Someone who meant enough to you that you would want to try doing things differently. To stick around. To risk your heart.'

I focused on the calming oasis of the little garden, the purple delphiniums shooting up towards the sky like flames, the lavender bushes, the smattering of tiny white daisies. The smell was intoxicating even despite Theo's unnerving silence.

'And how was the sex?' asked Melissa, ever blunt.

Theo groaned, clearly finding this question particularly mortifying.

'Great,' I said, quietly.

'And for you, Theo?'

'It was the best night of my life,' he said with a sigh. 'And I knew that because I didn't want to run away afterwards like I usually did. We stayed together until the morning. I felt like a normal, loveable human being for possibly the first time in my life. Hopeful for our future, actually. As though there might be a chance for it not to end in the kind of bitter conflict I was so terrified of.'

Melissa frowned. 'So what went wrong?'

'Scarlett ran out on me. I took a shower and when I got back, she was dressed already. Had her bag over her shoulder, as though she couldn't wait to get away.'

'Is that what happened from your perspective, Scarlett?'

'No it is not!' I said, put out that Theo was making out I was the bad guy here. Had he twisted it this much in his own mind that he'd started to believe it himself? 'He's missing out a vital part of the story.'

'Which part?' demanded Theo.

'The part where your phone rang repeatedly, while you were in the shower. And as you know, I'm always on high alert with my own family so although I didn't really think it was my place, I checked your phone, really quickly, in case it was urgent. In case somebody needed to get hold of you.'

'Nobody ever needs to get hold of me, Scarlett,' he said.

'Nobody except Poppy,' I said.

Melissa looked interested.

'He had a text from a woman called Poppy, saying she couldn't wait to see him that night followed by a string of red heart emojis,' I explained.

Theo looked like he was about to interject, but Melissa held her hand out to stop him.

'Let Scarlett finish, Theo. Scarlett, what did you think when you saw that message?'

I sighed, feeling a mixture of anger and sadness as I remembered how devastated I'd felt.

'I assumed he'd already lined up his next conquest – for that night. That he would be sleeping with me in the morning and Poppy in the afternoon.'

'It wasn't like that,' said Theo quietly.

I turned to him. 'I know things were bad for you growing up, but they were tough for me, too. I could never let myself be vulnerable, I had too many responsibilities, but I could be vulnerable with you. And I didn't feel the need to care for you, in fact, I felt cared for *by* you, which was a whole new experience. And yet the entire time you were hedging your bets, planning other dates on the same day we'd had sex. I was clearly just one of the women you were planning to have a night of fun with and then push away.'

Theo had his hand across his mouth. I might have felt bad for him under other circumstances. He'd clearly spent the last six years believing that he'd been blameless in all of this and now I'd laid the cards on the table and made him accountable for his actions. He'd probably convinced himself it was fine to shag multiple women at once, but my confidence had been so knocked that I'd ended up falling straight into the arms of Jackson Clark, who had never made me feel anything as deeply as Theo had.

'Theo, would you like to respond?' asked Melissa.

He put his hands in the prayer position, as though emphasising his point.

'Scarlett, I promise you that I had no idea you'd even seen that message. And I didn't meet up with Poppy that night, nor any other night. Our "date" or whatever you want to call it had been arranged weeks before but I'd already decided I didn't want to go because there was only one woman I wanted to be with, and that was you. And stupidly, I made assumptions of my own. That you'd regretted what we'd done. That I had nothing to offer you and you'd realised that and that's why you'd rushed off without so much as a word about seeing each other again.'

Now it was my turn to be shocked. It was a total misunderstanding, then? A set of mixed messages that could all have been solved with one phone call; one conversation. But instead, we'd both taken our childhood baggage and had let it colour our perspective, resulting in everything we'd started coming to a grinding halt. Instead of revelling in our success together, we'd spent the following months struggling through events and launches and signings with forced smiles and a hole where our hearts had once been connected. Once or twice I'd softened a little, tried to smooth things over, but I'd taken one look at Theo's face, which had seemed cold and closed off, and had decided that this was just how things were now. Carla had pushed for us to write a second book together, but we'd both categorically refused with no real explanation except that we'd fallen out. I didn't think Carla had ever entirely forgiven us.

'Is that why you shut me out of some of the book publicity?' I asked him.

'What do you mean?' he asked, seemingly genuinely confused.

'That interview you did for the magazine. You barely mentioned me at all, it was like you'd frozen me out completely.'

Theo shook his head. 'I was excited about the article, for both of us. I wanted the two of us to be featured equally, obviously, but for some reason the magazine duped me. They said they'd do your photo shoot at a later date, and your interview. I emphatically told them how closely we'd worked together on the novel, but they cut most of that out. And when the magazine was published, I wanted to reach out to you, but it was the night of the agency's summer party, do you remember? Jackson was stuck to you like glue. At one point, you were alone at the bar and I saw my chance, but then Carla swooped in, wanting to introduce me to someone, and when I looked for you afterwards, someone told me you and Jackson had already left. I assumed you were happy together, that I should back off and leave you to it.'

I pressed the heel of my hand against my forehead. All this time I thought he hated me, that I'd meant nothing to him. I was mad at myself, more than anything, for not having had the guts to try and work things out.

'This feels like a lot for both of you to take in,' said Melissa, sensing the drop in mood, the utter falling out of the bottom of my world.

I fumbled in my bag for some water, taking huge mouthfuls of it because I suddenly felt quite shaky and sick. Everything we'd believed about each other had been false. It was our own fault we'd ended up like this and nobody else's. My mind was reeling. I suddenly imagined what our lives might have looked like if I hadn't fled his apartment that day, if I'd just talked to him, told him that I'd seen Poppy's message, that I was scared of getting hurt, that I wanted to hear what he had to say. We could have enjoyed the success of *Little Boy Lost* together, as a team, instead of trying to avoid each other every time we were in the same room.

'Do you mind if I take a walk back on my own?' said Theo, turning to Melissa. 'I think I need some time for all of this to sink in.'

'Of course,' said Melissa. 'Why don't the two of you give each other some space and we can re-group at the activity tomorrow afternoon?'

'Fine,' I said, desperate to get away myself.

Except that Theo and I both started striding off in the

same direction at once and when I slowed my pace to let him pass, he did the same, and when I sped up, he lengthened his stride, too. Was he doing this on purpose?! Finally Theo stood still with his hands on his hips in frustration as I strutted off down a staircase, needing to put as much distance between us as possible. See, this was why it was much safer to put everyone else's feelings before my own. Because mine were complicated. And I didn't know what to do with them. And now we'd gone and stirred everything up, just as we'd found an easiness with each other. If you could call kissing each other and trying to pretend it hadn't happened easy. Stomping back into the centre of Cannes, I hoped that things would blow over eventually, once we'd both calmed down. They had to, because we'd missed several opportunities over the years, and this book we'd started was too good to let that happen again.

Chapter Twenty-Two

When I woke up the following morning I walked past the inter-connecting door between our rooms and ran my hand over it. I wanted to talk to him. There was nobody else who would understand the enormity of everything that had come to light in our session with Melissa because I, for one, had downplayed my relationship with Theo to every single person in my life. I'd chalked it up to experience because I was angry at myself for falling for someone who treated women the way I'd assumed he treated them. Now I knew more about him, I got it. It was fear that had been stopping him from taking things further, not arrogance or any of the other things I'd suspected. Without overthinking it (i.e. talking myself out of it) I ripped a page out of the notepad on the bedside table and scribbled a note. It had broken the ice between us last time we'd overstepped the mark, so maybe it could work its magic again.

Can we talk?

And then I marched over to the inter-connecting door, hesitated for a second, and pushed the note underneath.

I distracted myself by getting ready for the Zoom meeting Carla had organised for us that morning. Theo would be on the call, too, of course. As the minutes ticked on, I wondered if he'd read my note yet, and if so, why hadn't he replied?

What if he hadn't noticed it lying there, and I'd be thinking he was blanking me and he'd be thinking I hadn't reached out and we'd be back to square one?

Opening the Zoom link, I ran my fingers through my hair, smoothing out any errant knots, and then lunged down into my bag to slick on some lip gloss before popping back into the screen again and pressing Join Meeting. Theo was already there, as was Carla. I couldn't quite meet Theo's eye, not that it mattered because on Zoom, you couldn't tell who was looking at who, anyway.

'Guys!' exclaimed Carla, who was work-ready both in terms of make-up and attitude, despite it being only 7.30 a.m. in London.

'Hey,' I said.

'Morning,' said Theo, clearing his throat.

I still couldn't look at him.

'So I read your chapters as soon as you pinged them over yesterday morning,' she said, pausing for effect.

'And?' I said, eager to know, even if it was bad. I hoped it wouldn't be, but notes were notes and they weren't always what you wanted to hear but they were almost always for the good of the book.

'It's phenomenal!' she gushed. 'The two of you have done an outstanding job of starting this book with a bang. I couldn't stop reading it, turning page after page with no idea where the story was going but knowing I needed to find out and fast.'

I smiled to myself. The plotting had worked.

'And character-wise, what an interesting dynamic between the wife and the sister! One minute I believed everything one of them was saying, the next minute, I was totally behind the other. So multi-layered and realistic – after all, life isn't black and white, is it? We all have good bits and bad bits and you're really ensuring this comes across. Seriously guys, I'm majorly, *majorly* impressed.'

My eyes flickered to Theo's. I couldn't be certain of course, but I was sure he was looking at me, too. I smiled. He smiled back.

'I've taken the liberty of sending the first three chapters out to the list of UK and US editors I ran by you a couple of days ago, hoping to get the ball rolling. And suffice to say, a couple of them have already been in touch to say they want more of it. I think we're going to be talking about an auction here, or at the very least a lucrative early pre-empt.'

A pre-empt meant that somebody believed in it so much they wanted to offer a high advance to take it off the table. An auction involved publishers bidding each other, again pushing up the advance, sometimes by a huge amount. It was what I'd dreamed of for the last few years but hadn't quite known how to achieve. *Little Boy Lost* was acquired for a modest amount that, don't get me wrong, we'd been ecstatic about at the time. And then things had kind of exploded thanks to early word of mouth about the book and we'd ended up paying off our advances very quickly by publishing standards. But I'd always wanted the high of having a book sold at auction, and an announcement in the infamous trade magazine *The Bookseller* to shout from the rooftops about. With both of my solo books, I'd hoped *this* would be the one to get the industry excited about me again, but then the first one came out and it sold a reasonable amount, but it didn't blow my publishers away and my royalties remained average at best. And I was only assuming that sales for *The Mother-in-Law* would be much worse. But this felt different – Carla was never this enthusiastic and, more importantly, the editors she'd sent it to seemed to love it, too.

'That's great news,' said Theo. 'No pressure writing the rest of the book, then!'

'I don't care what you've been doing to create work this good. Perhaps it's even the couples retreat the two of you ended up on ...'

'It's not,' I stuttered.

'But whatever it is, keep doing it,' said Carla. 'It's working! Don't change a single thing.'

I chewed my lip, wondering whether that was going to be achievable now. Had too much been said? Had I ruined everything by bringing up the past in such detail? If I'd known this was going to happen, I would have stayed quiet until the bloody thing was written. It was just that despite my protestations to Carla, being here on the retreat, sampling therapy for the first time, *had* begun to change something inside of me. It was like I'd found my voice and suddenly I wasn't quite so afraid to use it.

'We're going to have another bestseller on our hands and it's going to be even bigger than your debut!' enthused Carla. 'I can feel it.'

Once the call had ended I didn't know what to do with myself. I paced up and down the room, feeling like I wanted to celebrate but not sure where I stood with Theo. I stared at the door between us, wondering what he was thinking, desperate to talk to him more than anybody else, but also scared to hear what he had to say. And then, as if he'd been standing on the other side of the wall, thinking much the same thing I had been, a note slid under the door right in front of my eyes. I swallowed hard, tentatively picking it up. Underneath my message about having a talk, he'd replied:

Sure. Fancy a walk on the promenade?

I grabbed a pen from the side and wrote back, attempting

to make my not-particularly-neat handwriting as legible as possible, so there could be no confusion.

See you downstairs in ten mins.

Cannes was beautiful in the early morning sun. I wondered whether that was why film stars had loved it so much through the ages, because the light was exceptionally flattering and would probably look amazing in photographs.

We walked downhill from the hotel into the centre of town, passing every shop you could imagine in Rue d'Antibes: *Zara, Fragonard, Massimo Dutti* and – my personal favourite – *Ladurée,* for macarons (I'd tried no less than five different flavours so far and wasn't intending to stop there). We made it to the beach in about fifteen minutes, turning left to walk along the front, past the back entrance to all the beach bars, including the one we'd pitched up at a few days earlier. Seagulls swooped and cawed above our heads as staff members set up for the day, placing tables and chairs out on the sand, ambient dance music already creating a breakfast beach-club scene. To our left was La Croisette and on the other side, the grand hotels I could only dream of staying in: Le Majestic, the palm-tree-flanked Carlton.

'So it went well with Carla,' I said as we passed a particularly glamorous couple wearing matching Balenciaga tracksuits. Who knew leisurewear could look so chic?

He nodded. 'You never know, really, do you, how well it's going to be received when you send it out there?'

'And Carla's tough, right? She'd tell us if it wasn't good enough.'

'There's no way she was saying any of that just to be nice. She must have meant every word,' he said, as though he was still a little bit in shock, as was I.

We walked in silence for a little while, the two of us

sporadically looking out to sea. A boat carrying some scuba divers was coming in and there were various yachts bobbing on the water further out. I wondered what kind of life these rich people had. Were they happier than I was? Would it really make my life better if I was more financially secure, like I thought it would? Or was it other things that made you truly happy? Like maintaining personal boundaries, and a good work/life balance and having fulfilling relationships in which everyone supported each other so that it wasn't just one person supporting the other time and time again.

'Looks like I might not have to urgently update my CV after all,' said Theo. 'I was beginning to worry I'd have to go back to my day job. Not sure if you remember, but I was working in a kitchen showroom when we met, and let's just say I'm not a natural salesperson ...'

I smiled to myself. 'Oh, come on, you can't have been that bad.'

'Want to bet? But on the other hand, I worked on commission, so there was some motivation to close the sale, but it was coming from a massively skewed place. I found it quite soul-destroying.'

'I'm with you on that,' I said. 'Remember my medical secretary gig?'

'Ah, yes,' he said. 'At least it got your typing speed up. I've heard you tapping away and I reckon you can probably type twice as quickly as I can.'

'Silver linings,' I said, surprised to hear Theo was worried about money, too.

I supposed it made sense – all the authors I knew were. Income was so sporadic and you could never count on anything. Occasionally something really good happened, like an unexpected foreign rights deal, and it would give your bank balance a temporary boost, but nothing could ever be planned for. I thought that sometimes I just needed to manage my money better. Or, more accurately, not use it to bail other people out when not only did it put me in a difficult position financially, but potentially it stopped them finally learning to work things out for themselves. I was thinking of Kate and Zach in particular, my not-so-little siblings, who sometimes I treated like kids who needed me, who relied on me to be a constant, a parent. But they were both nearly thirty now, and I was beginning to wonder whether it was me who had inadvertently held them back. Whether their general life skills might be less underdeveloped now if I hadn't always stepped in and made it all better for them.

'So we both need this to work, am I right?' said Theo. 'We need this book to get us a big advance and more than that, we need it to sell. We need supermarkets, we need airports. We need it all. Don't we?'

I nodded. 'Yes, exactly that.'

Theo stopped to take a photo of a huge yacht coming into the harbour.

'Want me to take one of you?' I asked, thinking that I really ought to post something on Instagram myself. After all, my day-to-day was currently about a hundred times more interesting to look at than it usually was.

'Believe it or not, I don't actually like having my photo taken,' he said, giving me a wry smile.

'Presumably you're saying believe it or not because you're phenomenally photogenic and look good in every single shot I've ever seen of you?' I said, teasing him.

'That's ... not what I meant,' he said, looking embarrassed. 'It's just that I have to post the odd shot of myself on socials because that's what people expect. But it's a part of the job I hate.'

'Although more fun than selling kitchens, presumably.'

'Well, quite. I remember feeling like working in the kitchen showroom defined me. I struggled to socialise at one point because my friends all had these careers they enjoyed and were doing well at and if we talked about me at all, even if they asked how my writing was going, I ended up feeling like a massive failure. I was quite introverted at one point, started turning invitations down, letting friendships slide, all that.'

I hid my surprise. To me he'd always seemed so popular and charismatic, and not like someone who cared what other people thought of him or his career choices.

'I'm sure they had no idea you felt that way,' I said.

He shrugged, taking another photo of the peninsula of Antibes up ahead.

'I don't think my friends thought badly of me, that's true, but it played into the narrative I told you about,' said Theo. 'The one started by my parents and made worse by my English teacher: that I wasn't good enough to make a success of being a writer. Now that I've done it, have had a taste of it, if you like, I never want to go back. Ever. It would be like they'd won.'

I stopped to look out towards the sand where a couple were holding hands, about to go in for a swim. Theo pointed at them.

'They're like our protagonists in an alternative universe where they don't hate each other and have affairs with each other's sisters,' he laughed.

'We've really got something here, haven't we, with this book?' I said.

We'd even come up with the entire plot for the second half now. Ethan's body would finally be found in a nearby reservoir. The police would arrest Caroline on suspicion of murder but would be forced to release her due to lack of evidence. And in a final showdown, Caroline's evil twin sister would try to kill her in order to keep her quiet, falling off a cliff and dying herself in the process.

'Which is what I wanted to talk to you about,' he said.

The lightness of a few moments ago was gone, blown out to sea on the breeze.

I nodded. 'Go on.'

He rubbed at his jaw. 'I've been thinking, and I reckon we should probably keep things strictly professional from here on in.'

My stomach dropped, I wasn't sure why. It felt like a rejection, I supposed, but when I took a few seconds to rationalise it, there was nothing to reject. I was in total agreement with him, and also felt like it was the most sensible way forward. So why did I feel actual, physical pain inside me, like I'd been repeatedly kicked in the guts?

'It's because of yesterday, isn't it?' I said.

He turned to face me.

'Scarlett, it's not just that. Please don't think you did anything wrong, because that's absolutely not where I'm coming from. At least we got to the bottom of what happened six years ago and we can stop blaming each other and chalk it up to bad timing and miscommunication.'

I nodded, willing myself not to look upset. There was no need. He was right, this was all for the best.

'We have a connection, there's no denying that,' said Theo, his voice softer now. 'And that kiss the other night ... I've been thinking about it. Too much, if I'm honest.'

Had he?

'It was quite something, wasn't it?' I said, smiling weakly.

'But we've got this massive opportunity,' he said. 'A second chance at the big time and I don't want to risk messing it up. Because as much as I think there might be something between us, I know myself all too well, and all the hang-ups I've discovered I've got are not suddenly going to go away overnight. And although being here with you and engaging with Melissa and the others has given me food for thought, I'm still not convinced that relationships are worth the risk. Look at everyone here, they're hardly advocates for happy, long-lasting relationships, are they?'

'No relationship runs smoothly all the time,' I said, disappointed that he felt like they should. 'But that doesn't mean it has to fail.'

'So what are you saying?' he asked.

'Nothing. I'm saying that I agree with you. That we should put the other night behind us and move on. Because for once, I need to put myself first, and that means protecting the career I love.'

He gently squeezed the top of my arm and it felt reassuring and yes, I felt a spark of something, but I knew, we both knew, now, that things couldn't go any further.

'It feels good to hear you say that,' said Theo. 'That you want this for yourself, too, not just for your family.'

'I'm trying.'

He dropped his hand. 'And I want you to know that the feelings I had for you six years ago have never totally gone away. So much so, that I went to call you a few times over the years, but always bottled it in the end. You know I dedicated my first solo book to you, right?'

'You did *what?*

He nodded. 'I wasn't brave enough to reach out, but I thought that maybe you'd see the dedication and know that you still meant something to me. And that maybe you'd be ballsier than I was and that *you'd* reach out to *me*. But by the time the book came out, Carla let slip that you were living with Jackson and I assumed you'd moved on to something that was better than what we'd had. Than anything I could ever give you.'

I dropped my eyes to the ground, overwhelmed, suddenly. He'd really done that, for me?

'I don't know what to say,' I said eventually, looking up at him.

'You'd really never seen it?' asked Theo.

I shook my head and sheepishly admitted the truth. 'I've never let myself read any of your books. It's how I deal best with feeling hurt about something – cut the source of pain out of my life completely and forever. It's the only way.'

He smiled. 'It's funny, I hated the idea of therapy at first. But it gets you thinking, doesn't it? About childhood, parents, the whole lot. And I feel like I understand myself a bit more after this week. And also, I think I understand you.'

'And at least we stopped at a kiss this time,' I said.

'Get us, making careful, considered decisions even while in the throes of lust.'

I laughed. 'My willpower is second to none.'

'You can say that again,' he said, grinning across at me.

'I liked you a lot back then,' I admitted to him, because it felt like I might as well, given that he'd been so open with me. 'And there's still something between us, I think, no matter how much I don't want there to be. But we're cut out to be writing partners, not romantic partners. And that's OK. As Carla said, we can't risk doing anything differently. Not a thing.'

Theo nodded. 'We'll write together, we'll finish the retreat, we'll focus on our careers and we won't let our feelings – whatever they are – get in the way.'

He held out his hand to shake on it.

'Deal?' he said.

'Deal,' I said, clasping his hand in mine and holding on to

it a tiny bit too long. It didn't matter because we both knew what we wanted now, and what we had to sacrifice to get it. And I pretty much ignored the fizz that ran along the length of my arm and across my chest and into my solar plexus as his fingers squeezed mine tight.

Chapter Twenty-Three

For the first time since we'd arrived, I'd given myself the morning off to relax. The book was in the back of my mind, as it always was when I was in the middle of something, but I was also reassured that we were in a good place with it, that we had our plan and that I could write quickly when I put my mind to it. I thought I deserved a few hours off to potter about. I went to the jacuzzi and balneotherapy on the roof again, I went for a walk around the local area spotting all manner of pampered pets, including a beautiful snowy white Samoyed lying in the window of an exclusive real estate agent. I went for a swim in the pool and I sat in the garden reading a book I hadn't written.

I hadn't seen much of Theo. He'd been around at breakfast, and he'd waved at me from across the dining room, but then instead of joining me he'd taken his food out to the courtyard and had sat alone, glued to his phone. And then when I was on my way back from my walk I spotted him leaving the hotel to head off for a run and we waved again. Was this how it would be now, the two of us waving at each other from afar? Because the annoying thing was, since we'd admitted that we still had feelings for each other but couldn't do anything about them, I'd been daydreaming about him even more. His beautiful eyes and chiselled jaw and muscular abs kept popping into my mind's eye at any given opportunity and adrenaline was constantly pumping through my veins in case I bumped into him and had to act like I hadn't just been imagining kissing him in the pool again (yes, that particular fantasy now recurred quite regularly).

At two o'clock we were summoned to the garden for Melissa's *Taboo Topics* class. I had no idea what the hell this was, and also thought that perhaps Theo and I should cut our losses and bow out of the retreat at this point. I was confident that I was only going to like him more as we became closer, not less. And that wasn't the plan, was it? It wasn't what we'd promised each other.

I walked across the garden to join the group who were sitting in and around the summer house at the bottom of the garden. The weather was particularly glorious and, wanting to make the most of our last couple of days in France, I'd worn a floral mini dress and flip-flops and sunglasses and my straw hat and suppressed the niggling thought that I'd made an extra effort because I wanted Theo to notice and to maybe feel a pang of regret about what might have been. I should probably have worn my baggiest leggings and a dirty T-shirt and then he wouldn't have looked at me twice, which was what I really wanted, wasn't it?

'Welcome Scarlett,' purred Melissa, directing me to a pair of sunbeds next to the orange tree where Theo was already sitting, looking devastatingly handsome as usual.

'Hi,' I said, perching on the end of the other lounger.

'Afternoon,' he replied. I couldn't help noticing that his eyes travelled down to my feet and then up and over my body until we made the most intense eye contact known to man.

I got some suncream out of my bag so that I had something to look at that wasn't him but then realised that massaging Ambre Solaire oil into my bare limbs probably wasn't the best course of action here. My nerve endings were on fire and as I stroked the oil into my shoulders, I could feel Theo actively not-watching me. At one point he put his head in his hands and I swiftly put my oil away. Bad idea.

'Right,' said Melissa. 'Taboo topics time. I am going to hand out a pack of cards to each pair. On every card, you'll find a thought-provoking question for your partner to answer. Just keep taking it in turns to pull a card until I ask you to stop.'

I glanced across at Claire who grinned at me. I'd noticed a change in her over the last couple of days and she seemed to be much more willing to get involved. Plus she and Rob were laughing more, which could only be a good thing. Meanwhile, the atmosphere between Theo and me felt different. Not in a bad way, exactly, but there was a tension in the air again that hadn't been there for a while. Perhaps having a laugh with the game would put things on an easier track again, although it would help if I could put my finger on exactly what the tension was about.

'Shall I start?' I said, picking up the cards Melissa had placed on the little table between us.

'If you have to,' said Theo, pressing a closed fist against his lips. His body language was clearly signalling to me that he did not want to be doing a talky task about feelings.

Soft French music began piping out of speakers I didn't even know existed and it would have been the perfect atmosphere for romance to blossom, except that romance was the opposite of what we were trying to achieve here. I made the decision there and then that this would be the last task we'd take part in. I opened the packet of cards, pulling one out, taking a breath before I read it.

'If you quit your job tomorrow, what would you do?'

This was good. Thinking about careers was as unsexy a

task we could hope for given the nature of the game and the fact that Melissa had come up with it.

'I'd never quit writing,' said Theo. 'If I couldn't produce novels anymore, I'd try writing something else. Perhaps I'd be a journalist. Or a poet.'

'I didn't know you wrote poetry,' I said, surprised.

'I don't,' he said. 'But never say never. Your turn,' he said, plucking a card from the pack.

He read the card through and hesitated, shifting on his lounger.

'Go ahead,' I said, although judging by the way he was squirming around it was a question that he didn't want to ask and I probably didn't want to answer.

'Is it our similarities that attract us to each other, or our differences?'

I immediately felt far too hot and began fanning myself with my hand which made not a jot of difference. How was I going to answer this?

'Um …' I said.

'Yeah,' said Theo, laughing lightly.

Maybe we could see the funny side of this.

'Well, I always thought we were very different,' I said tentatively. 'I used to admire your confidence and your single-mindedness and your ambition, all the things I felt I was lacking when I was in my twenties.'

Theo frowned. 'And now?'

'And now I think we're more similar than I'd thought. We're both afraid to let our guard down, and because I can see that in you, it makes it easier for me to not judge myself. To share things with you, but to not feel like I have to.'

'So you'd say it was our … similarities that attract you to me?' clarified Theo, looking at me hard.

'I think that's what I'm saying, yeah,' I said, although

my brain was fizzing so hard I couldn't think straight. All I could think about was his plump pink mouth and what it would feel like to run my thumb over his eyebrow and then about ripping his T-shirt clean off so that I could look at his upper body, really look at it. I shook my head, willing myself to focus on something else. Anything else.

'Your turn,' I said, pulling a card.

The words on the card burned into my retina. All I could see was the word SEX, flashing at me like a beacon.

'When you're ready,' said Theo, looking uncomfortable.

I coughed. 'OK. Brace yourself.'

He gave a terse nod.

'What non-sexual thing does your partner do that turns you on?' I asked.

The heat pulsated between us. I ran my tongue over my lips nervously. Theo seemed to be lost for words which I took as a sign that he was experiencing some of the same sensations I was. I supposed that the one thing guaranteed to create sexual tension was to decide that under no circumstances were you able to have sex with the person you desperately wanted to have sex with.

'I like the way you tuck your hair behind your ears when you're feeling anxious,' said Theo, at the exact moment I tucked a strand of hair behind my ear because I couldn't *bear* the tension and had to do something. 'And I like it when you sing in the shower.'

I swallowed. 'You cannot hear me singing in the shower.'

'I one hundred per cent can,' he said. 'Your voice is lovely.'

When I was under the shower head, steam engulfing me, I felt freer than at any other time and would sometimes imagine myself on a West End stage while I belted out my favourite show tunes. I'd always waited until I'd heard him leave his room before I jumped in the shower and crooned away to my heart's content, but I'd clearly got my timings all wrong, because he had *heard* me. Let the ground open up and swallow me immediately.

I draped one hand across my eyes. 'My humiliation is complete.'

And then Theo reached out and prised my fingers away from my face and that touch, that layering of Theo's skin on mine was too much and I let out a soft groan which he couldn't not have heard. Thankfully Melissa chose that particularly opportune moment to tinkle her bell and gather everyone together for feedback. Theo and I shot out of our seats, flushed and pretending that nothing untoward had happened. Luckily the hotel staff brought out some jugs of cucumber water that we all devoured, especially me, because I absolutely needed to cool off.

'Where are Theo and Justin going?' asked Claire, nodding towards the path leading round to the front of the hotel.

The two of them were disappearing down it and from here, it looked as though Theo was giving Justin some kind of pep talk. What were they up to?

'No idea,' I said, watching them until they were out of sight.

'How was your task?' asked Claire, refilling my water which I'd gulped down in about two seconds flat.

'Terrible,' I said. 'There was all this sexual tension.'

Claire laughed. 'Wasn't that the point?'

'For you and Rob, maybe,' I said. 'But Theo and I are supposed to be staying away from each other. We've made a pact to focus on the book and only the book. To not let any residual attraction between us get in the way.'

'But your pull towards each other is just too strong,' said Claire in a wistful voice. 'We can all see it. We can all feel it.'

I looked at her as though she was mad. 'Have you got vodka in your cucumber water?'

'No I haven't,' she said, cracking up. 'But it's obvious you want to rip each other's clothes off. Maybe you should just do it and get it out of your system and then you'd be able to concentrate on your book.'

'That's a terrible idea!' I screeched.

And anyway, it wouldn't work because I already knew that once wouldn't be enough. I knew how it felt to have sex with Theo and it wasn't a getting something out of your system kind of experience, it was a *I want this more and more every single day three times a day* sort of situation.

'Oh look, here they are,' said Claire.

Theo and Justin were heading back in our direction.

'What have you guys been up to?' I asked, squinting at Theo with suspicion as he came to stand next to me.

'You'll find out,' he said mysteriously.

Justin was now wearing a gorgeous navy blue designer suit that I was sure I'd seen Theo wear to a book event once. I watched as he walked up to Renee holding two glasses of champagne and handed one to her. Renee laughed nervously and looked quizzically over at me.

'What's going on?' I whispered to Theo.

'This is Justin being romantic,' he replied. 'Watch and learn.'

'Is that your suit he's wearing?'

'Might be.'

My eyes were drawn to the couple again as Justin asked Renee to accompany him to dinner in Monte Carlo that evening and revealed that they'd be travelling by helicopter. Everyone clapped and whooped, including me, and Renee, who looked over the moon.

'Did you help him put this together?' I asked Theo,

watching Justin lead a delighted Renee up to their room to get changed.

Theo shrugged. 'I simply helped him think about what romance meant to Renee. He reckoned it was grand gestures and a touch of princess glamour, so we came up with the Monte Carlo idea. Apparently there's a film set there that she loves.'

'Well, I'm very impressed,' I said.

'Good, because believe it or not I do have romantic thoughts of my own every now and again.'

I looked at him, scrutinising every part of his face. 'I guess I'll never know.'

My left hand was hanging by my side and whether it was him or me who moved I didn't know, but I felt my fingertips brush against his. It felt achingly good to touch him again, but this was the best I could hope for now, I supposed: the occasional brush up against each other, the odd lingering look. Nothing more, not now, not ever.

'We can't do this, Scarlett,' said Theo in a low, gravelly voice.

'I know,' I managed to stutter, tearing my hand away. 'It's OK. I understand.'

But although I could never admit it to him, I thought I might be the smallest bit heartbroken that we'd decided it was over before it had even begun.

Chapter Twenty-Four

'We must stay in touch,' said Claire, pulling a pen and paper out of her bag and scribbling a number and her email address on it. 'Here. Message me when we're all back. I need regular Theo and Scarlett updates to brighten up my otherwise very dull existence.'

I snorted. 'There'll be no updates to impart. Once the book's done, I probably won't see him again for dust.'

'You will. You'll have to do a book tour together, at the very least. That'll be romantic,' said Claire wistfully.

It was the penultimate day of the retreat and the nine of us had met up at a quaint traditional French restaurant in the old town for a farewell dinner. We'd been seated on the cobbled terrace of the restaurant, underneath a red awning. The tables were jauntily adorned with checked tablecloths and votive candles and it felt authentic and chic in a way that was both enticing and slightly intimidating because the menu was in French, the other patrons were French and the chalk board displayed words I'd never seen before in my life. I was going to have to use Google translate at this rate.

Once we'd all ordered – pan-fried salmon with potato dauphinoise for me, lamb shank for Theo and pasta with garlic for Claire – Melissa cleared her throat and tinkled her glass with the side of her knife, demanding our attention.

'Before we drink too much wine, I wanted to thank you all from the bottom of my heart for attending my couples retreat and for wholeheartedly throwing yourselves into everything I have asked of you. I hope that you've enjoyed it – although I realise that "enjoy" might be pushing it! – and that you feel that you've got something useful from everything we've shared together. Why don't we all say a few words about what we've discovered about ourselves and our partners over the course of the last ten days?'

Paul and Harmony, ever eager, went first with an overly saccharine account of how being here on the retreat had made them realise that they both needed to change, and that they had made a pact that things were going to be different when they returned to California. Paul was going to cut his hours a little, apparently, and Harmony was going to stop resorting to threats and find other ways to communicate her feelings to Paul.

Renee and Justin, fresh from their trip to Monte Carlo, were holding hands and beaming at each other. Justin vowed to keep finding ways to surprise Renee, and Renee was going to work on accepting that life doesn't have to be perfect all of the time, and neither does her boyfriend.

'And I'm done with the helicopter rides,' Justin jokily warned her, cracking up the table.

Claire and Rob went next and Claire recounted how she and her husband had found a newfound appreciation for each other and had remembered what they loved about each other. Rob admitted he needed to stop being so stagnant and start getting out of the house more, and Claire acknowledged that she wants to learn to appreciate the quiet times together and agreed to give Rob the space he sometimes needed.

'Theo and Scarlett, did you want to say a few words?' asked Melissa, looking at us hopefully.

As hosting a couples retreat went, we'd probably been the

participants from hell: didn't want to be there? Check. Not actually a couple? Check. Reluctant to talk about any actual feelings? Check, check, check.

'Scarlett, why don't you start. Let's hear how you've grown over the last ten days,' said Melissa kindly.

I looked at Theo, garnering strength from the kind, solid way he looked at me and the fact that I knew that despite everything, we'd been in this together.

'I've learned a lot about myself, actually. A surprising amount,' I said to the group who were watching me, clearly enthralled by the mini soap opera that had been playing out in front of their eyes every day for the last week and a half. Claire had declared that it was because of the will they/won't they element to our relationship, which I'd thought had all been in my head, but had clearly been obvious to absolutely everyone.

'For a start, I've come to the conclusion that I need to stop trying to be everything for everyone. I've realised that it's OK to put boundaries in place – around my time, especially – and around when I'm available on the phone – thank you for enforcing that, Melissa,' I said, making everyone laugh. 'I can even accept that I need to put myself first now and again. And in a way it's Theo who has made me see that, finally.'

I turned to face him, taking strength from his encouraging smile and the warmth of his eyes sparkling in the candlelight. 'So thank you, Theo.'

'Very good, Scarlett. That is amazing growth and hopefully you can continue to build on these foundations when you return home,' said Melissa. 'What about you, Theo?'

Theo was calm and still next to me, which was different for him. He wasn't squirming uncomfortably like he might once have done at the first sniff of having to open up.

'As you may have realised, I'm not usually one to talk about emotions,' he said. 'But it's been surprisingly cathartic to think about some of the difficulties I've had in the past.'

There was a collective rumble as people agreed with him.

'But as for romance, and I know that's what some of you were hoping for from Scarlett and me, we've made the decision to focus exclusively on our book from now on. We've got a huge career opportunity here and in order not to put that at risk, we have decided to keep our relationship strictly professional.'

I looked around the table. There were a few disappointed faces, one or two sceptical looks. Claire patted my knee in solidarity.

'It's what works best,' I said, supporting Theo's statement and willing myself to believe it at the same time.

'The book has to come first,' added Theo.

For a second it felt as though we were trying to convince ourselves more than the table, the entirety of which was looking at us as though we were about to change our minds right in front of their eyes. They must all be romantics at heart – they were here on a couples retreat, weren't they? Perhaps relationships were the most important thing to them and careers took second place, but it wasn't like that for Theo and me. We had the job of our dreams and the stakes were high and a messy on/off romance was one hundred per cent not on the agenda.

Luckily, our entrées were promptly served with a flourish and the table was suddenly full of steaming plates of pasta and fish glistening with olive oil and baskets of crusty bread and another bottle of Bordeaux that somebody had ordered. I was just about to tuck in when my phone rang.

Melissa gave me a jokey stern look

'I have been leaving it my room, honestly!' I insisted.

I was tempted to leave it ringing anyway – I did that quite a lot lately – but I'd texted Dad an hour or so ago and he hadn't replied yet. That wasn't massively unusual – the carer might be there and he'd be in the shower or eating dinner. But until I'd heard back from him I couldn't properly relax. I grabbed my phone from my bag. It was Kate. Without thinking I answered it, assuming she'd have some innocuous question about lawyers and that I'd be able to cut her short.

'Hey,' I said. 'I'm just out to dinner, can it wait?'

'Dad's had a fall,' she said, her voice light and breathy in a way I'd never heard it before.

I scraped back my chair and left the table immediately, pressing my finger against my ear to block out the sounds of other people having a good time when suddenly I wasn't.

'What happened?' I asked her.

'We're not sure. The carer found him. She thinks he'd been trying to get upstairs.'

My heart was hammering in my chest and my mouth had instantly gone gravelly and dry. I licked my lips.

'How is he?'

Kate hesitated for a second; enough time for me to assume the worst.

'He's dead, isn't he?' I said, my eyes filling with tears out of nowhere. It was like a tap had been turned on: all the worry and fear that something bad would happen had come to a head and was suddenly pouring out of me like an erupting volcano.

'He's not dead, for God's sake, Scarlett. Trust you to jump straight to the worst case scenario. He's in hospital, yes, but he's conscious and hasn't broken anything as far as they can tell. They're keeping him in for a few days for observation.'

'Oh,' I said, sniffing and wiping my running nose on the only available surface: the sleeve of my Breton top.

'Are you *crying*?' asked Kate, clearly incredulous that I was capable of demonstrating such vulnerability.

I went to deny it and then thought: Why should I?

'Yes,' I said. 'Yes, I am. I really thought you were going to tell me he'd died.'

I didn't think Kate knew what to say to that as she'd gone completely silent. How to render my sister mute: talk about my feelings instead of hers.

I turned to look back at the restaurant to see Theo striding towards me with his napkin flapping about in his hand. He rushed up to me, holding both of my shoulders, gripping them tight.

'What's happened? Is it your dad?'

I nodded, my face threatening to crumple into tears again. Bawling in front of Theo would not be my reaction of choice, shock or no shock.

'He's OK,' I mouthed. 'He had a fall, but he's all right.'

Theo mimed being relieved and I ended the call with Kate, letting her know that I'd be home as soon as I could, probably tomorrow morning now as I doubted I'd get a flight tonight. I suggested to Kate that she ought to be at the hospital with Dad, but of course she made some excuse about having her book club group round and not being able to cancel.

'What about Zach?' I asked. 'Can he get himself down there?'

'I'll ring him, but I can't guarantee he'll go,' she said.

'Well one of you is going to have to be with Dad at the hospital and I don't care which one!' I stated with conviction.

'Fine. But seriously, Scarlett, I don't know how you put up with him, you must have the patience of a saint to do everything you do. He's just so difficult all the time! So *negative*.'

'I know.'

I got it, of course I did, but he was our dad and we loved him so we had no choice but to carry on.

'I'll be there as soon as I can. But until then it's up to you two to take charge,' I reiterated.

Once I'd put the phone down, Theo looked at me with concern.

'Do you need to get home?'

I nodded, wiping a stray tear from the corner of one eye and hoping to God that Theo hadn't noticed. The familiar tug of guilt was in danger of engulfing me, showing me all the things I'd done wrong, all the ways I'd contributed to Dad's accident: I was too far away, I should never have left the country, I should be in Cambridge sorting everything out for everyone. I shouldn't be in the South of France having a nice time with nice people, one in particular. I'd got carried away out here, imagining that I could have a normal kind of life with a reasonable amount of freedom and the independence to do what I wanted with who I wanted when I wanted. I'd let my guard down and now look what had happened.

Theo slid his own phone out of his back pocket.

'I'll find you a flight,' he said, tapping on his keypad.

'I can do that,' I said, not wanting to put him out or – more importantly – for him to think I'd fallen apart and therefore couldn't manage to do any of this by myself.

'I'm perfectly aware that you can do it, Scarlett,' said Theo, his voice soft and soothing, 'but you have other things to get on with, I imagine. So let me do this one thing for you. Let me make things a little bit easier.'

I almost told him no, that I didn't need him, that he should go back to the dinner table and enjoy his meal. But there were new feelings in the mix, too: a realisation that he had noticed me and had picked up on the fact that I was momentarily struggling. That he was prepared to help me without question and that it didn't mean I was any less of a capable person. And wouldn't I have done the same for him, or anyone around that table? Of course I would have done, in a heartbeat. And so I let him google flights from Nice to London while I called Dad's local hospital, Addenbrookes. I managed to get through to the ward he was on and they told me he was comfortable and sleeping and that visiting times were the following day now, 2 p.m. until 8 p.m. I asked them to give him a message from me when he woke up: that I'd be there as soon as I could, that I was on my way and not to worry. And then, without over-thinking it, I texted Kate. She was probably fed up with me saying the same thing about three times, but I wanted to make sure she understood that for once she was going to have to be the one to step up.

Kate, Dad is sleeping now but somebody needs to get there at 2 p.m. sharp tomorrow to be with him. Either you or Zach. No excuses, he needs you.

I took a deep breath and pressed send, immediately, ignoring the feeling that I needed to add an addendum, something about me being there as soon as I could. If she knew I was on my way, she'd be likely to wait for me to swoop in and fix the situation, which was how our dynamic pretty much always played out. But the fact remained that Dad needed at least one of his children with him and if it couldn't be me, it would have to be one of the other grown adults he and Mum had produced.

'There's a BA flight tomorrow morning at 10.40 a.m., gets you into Heathrow at 11.45 a.m. UK time. Shall I book you a seat?' asked Theo, getting his credit card out of his pocket.

I'd pay him back, of course I would, but for now it felt

unbelievably good that he was here and that he was doing this for me. I smiled gratefully at him.

'Yes, please.'

Chapter Twenty-Five

The following morning at eight o'clock, Claire walked me out to the waiting taxi. Melissa came rushing out to say goodbye, too, pressing her card into my hand.

'I do individual therapy, too,' she said, winking at me.

I hugged her and Claire and when I looked up, Theo was there, looking all French Riviera chic in a Lacoste polo shirt and blue jeans and the suede desert boots he'd worn every day since we'd been here. I waved to Claire and Melissa as they rather unsubtly crept back into the hotel, presumably wanting to leave us to it.

'Did you get some sleep?' he asked.

I shook my head. 'Not much. Don't tell me you can hear me tossing and turning in bed as well as singing in the shower.'

He laughed. 'I just assumed. News like that isn't usually conducive to sleep.'

Picking up my suitcase for me, he put it in the boot of the taxi, slamming it shut again afterwards.

'I'm sorry to leave so suddenly,' I said. 'I haven't even had time to send you my latest couple of chapters.'

'Scarlett,' he said, touching me lightly on the arm. 'It doesn't matter. We can pick the book up again at any time, once your dad's better.'

'But I wouldn't want us to lose momentum,' I said anxiously.

'We won't,' he reassured me.

'Anyway, writing is just about the only thing that keeps me sane. If I'm going to be in Cambridge for the foreseeable future, I'm going to need to keep working,' I said, knowing that I wouldn't be able to get home to my flat in London any time soon. That I'd have to go straight to see Dad, with summery clothes and a bunch of inappropriate shoes in my suitcase.

'Let's stay in touch. By phone, or Zoom. Just let me know when you're ready for a call and we'll touch base, work out our next steps,' he said.

It felt strange to be separating, even though we would have been going home the day after tomorrow, anyway. I didn't like leaving things unfinished and our book was full of loose ends and not yet complete. Would we really work so well on it back home, miles apart, the sun and spirit of Cannes long forgotten?

'Stop worrying,' he said. 'I can see your mind ticking over, thinking that we won't end up finishing the book.'

I smiled. 'I never knew you could read minds.'

'I'm a man of many talents,' he teased. 'Seriously, though. Let's carry on sending each other chapters, just like we have been. I know it won't feel the same – I quite liked knowing you were next door, typing away at a rate of knots. It was inspiring. Stopped me procrastinating, which I have a tendency to do.'

The taxi driver stuck his head out of the window.

'You are ready, *Madame*?'

'*Oui*,' I said, opening the passenger door.

I turned to Theo.

'Thank you, by the way.'

'For what?' he asked.

'For helping me. With the flights. With my writing. With working out what needs to change in my life.'

He nodded. 'And thanks to you, I'm starting to see that conflict doesn't always have to be avoided at all costs. I think that's the biggest message I'm taking away from all of this.'

'Glad to be of assistance,' I told him.

He shook his head, smiling down at me. 'I never expected any of this when I got on that flight in London. In fact, I almost didn't get on it.'

I shuddered at the thought. It had all rested on both of us having the guts to turn up. If we hadn't, there'd have been no book. And we wouldn't be in each other's lives again, in any capacity at all. And I wouldn't have met Claire, who I hoped would be a friend for life. Nor would I have realised the importance of standing up for myself and working out what *I* needed. It had been an invaluable ten days all in all, a period of time I would never forget, no matter how things panned out afterwards.

'Is hugging part of the deal?' he asked, holding his arms out for me.

I walked into them, closing my eyes as he wrapped his arms around me and pulled me closer. I breathed in the familiar scent of him, my cheek resting against the soft cotton of his shirt, his heart beating so hard I could hear it. I didn't want to let him go.

'Have a safe flight back,' he whispered into my ear, his warm breath skimming my skin.

I peeled myself away from him, getting into the car, slamming the door shut.

'I'll call you,' I shouted out of the window as the taxi rolled out of the driveway, turning down the steep, orange tree-lined hill towards central Cannes.

Chapter Twenty-Six

Carla's name popped up on my phone and I sighed with resignation. I'd managed to avoid speaking to her since I'd been back in the UK, partly because I hadn't had time and partly because I hadn't told her about Dad. I didn't want her thinking I was going to go off the boil now I had stuff going on. I needed her to believe in me, and to want to sell the book as passionately as she had when she first read our chapters a few days ago. She wasn't the type of person to let personal issues get in the way of her work and although things weren't quite so cut and dried for me, it didn't mean that I wasn't going to deliver what I'd promised.

'Hi Carla,' I said brightly, trying to sound like the sort of writer who was totally in control of every aspect of her life.

'Scarlett! Are you back on British soil?'

'I am indeed,' I said.

'Want to schedule in a lunch?' she asked. 'I need to hear all about the retreat. I bet it was a melting pot of ideas. All those couples with marital problems screaming blue murder at each other.'

'It wasn't really like that,' I said, feeling the need to defend the people I'd spent the last week and a bit getting to know. 'They were actually very nice.'

'So, lunch?' said Carla, who had clearly lost interest already.

'I'm in Cambridge for a few days, actually,' I told her,

deciding I had nothing to hide. Surely she'd be sympathetic when she heard what was going on, and even if she wasn't, what could she possibly do about it?

'What on earth are you doing all the way up there?' asked Carla with an air of disgust.

'It's, like, fifty miles from London,' I said.

Carla was one of those people for whom the world revolved exclusively around the capital.

'Is everything all right? That's where your family are from, isn't it?' she asked.

'My dad's had a fall. But he's doing well. I'm just hanging around for a bit while he's still in hospital.'

Carla left it a beat or two. 'I do hope he's on the mend.'

Wait for it. I knew she would be dying to ask whether this was having an impact on my writing. And actually, it wasn't. Traditionally when I was staying at my dad's, I'd struggle to write anything decent because I felt paralysed with the weight of responsibility and instantly reverted to being a sad little nine-year-old girl/carer/surrogate mother. But this time, I'd felt differently. Possibly because my dad was being very well looked after elsewhere, but also because I thought my attitude had changed. And because I believed in this book and was actually enjoying writing my half of it, which was a welcome distraction from everything else going on.

'I hate to ask, but I've got editors chasing me almost every day asking about chapters. Do you know when you and Theo are intending to finish your first draft?' asked Carla.

Do not promise something you can't deliver, I told myself. It was something I did a lot, particularly with publishing types: I'd agree to something, a deadline I knew was tight, and then I'd burn myself out trying to meet it. But what would happen if I didn't do that? Was it feasible that I had every right to say no now and again? Nobody would get angry with me, surely, and even if they did, could I bear that? Could I stand my ground and say that more time was what I needed – within reason – and to hell with everyone else?

'We haven't got a definite date in mind,' I told her, finding a compromise. 'But we're plugging away on our chapters and we're in regular contact.'

'Hmmmn,' said Carla.

This clearly wasn't the answer she was looking for.

'I'm already under pressure with my dad in hospital, so I don't feel like giving myself the extra stress of an impending deadline. Sorry. But I do think Theo and I are still working well together. We've made progress since we sent you the chapters and we'll keep on making progress. Does that sound OK?'

I swallowed hard, not quite believing I was speaking to Carla so directly. I was usually terrified of upsetting her – I'd witnessed her shouting and screaming at people down the phone many a time and had never wanted to be on the receiving end of it. But today I'd decided to put mine and my dad's wellbeing and sanity ahead of trying to meet a deadline that simply wasn't achievable.

'No problem,' said Carla, sounding surprised. 'And thank you for being honest with me. Just keep me in the loop.'

'Of course,' I said. 'Now I'd better head off because I've got a Zoom call with Theo in five minutes.'

'Fine. Go,' said Carla. And then, just as I was about to hang up: 'Oh, and Scarlett? I'm very pleased that you and Theo are back on speaking terms. I never did know what happened the first time around, but you both seem much happier with each other in your lives. I hope the time away together was helpful. It certainly sounds like it was.'

With the Zoom to Theo about to start, I popped to the bathroom to tidy myself up. A dab of blusher and a smear of lipstick later and I was looking much more Zoom-ready, but also not as though I was trying too hard.

Theo, clearly a stickler for time-keeping, was already on the call waiting for me when I logged on. I'd plonked myself in front of the most bookish backdrop I could find, the bookcase in the hall that still housed some of the all-time favourite reads from my youth: *Anne of Green Gables, Rebecca, Pride and Prejudice*. I used to love the classics and had devoured them late at night, when I finally got to bed and had an undisturbed hour to myself before I nodded off, unless Kate woke having one of her nightmares and I had to go into her little box room and comfort her. She'd often cry out for our mum, which had been hard. What nine-year-old would know what to say in a situation like that? Which person, in fact, because there *were* no words of comfort when you were five and the person you loved most in the world wasn't there anymore.

'Hey,' said Theo, his lovely face filling my screen.

'Hello,' I said, grinning at the sight of him.

'How's your dad?' he asked, leaning forward as if he was trying to transport himself through the screen and into my hallway.

'Better. They've got him up and out of bed. He'll probably be home the day after tomorrow.'

'That's great news,' he said. 'Are you planning to hang around for a bit? Settle him back in?'

'Think so.'

I wanted to, of course I did. I wasn't just going to abandon him. But I also wanted to get back to London. I hadn't set eyes on my flat for over two weeks now, and I wanted to take advantage of my new determination to leave some things for Kate and Zach to deal with. If I wasn't around, they'd have to manage. I was planning to talk to them about it before Dad was discharged, but even getting them together in the same room to have the conversation seemed like an impossible task. How two people who currently had zero work commitments could be so busy all the time, I had no idea.

'Thanks for sending your next couple of chapters through,' said Theo. 'I thought they were brilliant, particularly the one leading into Ethan's body being found. There's a real shift in atmosphere from page one-fifteen onwards.'

'You don't think there's too much exposition?' I asked him. I sometimes had a tendency to throw in a ton of clunky information that I thought the reader needed to know rather than organically weaving it into the story.

'Not in my opinion. And your dialogue is spot on,' he said.

'Yours too, actually,' I said, looking at the print-out of the chapters he'd posted me because he knew I liked hard copies and that I didn't have a printer up here. 'I've marked up all the bits I really like with a pink highlighter. See, there's loads of them?' I said, holding a handful of pages up to the screen.

He looked pleased, until his phone rang and he glanced at the screen.

'Scarlett, sorry, do you mind if I take this?'

'No, go for it,' I said, immediately wondering what could be so urgent.

Theo turned off his camera, but his microphone flickered off then on again, so that although he probably thought he'd muted himself, I could actually hear every word he was saying.

Amanda, hi.

Yes. Seven o'clock on Wednesday would be perfect.
Can you message me your full address?
Lovely. I look forward to seeing you then.

My stomach dropped as I tried to read between the lines. He was going on a date on Wednesday, wasn't he, it was obvious? Under the table, I played with my fingernails – the beauty of Zoom was that I didn't have to show him the turmoil that was happening inside my head. The conversation had sounded a little stilted. Stilted but friendly. Meaning it was probably a new thing – their first date? It might not go anywhere, not that that mattered, because then there'd be other women, there always were. After all, what did I expect, that he was just going to sit around at home on his own? Just because that was what I was doing, just because going back on the dreaded dating apps hadn't even crossed my mind, didn't mean he had to do things the same way. So I brazened it out when he came back on screen and we chatted about the book for a bit longer and then we ended the call on a nice note. Of course I spent the rest of the night imagining him wining and dining some beautiful, talented woman who he would fall for on their Wednesday at 7 p.m. date while he forgot all about me.

I slept on it and felt mildly better the next morning. I'd managed to convince myself that it would be easier to get over him if he was dating somebody else, anyway. It would be out of my hands then, wouldn't it? There would be no more lingering looks between us or tentative touching of fingertips and then the unbearable pulling back on both sides. We'd know where we stood. And I could focus on myself and on the changes I wanted to make to my life. That thought spurred me on and I picked up my phone, finally texting my brother back about the uni accommodation.

Zach, sorry it took me so long to reply to your message, I was away with work and then there's all the stuff with Dad. Things are a bit up in the air at the moment with my books. I might be changing publishers, and I'm scrapping the book I was working on originally. I've got your course fees covered, but in terms of living arrangements etc. I think it's best if you sort that out yourself. Hope everything is well. Dad would love to see you x

Then, keen to strike while I was in a feisty mood, I called Kate, who as usual immediately launched into a rant about what terrible things Richard had done that week.

'He's refusing to give me any spending money,' she moaned. 'It's like he's using cash to control me because he knows I need it and he's going to make me beg for it.'

There had been something I'd been wanting to say to Kate for quite some time now but was so busy playing the ubiquitous comforting-big-sister role that I'd never quite got the words out. But enough was enough. I didn't think I could listen to another single conversation about Kate not having any money of her own.

'You could always get a job,' I said. 'Now the kids are at school. Something part-time, maybe?'

There, it was out there. She wasn't going to like it and for possibly the first time in my life, I really didn't care.

'But I've got the school run. How's that supposed to work?'

'I don't know. After school clubs or something. Lots of parents make it work.'

'And who's going to employ me, anyway? I barely scraped my A levels as you well know.'

Kate was throwing obstacles in the way thick and fast but I was not going to be defeated, not this time.

'There'll be something. What kind of industry are you interested in? Maybe narrow it down,' I suggested.

I could practically hear Kate spluttering at the injustice of it all. *A job? Her?!*

'I've never even thought about it.'

'Well maybe you should. Because then at least you wouldn't be relying on Richard to give you money. I think you'd feel a lot better about everything, actually, if you were a bit more independent financially.'

It felt good to tell her what was on my mind and to give her a few home truths. I had no idea why I'd never done it before.

'I suppose,' said Kate, sounding doubtful.

'Oh, and Dad's coming home the day after tomorrow,' I told her, on a roll now. 'I'll stick around for a few days, but after that you and Zach are going to have to take over. He's lost a bit of his confidence, as I'm sure you noticed the one time you visited him. So we need to build that back up. Let him know that he's doing really well and that he's capable of living by himself again, even if it feels difficult at times.'

And then instead of waiting for Kate to make excuses as to why she couldn't possibly get involved with Dad's care, I swiftly ended the call. I thought of Melissa and my friends on the retreat and Theo and about how we'd shared more of ourselves with each other than we had with our own families. And I missed them all in that moment, but especially Theo. And I didn't know what that meant and it was probably best that I didn't think too deeply about it, but I acknowledged it and then I sat down at my laptop, opened my work in progress and got back to my writing.

Chapter Twenty-Seven

Dad was more difficult than ever once he'd been discharged from hospital and was back home, and he had me running up and down the stairs finding this and fetching that. I cooked him all his favourite lunches and dinners but even that wasn't good enough. It felt like there was something on his mind, but of course he wasn't talking about it – supressing emotion clearly ran in the family. Making the decision to tackle it head-on, I made him a cup of tea and sat next to him on the sofa.

'Is everything all right, Dad?' I ventured.

'Can't imagine why it wouldn't be,' he grumbled.

'You seem a little … on edge,' I said gently. 'Is something worrying you?'

He did a huge, earth shuddering sigh. 'No more than usual.'

'You're sure? Because it must have been a bit of a shock, falling like that.'

'Why do you care? You'll be going back to London soon, won't you?'

Ah. Reading between the lines, he didn't want me to go and was nervous about what would happen when I did. But I also knew that as bad as I might feel about it, I had to get on with my own life. I was happy to speak to him every day and to organise things and do the usual admin for him, but I also needed to get back to London where I felt like I belonged.

'I'm writing a new book, Dad,' I said. 'Do you remember? With Theo Winters. I mentioned it before I left for France. We wrote *Little Boy Lost* together.'

'Hmmmn,' said Dad. 'Where are you going to find the time to look after me, then, if you're off writing another novel?'

'Dad, I'm really enjoying writing this book. And it's creating quite a buzz in the industry, apparently, which is not only good for me, but for us.'

'Fine. Go for it, then.'

Ploughing on, I decided to broach the subject of how difficult things had been for me when Mum died, a subject I'd only ever skirted around in the past.

'You know, I had to give up quite a lot when I was a child, Dad. I'm not sure if you remember, but you weren't yourself when Mum went, and Kate and Zach were too young to really know what was going on. I became a sort of substitute mother in a way, or at least that was what I felt I had to be. Not that I could ever live up to what Mum did for us all, of course, but I felt this constant pressure to try.'

'What are you getting at?' said Dad.

'I want you to know that I don't regret a single moment of it, and that I'd do it again in a heartbeat. But I'm not a kid anymore, I'm a grown woman with my own needs and my own desire to make something of my own life and to be happy. And so I want you to know that I'll always be here for you, for as long as you need me, but that also sometimes I might not be able to be as present as you might want me to be. And I'm going to speak to Kate and Zach about this, because I really need them to pull their weight a bit more. Does that sound fair?'

I had no idea how he was going to take any of this and winced internally as I waited to find out.

'All right. You've made your point,' he said gruffly.

Well, that could definitely have been worse. Maybe he needed some time for it all to sink in.

'We can chat about this some other time if you're not in the mood now,' I said, standing up and going back to the kitchen again. As I put the milk and sugar away I felt a bit tearful for some reason. This opening-up business wasn't easy, was it? Was this how people like Melissa and Harmony functioned, constantly teetering on the edge of bawling their eyes out? In some ways, I missed the emotional flatness of what I'd had before. But then I knew that I'd be missing out on leading a truly full and meaningful life if I continued to keep everyone at arm's length like I had been, and kept having relationships like the one I'd had with Jackson, to whom I didn't feel particularly connected, not really, but stayed with because I thought it might be marginally better than being on my own. I picked up my phone, scrolling through the messages Jackson had sent me that morning. It had been the strangest thing, particularly as we'd barely spoken since I'd moved out of the flat we'd shared a few months ago. He'd heard on the grapevine that Theo and I were working on something together.

I'm not sure it's a great idea to write with Theo Winters again. It could be a huge mistake for your career.

I'd read over it with confusion, trying to work out the context. Wondering why he cared so much. Was it an ego thing? Because he hadn't exactly seemed devastated when we broke up, but he knew Theo and I had once had a thing and maybe he'd assumed there was more to it than just the writing.

What makes you say that?

While I waited for him to reply I checked Theo's Instagram. When we'd first got back he'd posted a montage

318

of shots of Cannes, including one of the two of us working by the pool that Claire had taken, but there'd been nothing since. Suddenly I was craving pictures of him. I wanted to see his face again, even if it was a heavily filtered version of it on a small phone screen. Another message pinged through from Jackson.

You're never going to recreate the success of your first. And have you read his books lately?

I knew Jackson was forever slagging off other authors' work, but this was just plain unnecessary. He didn't 'do' commercial and I doubted very much he'd even read Theo's novels.

Theo is a brilliant writer and we work exceptionally well together. You've heard there's a lot of buzz about our book, presumably, otherwise you wouldn't have messaged me out of the blue like this?

I'd jabbed at the keypad, irritated now.

I could help you write something. Something more credible.

This was laughable. We had completely different writing styles and he'd never shown one iota of interest in us collaborating before.

Jackson, you're entitled to your own opinion, but I'm quite capable of making my own decisions, thank you.

I stared at my phone, tempted to delete his messages one by one but then deciding to save them in case I needed a reminder of my newfound assertiveness and how I needed to keep it up. And then the doorbell rang.

'Who's that?' called Dad, muting *Pointless* on the TV.

'Not sure,' I said, putting my phone on the kitchen counter and heading out to answer the door. It was most likely the Tesco delivery I'd ordered. I padded into the hallway and casually flung open the front door expecting a guy in a blue uniform brandishing crates of food.

There wasn't much light in Dad's hallway, so it took a second or two for my eyes to get accustomed to the brightness of outside and to acknowledge that it wasn't a delivery driver standing in front of me, it was Theo.

Shocked, I instinctively took a step back.

'Sorry, I didn't mean to scare you,' he said, smiling at me and also looking a bit nervous.

'You didn't,' I said, my body flooding with giddiness, confusion and an unexpected sense of relief.

'I thought I'd come and visit you, since you can't get down to London at the moment,' he said, shuffling about on the doorstep.

I smiled, leaning against the doorframe.

'You really did that? For me?'

'Now don't get panicky,' said Theo, holding out his hands. 'I know you don't need help and that you're perfectly capable of coping with all of this on your own. I just thought it might be nicer if you didn't have to. And also, selfishly, I miss writing with you around.'

This was too much.

'Have I done the wrong thing?' he asked, seemingly doubting himself suddenly.

'Definitely not,' I said. And then I had a panic that he would want to stay here and upstairs was a mess and the spare room was full of Dad's stuff and there were no spare sheets to even make up the sofa.

'Oh, and I'm in a hotel,' he said, as if reading my mind again. 'In town. The one down by the river with all the punts on the walls.'

'The Graduate?' I asked, relieved. Not because I didn't want to spend time with him, but because I didn't particularly want to spend time with him here. I wanted him to myself, I realised, away from all the family stress. And I realised now, looking at him, that I'd been deluding myself into thinking that I could just be his writing partner. If I was honest with myself, it had been more than that with us from the very beginning.

'That's the one,' he said.

I beamed at him. He'd come all the way to Cambridge (now I sounded like Carla!) for me. And whether it was as a friend or something else, I couldn't tell yet, but I wanted it to be more. There, I'd admitted it to myself. And perhaps later I would admit it to him.

'I'd like to take you out for dinner. If you want. If you can get away,' he said.

I nodded, a little too enthusiastically, probably, but I didn't care.

'I'd love that.'

'Good,' he said.

'Would you want to come in?'

He ran his hand through his slightly less-voluminous-than-usual hair. 'I don't want to intrude.'

'Oh, you're not,' I said, standing aside to let him into the hallway.

As I closed the door behind him, my arm brushed against his sleeve. In the darkness of the hallway we stood very close together for a second; very still. I could hear his breath and mine. I imagined sliding into his arms again, like I had when I'd said goodbye to him in Cannes, his body pressing into mine. Feeling safe, wanted, enough. I'd always secretly longed for someone – anyone! – to notice that I was struggling and to volunteer their help, despite me insisting I didn't need it. And Theo had done that, without me having to ask. Without me even realising that he was exactly what I needed all along.

'Scarlett? Who is it?' shouted Dad, not used to visitors arriving unannounced.

I beckoned Theo after me down the hallway.

'Dad, there's someone I want you to meet!' I called out, smiling at Theo over my shoulder.

'I'm honoured,' said Theo, following me.

'Just to warn you, my family can be quite dramatic,' I said, keeping my voice low. 'There might be some shouting at some point.'

'I think I can deal with that.'

'And crying?'

He winced. 'Really?'

'You'll be fine,' I said, ushering him into the lounge.

Later, we sat on leather bar stools around the stunning 1920s-style circular bar on the ground floor of Theo's hotel. He ordered us an Aperol Spritz each.

'A nod to Cannes,' he said when they arrived, clinking my glass.

'And to our reunion,' I said, clinking again for good measure.

Dad had been surprisingly upbeat in Theo's presence, clearly pleased to have a new face to talk to. While the two of them sat on the sofa and chatted about their shared lifelong adoration of Manchester United, I scrolled through the latest series of texts from my siblings – and for once they didn't make me want to tear my hair out. Zach had eventually responded positively to my message.

I hear you about your writing. Pretty unpredictable, huh? No worries, I'll sort housing out myself.

And a text from Kate had been similarly mind-boggling.

I've been thinking about your suggestion that I should get a part-time job and I've decided I'm going to train to

be a court clerk. That way I can tap up all the lawyers I meet
for free divorce advice!

I sipped at my Aperol Spritz.

'I have thanked you for coming up here to see me, haven't I?' I said with mock confusion.

'I believe you have, yes, several times.'

I took a slow breath in, quietening the butterflies in my stomach.

'There was something I've been meaning to ask you, actually,' I said.

'Anything.'

I took a second, thinking about the promise I'd made to myself to be honest with people from here on in, and especially to be honest with Theo.

'Are you seeing someone?'

He frowned. 'Why would you think that?'

'Your meeting. I heard you arranging it a couple of weeks ago, when we were on a Zoom call. I suppose I put two and two together.'

He laughed softly. 'Ah. Well, I have been meeting someone.'

I knew it.

'That's fine, honestly. I don't want you to think that—'

'It's a therapist, Scarlett, not a date.'

I widened my eyes, feeling foolish for about a second and then realising there was no need.

'Did I hear that correctly?' I said, shaking my head in astonishment. 'You, Theo Winters, have voluntarily been going to therapy?'

'What can I say? I'm a convert,' he said. 'I realised, after the retreat, that I'd been living a sort of half-life. Too scared to put my head above the water because I thought that relationships were difficult and unsafe and not worth the immense fear of being hurt.'

'How's it going?' I asked gently. I knew how difficult it must be for him and how much this must mean he wanted things to change.

'It's tough, I won't lie. Scary as Melissa was at times, she has nothing on my new therapist!'

Soft jazz music played in the background and with the sounds of cocktails being shaken and subdued chatter it felt like a good place to tell him how I really felt about him.

'Have you given any thought to us? To what you want this to be?' I asked, indicating the space between the two of us, the uncertainty around whether we were friends or something more or nothing at all.

He propped his elbow on the bar, really looking at me.

'I'd be lying if I said I hadn't fallen for you, Scarlett. If I'm honest, it started six years ago and it's never stopped, not really. And I came to Cambridge partly to make sure that you were OK, but also to finally tell you how I feel about you.'

'But I thought—'

'I know what we said, the pact we made,' he said, reaching out to take my hand. 'But this last couple of weeks without you has made me realise that having a professional relationship with you isn't enough. I love writing with you, but I also love swimming with you, and walking on the beach with you and sweating it out in a sauna with you, and catching your eye in a crowded room because wherever you are, I can somehow always see you. All of that.'

I let myself take all of this in, but really I wanted to jump out of my seat and shout from the rooftops: *He feels the same way I do! He's in to me, too!*

'I was actually planning to say a version of the same thing

324

to you,' I said, reaching out to run my thumb over his cheek, like I'd thought about doing so many times before. 'It was just taking me a bit longer to work up to it.'

'No rush,' said Theo. 'These are big revelations we're making, here. Melissa would be exceptionally proud.'

'But how would it work? There's so much riding on us putting the best book of our lives out there. Can we really risk complicating things?'

He nodded. 'I know, and I've thought about that a lot. In fact I haven't been thinking about much else.'

I smiled. 'You've been procrastinating again, haven't you?'

He grinned at me. 'Caught red-handed.'

I laughed, reaching for him again.

'Surely there must be other writing duos out there who are also a couple. Mustn't there?' I said, needing reassurance that it could work.

He nodded. 'There's a couple at my publishers who write romcom together. And I know two sets of siblings who co-write, although that's a different dynamic, obviously, but still. It can work. And honestly? I'm prepared to do anything to make it happen. Because I want us to be together properly, Scarlett. As partners, not just as writing partners.'

And then he leaned in and kissed me, tentatively at first, making sure it was what I wanted. It was, obviously. I tangled my fingers up in his hair, kissing him back, inhaling his delicious scent and the achingly familiar feel of his hands on my waist.

'I hear the bedrooms are very nice here,' I said, breathless already. I wasn't in to public displays of affection, plus I wanted to make the most of this moment and we could hardly do that here.

'Mmmmn,' he replied, taking my hand and pulling me up with him. 'I should probably show you.'

His room was on the ground floor. We walked down a long glass-walled corridor to get there, my hand comfortingly in his.

'This is me,' he said, stopping outside a door and buzzing us through with his key card.

We were kissing again before the door even clicked shut behind us. He led me over to the bed, unzipping my dress as we went. I let it fall to the floor, kicking off my shoes, pulling his shirt out of his jeans, running my hands under the hem.

'I wanted to do this every single time we walked back to our hotel rooms in Cannes together,' he said, unhooking my bra strap with one hand.

I fumbled with his belt buckle, impatiently ripping open the fly of his jeans, easing them over his hips. Then he picked me up and lowered me down on the bed, easing himself on top of me.

'This is all very romantic,' I said, laughing softly.

'Told you I had it in me,' he whispered.

I closed my eyes, feeling his hot breath on my neck, then my shoulders, then my stomach as he moved slowly down my body. I arched my back with pleasure, knowing for a fact that nothing had ever felt quite as right as this.

Epilogue

Three Months Later

As Theo popped the cork on a bottle of champagne, I could barely contain my excitement.

'I'd like to say a few words,' said Carla, perching on her desk and holding out her glass for Theo to fill.

'The floor is all yours,' said Theo.

'So as you've probably gathered by now, I have some very, very good news for you both.'

My whole body tingled with anticipation and I put my hand in Theo's, squeezing his fingers tight. Whatever happened, we were in this together.

'Don't keep us waiting, Carla,' I said, 'my nerves can't stand it.'

She took a deep, dramatic breath. 'OK. Brace yourselves. We have had multiple UK offers for two hundred and fifty thousand pounds for *The Couple on the Beach* and I'm confident I can get that bumped up even further for you when we go to auction. Editors at the big five publishing houses are going batshit *crazy* about the fact that you've not just reunited as a writing duo, but that you're a romantic duo now as well. Your relationship is literally a publicity goldmine. Seriously, guys – my hunch is that this is going to be even bigger than *Little Boy Lost*!'

I let the news sink in while Theo almost choked on his

champagne. A quarter of a million pounds? For a book idea we came up with walking along the promenade in Cannes while on a retreat neither of us wanted to be on? And then I expressed myself in the only way I knew how and let out a deafening squeal and Theo cheered and lifted me up and spun me around and then we both hugged Carla, champagne spilling over the tops of all our glasses, me nearly in tears and even Carla looking a tiny bit emotional.

'You'll be able to sort out your dad's house,' said Theo, pressing his forehead against mine.

I kissed him gently on the mouth.

'And you won't have to go back to selling kitchens.'

The last few months had been spent living in each other's pockets. There had been a few blips, of course – Dad was finding it hard to get his head around the fact that I wasn't at his beck and call 24/7 and I'd disagreed with Theo once or twice about the book, mainly towards the end when we'd had to tie all the storylines together and Theo was being a stickler for leaving nothing unexplained and I'd thought it was fine to leave a couple of loose threads here and there for the reader to come to their own conclusion over. But we'd always got through it, by giving each other space and then communicating how we felt about it.

Carla bustled about, refilling our glasses, giving us details of all the deals we'd been offered. 'I retained world rights, as you know, and have already had a lot of interest in the US, in fact two publishing houses are taking it to acquisitions imminently. I'm hopeful we'll have a bidding war by the end of the week.'

Acquisitions, that mysterious meeting where an editor pitches a book they love to the rest of the team – senior management, marketing, publicity, sales. It was a good sign if a book got that far.

'Congratulations, guys,' said Carla. 'This is so well-deserved. When I sent you off on that retreat, I had no idea that this was how things were going to turn out. But look what's happened – a romance *and* a book deal. I couldn't be happier for the two of you.'

Theo's therapy was going so well that I was considering contacting Melissa – who was currently in San Francisco according to her Instagram feed – to see if she and I could meet for some sessions online. And Claire and I had been in regular contact and she'd finally revealed what Theo had told her about his feelings for me that night at the anti-speed-dating event, although it was nothing I didn't already know now. Zach – who Theo had bonded with, as well as the rest of my family – had finally got his shit together and was working flat out on his course. Kate's marriage was as rocky as ever, but she was doing her court clerk training and was loving it and wished she'd tried this work lark sooner. Alexa was doing better at medical school and because she felt more on top of her work, the panic attacks were less frequent, although not gone altogether. And Petra was still in the infertility trenches, but at least Dan was being more supportive and had given up alcohol in solidarity. All in all, my friends and family were doing pretty well without me micro-managing their every move, freeing up more time for me to think about my own life and even to spend the odd evening relaxing with Theo and doing absolutely nothing.

As I looked at a proud Carla smiling at us, as though she was pleased with herself about something, the penny dropped and I narrowed my eyes at her.

'Carla, did you know it was a couples retreat all along?' I asked her.

Theo looked surprised. 'You didn't!'

She smirked. 'You got me.'

Theo and I sputtered with indignation, which quickly turned to laughter.

'To my two favourite clients,' said Carla, raising her glass.

'To couples retreats,' I added, raising my own.

'To devious agents,' Theo offered with a grin. 'And to therapy. But most of all,' he said, turning to me and touching his glass to mine, 'to us. We make one hell of a team.'

Acknowledgements

I've loved every minute of writing this book, and it might just be my favourite so far. So many thanks to my literary agent, Hannah, who was as enthusiastic about the story as I was from the off – I'm so grateful for all your support and advice, and your calming approach to facing the inevitable challenges! A shout out to everyone at Hardman & Swainson, particularly Hana and Aaminah. Thanks, too, to the lovely team at Orion, to whom I will always be immensely grateful for making my dreams come true – a special mention must go to the two brilliant editors who worked on this book, Rhea Kurien and Sanah Ahmed. Thanks to my writer friends, without whom I would have lost the plot completely at some point, probably, especially Caroline Khoury, Nicole Kennedy, Sara Jafari, James Bailey, the screenwriting crew, Zoë Folbigg, Kathleen Whyman, Olivia Beirne and the Debut 20s! And to all the librarians (especially the brilliant Mark Nagle at Barnet Libraries!), book bloggers, bookstagrammers and readers who have been so supportive over the years and who have taken the time to post the most beautiful photos and reviews of my books – I really do appreciate it. Thank you to Connie, Ora, Kay and Julia, the therapists I've been lucky enough to know and who inspired me to create the character of Melissa – her scenes were always so much fun to write! A huge thanks to Gabriel and Robbie for joining me on my research trip to Cannes, and for their constant love and encouragement. And finally, thank you to friends, family and colleagues who have helped make the writing of this book such a pleasure, especially Louise, Alex, Alyson, Jan, Ads, Laura, Margo, Matthew, Helen and Mum. And with love to my dad, of course, always.

Credits

Lorraine Brown and Orion Fiction would like to thank everyone at Orion who worked on the publication of *Couples Retreat* in the UK.

Editorial
Rhea Kurien
Sanah Ahmed

Copyeditor
Francine Brody

Proofreader
Laetitia Grant

Audio
Paul Stark
Jake Alderson

Contracts
Anne Goddard
Dan Herron
Ellie Bowker

Marketing
Ellie Nightingale

Design
Nick Shah
Charlotte Abrams-Simpson
Joanna Ridley

Editorial Management
Charlie Panayiotou
Jane Hughes
Bartley Shaw
Tamara Morriss

Finance
Jasdip Nandra
Nick Gibson
Sue Baker

Publicity
Sian Baldwin

Production
Ruth Sharvell

Sales
Jen Wilson
Esther Waters
Victoria Laws
Toluwalope Ayo-Ajala
Rachael Hum
Anna Egelstaff

Sinead White
Georgina Cutler

Operations
Jo Jacobs
Sharon Willis

Could one split second change her life forever?

Hannah and Si are in love and on the same track - that is,
until their train divides on the way to a wedding.
The next morning, Hannah wakes up in Paris and realises
that her boyfriend (and her ticket) are 300 miles away in
Amsterdam!

But then Hannah meets Léo on the station platform,
and he's everything Si isn't. Spending the day with him in
Paris forces Hannah to question how well she really
knows herself - and whether, sometimes, you need to go
in the wrong direction to find everything you've been
looking for …

'Fresh, modern, and totally charming, this is a romance-lover's dream!'
Laura Jane Williams

Sometimes love is just around the corner ...

Rebecca isn't looking for love. She's perfectly happy with her high-flying city job, gorgeous flat overlooking Hampstead Heath and fortnightly fling with the hot CEO. She's certainly not interested in the hot actor neighbour who's just moved in opposite ...

Jack is still looking for his big break. It turns out being the star talent at drama school doesn't give you a golden ticket to Hollywood, after all. The last thing he needs is any distractions right now – especially not the uptight, power-suit-wearing girl next door.

They might live only a few metres away from each other, but their worlds couldn't be further apart, plus opposites don't really attract ... do they?

A fiancé. An old flame. And five days in Florence …

Maddie is over the moon when her boyfriend Nick
proposes in Paris. And spending five days in Florence with
his family sounds like the perfect way to get to know her
future in-laws.

But Maddie is in for a rude awakening. Nick's parents are
too posh for words, his daughter doesn't want to know
her – and just why has his ex-wife come along?! And if
that wasn't complicated enough, who should be at the same
boutique hotel but Aidan, the one that got away two years
ago …

Who knew so much could happen in just five days in
Florence?